THE EARTHMIGHT WAR

THE ANNALS OF THE LAST EMISSARY

BOOK TWO

Other Works by
J. Jason Hicks

Fiction

Ruinwaster's Bane:
The Annals of the Last Emissary
Book One

Nonfiction

The War of Leadership:
Hard Lessons and Practical Truths for
Surviving in and Beyond Leadership

THE EARTHMIGHT WAR

THE ANNALS OF THE LAST EMISSARY

BOOK TWO

J. JASON HICKS

DASMURWIL PROPERTIES LLC

Tucson, Arizona
Eden Prairie, Minnesota
New York, New York

For information about this title or to order other books
and/or electronic media, contact the publisher:

Dasmurwil Properties LLC
Tucson, Arizona USA
jjasonhicks.com
linktr.ee/jjasonhicks

Cover art by Jeff Brown
Cover design by Jeff Brown

Book interior design by the Book Cover Whisperer:
OpenBookDesign.biz

Original map design by J. Jason Hicks

Digital map design by Ryan Thompson

Digital/Leather map design by Sarah Edwards

Names: Hicks, J. Jason, Author Title: The Earthmight War / J. Jason Hicks
Identifiers: LCCN 2025913697 | ISBN 978-1-960481-00-9 (hardcover) |
ISBN 978-1-960481-01-6 (paperback) | ISBN 978-1-960481-02-3 (eBook)
Series: The Annals of the Last Emissary
Subjects: | BISAC: FICTION / Fantasy / Epic | GSAFD: Fantasy Fiction.
LC Record available at https://lccn.loc.gov/2025913697

Library of Congress Control Number: 2025913697

978-1-960481-01-6 Paperback
978-1-960481-00-9 Hardcover
978-1-960481-02-3 eBook
978-1-960481-03-0 Audiobook

FIRST EDITION
OCTOBER, 2025

*For
Kris, Mike, and Paul*

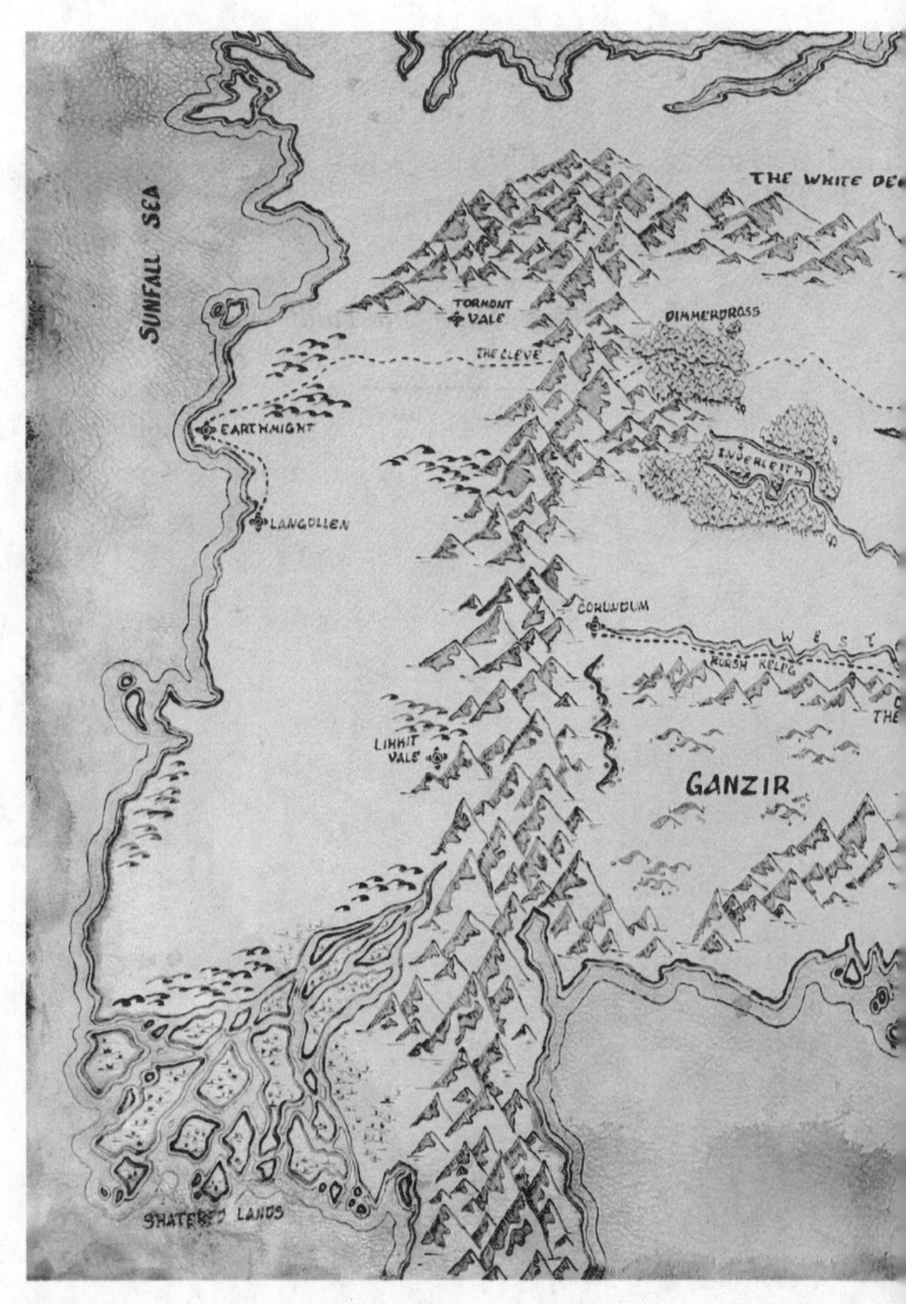

SUNFALL SEA
THE WHITE DE...
TORMONT VALE
DIMMERDROSS
THE CLEVE
EARTHMIGHT
INVERLEITH
LANGOLLEN
CORUNDUM
WEST
KURSH KELPG
THE
LIHHIT VALE
GANZIR
SHATTERED LANDS

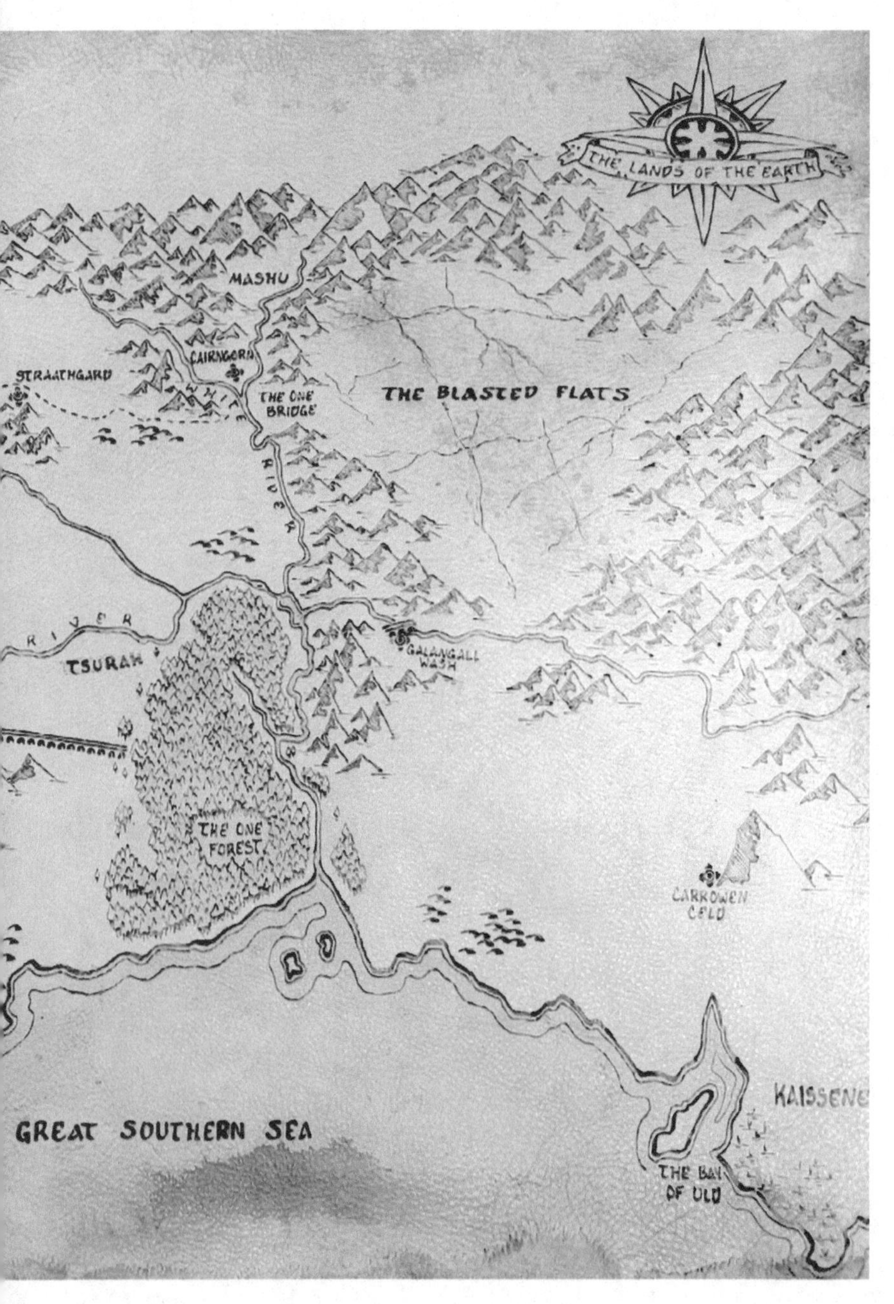

THE LANDS OF THE EARTH
MASHU
STRAATHGARD
CAIRNGORA
THE ONE BRIDGE
THE BLASTED FLATS
WHITE RIVER
RIVER
TSURAN
GALANGALL WASH
THE ONE FOREST
CARROWEN CELD
KAISSENE
GREAT SOUTHERN SEA
THE BAY OF ULU

Life begets life

Life preserves life

Life adapts to the world,

and the world adapts to life

The earth yields plants

Trees and plants bear fruit

according to their kind

Seed to root, seed to life

Seeds, earth, and life are intertwined

Love and life are intertwined

Life and death are intertwined

Creation is a process and a principle

The process reveals the principle

Tenets from the Law of Creation

CONTENTS

PART I

AFTERMATH

1

STONE FINDER

A world-ending eruption of light and power had blasted him out of existence. The shattered debris of his soul was scattered across the darkest spaces in the void.

As the aftershocks of cataclysm and ruin receded, only the faint pulse of his heart remained. His chest rose and fell, and that rhythm told him one thing: he had not yet passed into the White Earth. There was no context for who he was or what his life might have been, but he was flesh and bone still, ignorant of himself, but solid.

Stubborn aches and taut stiffness defined the precincts of his body. Ribs groaned in layers of pain. His legs were sore from disuse and deep bone bruises. He was pummeled as if he had tumbled down a cliff. Those various pains assembled him more clearly than any sensation he had about who he was.

One particularly sharp hurt drew his attention. He pulled his arm up to inspect the wrist. Crusted eyes fluttered open stubbornly as he found the bandage. Shock staggered him, and if he hadn't been lying down, he would have surely fallen.

His whole arm was grisly. A coat of sickly gray and purple flesh covered it. Veins and tendons snaked beneath the translucent, gruesome skin. Scabs and scars pockmarked his arm everywhere. The bandage seemed ridiculous compared with the state of his arm.

As he inspected it, pieces of his life started to come back, borne by the memory of the source and reason for the horrible wound. A grief-drenched decision to attempt a forbidden, arcane rite to honor someone had driven him. His dead father. He was his son. Sairik's son, Aenguz. His father had been the lord and leader of their people. Now, *he* was their leader. Those facts were the first fundamental pieces of who he was, but where was he?

Aenguz lay in a stall segregated by crystal walls. It was at once familiar and foreign. He wasn't home, but something about the stall was familiar. Wooden chairs sat on either side of the bed, facing him. It looked like they were waiting, like others had been watching him. How long had he been out?

There was a stall opposite that reflected his own, but the space was unused. His eyes were drawn up to the sheer yellow-and-white crystal wall.

A contoured sculpture, carved in relief, ran to the left and right, out of sight in both directions. Long-faced animals, their heads and necks only, crowded together. They surged and seethed to the left. Hair on the spines of their necks was tossed and swirled by implied wind. Wild, intelligent eyes gave each animal its own personality, its own look of terror, bravery, or joy. Their mouths gaped and heaved. They chattered, or howled, silently, emulating whatever sound they might have made.

The color of the crystal and the striations within that ran on a bias were somewhat familiar, but he couldn't place them.

He rolled up to sit on the edge of the bed. He inspected the yellow-green bruises elsewhere on his body. Old scars reminded him of hard griefs and brutal losses. As he scratched his head, he felt the scar around his neck. The memory of his capture and his journey across the Lands of the Earth was ordering slowly, regretfully, into place.

He had traveled to Corundum. This had to be Corundum, but he was never in this space.

A short, stocky woman came into his stall. Confidence and concern imbued her gait. She wore a mustard-colored frock and a simple white apron. Her long brown hair was drawn back in a smooth ponytail. Her face reminded him of someone, but he couldn't place it.

"I thought I heard you. How do you feel?" She sounded like a concerned mother.

"Sore. Parched. Hungry." The words scraped out.

She went to the table beside his bed, poured a cup of water, and urged him to drink. As he drank, she said, "We were worried about you. You have been unconscious for a long time." She filled his cup again.

He emptied it a second time, then asked, "Where am I?"

"You are in the infirmary in Corundum. Your friends will be glad to know you are awake. Let me send a runner for Lord Lokah." She stepped to the mouth of the stall and called for a runner. A young, proud girl darted up to the woman. Brown leggings covered lithe, muscled legs. She wore a green short-sleeved blouse. A wide belt held it tight to her body. It looked like a uniform of some sort. "Go and find Lord Lokah. Check the sanctum first. When you find him, tell him his lord is awake. The Stone Finder is awake."

She nodded once tightly. "Yes, Kikey."

Before she left, Kikey added, "And find Lord Prince Legerohn. He insisted we tell him once the Stone Finder was awake."

Stone Finder? That name didn't make sense. Another name, a different one, came to him - an unwanted one. The Last Emissary.

He had been charged to deliver a dire message of ruin and revenge.

Lord Morgrom, or the Flayer, as Aenguz's people called him, had forced him to bear the message to Corundum. Malefic and puissant, Lord Morgrom wanted vengeance for his defeat in the Last Battle. He wanted to abrogate the Law of Creation. He had given the lands, the waters, and even the air to his servants. He had called the Remnant and the people of the earth squatters.

"How long have I been here?"

Kikey sat down and inspected his wrist. "You have been unconscious since your friends brought you here five days ago. You are one of our last patients."

More confusion rattled the already loose memories. "Last patients? What happened?"

"We were attacked."

"What?! By whom?!" Panic kicked his heart.

"Horrible creatures. Erebim and Tsurah. They came upon the Stair Guard unawares, but my father gave defense to Corundum. My father saved us." A solemn pride filled her eyes, and then grief brought them down again to his wrist. She unwrapped the bandage and inspected the scars beneath. She dabbed some ointment in places.

The *mithrite* chain that secured his weapon had caused this wound.

"Where is my weapon?"

"It is in the sanctum with the Dagba Stone."

"The sanctum? The Dagba Stone?"

"It is in a safe place high up in Corundum."

"And the chain?"

"I am sure Lord Lokah or Prince Legerohn would know. What happened to your arm?" she asked as she inspected it. "I have never seen a wound like this."

The memory surfaced like an exposed root. He didn't want to recall the arrogance and grief that drove him to break the law and attempt the rite that upended his life. All he could muster for her was the fact of his father's death. "I was attempting to honor my father with the sacred metal of the Mashu."

She met his eyes again and offered a look of quiet compassion.

"Who is your father?" he asked.

"He was Stair Mark Uran."

Now he saw the similarities in her face and around her eyes. The stern Stair Mark had confronted him on the old road that led to Corundum. He had barred Aenguz's path and called him a foe. He could have killed the company right there, but he didn't. He demanded that Aenguz lay down his weapon, then he ordered one of his men to take it up. But Aenguz weighed it down with words of lore, and it wouldn't budge. With that act, Uran knew enough to know that Aenguz was an Akkeidii and also a friend to the Lands of the Earth. He guided the depleted company Aenguz led up to Corundum into an audience with the Counsel Lords and the Mono Lord. There, he completed his charge and delivered the message from Lord Morgrom. Uran had allowed it to happen.

"I remember him. I only knew him briefly. He could have killed us, but he held true to his duty. He was honorable and wise."

Kikey smiled at this, but it only brought more grief to her eyes. "He was." She stood up and clutched the bandage. "Let me get you some clothes."

She left and brought back something for him to wear. She set the clothes on the edge of the bed and laid her hand on them in a kind of blessing, then left him to dress.

2

CONUNDRUM

The newly formed talisman lay before Lokah on a slab of wood in the middle of the long table. The Dagba Stone gripped Aenguz's weapon firmly, as if his *montmorillionite* had grown into and through it.

The three-armed Dagba Stone reached around the hook and the spike at the head of Aenguz's weapon and gripped it like a fist. The arms met at an oblong layer with a round nub on top. It looked like a kind of cochlea or valve, like it was shaped or formed for some other purpose in some other context. Thin, irregular streaks of gray wisped through the white talisman like smoke trails. A breath of faint red colored a third of it at a random angle, as if it had accidentally touched some diluted dye.

How did Aenguz lodge the stone onto his weapon? The question gnawed at him, haunted him. Why did he do it? The conundrum made him question his skill as a loremaster for *montmorillionite*. He had gone over The Lay of *Montmorillionite* a hundred times, but there was nothing in the couplets that accounted for this, no reorganizing of the order that could cause this oddity. He needed more information. He needed to go deeper into the lore. He really needed Aenguz to wake up so that he could share what he had done. Lokah needed to know what Aenguz knew.

If he hadn't already touched the talisman out of necessity, he would have been cautious about touching it now. The moment had come after the Battle of Corundum.

Mandavu had hauled Aenguz around the perilous ring of Mimirmere to the narrow stairs that led up to the entrance of Corundum.

"He's alive!" Mandavu had shouted over the roar of the awakened waters around the keep. Then he had called to Lokah, "Secure his weapon!"

The weapon had swung below the water from Aenguz's wrist at the end of the *mithrite* chain - the one Legerohn had given him. Cuts had crisscrossed along the side of Mandavu's calf. In that chaotic moment, the strangeness of that had not fully registered. They had all been too shocked and relieved to have found Aenguz after the eruption that shook Corundum. As an Akkeidii Warrior, Aenguz's *montmorillionite* should have been dull against Mandavu's skin.

He had grabbed the chain and hauled the weapon out of the water while the others had pulled Aenguz's naked, lifeless form onto the stairs. In the pandemonium, he hadn't totally noticed the inertness of the metal. The oddity of the strange smooth stone locked onto the end of it had drawn his attention, not the absence of the *feel* of the sacred metal. Alone and quiet as he was now, he would have sensed it right away.

Once they had gotten him to the infirmary, it was the reactions of the healers to Aenguz's weapon that had brought his focus more closely to it. As they had tended to Mandavu's leg and covered Aenguz, he had noticed the puzzled looks they gave the stone.

Kachota had blurted out, "Is that...?" Mandavu's brother always spoke the first thing that came to his mind. He was a warrior, and quick action was in his blood.

Mandavu had cut him off and said to Lokah, "You'd better get that out of here. Go."

"Where?"

"Just go."

Lokah had loosened the *mithrite* chain from Aenguz's wrist and left quickly, holding the weapon close to his chest. He had had no idea where to go except the room where they had been led when they had first reached Corundum.

He had left the cacophony behind and walked up to the room high up in the crystal citadel. The halls had quieted quickly. Every person had been down near the entrance, first to repel the attack, and then to help in the wake of the released waters. It had gone against his warrior training to move away from the fray. But in a way, he had also been running toward a new unknown terror, a stark mystery that had not fully materialized. Alone, in the empty corridors, the change in Aenguz's weapon had been more pronounced.

He had tried using a simple power to call some small light from it, but nothing had come. It was undeniable that something was amiss with the *montmorillionite*.

He had reached the hallway where the squad of Stair Guard had been stationed to keep them in their rooms when they first arrived at Corundum. He had climbed the narrow stairs and entered the room they had all gathered in on the night Aenguz left and disappeared.

When he had set the weapon on the table, he had spoken the words of lore to weigh it down and keep it safe - the same words of lore he had used to save their lives and anchor them to the floor when the waters had come and flooded the entrance of Corundum. But nothing had happened. He had lifted the metal easily. The stone nullified the essential power from Aenguz's *montmorillionite*. It had released the waters and dispelled the Glaize. It had done this to the sacred metal. What else had it done? What else was affected? Lokah had closed the door behind him. It was the only means at the time to keep the dead talisman safe.

It had been five days since they found Aenguz, and he was still unconscious. Alive, but unconscious. There were no answers forthcoming from him.

In that time, Lokah had learned through Legerohn about the other damage to Corundum caused by the Dagba Stone. The massive eruption that had released the waters had shaken the keep to its foundation.

While the others had helped to clear the fallen trees outside Corundum caused by the avalanche of water, the Moresi leader had taken on the task of inspecting the damage within the keep - cracks in the foundation walls, rocks that had fallen from ceilings in different chambers. And the most serious damage of all, the loss of the Vaults of Corundum. Shallow water now filled the end of the hidden corridor that led to it. Even the large stone doors were cracked and broken.

The counterpoint of the stone's power affirmed for Lokah the power of *montmorillionite*. Only something so powerful could nullify the power of the sacred metal. The two powers interlocked might make for a deeper lore that he could not plumb. The thought of it overwhelmed him.

And there was another power that the stone raised by virtue of its presence alone: belief. Word had spread through the stewards about the Dagba Stone. The people of Corundum had found out about it, and they wanted to see it and touch it.

He picked the weapon up and set it into the slab of wood so that it could stand upright. It was the simplest care he could provide for it. He set shaped pieces of wood over the exposed edges, and another cylindrical piece over the spike. It looked odd being protected in that way, encased in wood, as it were, but too many hands had been cut.

There was a knock on the crystal door. The Stair Guard opened it and let in a young girl. She was out of breath. "Lord Lokah," she panted. "The Stone Finder is awake."

Finally, some answers.

3

SILVER BONE, KNOTTED STONE

Aenguz was sliding on his boots when Lokah arrived. He hurried into the stall, breathless. "Aenguz!" He rushed up and grabbed his shoulder, as if to confirm what he saw. He pulled back and said, "We were worried you might not wake up."

Aenguz was used to seeing Lokah in the bone-white tarp he had worn across the Lands of the Earth on their journey to Corundum. And the last time he'd seen him was high up in Corundum in a beige robe and wrapped in bandages. Seeing him dressed in clothes now was jarring.

"I was out for five days?" Aenguz asked.

"It has been nine days since you descended into the Well of Sorrows."

"Nine days? What happened here?"

"We were attacked by Erebim and Tsurah. There was an Urning."

"I should have been here," Aenguz chastised himself. "Is everyone alright? Is anyone hurt?"

"None of us were hurt - drowned a little, but not hurt. Mandavu, Kachota, Legerohn, and the others are all fine."

Aenguz's curiosity was devouring him whole. "Tell me everything. And I need to get to my weapon."

"Come, I will show you."

Uran's daughter bid Aenguz farewell. "I will see you at the victory feast tonight?"

Aenguz looked at Lokah.

"He will be there," Lokah answered.

As they walked past the empty stalls, Aenguz was drawn to the mural again.

Lokah studied Aenguz for a moment and then looked at the mural. "They are horses."

"Horses?"

"A race of herd animals. These were stables at one time. Apparently, the old Counsel Lords rode them to travel abroad in the Lands of the Earth. That was before the Last Battle."

"They look like wild, fearless roe deer does." Aenguz searched their lines and creases. The crystal surged to life beneath the racing herd.

"Can you imagine riding one?" Lokah rolled his head.

They left the infirmary, and Lokah took Aenguz to the entryway between the refectory and the entrance of Corundum. He navigated to a place where they could see down into the entrance and across into the vast space. Both were a bustle of activity. The smell of roasting meat and baking bread drew his eyes to the kitchens spread out behind a long crystalline countertop.

Tablecloths were being laid on the long tables. Dishes and bowls were being set out with precision. Centerpieces of yellow and white flowers were being primped and shaped.

Half of the vast hall was left untouched, except for two tables set apart from the rest. One had a burgundy tablecloth, and another had a pale blue tablecloth. There were no flowers, just gray plates and black goblets.

Just beyond the two tables, another table was crushed beneath a man-sized boulder. The broken shards of the crystal table looked like broken bones.

"The whole keep shook," Lokah said, attempting to answer the question in Aenguz's eyes. "Prince Legerohn has been inspecting Corundum for faults and cracks, seeing what is safe and what is perilous."

People walked by and glanced at the pair. When they saw Aenguz, they looked again. They stared longer as they hurried by, as if they were looking at a ghost.

"You were thought to be dead."

He had felt something akin to death in the caverns below when the Dagba Stone erupted with power. He was removed from his body, but tendrils of *montmorillionite* held spirit and flesh together and would not let go.

"We secured a way across the river." Lokah pointed to two braziers that were stacked and weighted down with hunks of crystal. Ropes were wrapped in and around them and stretched out of sight. The white noise of rushing water forced those working below to shout to one another. People were queued up to cross on the rope lines. Supplies were being stacked to go over, and other supplies were being brought back across.

"See there..." Lokah pointed to the far wall below. "That is how far up the water came."

Near the ceiling of the entrance was a slimy line of black bits and flecks of green.

"By Grieg," Aenguz breathed.

"It took out many of the Stair Guard and all of the Counsel Lords, except for Lana and the Azari Stroud."

"The Stair Mark. Uran."

"Yes. Uran was lost. Pogacar is the Stair Mark now."

"I should have been here. I should have been fighting with you."

"There was little fighting. And if you had not been below with the Dagba Stone, we would all be dead. An Urning was about to enter the keep."

"An Urning was here?"

"And Tsurah. The water took them all away. It saved the keep."

He hadn't imagined that Corundum would be attacked. He never would have left if there was such a threat.

They turned from the chaos and traffic. Aenguz followed Lokah up into Corundum. The halls were familiar. They were the only halls he knew in the crystal citadel. The last time he had taken this path was when Counsel Lord Bremball had led them up to a room where the Counsel Lords meant to hold them prisoner until they could seal the Well of Sorrows. They had been so foolish to be led unwittingly into their cells. If the Counsel Lords had had different intentions, the whole company might have been imprisoned forever, or killed.

Lokah walked confidently through the halls, turning and climbing up the series of stairs higher and higher into the keep. He recounted the final moments of the battle, the events of Aenguz's rescue, and his discovery of the Dagba Stone.

High up in the keep, they came to a hallway with a reverent queue of women, mouthing something silently like a kind of prayer.

They looked deflated when they saw Lokah. But when they saw Aenguz, a quiet awe filled their eyes. Some whispered, "Stone Finder," as he passed. A hand reached out and touched him as he climbed the stairs. It startled him. At the top of the stairs, Lokah greeted the lone Stair Guard.

"Back so soon?" Then the sentry saw Aenguz. "Oh."

He raised a hand to the people waiting in the hall. An indistinct groan slipped from them. Then the sentry peered in and waited. He gestured for the middle-aged couple to come out. Tears were in their eyes. They left the stone and barely looked at Aenguz and Lokah as they left. The old man guided their way. They walked down the narrow hall wrapped in each other's arms.

The sentry stepped out and made way for Aenguz and Lokah. They walked in, and Lokah closed the door behind them.

"I've been here all morning. Because you found the stone, I get to have access to it whenever I want."

It looked clumsy and awkward with raw hunks of wood covering the sharp edges. Standing upright in the slab of wood, it seemed odd. And there was the Dagba Stone, lodged impossibly onto it. There was something else different and strange about it. He reached out to take off the protective coverings.

"Be careful. It's sharp." Lokah held up his fingers to show the straight scars.

Aenguz took the wood pieces off. Then he removed the blade and laid the weapon down on the wooden slab. Something was different about it. The weapon had changed. The shaft had attenuated slightly along the middle. It looked more like a long bone. The dagger at the hilt had changed, bent more than he remembered. The hook at the head curved differently. The tip of the axe-head waved like a flame tongue. The weapon seemed longer. It had *grown* and *changed*. The only lore that could do that to *montmorillionite* was time. Years. Decades.

He looked at Lokah as he said, "It has changed."

"I thought so, but I could not be sure," Lokah answered.

Aenguz reached out to touch the Dagba Stone. "Is it safe?"

"Yes. How did you do it?"

Aenguz touched the smooth surface of the Dagba Stone.

"I didn't do anything. It was in a small pocket of rock. The metal signaled me to it. But I could not reach it with my arm. I reached in to hook it."

"And then?"

"And then, light and power and water."

"So, you did not use words of lore to lock it on there."

Aenguz shook his head.

He grasped his weapon, hoping for the thin tremor of life and power. But there was no thrum, no lore, no life in his *montmorillionite*. The weight of the Dagba Stone threw it off balance too. He squeezed harder, as if to reach further into it, but there was nothing. It was as dull and inert as a common blade.

"How do we get it off?"

"I thought *you* would know."

Aenguz turned to the door.

"Wait," Lokah said. "You cannot take it. They will follow the stone wherever it goes. They will line up outside your quarters. You will never be alone."

"What power do they think it possesses?"

"They think it cures the blight. They think it will cure their wombs. They pray for children."

"Will I be able to take it with me? I cannot go back to the Mashu without it."

"I know."

The gravity and consternation in Lokah's eyes mirrored the tightness in his own.

He left his weapon behind, and any answers it might have held. The vagaries of his dreamlike mind left the sensation that he had been forced to leave a limb behind. As surreal as it seemed, it was like he had been late for a trial, and the judgement had been pronounced. Part of himself would have to be sacrificed. It left him unbalanced as he listed away from the line of women. The adulation and awe in their eyes didn't reach him; it seemed more like shame and scorn.

4

THE DIVINE OCULUM

Aenguz followed Lokah down the maze of stairs and hallways to the lower levels of Corundum. Everyone else from their company had adjacent rooms down the same hallway. They were all close by. Lokah turned down a corridor and pushed open the door to Aenguz's suite. A small dining table was in the center of the main room. The empty silver-banded scabbard lay on the table, and beside it, the *mithrite* chain - Legerohn's gift to him, and the means of their escape from the Sallow.

The empty scabbard jolted him back to his grandparents' home, the memory of his father's own empty scabbard on their dining table, and the iron-bound box on top of it where his bones lay. Two scabbards bereft of their *montmorillionite*. One man dead, the other half out of life.

Lokah gave Aenguz a terse Akkeidii introduction to his suite. In the water room, he showed Aenguz the stone valves that, when turned, let fresh cold mountain water into a basin and also a bath.

"The walls seem lighter," he said as he opened and closed the valve.

"They are. And they are getting lighter over time." They walked back to the main room.

The walls had changed. Their clothes had changed. Life had moved on, was moving on without him. The journey to deliver the message was over. He had survived. They had survived, but too many had still died on his account.

He had fulfilled the charge of the Last Emissary. Thoughts of his home in the Mashu tempted him. Maybe he would feel more like a leader back among his own people and in the role he had won via the Challenge, but the riddle of his stone-locked weapon anchored in that slab of wood kept the Mashu as far away as it literally was from Corundum.

Lokah was half in his own thoughts as much as Aenguz. They seemed to both be caught in the grip of their shared circumstance.

When Stroud appeared at the door, they both came out of their reveries with a start. The Azari stood in the doorway, legs apart, with his simple plain tunic. It seemed at once out of time from some ancient fashion, and also timeless. His black hair was cropped short, and motes of white marked it, as if he had been caught in a sudden snowfall and the stubborn flakes refused to melt. His eyes were set deep within the sharp cuts on his flat face, his eyelids level with his brow. His eyes were enigmatic and black as obsidian. "The Mono Lord would see you, Message Bearer."

Aenguz looked to Lokah for an answer, but the Kriel had none. He walked toward the Azari. Stroud pivoted tightly and led Aenguz down the hall.

They walked past the refectory and the strong smells of roasted meat and baked bread. His stomach growled as they weaved through the people moving between the entrance and the dining hall. More eyes fell on him again as he passed; curious and strange glances followed him. The din of the rushing waters added to the bustle and chaos at the entrance. As Stroud led on, the noise dwindled until the whitening walls consumed the sound altogether.

They passed a Stair Guard and found themselves alone in the long hallway. Farther on, they came upon another Stair Guard. She stood at attention at the base of a stair that led up the wall to their left. Stroud did not acknowledge her as they passed. She held still, at attention, except for her eyes. Fear and uncertainty filled her tight gaze, as if she were looking upon a living myth, something that might change form or explode into something altogether different that could consume them all.

The corridor angled gently downward. They came to a simple door carved from a gray, yellow, and azure stone. A relief sculpture of imperfect circles was carved into the door. Stroud turned and spoke without preamble. "You are about to enter the Divine Oculum. Do not try to take in the entire space in one glance. Keep your eyes to the right. The Glaize has been removed."

Aenguz detected a hint of accusation in Stroud's flat tone.

"The Divine Oculum is too much to take in all at once. And there is much to explain and understand. The Mono Lord asked me to prepare you."

Aenguz searched Stroud's dark eyes for an inkling of what the Azari meant in order to prepare himself.

"You may become disoriented. Look to the floor to steady yourself. You do not need to look at the whole Oculum at once."

"How do you endure the effects?" Aenguz asked.

"I am Azari. I see what must be seen."

Aenguz's question and curiosity held the enigmatic sentinel.

"I possess the One Sight. I am bound by it. However, I am the only Azari here."

"The One Sight?" Aenguz asked.

"A remnant power of the Remnant Azari. Our last bond to our former life. If there were other Azari here, we would all share in what the others saw. We were the Eyes of the World. After Oblivion's first victory, ushering in the fall of the One Race, we were left caught … in between."

Stroud pushed in the door and guided Aenguz to his right, pointing him to the rough labradorite wall. Soon, smooth imperfect circles met them. The floor curved in an arc and ran off to his left away from the wall. The chamber smelled like cold stone.

Aenguz began to look up. A silent admonition from Stroud kept him from taking in the whole height.

A Stair Guard stood before them. A trick of the perspective made it look like the lower half of her body was trapped within the stone floor. As he came close, he saw the large tiers that stepped down to the true bottom of the curved wall. She wore no helmet but was dressed in thick armored leathers and a burgundy cloak. She looked back at them and returned to look down at the window below her. Were women members of the Stair Guard before his arrival? Their numbers must be severely depleted. Akkeidii would never allow their women to fight, but with an exigency great enough, perhaps such edicts were pointless. Why wouldn't women want to fight for their own people, protection, and safety?

Stroud led Aenguz along the floor to a place behind her. Lines fanned beneath their feet and pointed at the windows. He directed him to look down over her shoulder. Aenguz could see the narrow cliff that ran at the top of the lower Stair of Forhnthulen. A cluster of small windows showed different views of the same cliff. Sunlight poured in at dawn. Night darkened other windows. Starlight silvered the shadows and cast an aura around a solitary fire. Another window had a cable or a rope running down the middle on the outside. Through that window, the cliff teemed. Fires burned. Strange tents made up an encampment. A small army worked along the length of the ledge. Felled trees were rolled and cut. Piles of wood for fires were stacked along the edge. Strawmen were being erected. The Stair Guard kept an eye on her comrades and another window that showed the last half mile of the Rursh Keleg. The Wester surged vibrantly with liberated waters alongside the old road.

It caused a disorienting dissonance in him. Smoke from the fires should have seeped in. The sound and feel of wind should have buffeted the round windows. The crash of water was empty, just beyond hearing, lost to another time. The windows roiled and churned, but the Divine Oculum was as still and quiet as a chapel.

"The ropes show which windows look out onto now."

Aenguz saw one of the windows at night showing the vertical cord cutting it in half. "What about that one?"

"That window only recently changed."

Changed? Aenguz wondered, lifting his gaze from the cavity below. Before him, images of the Spine appeared, fractured like a shattered mirror with rounded edges. He was drawn away from the towering mountains and saw a shimmering turquoise underwater world. An aqua marine dreamland with spiny rock-like flowers and strange, colorful creatures. Groups of fish weaved and flowed with the languid pulse of the water.

"That is the Great Southern Sea."

"But the Great Southern Sea is leagues from here."

"Distance is a small matter for the Oculum. Come."

Stroud led him along the rounded edge of the chamber near to the center. Soon, the windows began to fill with scenes of the blustering falls that poured off of Mimirmere, where Aenguz had been rescued. There were a few small scenes of the prior view. Frozen water from

Morgrom's hand. A yellow ribbon of the Wester. But overall, the scenes were of rapids pouring out of the mouth at the underside of Corundum.

Stroud pointed to a window overlooking the falls. A piece of red cloth was wedged in the frame at the corner. The view overlooking the Lands was breathtaking. It was the height of summer, the same light that met the Stair Guard on the cliff. A small group of birds whirled out over the falls. A thin line of yellow colored their wings. They swooped and played, dodging one another and dipping into the spray that came off the crest of the falls. Aenguz looked to Stroud, but the Azari's eyes remained fixed. Aenguz looked back and noticed that no rope line broke the window. Then the birds came into the scene again, playing their child-like game. Then the pattern emerged. The same birds. The same banks and turns. The same play looped again, and their play repeated.

"By Grieg," Aenguz uttered. "What is this? What are we seeing?"

"The Divine Oculum is not fixed."

Stroud remained silent as if his words were enough.

"The floor will help you regain yourself. Focus on one thing. Do not try to consume it all.

"These are the attributes of the Divine Oculum; windows can change, scenes of the past and the future and the present, vistas of near places and faraway lands, the same scenes repeated over and over again, and more. The Oculum is a mystery."

The Azari led him away from the wall of irregular windows. He pointed at the floor. "These lines point out in all directions toward the east, south, and north." He led Aenguz to the mound of varying crystal rock at the back of the chamber. Aenguz was grateful for the reprieve. His mind was turning, but the lines grounded him.

Stairs were carved into the jagged slope. They followed the contour of the rock rather than straight lines up. Women in beige robes stood at points on the inner crystal mound. They looked up at the wall behind

Aenguz and Legerohn and then scrawled notes on sheafs of parchment on the podiums they stood at.

"The windows look out across time. From times before and times to come. The former work of the Counsel Lords is renewed now that the Glaize has been lifted."

Lana strode heavily toward them from around the edge of the raw crystal. The hollows of her eyes were gray, as if she had knuckled ash into her sockets. Her whole body sagged with exhaustion. Her brilliant red hair was the color of late autumn leaves, the red all but sapped out of them. It was shorter than Aenguz remembered, but he couldn't be sure as it was drawn back. Her blue robe was frayed at the sleeves. Blots and stains also marked the Counsel Lord's cloak. It revealed glimpses of her bare arms. Bruises and scrapes splashed like awkward paint. If she had made no time for sleep, she had made no time to wash her clothes. In spite of all of it, her eyes held a focus and intensity. She looked like hard discipline had kept her together, barely. When she spoke, the gravel in her tone revealed a glimpse of her extremity.

"Have you explained what the Divine Oculum shows? Have you shown him what it does?" she asked Stroud.

The impassive Azari stated simply, "Yes, Mono Lord."

"There is much here that we do not know, but there are some things that you must see. Are you able to continue?" She looked squarely at Aenguz.

"I am well enough to continue." His brusqueness was directed at himself. He wanted his mind back from the dreaminess that still clung to it.

"Follow me. Keep your eyes on the stairs." She led the men up into the irregular stair of the glass hillock.

"When the Glaize was cleared, the power of the Divine Oculum was revealed. The Counsel Lords learned of the power only as teachings from these tomes that were passed down to us through the generations from the Counsel Lords of old. But we never witnessed the power for ourselves. We saw glimpses when the Mono Lord would fight the mist and peer out a window to watch the Rursh Keleg to aid the Stair Guard. And we in turn would battle the Glaize as a form of training with our staffs, but not much more than that."

The glint and color of the crystal dimmed and made the agate look like muddy rock as they climbed. The atmosphere changed as if dusk had suddenly drawn upon the Divine Oculum, but it was just after midday.

The frayed Mono Lord continued up to a pocket of varied crystal that held a pedestal. From behind, she looked to be bearing an invisible burden. Her back was bent with exhaustion.

A short woman in a beige robe stood at attention away from the pedestal. She held her shoulders square. She was no longer a child. The first flower of womanhood radiated confidently from her. She was formidable in her way, and it added to her stern beauty. She studied Aenguz while Lana spoke. "This is Saissha. She is an initiate learning the ways of becoming a Counsel Lord."

Lana indicated a thick tome tucked in a pocket underneath the crystal desktop. Sheafs of rough-edged paper were stacked on top. A polished wooden arm held smaller tooled arms and at their tips were various lenses. Green, rose, and pale yellow lenses were fashioned into the tips. They fanned out like a small peacock's tail.

"We are re-learning how to understand and interpret the Divine Oculum," Saissha started. "We look to see what is near and far. When do day and night fall. What is now and what is past. What could be the future and what might be the extremes of the Earth's ages. And what images the Oculum chooses to repeat."

"I will not waste our time telling you how the initiates piece together the moon and stars and the life of trees and the images near and far to decipher what the Oculum reveals," Lana continued. "It is an imperfect practice, and we are new to it, but this is what the old Counsel Lords did. These ancient tomes hold notes of what they saw and recorded. These various points and lenses allow us to focus on details of scenes. We take all of this together to determine what we might be looking on. This is where my first question of you lies. Since you have traveled in the east, what you saw there might help us uncover what the glass is showing us and *when it is*."

She gestured for him to handle the rock to brace himself. Then she took a deep breath and looked up at the wall of oculars at the north end of the Divine Oculum.

Darkness filled most of the windows with blots of night. Fires dotted the land. There were motes of daylight here and there. Snow was stamped and sooty. Thick gray clouds made any of the days seem static and trapped in a morose timelessness. There was blood. Fields of dead with black vultures working among the corpses. Some were human. Some were Erebim. Some of the windows were covered with hastily fitted tarps. A dark army milled and seethed on a trampled plain.

"Look there. This is your message revealed, Message Bearer. The Divider's armies will move in the north on the Lands of the Earth."

"Is this now?" Pressure grew in Aenguz's chest. The thumps were capstones dropping into place.

"No. See that window?" A cable dropped across a view of summer green and folding plains.

"When is this?"

"It is not the past. If your message is true, then this is the future that awaits us."

An army of Erebim were terrifying in their own right. But it was what led them that terrified him more. "Have you seen any Urnings? Any Ruinwasters?"

"Yes. We have seen the floating specters. But the Ruinwasters are disembodied spirits."

That was true. He struggled for a way to describe what he had seen on the Cairngorm. A monstrosity had climbed out of the profane pit on the southernmost tip of the Mashu. Oily ill sluiced off of it from the hole it crawled out of. Then it vanished with the Urning who summoned it.

At the second summoning at the edge of the City of the Sho-tah, he didn't see any form there. He had tried to stop the Urning's ceremony, but he had a nagging suspicion that he had been too late and that another of the five was free.

Each had different powers, different potencies. The Chosen Freeholder, Mere Gurudev, had told him that Tycho Ruinwaster was the most dire of them all. She had said that if he was free, the Earth would already be in ruin.

"At least two are free, but I do not know what form they might have taken. I will come back and help to search later." Though he didn't know how he might find them.

"That would help."

Lana turned to a window that was filled with fire. Dry heat, wicked flames, and an unchecked conflagration devoured the green boughs and brown trunks.

"What is this?"

"We think that is Inverlieth."

Aenguz ached for his friend and what he must have felt seeing such a sight.

"Has Legerohn seen this?"

"Yes." Her eyes sagged. "He is ready to return to Inverlieth, but he would not leave while you were asleep."

It must have torn him apart. Aenguz could only imagine how it must have felt.

"We think you may understand this," she said. Her tone dropped.

She directed Aenguz to a lens on the podium. It took him a moment to orient within the scene. Silver flashes glinted in a nest of sharp mountains, like brief dots of lightning, a creche of stars. The silver light was familiar; it was *montmorillionite*. The flashes of light were the responses of the sacred metal to a dying warrior. It was night in the narrow image, so it was out of sync with the current time. He looked away and down at the lines on the floor.

"Is this the Mashu?"

"I believe so," Saissha said. "The image repeats; it is not ongoing. I have only seen one night, but the location appears to be your home."

"There is more," Lana interjected. She pointed to another yellow lens.

He drew in close, curious about the strange contraption and power. The room shifted as he righted himself with the image. There was a sea of churning and roiling Erebim. They clawed and fought wildly over one another to reach a prize. In the midst of them was an open pocket. An invisible barrier held the Erebim back.

A man drew another by a cord. A prisoner. The bound man lumbered behind. His head lolled like it might fall off. They were both Akkeidii with their long black hair, wide shoulders, and thick legs. The leader wore a black scabbard on his back. It was marked with silver bands. It looked like his own scabbard - the one gifted from Mere Gurudev. In the leader's other hand was a weapon - *his weapon*, raised high before him. Something was knotted at its head. It was the Dagba Stone.

The scene hiccupped and continued. It looked like an eternal march on the plains of the Black Earth. The chamber turned on him hard, balance fled, and he joined the darkness.

5

A DESPERATE PLEA

When his eyes fluttered open, Aenguz saw Stroud peering into him as if he could see the deepest precincts of his soul. Stroud held him firmly until he could sense Aenguz had found his equilibrium.

The Divine Oculum, *montmorillionite*, and the Dagba Stone were wreaking havoc on the orienting elements of his mind. His jaw flexed and his teeth clenched as if they might provide balance. If he had eaten anything, he might have wretched. He drew on his warrior's will to master himself.

Lana led them down and out of the darkest part of the Divine Oculum. Stroud held and guided Aenguz. She led the way to an unobtrusive door on the other side of the chamber.

The room inside was a kind of antechamber of crystal and stone. It looked like it had been newly restored to usefulness. A door was on the opposite wall, but it looked like it hadn't been opened in an age. There were shelves carved out of the stone, thick with dust, and a few boxes in the corner that looked so new in the space as to be out of place. Lana's braided staff rested in a tripod near the wall.

Aenguz shook off Stroud. Lana closed the door behind them. Though there was little sound in the Divine Oculum, this chamber was even quieter, as if they had stepped into a tomb.

Vast powers were taking their toll. They were taking Aenguz away from himself. The inscrutable needs of those forces were channeling through him as if he were a necessary conduit. Time too was a force that weighed and pressed on him. Morgrom had meted out explicit times for his will to come to pass. According to the Divine Oculum, creation was already bending under his will. There were only a few seasons left before Morgrom's closest warnings came to pass. His vengeance on those he blamed for his defeat was unfolding. His control over the earth was expanding. Aenguz began to truly worry that his mind might not hold. He would have to find a new way to endure.

He had fulfilled the task assigned to him as the Last Emissary by Morgrom. Now was the time for practical action, for fighting. Now was the time to marshal armies. Now was the time for war. After what he saw in the Divine Oculum, he wondered if he could even reach the Mashu to field that kind of resistance.

Lana laid a hand on Aenguz. She asked silently if he was all right.

Aenguz nodded, though uncertainty still held him.

Lana walked to where her staff was perched. "I did not ever expect to be the Mono Lord. My life was in the Vaults of Corundum and with the seeds stored there. I assumed I would support the next Mono Lord." Her gaze flickered and went distant. "Alas, extremity has called something else of me. I am learning to take the mantle of my new role." She looked at her staff as if it were not enough, as if it were a paltry thing.

"I am grateful to you," she said to Aenguz. "We could not have survived if you were not here. And we would not have the Dagba Stone." It added some relief to her gratitude.

"Lord Aenguz, Message Bearer, and Stone Finder. That you stand here now after what the stone did." Lana shook her head slowly. "I do not know how you are alive."

He couldn't process that fact either. He had been lost, trapped beneath the keep. He was dislocated from himself and beyond sleep. Then an inconceivable flash of light. And then he was awake in a bed in Corundum. *Montmorillionite* had something to do with it, but as to how, or what it might mean for his life, he couldn't guess.

"I would ask the same thing of you that I ask Prince Legerohn. Will you send men to Corundum to help defend us?"

The Mashu and Akkeidii were too far away to help. Even traveling directly via the northern route with no Erebim horde in between, the distance was still vast. And who knew when the hordes of Erebim would cross onto the plains? There would not be enough in their party to fight their way home, based on what he had seen in the windows.

And the question of the Dagba Stone still remained. He would need time with Lokah to try to remove it so that he could take his weapon. After what he had seen in the Divine Oculum, traveling across the war-scarred plain north of Inverlieth would be reckless at best. And he certainly couldn't take the Dagba Stone into that kind of peril. But would she really let him leave with it?

He was going home one way or another. "Of course, I will send Akkeidii warriors." They both seemed to know that it was a futile ask, and based on what they had seen in the Oculum, it might well not matter. An army stood between Corundum and the Two Lands of the Mashu. It wasn't there now, but by the time he left to go home, who could say?

Lana seemed to understand Aenguz's response. "Lord Legerohn has said that you will not travel alone to Grieg's Gate. You will be warded by his finest fighters. He owes a life debt to you and the others you saved. He means to honor it. He said that he would see that you are brought safely back to the Mashu."

They had been through so much together since their time on the Sallow's *cog*. They had come to trust each other in a way that went beyond friendship. Trust had forged a different kind of bond. Legerohn's commitment to Aenguz to carry the message to Corundum when his own mission to the One Forest had failed had kept the Moresi Prince away from his home far longer than he had anticipated - far longer than Aenguz and the others. They had survived much together. The fact that he remained on Aenguz's behalf in spite of what he had seen confirmed what he knew about the honor that made up Legerohn's constitution.

"What of the needs of the message?" Stroud asked. "The warning for the One King and the One Army?"

"Yes, help may be found in the Lower Lands," Lana replied.

Stroud recited the part of the message concerning the One King and the One Army. His voice dropped to a lower tone as he spoke.

"'*Five seasons will not pass before Earthmight is under siege and the One King's army is lost.*'"

"If we could reach Earthmight and deliver the message to the One King, we could implore him to bring the One Army. The people of the Lower Lands must be warned too. He bears the responsibility to ward all the Lands of the Earth. The One Army could help us and Inverlieth and the Akkeidii. It might be the only thing that could stand against such a force." She inclined her head toward the wall of windows beyond the door.

Aenguz remembered the words. They still burned in his mind. He tried to reason himself away from the responsibility. A musing from Morgrom. Aenguz's charge was to bring the message to Corundum. There was no specific charge to warn the One King. Morgrom was merely reveling in his malevolent plans for revenge. Aenguz had served the charge of the Last Emissary.

"What of the Cleve?" Stroud asked flatly.

Lana bristled as if this were a familiar argument between the pair. "It must be tried, but not even Prince Legerohn will attempt it."

Stroud turned to Aenguz and dropped his tone an octave. His inflections matched the Prince's. "'I would assign a hundred, two hundred men to see Aenguz home safely, but I will not hazard the Cleve. I will not risk a single Moresi to attempt the Dimmerdross or cross into it.'"

Lana fell into herself. She looked at Stroud and then said to them, "Will the Divider's words come to pass then? Will Corundum fall and with it the last hope of the Lands of the Earth?"

6

REUNION

Aenguz felt Stroud behind him like a tangible shadow as he walked down a long hall on the north side of Corundum. The Azari had ushered him out of the room and the Divine Oculum. He let Aenguz pass and he followed him, almost as if he was positioning himself between Aenguz and the Divine Oculum or the Mono Lord.

Aenguz came to a different entrance to the main refectory and made his way through the rows of unmade tables. When he walked near the shattered table, he looked up into the jagged ceiling and wondered if another hunk of crystal might fall. He skirted the pale blue and burgundy dressed tables. Ghosts dined there on empty plates and empty goblets. As he moved in among the long tables being set for the living, eyes studied him with long unbroken stares. Suspicious whispers followed in his wake.

Stroud's recitation followed him through the corridors and the refectory just like the silent Azari did at his back. What could he do? Earthmight and the One King were beyond reach. He didn't even know how dire the situation was in Corundum. How long would it take to undo the Dagba Stone from his weapon? How long would it take to reach the Mashu? They had been gone so long from their home. The Akkeidii must think they were all dead. His grandparents, Selene, his betrothed, must all think that he and the others were dead and lost. Who could say how near to now those images were in the Divine Oculum? And what could those flashes mean other than dying warriors, battle, or war?

Once he reached the top of the stairs that led to his suite, Stroud was gone. Laughter was coming from his room as he approached. He pushed open the door and saw all of his friends gathered in the cozy apartment.

The old makeshift clothes they had worn were gone from them. The crude, ratty ponchos they had made from the canvas on the Sallow's *cog* were gone.

"Ah, there he is!" Mandavu joked about the detour to the infirmary before sending another runner off to find Aenguz's whereabouts.

"Quick, block the window! Do not give him another way out," Kachota seconded.

They wore loose gray shirts and leather leggings. They were covered in wood dust and wood chips, and they were slick with sweat.

His friends all came in around him. Smiles and laughter enveloped him as they shook their found leader.

"You are one tough Sidor," Kachota said.

Legerohn laughed through his broad smile. He looked regal. His tuft of dark hair was cropped short. A soft gray veneer was emerging beneath the tight black curls. His scraggly beard was gone. His clothes were clean and tailored. He wore a burgundy shirt and dark brown leggings. Like Lokah, gone was the beige robe he had last seen him in and the canvas poncho he had grown used to seeing him in during their journey across the Lands of the Earth.

Mond, Legerohn's First. The old soldier looked to be rough-sculpted out of oak. Stokke was dressed in similar clothes and, like the others, was covered in wood chips and saw dust. Chimere, the hobbled young Moresi, was injured on their escape from the City of the Sho-tah and their long walk to Corundum. It had left him with a persistent limp that was slow to heal. He was clean and dressed too in burgundy and brown, and his thin frame bore the clothes loosely.

They looked so different to him, like a year had passed.

"How do you feel, my friend?" Legerohn asked.

"Sore and hungry."

They laughed at this. Aenguz smiled. It seemed too like a year had passed since he had smiled or laughed.

"Well, it is a good thing that there will be a feast tonight."

They pulled back and gave him space. Their mirth still encircled him.

His brief bit of joy was replaced by his self-castigation. "I should have been with you at the battle."

"While you were scratching your back on the bottom of Corundum, we were holding back the horde." They all laughed at this. Chimere less so. His sprained ankle had kept him out of the fray, but he helped in other ways.

"The water did the work."

"We all drowned a little. You drowned too, just in a different spot."

"Lokah saved us."

They all looked at Lokah and their appreciation calmed their laughter.

"*Montmorillion* lore saved us."

"The whole keep shook. Did you see that stone in the dining hall?"

"I did."

"That happened all over Corundum and more besides."

"Corundum is strong. That it still clings to the side of the Spine is no small miracle," Legerohn added.

"What happened down there?" Kachota asked Aenguz.

"I do not know. *Montmorillionite*," was all he could say. And the laughter rose up again. Lokah laughed too, but his eyes were fraught and complicated.

"What have you all been doing?" Aenguz asked.

"Clearing the trees."

"Of dead Erebim and Tsurah."

"How many were there?"

Their guesses ranged from scores to hundreds. The attack had come so quickly that they gave all their attention to readying for battle and not for taking an accurate count. There were enough to overtake Corundum.

"We gave their dead back to the falls and the Wester."

This added a grim tone to their ebullient laughter.

"We have also been helping with the defense of the stairs. Setting snares, building gates, sharpening axes, warding the cliff."

"The water took down many trees," Mond said. "The risk of fire would be great next summer."

Next summer. There might not be a next summer, Aenguz thought.

"Chimere has been helping me here to catalog the cracks in Corundum along with some of the men who know the keep."

"But now we can go home, right, Tahnka?" Stokke asked.

"Yes, now we may return to Inverlieth," Legerohn answered.

Relief, like a deep exhale, washed over them, bringing a sense of accomplishment, and hope quieted their laughter and stilled their mirth. It left them with a satisfied joy that said "Finally."

"And we will take a safer road this time," Legerohn added.

His comment brought back the kind of laughter among friends who had endured hard miles and hard burdens together. Their eyes gleamed with the bond that only brothers in arms share.

Aenguz could see it. He felt it though he was slightly removed due to his lost time in the Ganzir and the five days out of life while he recovered in the infirmary. Still, it made him happy. It was like the brotherhood he shared with the Sidor warriors back in the Mashu.

"You will be our guests in Inverlieth." Legerohn grabbed Aenguz's shoulder. His mirth turned into a piercing gaze as he stared into Aenguz's eyes. He had seen what Aenguz had seen in the Divine Oculum, his eyes said but now was not the time to discuss it. Aenguz understood, and he put the matter away and let joy continue.

The Moresi expounded about their celebrations to come in Inverlieth, Stokke most of all. Chimere's complexion changed when he talked about the great Gildelmun trees there and how they held up the sky.

"Mond," Legerohn commanded, "make preparations. We will leave as soon as we are ready."

"Your words, my will, Tahnka."

This brought another "whoop" from Stokke, but Legerohn was not done. "We have a celebration to attend to honor the dead and celebrate our victory. Go and make yourselves ready."

Kachota turned to the balcony and closed the windowed doors. The others looked at him quizzically. "Just to make sure he uses the door and not the window again."

Belly laughs were more a exhalation of relief. There had been little hope when he left. And all hope had been lost when those days went by with no word from Aenguz before the attack. Tears moistened Mandavu's eyes. Aenguz had survived. They all had survived. Laughter followed them out of his suite.

Legerohn held the door for them and then quietly shut the door.

"How are you feeling, my friend?"

"I am still trying to understand the world I find myself in. So much has changed. There was an attack. You all look so different. And the

Oculum... You saw what the Divine Oculum showed of your home. Why did you not leave right away?"

"I wouldn't leave you until I knew you were awake and well. And Corundum needs help. And we needed our own time to heal."

"You didn't tell them."

"Do you know how you would relate what you saw? No one is allowed in the Divine Oculum save Lana, Stroud, and the initiates that help to decipher it."

Aenguz barely understood what he witnessed there. He believed what he saw, but independent of the chamber itself, he struggled to think of a way to explain what he saw. In its own way, it was like the message that Morgrom had given him. He had been sure at that time too that no one would believe him.

"What can we do?"

"We return home, marshal our men, join our forces as soon as possible, and send men here to help defend Corundum."

"You saw what the northern plains looked like."

"That is why I am so grateful that you are awake. It is still summer. We can reach Inverlieth easily before the trees prepare for winter." Legerohn's smile faded. "It is a different matter for you. I am afraid your time in Inverlieth will be short. I would have arranged a hero's welcome for you for saving what remains of the mission to the One Forest. I will see that you, Lokah, Mandavu, and Kachota are warded on your journey to the Mashu, but I do not know, even with that, if you can reach your home before winter."

"Or before that army takes the northern plains."

Legerohn looked at him with a finality that Aenguz recognized. It was the same conviction that set the terms of their passage through the One Forest.

"I have another problem."

"What problem?"

"I need more time to learn how to remove the Dagba Stone from my weapon. I do not know how long that will take."

"My friend, I cannot wait any longer to return home. Already I have been gone too long."

"I know. But can you give me a little time to try and remove the stone from my weapon?"

"Why not take it with you?"

"I am not sure the Mono Lord, or the people for that matter, would let me. And I don't know if I should risk taking it out into the Lands. It may draw more peril than aid. I fear that Morgrom knows that the stone has been found."

"How could you know such a thing?"

"So much power must draw his attention. Certainly, a power he recognizes and craves."

Legerohn considered Aenguz. Creases crowded around his eyes. His head tilted slightly as if he were trying to get a better look in between Aenguz's words.

"What of your men? What do they think? Who is your First? Lokah? They may have some insights. You do not have to take this all on alone. You are the Lord of the Akkeidii."

How could he explain Akkeidii ritual and tradition? How could he translate the edicts of the Challenge and the choices that brought him to it? How could he tell the Prince of the Moresi that he didn't have a First or an Honored Guard or any of the hierarchy that an Akkeidii ruler would have. His title was as near to meaningless as he could imagine.

"I have not named a First."

Legerohn waited patiently.

He drew in a deep breath and hoped that his exhale would bear the truth out. A large measure of his life that had been lost to the veil of delirium was organizing back into place. He began by telling Legerohn about the Champions and how they were chosen. Honoring the memory of the Champions seemed like the only appropriate place to start. Then he worked back and explained the purpose of the Challenge. Legerohn had seen how Lokah had sworn his allegiance to Aenguz on the banks of the Wester.

He did not go into the detail about how Sairik died. The trauma of that moment was housed in a vault deep within. He did not have the strength or the will to open it. It was enough that his father was gone.

He did not digress into Akkeidii mysticism. He merely raised his arm to show that this was the outcome of trying to honor his dead father. It was gravid with answers for Aenguz, but for Legerohn, only the surface effect of his mottled arm made Aenguz's point.

It was what led to the Challenge and their trek to the Cairngorm. He had expected to die at Mandavu's hand. But the night before the Challenge they were caught by the power of the Urning.

He told the Prince about the crimes of the Erebim and the horrors of the Cairngorm. "I saw a Ruinwaster emerge from the Black Earth."

Legerohn's eyes widened into a shock Aenguz barely recognized. Revulsion contorted them.

Then he told him how they were spirited across the One Bridge and how they all came to be taken as prisoners and delivered to the *cog*.

"I have not been a leader. More of us died than are alive. I hold the title just barely, but I do not hold much else - at least, not in a formal way, in an Akkeidii way. I saved only a fraction of the Champions in service of Morgrom's charge to me as the Last Emissary. I have been that longer than I have been Lord of the Akkeidii."

Legerohn reached out to Aenguz. "You are more a leader than you realize. Only the most difficult decisions come to leaders. I too have lost many men in service of a call we could not see to help the One Forest. What else could we do? Avoid peril and risk the world? For leaders, the choices are always difficult. For leaders, the stakes are always high.

"I know that no words of mine can make you feel like a leader. Only you can do that. And know that you are not alone. That is the gift of leading men. You have help at your hands. 'Close as bark,' we say in Inverlieth. Let your men bear some of your burden. Then, perhaps a way forward will become clear for you."

——◆——

THE PROCESSIONS INTO THE refectory were solemn. A runner led Aenguz and Legerohn with the freshened and clean-clothed Akkeidii and Moresi. She led them proudly to a dressed table at the edge of the boundary between the clothed tables and the scores of empty ones beyond. The boulder-crushed table and the empty blue and burgundy tables were in that space.

Mono Lord Lana led the new Stair Mark Pogacar, his Step Mark Einki, and a dozen or more Stair Guard from the entryway beyond the empty space to the table beside them.

All the denizens of Corundum stood. Even the small children that were there clung to their parents' legs in a kind of reverence they barely grasped.

Lana looked resplendent in her new Mono Lord's cloak. It was as blue as the labradorite in the Divine Oculum. A white stole embroidered with runes or letters was draped over her. Her braided staff gleamed, as if it had been recently polished. Her hair shone as it had when he first saw her, large red curls spilling onto her shoulders. A faint, nervous smile played on her lips as she tried to take on the solemn presence of her new office.

Stair Mark Pogacar wore grieves on his forearms along with his burgundy cloak and oiled, padded leathers. His light hair was smoothed atop his head.

The last murmurs and shuffles quieted. All eyes were on the new Mono Lord. She scanned the assembly and then drew in a deep breath that looked almost like a sigh.

"Corundum is forever changed. *Life adapts to the world.* But Corundum remains. *And the world adapts to life.* We loved the Counsel Lords and Stair Guard. *Love binds life.* We loved and honored Mono Lord Venrahl and Stair Mark Uran. They gave their lives to preserve our lives, to preserve Corundum. *Life and death are intertwined.*"

"*Life and death are intertwined,*" the solemn men and women of Corundum recited back to Lana.

"Let us honor and remember them. Honor their sacrifice. Remember their lives. *Life begets life.* We are alive and the tenets of the Law of Creation tell us that they are alive in us, in our memories."

Then, she and Pogacar moved away from the table and walked to the head of the blue and burgundy tables respectively. The crushed table set an ominous backdrop behind them. They held their goblets as if they were saluting the dead. "Hail to the honored heroes of Corundum." Then they raised them to the host again and everyone drank.

Aenguz took his crystal mug, raised it to them and the men at their table, and sipped the honey-flavored spring ale.

Then the pair returned to their tables. She gestured for the host to sit. Legerohn pressed Aenguz's arm slyly to keep him from sitting. She raised her goblet toward Aenguz and Legerohn. "We welcome the Lord Prince Legerohn, Ruler of the Moresi, and we thank him and his men for their help in the Battle of Corundum. And we thank him for his generous aid of soldiers for Corundum."

Everyone drank.

"We welcome Lord Aenguz, Lord of the Akkeidii, the Last Emissary,

Message Bearer, and Stone Finder. We thank him for returning the Dagba Stone to us. And we thank the Akkeidii warriors who fought in the Battle of Corundum and for the aid they have provided since our victory. We thank Lord Aenguz for the the promise of warriors to preserve Corundum."

Aenguz wondered if the denizens of Corundum knew how futile that promise was.

"Raise your crystal one more time for those who have been chosen for the embassy of Corundum. Counsel Lord Saissha will lead the embassy and Step Mark Einki will ward her to pass through the Cleve and beseech the One King to send us aid as well. The Divider will not find an undefended Corundum should he dare to return."

The Stair Guard called out with an "ah-whoop!" and they drank again. There was no keeping the host quiet now. A raucous chatter thrummed beneath the sounds of celebration. The kitchen moved into action and food was brought out in a line to all the tables. Music was started by players beside the kitchen.

Aenguz turned to Legerohn and asked in the cocoon of noise that rose at their table and in the vast hall, "Did she not understand your warning about the Cleve?"

The Prince smoldered. "I told her I would not risk one Moresi to enter the Dimmerdross or the Cleve. It is not safe."

"Why is she sending an embassy?"

"She is desperate. See how few remain. How can she send more away?" he said partly to Aenguz and partly to himself.

"Is this everyone?"

"There is a complement guarding the Stair of Forhnthulen, but not many more. You see all the Stair Guard are armed and ready."

"You, we, have to stop her."

"She is the Mono Lord of Corundum. What can I say? What can you say? How would you dissuade her?"

Aenguz didn't have an answer. His life had come back into focus, but the world around him was uncertain. He needed other pieces to understand what had changed and how it had changed beyond what Lokah and Legerohn had told him. He needed to unravel the mystery of the stone and the world it had unwittingly altered. The world *he* had altered.

7

BROKEN STAIR

The days following the victory feast blurred for Aenguz. Initiates called him back to the Divine Oculum to help decipher the shifting images in the windows. The Mono Lord's decision to send an embassy delayed Legerohn's departure, though Aenguz had no idea for how long. He was compelled to dissuade her. Each day felt like weeks as he and the others sifted through images that spanned months and years or more.

While there were several questions about the happenings in the east, Lana commanded the initiates to look through the northernmost windows of the Divine Oculum for anything that would help or presage the course of the embassy. They looked for any sign of the mission in the windows. Perhaps the decision was too new; the windows showed nothing. If Legerohn was right, the embassy's journey into the Cleve might be their last, and the doom of Earthmight might come without warning.

When he was pulled away to look east, Saissha stayed with the other initiates and continued to look from different podiums through different oculars to find any clue. She was well aware that she faced death.

Aenguz stole moments to look at the battlefields and armies for any signs of Ruinwasters or Urnings. At one point, he saw an armored *trullen*. The cursed offspring of the Hyrrokkin looked to be intelligent and fierce. It was nothing like the dull creature he had glimpsed in the City of the Sho-tah. He attempted to tally counts of the dark host, but it was futile.

Lana's gratitude for the retrieved Dagba Stone left Aenguz even more worried that he would have to leave his weapon behind. It was something he didn't think he could do.

He spent time with and without Lokah in the sanctum at off hours. He was loathe to delay Legerohn, and he wanted to join him in Inverlieth. If they went together, they could see the embassy safely to Inverlieth and perhaps fortify their courage as much as possible before they ventured into the forest that Legerohn and Chimere cursed about. Perhaps the Mono Lord thought that the Prince would change his mind. Aenguz could only speculate.

He and Lokah tried every song in The Lay of *Montmorillionite* to separate the stone from his weapon. They discussed all the other branches of *Morillion* lore they knew. There were only two options that they arrived at after days of study and pondering. One was that a forge might help. But there was no *montmorillionite* forge in Corundum. The other was exercising the final power that the sacred metal had - the bond between itself and the warrior who forged it. Aenguz's death might release the bond between the two and the stone might be freed. "I would rather be alive than dead," Aenguz said mock seriously. They both laughed, but it left the puzzle firmly in place.

One morning, before the initiates came, he decided to inspect the defenses on the stairs. He woke up early from elusive dreams caused, he guessed, by all the images in the Divine Oculum and all the memories of his journey across the Lands of the Earth.

The curtains opened onto a crisp morning. Summer was still here, but cold air poured off the Spine and hinted at the season's end.

Below, birds chirped and sang among the line of fallen trees that ran alongside Corundum. They looked to be picking up the pieces from the wave of water that had crashed down the mountainside. Toppled nests, ruined seed stores, and long-held perches were now gone. In the distance, he heard men talking and the first sounds of rending and chopping.

He went to refresh himself, and he marveled at the valve that channeled water into Corundum. This too must have been frozen like the water around and beneath Corundum until he touched the stone.

He donned the gifted clothes. He touched the *mithrite* chain and fingered the silver bands on the scabbard before he left the modest suite. He wished he had Mere Gurudev to provide some insight to him. The Chosen Freeholder had gifted him with so much more than the repurposed scabbard.

Out in the hallway, he found Kachota. Aenguz saw the handles of his *montmorillionite* axes. They poked up out of a leather bag, a sheath of sorts.

Mandavu's younger brother greeted Aenguz with an alert nod and sharp eyes.

Mandavu had set a watch on Aenguz once he left the infirmary. He recalled his first conversation with Kachota when he asked, "Is it safe?"

"Mandavu is wary. With the Dagba Stone found, you, *we*, may no longer be necessary. They imprisoned us once."

"What do *you* think?"

"I think they are too busy recovering from the battle and the flood." Kachota looked past Aenguz at some people leaving their rooms farther down the hall.

Could they really be in jeopardy? They had been fooled once before.

"I want to go see the work of the defenses on the stairs."

Kachota nodded.

They woke Mandavu and Lokah. Mond, Legerohn's First answered the door immediately. The old, hard Moresi soldier opened the door and greeted them as if he hadn't slept. He appeared ready for any order. Stokke opened his door bright as the dawn. Mond informed them that Legerohn and Chimere, the young Moresi mystic and healer, were already gone working to catalog the damage done to Corundum.

The six men went down to the entrance to Corundum. The area was a busy station. Men and women worked amid piles of supplies. A steady stream of people walked up and down the solitary stair that connected the entrance to the refectory. The last two braziers were stacked together in the center of the entrance. They looked like giant stone hands back-to-back. They cupped huge raw hunks of crystal. The other four braziers had been lost to the flood. Lines were wrapped and knotted in and around the braziers and boulders. They stretched across the loud river to a massive felled tree that crossed the boulevard. A small team of Stair Guard manned both ends of the rope lines.

The people had become familiar with the Akkeidii and Moresi and paid little heed to them. But when they saw Aenguz, a strange admixture of curiosity and fear came over them. Some stared openly. Others stole glances as they worked on their tasks organizing and staging the supplies. All of them veered away as if Aenguz carried some contagion.

Mandavu greeted the men by the braziers. All of them were going to cross. The team of men moved into action.

A line was tied around Kachota's waist. Mandavu took a sack, and he and Lokah slid their weapons in handle first, cinched it tight, and slung it over Kachota's shoulder.

Then, Kachota stood on the rope, grabbed the second at his head, and made his way to the edge. The two Stair Guard held the line at his waist. The other end of that line led to another pair of Stair Guard on the other side.

Mandavu's younger brother inched out over the white rush. He sashayed across the line, holding himself firm. The teams fed the safety line as he crossed.

The ropes stretched far over the ground on the further side to the felled tree. Kachota stepped off easily, the rope around his waist was undone, and the line was pulled back to the entrance.

One by one, the others made their way across the twin rope lines. Mond and Stokke went in turn. Mandavu and Lokah moved in once it was Aenguz's turn. They took over securing the line at his waist. They were going to make certain they didn't lose him to the rapids.

Aenguz moved along the lines and then came to the edge. The surge and spray were disarming. When he had arrived at Corundum, the water was still as glass under his feet. They crossed on planks that wove between hunks of rock half in and half out of the frozen water.

A river of cold air pushed around him as he shuffled across. He had crossed rivers in the Mashu in a similar way during warrior training. It was not new, but it had been a long time since he had done this kind of crossing.

Kachota helped undo the line on the other side and they waited with Mond and Stokke while Mandavu and Lokah crossed. They took back their scabbardless weapons and made their way through the blocked boulevard.

The slope above was a swath of felled trees. It was a familiar sight though due to different causes. After winters in the Mashu, minor avalanches would plow down long paths of trees here and there in places. But this was summer, and an avalanche of water had done this recently. The sheer side of the citadel was visible. It rose like an impenetrable wall. Small teams of men were up among the trees, hacking and sawing at the fallen trunks. The sound of rent branches punctuated through the roar of the river. Aenguz could hear more chopping and rending on the slope below, out of sight. Here, Morgrom's power, undone by the Dagba Stone, was intertwined. Creation and destruction intermixed. So much had happened while he was out. A whole season seemed to have passed, but it had only been a dozen or so days.

The boulevard leading away from Corundum was barred by fallen smooth-trunked trees. Some had been cut and cleared, but the six men still had to climb over, under, and around the trees to get clear of the fallen line.

The line of broken trees stopped abruptly, and the boulevard looked much like it had when Aenguz first arrived. The Glaize had hidden the keep beyond in a thick fog. The stately trees next to the stumps were still intact, and the view to the opening of Corundum was now clear.

Once clear of the fall line, they stopped and produced their weapons so that the other men could sharpen their axes against the harder *montmorillionite*. Mond and Kachota talked about the wall of water that rushed down, but more of the aftermath. They themselves had nearly drowned. Stokke added his own awe to the story about how the water took the Erebim and Tsurah away, how the Urning had nearly crossed but was unable to resist the massive wave of water.

They came to the wide stone veranda and stairs that marked the head of the Stair of Forhnthulen. Aenguz looked out through the opening in the green trees onto the haze that rested on distant lands. The weaving line of the Wester popped in and out of view like a glinting thread.

They continued down the winding path amid the pine trees and giant boulders. Hacking to their left and the calls of others working along the slope to clear the fallen trees were cupped by the rush of the cascading falls. The odor of fresh-cut pine comprised the majority of the new atmosphere.

The grade of the stair lessened, and the group came onto the flat of the wider area of the middle watch. Ahead, a dozen Stair Guard stacked stones to narrow the pathway. Aenguz recalled the simple lean-to and the shrouded pocket where Stair Guard maintained the watch post. He recalled the eyes beneath the helmets that had studied him as he passed on his way up to the keep to deliver Morgrom's message.

To his right, the area was cleared. They were setting stones adjacent to the natural rock, extending it into the clearing for the foundation of a wider structure. They worked diligently, covered in sweat and bark and stone dust. Stacks of wood had been cut and stacked, clearing and widening the space. A pair of large corallel tents were set back against the tree line. The soldiers' stern conversations quieted and silenced when they saw Aenguz and the Akkeidii. Anger seethed in their eyes. Their faces mimicked the rough stone they worked to set.

Aenguz wondered how welcomed he would be if he were forced to stay in Corundum. He saw a small alcove that held a collection of small wide-mouthed stoneware crocks. Blue and white flowers and bits of crystal were set carefully in them, and they rested on a strip of burgundy cloth.

Mandavu nodded to the soldiers, as did Mond. Lokah kept his eyes forward, and the whole company went by without a word. Scraping stones and angry grumbles followed them out of sight.

"They are upset with Lokah. With what he did to them," Mandavu said.

"Many did not hear the warning horn. Their ears had not recovered from what Lokah did," Kachota added.

Aenguz turned back to Lokah, but the Kriel shrugged it off and refused to enlighten Aenguz. They might hear his reply and be reminded of what he had done.

"They are bitter about what the Erebim did to the men of the watch. They are angry about all of the men lost in the flood. They are still grieving, but they are turning that grief into preparation for their defense," Mond said matter-of-factly. War was war to Legerohn's First.

They continued down the final distance of the mid stair. The final steps were cut out of the gut rock. Aenguz entered the cool channel of stone and then exited onto the flat cliff that marked the top of the lower stair of Forhnthulen, the switchback stairs that ran down the face of the tall cliff to the barren plain below.

Scores of men and Stair Guard worked in a harried chaos. To his right, a dozen or more corallel tents were set. Smoke trailed from cook fires. Against the near rock wall in a rarefied space was a pile of stones. A round cairn. Four spears were set in it, and stone crocks filled with flowers and trinkets were placed carefully beside it. The men working above and the memorial here reminded Aenguz of the cairn the company had set on the shores of the Wester. Those deaths were his fault. These deaths were his fault. He wished he had warriors here already so that he would not feel so outnumbered and outmanned.

A path led from the stairs in the channel of rock to the head of the lower switchback stair. The scrub was trampled or cleared on either side. Logs were piled up and blocked the footings at the top of the stair and to the only entrance to the top of the cliff and Corundum. Along the edge, men worked at fashioning straw men. Sentinels of wood and stone robed in burgundy. Smooth branches shaped to look like spears at their sides. Piles of chopped wood were in between to feed fires at the edge. Fiery embers that could be pushed over onto invaders. Eyes continually peered down and outward as if a threat could come at any moment.

To his left, a wall of white marked the edge of the cliff. A waterfall raged down. The steady roar forced them to yell or call out. Men worked near that edge at trunks that had been pulled or lowered down off the slope. Wood was chopped, and some carpenters set up crude tables to fashion chairs, stools, or boxes - things they needed there on the cliff or for the citadel above.

Mandavu searched out a group of Stair Guard near the pile of trunks at the head of the stair before them. He led the group to it.

Stair Mark Pogacar was surrounded by men. He answered questions, gave orders, and sent them back to whatever quarter of the cliff they had come from. Many were young boys. Many seemed proud and nervous, overwhelmed by their new responsibilities.

Aenguz recalled Pogacar from their first meeting on the Rursh Keleg. He was the Step Mark who had been ordered to take up Aenguz's weapon, but the mystical metal had held firm. It was the proof that Stair Mark Uran needed to confirm that Aenguz was an Akkeidii. Now, Uran was gone, and Pogacar had taken his place. Einki was next to him. He had been promoted into Pogacar's former role.

The reaction to the Akkeidii and Moresi was mixed. Some looked on in awe and some seethed. Pogacar dismissed all but Einki as Aenguz and the others approached.

"How can we help?" Aenguz offered.

"Get on your way and send men as soon as possible. We have men warding the lower, middle, and upper stairs. We have others searching for the dead along the banks of the Wester. Women fill the gaps in our ranks. And now we have to send more Stair Guard on an embassy to the Lower Lands. There were not enough before the Battle of Corundum. How can I hope to defend it now? Leave. Send men. Now."

"The Prince will send Moresi once we return to Inverlieth," Mond said.

"When do you depart?"

"Soon," was all Mond said.

It was Aenguz who was delaying him, delaying them.

Pogacar asked Aenguz, "How long before your men can get here from your Lands?"

Aenguz had no answer for him. His road here was not direct. He couldn't even guess how long it would take. He only knew that it would not be quick enough.

"We will leave with the Prince and make all haste for the Mashu once we reach Inverlieth." Aenguz wondered about the mural of the horses and suddenly wished he had a faster means to bring help back to Pogacar's men.

Pogacar's eyes softened. "Prince Legerohn has been a great friend and ally to us. I trust your journey will be swift. We will man the stair as we have always done and await your arrival."

Aenguz looked at the falls and the towers of the Spine. Suddenly, he wondered how they would get north of the Wester. The river was wide and the current clearly swift, even from the cliff. "Is there a way to cross the Wester?"

"The stairs on the other side of Corundum are gone," Lokah said. "They will have to find a path through the mountains."

"What about a raft?" Aenguz asked.

"We have the wood. It would just be a matter of time and men." Pogacar said *men* with such derision, Aenguz almost stepped back. "It would still be difficult to cross."

Aenguz nodded at that. More delay. He wasn't ready or able to leave yet. And for the defense of Corundum, he needed to go right away.

8

FIRST OF THE
HONORED GUARD

The knotted Dagba Stone, the images in the Divine Oculum, and the pressure to let Legerohn go to Inverlieth weighed down on Aenguz as if Corundum pressed down on him. The purpose and the futility of the embassy troubled him deeply. It was a suicide mission that would leave Corundum even more depleted. He understood the strain and desperation that drove Mono Lord Lana to the decision. The whole weight of the crystal citadel seemed to crush down on him as if he had never escaped the cataclysm beneath it.

He lay awake at night in the small bedroom, turning over the problems again and again. Legerohn's words about leadership echoed in his mind. Recollections of his father before his death and the things he had tried to teach him resurfaced, along with the memory of the impossible challenges and choices he had faced on his long trek across the Lands of the Earth. All of it left him tossed about like the waters that had carried him free. But they had also nearly drowned him.

He wanted to go home. With Legerohn's men, they could feel safe and sure that they could make it. But Lana's plea and Corundum's plight were too grave. The futile course of the embassy would lead to failure. If he left them now, they would all be lost for certain. He was closer to Earthmight now than to the Mashu. And there was the burden of the final part of the message, the warning to the One King. There was hope in reaching the One King and securing the help of the One Army. He could save Corundum. He could save Inverlieth. If he accepted his responsibility as a leader, he might overcome the dire yoke of being the Last Emissary.

What about Selene? What kind of life could he offer her? If he accepted his responsibility, it would take him further from her for an even longer period of time. If he didn't relieve the burden of being the Last Emissary, who would she be next to him? It was all too much. He would have to forgo his yearning for Selene for her own good. His responsibilities did not leave room for her. The powers that warred over him and through him did not account at all for his wants or loves. With all of the demands on him, what life could he hope to have? What kind of life could he hope to have with her? She could still have a life with someone else. He might not make it to Earthmight, never mind returning to the Mashu. Best to let her go. But the pain of that sacrifice was acute.

The next morning, he replayed all of the decisions he came to through his sleepless night. The gray morning did nothing to give him a feeling that he had made the right choices. Too much was still murky. Too much relied on good fortune and hope. But what he planned, to deliver the message and get help from the One Army, was the only option available to him. He would need the others to solve the rest. But how would they react to his plans for them? They were just a collection of Akkeidii. He was barely a leader to them. Would they accept him as one now?

He found Lokah in the hall, keeping watch. "Where are Mandavu and Kachota?"

Lokah pointed to two doors.

"Get your weapon and follow me." Aenguz knocked on the doors. Each brother was groggy. Aenguz told them to get their weapons and follow him.

He led them up into the keep. Soon, they reached the line of people waiting to see the Dagba Stone. The line seemed longer. He walked past them and ignored the whispers of "Stone Finder" as he climbed the stairs.

The old Stair Guard stiffened as Aenguz and the Akkeidii approached. Surprise akin to fear tightened his eyes. Aenguz brushed past the guard's question about needed time with the stone.

Four determined Akkeidii stood silently around the mother and daughter who wept before the raised Dagba Stone. They wiped their tears away and left quickly. Kachota closed the door behind them.

The three warriors had questions in their eyes, but they held at attention before Aenguz. He studied each of them and acknowledged them. Then he began, "You swore to help bear the message to Corundum. Through the trials of the One Forest and the City of the Sho-tah, and the long leagues of the Rursh Keleg, you honored the words and faith of your oaths." He pulled the awkward weapon from the wood slab and held it before him. The wood pieces covering the edges and the Dagba Stone ensconced on top made it childish and odd. Then, he continued, "Here now, I hold your oaths fulfilled."

The three straightened. Their uncertainty of what Aenguz was doing did not wholly mask the release that softened their shoulders.

"Where you have traveled, what you have survived, would be worthy of story and song among our people. You have done more than any Akkeidii in recent times. If we were in the Valley of Gathering, I would command the Lord of the Stonemages to enter your names and accomplishments onto the wall along with all the other Akkeidii heroes stretching back to Grieg Sidor and the Venture."

Acknowledgment and pride filled their chests. Kachota looked at his older brother and both shared a smile.

"When we departed the shores of the Wester, we were divided Champions. The edicts of the Challenge and the promise of war placed demands on us that drove us away from home and across the Lands of the Earth. They were things we could not control."

Mandavu interrupted, "Aenguz, I am not the same person I was on the banks of the Wester. My grief for the fallen Champions and anger towards you and our straits left me unable to swear my allegiance to you."

Aenguz stopped him. "Your actions have shown more faith than any words you might have said then or now."

"Then let me swear it for the Makans too. You are our lord and the Lord of the Akkeidii."

Kachota spoke up then too, "Aye, I swear it too. You have saved my life and our lives more than once. That alone would compel me, but the trials you have endured... You stand as a Sidor worthy of the line of Grieg Sidor. You have my axes."

Aenguz nodded and thanked them. It was not what he was looking for, but he accepted their oaths.

"However, I am still the Last Emissary." He let that fact resonate with them.

"But I am also your lord." The words still seemed strange to him. "Both of those demands pull me in different directions. And now more problems face us: Corundum's defense, our absence from the Mashu, and the fate of the One Army and indeed all the Lands of the Earth. I need you now even more than I did when we fled the

Wester. More than that, the world needs you. We are Akkeidii, and we must set our mettle against the Flayer." The weight of that pronouncement kept them clear and focused, and the room fell into a quiet, sacred calm.

"Mandavu, my life will come under threat as both Lord of the Akkeidii and the Last Emissary. I will need your protection. I select you to be my First. And I charge you with leading the Honored Guard that wards my life."

Mandavu's eyes fluttered. Shock and confusion drew strange wrinkles between his eyes. He looked at Lokah and Kachota and back to Aenguz, as if he hoped an explanation might come from one of them.

Aenguz held out his encumbered weapon. Mandavu reached out slowly and gripped the shaft. A wave of commotion and consideration moved behind his eyes. He seemed to be processing the gravity of what he was about to say. He was about to commit his life. It was an honor due to a brother or a friend.

He pleaded silently across the stone for Aenguz to make his choice make sense to him. Mandavu had planned, had expected, to hear his brother say the oath to him. He had intended to kill Aenguz and rule the Akkeidii. If Mandavu recited the oath, it would change the course, meaning, and purpose of his life, his dreams, his father's dreams for him. Now he was about to be a First. Aenguz could feel the inchoate turmoil in him.

"What say you?"

Mandavu seemed to be processing that Aenguz had done more than any Akkeidii in living memory. He was more akin to Grieg Sidor than Sairik, the former Lord of the Akkeidii. If he was a hero on par with Grieg Sidor, what might be asked of his First? Aenguz was glad Mandavu seemed to be considering all of this and didn't jump right away into this charge.

"If I am to be your First, then there can be no more going off alone without me."

"I hear you."

Mandavu recited the oath of the First of the Honored Guard. "I, Mandavu, son of Warrum…" he began. The walls of their one-time cell, now turned sacred place, became rarefied for another reason: the Oath of the First of the Honored Guard was being recited here for the first time ever. He would be Aenguz's closest councilor and responsible for Aenguz's life.

The oath was short but absolute. He would command the Honored Guard, whose sole purpose was to protect the life of the leader of the Akkeidii, to carry out his orders and execute his will. He swore by the old heroes and the forefathers of all the clans. He swore by the Mashu and the Two Lands and the Twin Rivers. He swore his life with such gravity that it looked like the giant might turn to stone.

He released Aenguz's weapon and placed the tip of his mace on the ground before him. He tilted the handle toward Aenguz. Aenguz transferred his weapon to his marred left hand and reached out with his right to grab the handle. He looked at Mandavu squarely. There was no superiority, no arrogance, only a gratitude that he could not fully understand.

There would be perils and trials ahead that neither of them could conceive. There would be places that Mandavu could not follow. Aenguz's charge from Morgrom had already confirmed that. Mandavu's protective role over his lord would be unquestionably hard if not im-possible to keep. And the price of his life would be near to the surface at all times. The possibilities and exigencies of their new relationship mixed between them. Aenguz accepted Mandavu's weapon and then released his grip.

Mandavu pulled the mace back. His complexion had changed. The wrinkles and uncertainty were gone. He looked at his brother and named him the first member of the Honored Guard - his Hand, a lieutenant to help him execute his orders in service of Aenguz.

"I will need your help too, Lokah. You too are chosen for the Honored Guard."

Lokah nodded, stern but crestfallen. Aenguz guessed what he might be feeling. As a Kriel from the line of Hernus Kriel, who had been the best friend to Grieg Sidor the Venturer, he was the obvious choice to be Aenguz's First. But with Aenguz's decision, he was left out of that ancient role. In some way, he was not worthy. Lokah looked downcast, like he had failed his clan. But Aenguz had something else in mind for Lokah.

"Lokah, we will all have to take on multiple responsibilities. I have another role for you. I name you as my loremaster. You will be the loremaster for the Ruler of the Akkeidii. You will aid me and learn to master the mysteries of *montmorillion* lore and ward my weapon and all of our *montmorillionite*. You are now the weapons master for me and for us all. And you are charged with finding a way to get this stone off of my weapon."

Lokah's eyes froze in shock. The shift in the charge paralyzed him for a moment. Aenguz held his weapon out for Lokah to touch. The implications of what Aenguz asked of him clouded his complexion. Aenguz could not read what internal searching Lokah might be doing. His hand came up reflexively, but neither fast nor slow. He hesitated briefly as he contemplated what the charge and the task might mean. His eyes dropped to the stone and the weapon and took them both in with a new weight. Then, he gripped it. "I am honored to be your loremaster, my lord."

Mandavu and Kachota presented their weapons to Lokah. He set his sword down and examined them closely, as if to incuse every detail of each weapon. He was responsible for all of their weapons now, and

Aenguz's most of all. The sacred metal was rare and valuable, and he was now their chief steward.

The solemn Akkeidii ceremonies were complete. They waited on Aenguz's words and his first orders to them in their new roles.

"I know you want to go home. I want to go home. After what I saw in the Divine Oculum, I ache to warn our people. They are closer to this threat than anyone else in all the Lands. But Corundum is in dire need, and it will take a long time to get help from there. And the charge of the Last Emissary still holds me. The message compels me to warn the One King and the One Army.

"Legerohn is planning to send Moresi warriors here to protect Corundum, but he will not attempt the Dimmerdross or the Cleve. The Mono Lord prepares an embassy to cross the Cleve and travel to Earthmight and gain the aid of the One King and the One Army. The One King and the Lower Lands must be warned. I trust Legerohn. If he would not risk the Moresi, then I will not risk the Akkeidii. Therefore…" Aenguz walked to the curtains and drew them back with a firm sweep. "We will join the Mono Lord's embassy, but we will lead them over the Spine. I will go to the Mono Lord and dissuade her from the Cleve. And I will tell her how, with Akkeidii help, we will cross the mountains. No one has passed over the Spine before, but we are suited for it." The gray wall of the Spine undulated imperviously into the distance. The tips of the pines gave up their climb against the high, hard granite. "With the warning delivered and the One King and One Army at our side, we will breach the Cleve and bring help to the Upper Lands."

"As you command," the three replied, though uncertainty tinged their tone.

Aenguz faced Mandavu directly as if he were talking to him alone. "Word must be sent to the Mashu. First of the Honored Guard, send word to the clan lords of what we plan to do. Send word so that they may know that we are alive, and of all that we have endured and seen in the Lands of the Earth. Send word to them that their lord commands that they ready the army. War is upon the Lands of the Earth and the Akkeidii must be ready for my orders."

Mandavu's eyes contorted. Realization flexed them. He could not leave Aenguz's side, nor could Lokah. His only option wrenched him. He turned to his brother. "Kachota, you will return to the Mashu and give account to the clan lords of all that we have seen and all that has happened. Tell them who has lived and who has died."

"Brother…" A cold shock washed over Kachota's face. "Aenguz," he pleaded. "Do not send me from you."

"Lord," Mandavu corrected his brother. Then he added, "Would you disobey my first order?"

Kachota begged quietly, but he held his tongue and shook his head. Mandavu glowered at his brother.

Kachota eked out, "By your will, it will be done."

Mandavu relaxed and faced Aenguz again.

"Kachota will bear word to our kinsmen." A low chord of pain like a tremor hummed through his words.

Aenguz's heart stung for Kachota and Mandavu. Separating brothers was no small matter. There were so few among the Akkeidii. He had a plan on how to bring Kachota back from his sinking despair.

He faced Kachota as if he were addressing him for the first time since learning of Mandavu's choice. He played at a formality in their new roles. "Kachota, I understand you will be returning to the Mashu. You will act as my ambassador in Inverlieth. You will represent all the Akkeidii. You will represent your lord."

Kachota rose up. His chest filled. His eyes widened and grew serious.

"You will accompany the Moresi to Inverlieth. I will have more words for you to bear before you go. Your stay in Inverlieth will be brief. I will talk with Legerohn and see that you have all the men you need to make it safely back to the Mashu."

Acknowledgment of the honor bestowed on him gave Kachota a new kind of wonder - a task more weighty than he could have imagined. He straightened another notch as if a mantle had been placed on his shoulders. He nodded and answered firmly, "Yes, my lord. It will be done."

Mandavu indulged in a proud smile.

"Make ready to prepare for our departure. I will go now and tell Legerohn. And I will go and talk to the Mono Lord."

9

ALLIANCE

Aenguz left the sanctum and found a runner in the refectory who guided him up the stairs on the far side of the dining hall and led him to the roof of Corundum. The squat agate forest appeared different in the daylight. The last time he had seen it, it was under the cover of night, crawling across it on his way to the Well of Sorrows. A lot had changed since then.

They doubled back and walked toward the front of Corundum. She led him down steps to a wide circular platform. Lines ran in deliberate paths around the surface. Hunks of jagged crystal were spaced around like a makeshift crenellation. A rope was wound around each of them and they draped down out of sight over the edge.

Legerohn stood with some stocky men. They peered over the side to the north face of Corundum. They seemed to be mulling the integrity of the crystal.

Aenguz left the runner behind and walked over to the Prince. "Legerohn, a word."

The men looked at Aenguz and then to the Prince. "I will find you later." They left the two men alone.

"I am planning to go with the embassy."

Legerohn chewed on Aenguz's statement. "I will not commit my men even if you go."

"I am not asking you to. I believe you when you say that it would be foolish to try. I have another way." Aenguz turned to the Spine. "I plan to cross the Spine from here." The sharp gray peaks glowered down at them. "I am going to persuade her that it is the better way, a safer way."

"Is it?"

"We are Akkeidii. The mountains do not daunt us."

Legerohn considered him. His eyes worked as his mind processed Aenguz's words. Finally, he said, "You know the mountains better than I. You have gone into greater danger before, but it still worries me."

"Mandavu, Kachota, and Lokah are making preparations to cross. We have experience bearing supplies into the mountains. We will help deliver the Mono Lord's plea. It still falls to me to deliver the warning in the message to the One King. With the One King and the One Army, we will attempt the Cleve and purge the Dimmerdross. We will then join you in Inverlieth."

Legerohn's lips pursed and flexed, but he said nothing.

"I have named Mandavu my First and charged Kachota with bearing word to the Mashu. With good fortune, the Akkeidii will join us before any harm befalls Inverlieth or Corundum. Will you receive him in Inverlieth and see him safely across the northern plains?"

Legerohn turned and looked out over the green lands north of the Wester. Dense forest covered the tight foothills along the Spine. A vast swath of grasslands and prairie fanned out to the north. The Wester glinted to the right and ran off into the east. The Moresi Prince seemed to be searching for any hint of his homeland. Then, he turned back to Aenguz. "Of course, Kachota will be welcome in Inverlieth. Mond and Chimere will see him there. Unfortunately, the celebrations will be short. My men will accompany him safely to the Mashu."

Aenguz could see that Legerohn had more to say. He made his promise to Aenguz for Kachota with an uncertain tone. "My friend, I still will not leave you alone to this task. And if this embassy is to have the weight of the Remnant and the free peoples of the Upper Lands, the Prince of the Moresi will add his appeal to yours and the Mono Lord's."

"No, you do not need to do that," Aenguz objected. "Return to Inverlieth, ready your men for our return."

"Whoever the Mono Lord sends can only speak to the Battle of Corundum and the victory here. You and Mandavu and Lokah would act as only one voice for what we have both seen in the east of the Erebim and the Sallow and the Tsurah, but not what my men experienced before that. How would an emissary from Corundum explain the Divine Oculum and the images unbound by time? And you, my friend, are still the Last Emissary. Your words may not be well received by the One King. I will add my words to yours. That way, the plight of the Upper Lands will have as many voices as will be heard."

Aenguz searched the air around Legerohn as he contemplated the Prince's words.

Legerohn continued, "Mond can ready Inverlieth. He will see to it that we are ready for the One Army's arrival."

Aenguz didn't want to risk his friend, but he could not counter the Prince's reasoning.

"I will accompany you," Legerohn said unequivocally.

Aenguz's relief was so unexpected that he half laughed and clapped the Prince on the arm.

Legerohn asked, "I know how important your weapon is to you. Will you leave it here with the Dagba Stone?"

"I have charged Lokah with removing the Dagba Stone."

"What if he cannot remove it?"

"I am not sure if the Mono Lord would let me take the Dagba Stone with it."

Part of Aenguz wanted to leave it as recompense. It might make up for the loss of so many Stair Guard, might make up for the destruction it had caused. It might be the single best thing to protect Corundum, if Lana could uncover how to use it. However, there were no other Counsel Lords to help her. And it might draw the full might of Morgrom's forces right to the steps of Forhnthulen. If she could not use the Keystone of Creation, it would only act as the means of their doom, whether it was attached to his weapon or not.

The Dagba Stone had been at the heart of Corundum for an age. She had every right to claim it as their own. He had only found it. If it were not attached to his weapon, would he have any claim to it at all? Would she even allow him to leave with it? Would the people of Corundum? He hoped Lokah could find an answer so that he could avoid the problem altogether.

Legerohn searched for the runner. He called to the runner and sent her on ahead to find Mond. Aenguz walked with him to the door that led back into the keep.

"As I said on the shores of the Wester, I will not leave you alone with this task. The fate of the Remnant and the peoples of the Lands depends on the One Army." Legerohn's smile was reassuring.

After he left, Aenguz remained and took in the sharp towering gray granite of the Spine. He followed the winding path through the short crystal forest toward the wall. He came upon the sealed mouth of the Well of Sorrows. An empty scaffolding of wooden beams marked the spot. A shallow cup filled with pulverized tourmaline rested next to it. He found the line he used to climb down into the hole. Had he made the right decision?

He left the sealed well and followed the path to the farthest edge of Corundum. The outflow from the tip of a long lake split where crystal met stone. A crude stone bridge crossed the left branch and led to the rocky shore. There was evidence of a second bridge to the right, but it was broken. Water poured over the broken bridge stones.

Ringing the clear blue-gray lake and the exposed rocky shore was a sheer wall of snow. It looked to be cut away. On the distant farther shore, there was a fold between the treeless peaks. That is where they would cross. This is where they would depart for the Lower Lands. His will met the will of the Spine. It had to be safer than the forest to the north. It had to. But first, he had to convince Mono Lord Lana.

10

MONO LORD

Aenguz returned to the refectory and asked a cook for the Mono Lord. He waited by the kitchen and ate some cheese and bread to stave off his morning hunger. He moved out of the way of the bustle around the kitchen. Some stared at him until their eyes met, and then they looked away quickly. They were either too afraid or too unsure of him or what he was to say anything. A pocket of quiet grew around Aenguz. Soon, Stroud appeared. The Azari walked up to Aenguz and said, "I will take you to the Mono Lord."

Stroud led Aenguz through a corridor on the north side of the keep. The hall led eventually down a shallow series of stairs and flats past a set of evenly spaced doors. Stroud led him all the way to the bottom, pulled at the door, and ushered Aenguz in.

The smell of stale must like old stone met him. Dim ambient light withheld the depths of the space. In the dark open area before him, a massive boulder the height of two men gaveled the floor. The damaged floor was a swirl of green malachite. Veins of bright yellow and jots of night shade opal complemented the green. The darkly colorful ceiling was jagged like the roof of Corundum. A vacant space marked the spot where the boulder was. If light were cast upward, the whole ceiling would be a chandelier fit for giants or Hyrrokkin.

Rings of seats rose up to his left. Two other large boulders crushed down on the rows at different points and sat like unwanted guests. A shelf of rock hung halfway above the rows out into a balcony, and another above that.

A moment of trauma and devastation inculcated for all time.

To his right was a semi-circular stage. A crystal table sat on top and mirrored the same curve. High-backed crystalline chairs, vaulted on a slight bias, ringed the table evenly. Black cloths like cerements were draped over the tall-backed chairs.

Mono Lord Lana was folding one of the black cloths on the table. In the dim light, in her blue robe, she looked like a specter of the living trapped in a world of the dead. Its darkness could not wholly mask the aura of her grief and loss. The realm of death seemed to be coaxing her into its bosom, urging her, tempting her to stay. She drew the black fabric off the chair carefully, draped it on the tabletop, and folded it deliberately, checking the edges and corners.

Aenguz walked reverently, positioning himself before her like a pro se defendant. Stroud stayed behind, but his gaze never left Aenguz's back. He was as impervious as the fallen megalith before him. Aenguz did not want to intrude on her dour ritual. Also, this was probably a rare moment of peace in her now hectic days.

Lana finished her folding and summoned a sad, forced smile. "You wanted to see me."

"Yes, I wanted to talk with you about the embassy you plan to send to Earthmight."

"Yes."

"I trust Prince Legerohn when he says the Dimmerdross and the Cleve are not safe."

"It is the most direct route."

"Perhaps not."

Her head tilted slightly. Her eyes clenched.

"I have another option - a safer one. I still bear words of warning for the One King. We are already high up in the mountains. If you will agree, the Akkeidii will guide the embassy over the Spine."

The relief she seemed to hope for turned to shadows of anger. "The Spine has never been crossed. The Spine is like the end of the world to us. How can you believe that you can cross it?"

"We are Akkeidii. We were born in the Mashu. We live and train in the mountains. We know how to navigate them. By climbing through the Spine, we will avoid the perils of the Dimmerdross and Cleve altogether."

"Or you may die in the Spine."

That was a possibility. "We may. Mountains are perilous. But the Cleve is death for certain. In the Spine, we have a chance. Legerohn is willing to go with us. And summer is the best time to go." He assured her that Mond would return to Inverlieth to send men back to Corundum. He would send Kachota on to the Mashu to get Akkeidii warriors. "With good fortune, we will meet Morgrom's army with the One Army and the Moresi army. The Akkeidii may be late to the battle, but they will make their presence known."

Lana studied him. She walked around the table and came down a short stair at the edge of the dais. "Both options are dangerous; whether one is more dangerous than the other, I cannot say. It may be that it is time for the Cleve to be breached, just like it was time for the Dagba Stone to be found. The Spine is the edge of the world. Who knows if you can cross it? How do you know you will come out into the Lower Lands? Who knows if the Lower Lands remain beyond?"

"An unknown danger may afford a way that a known danger will not." Aenguz did not move.

She came up smoothly to Aenguz. Calculation replaced the grief on her face. Stroud was suddenly in Aenguz's periphery as if he had always been there.

"Do you truly believe you can cross the Spine and preserve the embassy?"

"I do." It was a reckless promise, but it might be the only thing that would get her to change her mind.

Lana contemplated a moment longer. She stared into his eyes to gauge him. Finally, she answered, "Very well. The embassy of Corundum will go over the Spine. It was a hard decision to send Saissha and Einki into certain peril, but I had no other option."

Aenguz breathed out, not realizing he had been holding his breath. His heart was thumping hard. Relief coursed through him, but then another matter, a more difficult matter, seized him again and tightened his breath.

"Is there anything else?"

Was there a way to make her understand? His words blurted out, "I cannot go without my weapon. I am an Akkeidii and a Warrior. There is no accommodation in my oath or faith for the abandonment of my *montmorillionite* weapon."

Her eyes narrowed. She did not appear surprised by his words. "You are also the Stone Finder and the Message Bearer, Last Emissary to the Divider. Obligations change. I was the seedmaster of Corundum and would have been more than content to follow that discipline in counting and storing the seeds until the end of my days upon the Lands of the Earth. The Dagba Stone has been here since the Last Battle. Corundum has been its resting place for eons. Look what it has done since it was found. It has changed much here." The boulder sustained her assertion.

"Perhaps you were meant to become something else," Lana posited.

"I have become something else. I might do more than I could have ever conceived of as the Mono Lord than I could as Corundum's seedmaster."

"Would you attempt a journey like this without your staff?"

Lana turned her head to find it behind the table, but she did not answer.

"I am the Lord of the Akkeidii. I could not command the Akkeidii without my *montmorillionite*. I could not remain its ruler or a Warrior or even set foot beyond Grieg's Gate without it." That was, if he even lived to return home at all.

Lana regrouped and walked a few steps to put the boulder behind her. Both Mono Lord and megalith towered over him. Stroud was out of sight, but he seemed nearer at his back.

"Have you considered the message you delivered?"

Have I considered it?! A tsunami of rage and self-castigation rose up to drown him. "The message and his words have never left me!"

"I do not mean the words themselves; I mean the Divider's intent around them."

"Doom. Doom to the Remnant. Doom to the people of Earth. Ruinwasters free and unchecked on the Lands to enact *his* will. That is his intent, his sole desire."

"And what could one Ruinwaster do?" she asked calmly.

Vitriol scored each word as he said, "'*One Ruinwaster alone would be enough to rend the Vaults of Corundum.*'"

The Mono Lord accused him. The boulder accused him. The gallery was an indictment, the whole state of Corundum an indictment. The lost seed vaults lay empty below him. The dead Stair Guard, the drowned Counsel Lords, all of it prosecuted him.

"Perhaps *you* are the doom you warn about."

Her accusation shocked him. In that moment, he might have killed her - was capable of killing her. Part of him wanted to reach out and strike her. The rage overwhelmed and shocked him. He was not a Ruinwaster. He was just the Last Emissary. Unwanted. Unbidden. But it was perhaps the truth of what she suggested that angered him most. His face flushed. He couldn't look at her. Stroud was in his periphery as if he had always been there.

Aenguz strained to master himself and unhook his rage.

"What would you do with the Dagba Stone if you wielded it?"

It was the same question Bremball had asked him when he led them up into the keep. Aenguz didn't have an answer, but he didn't want the stone for himself. He wanted the Counsel Lords to have it, wanted them to use it. "I do not want the stone. I wanted you to have it, but it's locked on my weapon. And I cannot leave my weapon."

Lana continued, "But what would you do if you could master it? What would you do with it?"

"I do not know. Remove the blight. Destroy the Flayer. I have no idea how to use it."

"You could alter much more with the Keystone of Creation."

"I only ever wanted to please my father and be a good leader for the Akkeidii. I love my home. I want to return there. But I don't know if there will be a Mashu to rule if I do not get help. My whole life is in the Mashu. I never wanted any of this. I want to get out from under being his Last Emissary. I want to save my home, and if that means saving the Earth and using the Dagba Stone to do so, then that is what I would do with it."

He couldn't tell if she accepted his answer. He was drained from opening up to her and articulating something so deep inside about himself. He felt like he was defending his life.

"Are you able and willing to protect the Dagba Stone at all costs?

Are you willing to sacrifice yourself for its sake? Are you sure that would be enough to protect it?"

"If I fail - if we fail in crossing the Spine - it will be lost again in the high reaches where no one may find it. If I reach Earthmight, it will be better protected there than it is here. You and I both know it is not safe here. If I take it from here, the images in the Divine Oculum might change. It cannot be where Saissha saw it surrounded by Erebim.

"I will keep it safe until you or someone wise knows how to use it to stop Lord Morgrom. Since it has found its way onto my weapon, I will take responsibility for it. I will protect it, if needs be, with my life."

Lana's eyes were tight and intense. She looked down as if she had unintentionally trampled flowers. When she looked up, the aura of her eyes changed and became grave. "I will not remove it from the sanctum, but I will not stop you. If you take your weapon and the Dagba Stone with it, you cannot move it to some other place in Corundum and keep it. If you take the Dagba Stone, you must leave Corundum immediately and forever."

11

DEPARTURE

With the knowledge of the new course shared, the efforts of everyone in Corundum rallied around readying the embassy to cross over the Spine. Work began on three sleds that would bear the supplies and tents the company would need in the mountains. It was Mandavu's idea, but Aenguz gave the order.

Kachota oversaw their construction. They were based on Akkeidii design. The carpenters relished the challenge to try to interpret Kachota's description of the sled. Like flat-bottomed boats with four gunwales, two in front and two in back, four men could bear the sleds with straps that fit over their shoulders. Wooden rails ran along the bottom, allowing them to haul the sleds with ease whenever they encountered snow. They had to be both sturdy and light. Everything they might need was discussed and argued over in order to fit in the most efficient manner. Einki was fastidious about each piece. The Step Mark of the embassy had an ability to catalog everything. He seemed able to list out every tool, every component, the count of each piece of their supplies.

Pogacar and Einki selected the Stair Guard from among the

volunteers. When they had learned that they must either have a child or at least be mated, it accelerated courtships that had been pushed back due to the work in defending Corundum. It also kept the younger boys out of the pool of eligible volunteers. This gave no small relief to their parents.

In a boon of hope, a small contingent of Stair Guard returned from their search on the Rursh Keleg with a Counsel Lord's staff. The rest of their company remained on the old road to honor and inter the dead. It was not old Mono Lord Venrahl's staff, so Lana blessed it and gave it to Saissha for her journey.

The embassy was ready to leave ten days later. A final day of rest was given to the members of the embassy for goodbyes. On the last night, a farewell feast was held in a large room off of the refectory. The Stair Guard who had worked side by side with the Akkeidii and Moresi presented them with burgundy cloaks as thank you gifts. To Mandavu, Lokah, and Kachota, they gave scabbards for their weapons to thank them not only for their strength and sweat, but also for the honing ability their hard *montmorillionite* possessed. Sharp axes made the work of clearing the side of Corundum much easier.

They did not give a scabbard to Aenguz. He wondered if they remembered his own silver-banded scabbard, or if they had simply assumed that his weapon was staying in Corundum. They presented him with a Stair Guard sword and scabbard. It had been found among the rocks on the cliff and was honed to a razor's edge. The Akkeidii accepted the gifts graciously, though it was a warrior's responsibility to craft and tool his own scabbard. But there was not time for such things. These would be temporary gifts until Mandavu, Lokah, and Kachota could craft their own.

The next day, Aenguz closed the doors to the balcony and adjusted the curtains in his room. He made sure that not a drop poured out from the stone valves. He adjusted the chairs around the table again and again to make sure they were squarely set. The room looked like it had when Lokah brought him here those many days before. Once he left, it would look like he had never been there at all. When he left, he was never coming back to this room or to Corundum again.

He was still inspecting the room when a short knock came at the door. He nearly jumped. Aenguz walked to the door, collected himself, and let Mandavu in.

"It is time."

"Do you have it?"

"Yes."

Aenguz donned his silver-banded scabbard from Mere Gurudev. He draped the burgundy cloak over it.

Mandavu inspected the bulge. "It will do."

Aenguz's heart started working its way up into his throat. They left the suite and turned to the interior of the keep. The yellow tint was nearly gone from the walls and the white strata beneath dispelled the shadows from the corners.

Mandavu led the way as they climbed up the stairs into the keep. Even though his First was on high alert and ready for anything, he emanated a stoic calm.

When they reached the base of the stairs, Aenguz's heart choked his throat. He was sure they would be able to hear the pounding when he passed.

The line waiting to see the stone was shorter. Many people were on top of Corundum gathered, to bid farewell to the embassy. Others were down on the cliff, continuing the work of manning the defense of the Stair of Forhnthulen.

Two Stair Guard stood at attention outside the hallowed room. They straightened as Mandavu and Aenguz approached.

"A last time with the stone?" one guard asked.

"It is Akkeidii tradition to bid farewell to a weapon before leaving it," Mandavu said.

One guard raised a hand to the next people in line, signaling for them to wait. The other stood in the doorway to quietly usher the three women out of the room. A grandmother, mother, and daughter all cried, but their tears were tears of joy. They clung to one another. As they left, they thanked Aenguz, calling him Stone Finder. When they were out, the guard stood to the side and let the Akkeidii in.

"This is a sacred rite. Do not disturb us," Mandavu said and closed the door behind them.

Aenguz's wood-covered weapon stood poised upright on the slab.

He unslung his scabbard and set it on the table. He wiggled his weapon out of the wood. He pressed the protective pieces tightly onto all the edges. Then he slid it carefully and quietly into the scabbard. A giant's drum pounded in his head. Sweat tickled his face. He pulled the flap over the stone. It didn't close. Panic flooded him. He pulled on the leather. Mandavu grabbed the scabbard and shook it hard once. Then he gave it back to Aenguz. Aenguz thumbed the placket through the silver button. His weapon fit snugly into Mere's gift. He looked at Mandavu. His First panted, but Mandavu had a slight smile. Aenguz's heart seemed to be escaping from his chest. He slung the scabbard over his back and under the cloak.

Then, Mandavu reached around beneath his cloak and pulled out Kachota's axe. He leaned into it and pressed it deep down into the wood slab.

Then Aenguz uttered words of lore:

"Ever clean, ever new, ever bright..."

His throat broke, his mind was frantic. He took a breath and started again.

"Ever clean, ever new, ever bright
Earth's first star to dispel the night."

White light came to the axe. He spoke a few more couplets to intensify the brightness. Then he added a few lines to call a chime from the weapon. The sanctum glowed. The chime echoed in the rarefied room.

"Ready?" Mandavu asked.

Aenguz nodded.

"Let me go first, then get in front of me. I will close the door behind us."

Aenguz nodded again. He wiped his face and took several deep breaths.

Mandavu opened the door. Light and sound poured into the hallway. He towered over the guards and blocked their view. He told them that it would take some time for the metal to quiet. Under no circumstances was he to let anyone into the room until both the light and the sound had died. It would not harm the stone, but it might be dangerous for them.

The guards stared up and acknowledged the giant Makan as if they had been given the most terrifying orders of their lives.

Aenguz walked out behind Mandavu. He was sure they all knew what he had under his cloak, but the people's eyes remained fixed on the light as if they had just witnessed something mystical from the stone.

Mandavu closed the door to the sanctum, and Aenguz led the way down. Every time someone uttered, "Stone Finder," his heart dropped like he had been caught - like their next words were going to be, "He has the stone!"

They made their way back down and through the refectory. Aenguz was convinced that they were all suspicious of him, as if they knew what he carried.

They wound their way through the mix of stairs and halls to the door out of the keep and onto the roof. The wall of the Spine greeted them and seemed to lean toward them, warning them. They strode past the Well of Sorrows. Mandavu glared at the tourmaline plug as if to say, *"If only I had more time."*

They wended their way through the squat agate forest until they saw a gathering of people. They parted as Aenguz and Mandavu came up. Kachota, Mond, and Stokke met the pair near the front of the gathering. Mandavu clapped his brother's shoulder. Kachota nodded. They shared a brief, almost compulsory goodbye. Whatever real words of farewell they had, they had shared together in private the night before.

Kachota gave Aenguz a proud, "My lord". Aenguz nodded. He was too focused on the talisman beneath his cloak to tell him anything else. He had given his new ambassador all the advice needed for his journey to Inverlieth and all the words he wanted to send back to the Mashu.

Mond and Stokke wished Aenguz and Mandavu farewell. They assured them that Kachota would be in safe hands. Mandavu thanked the old salt for keeping his brother in his stead, and Stokke too. Aenguz nodded and smiled as well, though he was certain that if he spoke, his nervous tone would betray him. What might the people of Corundum do if they knew he had taken the Dagba Stone?

At the front of the group, just before the bridge, was the Mono Lord. Stroud stood beside her. Pogacar was with them. He gave his final few bits of advice to Einki. The proud Step Mark nodded and seemed to gain some final assurance from Pogacar. They glanced at Aenguz and Mandavu as the pair passed. The pair blended in with the final few Stair Guard who moved to and fro over the bridge.

Aenguz held his breath until they crossed the primitive bridge to where the embassy assembled. Saissha gave them a tight smile, found staff in hand, shoulders square, and then returned her gaze to the only life she had ever known.

Prince Legerohn and Chimere flanked her. Aenguz slipped in next to Lokah and tried to blend in with the fifteen Stair Guard who were chosen for the embassy. Einki followed after the Akkeidii and looked over the men in his charge and the three sleds. Then he took his place next to the Prince and Counsel Lord Saissha. The men towered around her, but she still seemed tall among them.

Then suddenly, surprisingly, Stroud left the Mono Lord's side. He pivoted like he was stepping out of formation. Aenguz's heart stopped. Stroud crossed the bridge and took a position right next to Saissha. This was it. He knew. Aenguz was caught. But Stroud said nothing. The Azari was coming with them. That was almost more unsettling.

The benediction the Mono Lord gave was brief. The gurgling waters lifted her words up. She called on the powers of the earth to see them safely over the Spine and to aid their journey to Earthmight. She uttered a potent blessing for a quick delivery of the message and a quicker return. They would all be waiting for them in Corundum.

Saissha thanked the Mono Lord on behalf of the embassy across the bridge. A chill wind was at her back. Then Saissha led the embassy out along the rocky shore of the wide lake. Stroud and the Prince walked with her, then Chimere, Mandavu, Aenguz, and Lokah followed behind.

Einki called the Stair Guard of the embassy to life. Twelve men, four for each sled. They slid the collars over their shoulders and hoisted up the bulging, laden sleds. Einki, his Step Mark, and another Stair Guard held point for each sled, acting as a set of eyes for the bearers. Fifteen Stair Guard in all.

They made their way slowly around the empty, rocky shore of the long lake. When they reached the far end, Saissha turned and gave a final farewell to the Mono Lord and the onlookers at the other end of the lake. She waved her new staff, and Aenguz could see the Mono Lord standing on the bridge, her arms wide as if to gather all the power of the earth and creation to pass over to them.

The company climbed up through the channel that had been carved in the snow. Once they were beyond the sight of the others, Saissha took off her robe to reveal her form-fitting mountaineering clothes. She folded her blue robe and gave it to Einki, along with her staff. He stowed it under the canvas and ropes of the sled he oversaw.

Mandavu unslung his gifted scabbard and handed it to Lokah. Aenguz undid his from under his cloak and gave it to his loremaster. The Kriel took them both, but Aenguz's more carefully, and stowed them with his own weapon on the last sled. No one except Saissha paid much attention to what the Akkeidii did.

A few other adjustments were made by the Stair Guard, and then the sleds were pulled across the snow up over the tight pass between the peaks into a wilderness never before ventured into.

12

WINTER'S SPINE

Aenguz led the embassy up into the stark gray peaks of the Spine. He talked with Mandavu and Lokah about the surest paths to the lowest points between the folds in the mountains. They would confer with Saissha and Einki about their proposed course and then the day's climb would begin. When they made camp at the end of each day, they surveyed the rugged wilderness and mulled the best course amid seemingly impossible choices.

Saissha was an able climber. Her blue robe and the gifted, braided Counsel Lord's staff were packed away on one of the three sleds that the coterie of Stair Guard bore. She looked like a mountaineer scout and not one of the defenders of the Lands of the Earth.

She volunteered to climb ahead with Mandavu to check narrow high passes and steep cliff walls. "She is easy to lift, and she has strong hands," he said of her.

They would go on ahead with Mandavu bearing the rope. Their only agreement, which became an edict for them, was to not turn back. Coming back out on the eastern face of the Spine south of Corundum would crush them. It was the only charge the pair took with them when they scouted the way.

However, the lowest points drove them southward. Even if they entertained the idea of going back, it wasn't certain that they could make it. The Spine seemed determined to prevent their crossing either way. They moved among the clouds and were shredded along with them as they climbed.

The day the embassy from Corundum reached the stark valley, the sky was so blue and so near that it seemed like they could drink from it. The company was exhausted from days of thwarted climbing. By the time they reached the bottom of the hollow, Aenguz determined that they all needed a rest.

Three disparate peaks enclosed the steep hollow. The sharp gray mountain they had climbed around was like all the mountains they had seen the days before since departing the citadel. The mountain to the west was brown and formidable but not as severe as the sheer gray peaks. To the south and east, a lithified cliff walled the valley. Vertical lines of colored strata looked like rows of giant spears left unused and forgotten. A thin opening marked the middle like a pass, but it was dark and foreboding. It might be a pass, but it led the wrong way. The change in the complexion of the three mountains and the clear sky was a cause for guarded hope. It was a logical place for the company to rest, even though it was still midday. But that was not the only reason.

Legerohn trailed down the slope behind the company. His arm was draped over Chimere. The leaders of the embassy assembled as the Stair Guard lowered the sleds.

"He needs to rest," Aenguz said.

"Rest will not help him," Lokah countered.

"He is not doing well," Saissha pleaded with the Akkeidii. She saw how the Prince was deteriorating. She shared a tent with him and

Stroud, though the Azari never slept. "Chimere tries to get him to eat, but he insists he is not hungry. Whenever he does eat, Legerohn brings up anything he swallows."

"We have tried everything in our stores for his head pain," Einki said. The Step Mark was as wracked as Saissha.

"He has mountain sickness," Aenguz said with a grimace. "The only answer is to get him off of this mountain. This is the first break we have seen so far, and that pass looks promising," he said as he searched for a way out and down as much as an answer for Legerohn's condition. He asked Einki, "Can you build a litter with what you have in the sleds?"

The Step Mark seemed to catalog and inventory each and every item in a few brief moments while his eyes worked. His lips moved as if he were counting to himself. He had seen to every piece of equipment, tool, and food store that was packed on the sleds. "We could perhaps repurpose one of the tents, but it will make for tight quarters for the Stair Guard." Fifteen Stair Guard made up their complement.

"See what you can do. We may have to carry him." Aenguz buried his dejection. They were no closer to the Lower Lands and his marvelous plan was about to cost his friend his life.

He turned to Mandavu. "Go and check the pass. If it looks good, we will make for it in the morning." Aenguz deferred to Saissha, mindful of her role.

"Make camp," she ordered Einki. "And get Legerohn in to lie down as soon as you can. Mandavu and I will inspect the pass."

"Yes, Counsel Lord." Einki called orders to the others.

Mandavu and Saissha hiked ahead across the snowpack to the rock field while the Stair Guard raised the corallel tents and made camp.

Aenguz and Lokah walked back to meet the Prince and Chimere. Stroud went with them. They relieved Chimere of his burden. His limp had never fully gone away. Stroud moved to help Chimere, but he shrugged the Azari off. He was too proud to add to their burden. Aenguz and Lokah shouldered Legerohn and walked the Prince down to the bottom of the hollow. When the tent was raised, Chimere helped him in.

That had been four days ago.

The Akkeidii were used to hunkering down during a blizzard. The only regret they had was that they carried no ale, lager, or even mead with them to help pass the time. Everything they needed for the crossing was packed onto the three sleds, and there was no extra room for unnecessary items, despite Mandavu's protestations before they left.

Summer storms in the mountains of the Mashu were not uncommon for the Akkeidii. They were brief and rarely severe. They never lasted longer than a full day.

But this storm seemed misplaced. It should have passed already. It was more like an unrelenting blizzard than a summer squall. It might have easily been the heart of winter. It was only by virtue of it being summer that they attempted the Spine at all. After two days, Aenguz was concerned, but this was the Spine, and no one had climbed here before.

Aenguz ordered a winter watch to be set. The Stair Guard would determine a rotation to check the tents and clear the snow between them during the day. At nightfall, Mandavu and Lokah would make the rounds. Besides checking their number, the warriors would melt snow for water with their *montmorillionite* weapons. They also conjured up heat to warm their blankets, coats, and cloaks. It bolstered the meager heat generated by their careful stump fires.

Mandavu or Lokah would share anything they had heard or seen in the storm, and vice versa. Predators were a concern, but they were more interested in signs that the storm was shifting. The Stair Guard would ask, "If there was a plan?" Or, "How would they get clear of the tempest?" But Mandavu and Lokah had seen little to report, either to them or back to Aenguz. The Stair Guard were grateful for the visits and the warmth. They were hardy and urgent, but waiting did not suit them.

Aenguz shared their concern. How would they get clear? And time was not on their side. He had been delayed in Corundum while he tried to remove the stone and decide how to help the embassy. And now they had already been in the Spine longer than he had anticipated. Another season would pass before they reached Earthmight, if they even reached it. Not much time to marshal an army and return to the Upper Lands.

Five seasons will not pass before Earthmight is under siege and the One King's army is lost.

13

A FINAL HOPE

On the fifth day of the storm, Aenguz gave voice to his concern. Akkeidii toughness clashed with the harsh reality. Lokah and Mandavu seemed relieved by Aenguz's confession. They had joked about the storm, and they did not want to show weakness in front of their lord. On his next visit to check on Legerohn, Aenguz spoke to Saissha about his concern. The fluttering tent walls served to confirm his fears. The storm seemed unnatural, and there seemed to be no end in sight.

"What if I used my staff to counter the storm?" she posited.

Aenguz had no answer for her. He didn't have any explicit knowledge of the braided staff's power beyond what the Mono Lord had done when Aenguz delivered the message to the Counsel Lords. The large entryway to Corundum had filled suddenly with a bright blue flourish of energy that nearly blinded him. It was a considerable power, but it was the only one he knew.

"What about the Dagba Stone?" she suggested.

"There is no power at all in my weapon or the stone."

"What about theirs?" She gestured toward Mandavu and indirectly to Lokah in the tent beyond.

"I do not know. Let me discuss it with Lokah."

Aenguz and Mandavu brought the question back to their loremaster. They pondered over The Lay of *Montmorillionite* for a combination of couplets that might help them. They hoped to find way to draw out of the sacred metal some means to dispel the storm. Mandavu listened mostly and grunted following their esoteric reasoning. He did not delve so deeply into the lore as Aenguz and Lokah did, but he could follow what they were doing. There was nothing immediately available in the lore that would counter the weather. It was a local power, mostly, a bond between weapon and creator informed by their time together. Only the forbidden clashing of *montmorillionite* weapons would bring about such a large explosion of power, but it was erratic, and they might not survive that particular expression of *montmorillionite's* force. It seemed like too big a risk. Up in the mountains in a storm, if one or both of them were injured, any help would be limited to what they bore with them.

They came up with something to try that would call a power to expand into a wider protective circle. It might offer a way to shield the company. But such a force could not be sustained.

Aenguz seethed at the powerlessness of his weapon. The lodged Dagba Stone turned both talismans into useless artifacts of stone and metal. Their *montmorillionite* might not hold an answer, but certainly if the Dagba Stone were free, the Keystone of Creation would offer something to quell the storm's fury. He had seen what it had done and unleashed firsthand. It had dispelled the sempiternal Glaize around Corundum and released the stilled waters that encased it too. But there seemed to be no way to access it, at least, not in its current state. His success at finding the stone had turned so quickly into failure.

It had been his idea to lead them into the Spine, and now he faced the grim reality that they might die and the embassy could fail. Without the embassy, no help would come from the One Army. He had no way to help. He was as useless as his weapon.

If Saissha's approach were successful, then maybe his own inadequacy might not come into focus. Mandavu went back to Saissha's tent and told her that they would attempt something the next day. Word was passed to the Stair Guard.

In the morning, the leaders of the embassy gathered beyond the cluster of corallel tents. The sun only served to illuminate the opaque clouds. Saissha bore her staff, gifted from the Mono Lord, out a short way from them. Mandavu shouted into the storm, "That is far enough!" He did not want her out of his sight.

Whatever words she was taught, whatever conjuration from the Law of Creation she used, none could hear over the wail and rip of the storm. Flashes of pale blue arced in fits and starts. The wind was disrupted slightly. She waved the braided staff and heaved and strained out into the tempest. A small further power came out like a bloom of sorts, but the wind resumed unabated, and she trudged back through the snow to them. Self-castigation marked her face like a scar. Mandavu trudged out to his diminutive climbing partner and helped her back.

Then Lokah and Mandavu lunged out through the wind and snow to a safe distance from the others. They moved out just on the edge of Aenguz's view. They stood apart. They must have looked strange to the others in their thick coats, their weapons poised before them. Their words, too, did not reach back, but Aenguz recited the lines along with them. He uttered them in allegiance along with his brother-friends.

> *"Preserve the life that preserves you.*
> *Draw forth the force above and through.*
> *Lines of life and lines of power,*
> *Shield us in this dire hour."*

Aenguz echoed them as they recited the rest of the couplets.

Soon the space around Mandavu and Lokah became clear. Their hair and the fur on their long coats stilled. They stood and chanted in a calm pocket. The storm tried to reach them and railed against the new power. No snow or ice fell on them.

Aenguz willed their efforts to work. He hoped he wouldn't have to attempt what would be required, what they had agreed to if Lokah and Mandavu failed.

The pocket did not reach back to Aenguz, and it did not last. The storm closed in on the pair again, and they returned to the leaders.

"Come. Rest," Aenguz commanded as he ushered them back to their tent. They would need time to recover before they could try what they meant to attempt next. The leaders all returned to their tents and agreed to return later in the day.

Lokah and Mandavu took as much rest as they could. Urgency permeated the tenor of the whole company. The Stair Guard who looked in on them gathered the state of the Akkeidii and verified that something would be attempted later in the day.

Aenguz withdrew from Lokah and Mandavu within the tent. He wondered about the source and cause of the storm, wondered about what he had inadvertently called forth from the stone when he snatched it from the pocket of rock beneath the crystal citadel. What else had he released when he touched the stone with his weapon? Another fear gripped him: he believed that Morgrom was aware of the Dagba Stone's awakening. How could he not know that it was found and awake?

Lokah asked with a febrile tone, "What is it?" Even depleted as he was, he still held concern for Aenguz and curiosity for the mysteries of the sacred metal.

"I believe the Flayer is aware that the stone has been found. I was hoping to keep our passage a secret from him."

Lokah considered this. His eyes worked as if he were pondering the breadth and reach of Morgrom's power. "It may be better for Corundum if he learns that the stone is no longer there."

He was right, of course. It would be better for Corundum, but it would be more dangerous for them. They both acknowledged that fact silently between them. Lokah closed his eyes and drifted back to sleep.

Aenguz didn't want to acknowledge that the only way to possibly separate the Dagba Stone from his *montmorillionite* was to leverage the final immutable law of *montmorillion* lore that bound the weapon to its master. Only his death would affect the shape of the metal. It would shift its state into a liquid, so that it could return to its source deep within the earth. But only his death could prove the point. But if that final power was stripped from his weapon, like all the other powers, then the path of the Last Emissary would end high up in the distant mountains. And Lokah and Mandavu would become targets for Morgrom's ire, and the Dagba Stone could fall into anyone's hands. His promises and poor choices would die with him in a tomb of ice.

They gathered again outside the tents in the looming darkness. Lokah and Mandavu stood before Aenguz. They kept a dim light alive in their weapons. They were saving their strength for what was coming next. They had shared the plan and the reasoning for it with Saissha. She, like the rest, had experienced the power of the Dagba Stone firsthand. Risking life to preserve life was new doctrine that stood in conflict with the Law of Creation, but they would all die here - and Legerohn first of all - if they did nothing. She stood next to Mandavu and readied her staff to add her light to the others.

The Moresi leader insisted on being there. Chimere wrapped an arm around the Prince to hold him steady against the wind. Legerohn's dark skin looked pale and sallow. His persistent headaches knotted his face, his right eye squinted against the pain.

Stroud stood stolid against the storm as if he were impervious to it. He wore a thin covering over his plain tunic. He stared at Aenguz as if he meant to remember every aspect of his face. The thrashing snow and blasting ice were nothing to him. His eyes narrowed slightly, but Aenguz was certain that the Azari didn't blink.

The Stair Guard were left in their tents. They could offer no help here. Only the Step Mark of the embassy, Einki, and his second stood with the others.

Aenguz looked at Mandavu and Lokah and nodded.

"This is the only time I will allow it. Otherwise, our agreement still holds," his First said.

Aenguz nodded.

"Keep the lights apart. If you only see one, then you've drifted too far to one side or the other," Lokah said.

Aenguz met Lokah's eyes.

"Be wary, there might be animals hiding from the storm up there too," Mandavu cautioned.

"Start your stump fire first."

If his own weapon were not mute, he would have all the heat and light he could need.

"If nothing happens, wait for daylight and then come back down. We..." Lokah turned his head to the side, indicating all of them. "... will take turns keeping watch for you on the morrow."

Aenguz steeled himself. "Thank you, brothers."

They stared at one another. They had been in a similar situation on the balcony in Corundum when Aenguz planned to attempt the impossible and enter into the Well of Sorrows. He had hoped to delay the Counsel Lords from sealing the well. He had nearly died, but instead he found the Dagba Stone and unleashed chaos.

Much had changed for the three of them since then. They were no longer just a group of Akkeidii fleeing across the Lands of the Earth to deliver the message Morgrom had given him. Their roles and responsibilities had changed. Mandavu as Aenguz's First and Lokah as his loremaster made up the structure around Aenguz, their lord and the Ruler of the Akkeidii.

The two began their chant from The Lay of *Montmorillionite*:

> *Light in the dark and in the hand.*
> *Pow'r concentrated from the Lands.*
> *Ev'r keen, ever new, ever bright*
> *Earth's first star to dispel the night.*

Mandavu's mace and Lokah's sword began to glow. Brighter and brighter the light rose. They spoke in rhythm, calling forth the cryptic light from deep within the metal. The light was being drawn from all *montmorillionite*, except his own, which seemed dead to his touch. He kept it in his scabbard, gifted to him by the Chosen Freeholder from the Oasis of Ganzir, and tried not to let the weight of its implications carry him down into the snow.

The two Akkeidii were clear and bright. They closed their eyes against the light. Legerohn covered his eyes. Chimere hid his face. Saissha buried her eyes in the crook of her elbow. The two Stair Guard leaders closed their eyes and bent their heads down. Stroud watched Aenguz. His eyes were thin slits in his flat face.

Aenguz turned away from the light and made his way through the thick snow toward the cleft in the monolith. If he was going to attempt to unleash the stone's power, he would do it in the safest place, farthest from the embassy.

14

DIVIDED EMBASSY

mbient light dispelled the stubborn shadow in the cleft. Aenguz couldn't recall when he fell asleep or for how long. Habit had him chant the words of lore to draw heat from his weapon, but it was useless. He woke to a stinging chill on his face and fingers. He found the stump. It had burned down to a pile of black charcoal. That was strange; it should still be intact, still be burning.

Images and impressions of a strange, seismic bright power clung to him, not quite like a dream. There were flashes, the whirl of vertigo, and a dislocating disorientation as if he stood uncomfortably outside of himself. Expansion and contraction, silver white light and vast deep black.

The storm was gone, and the light showed that the sky was clear. Had the stone ended the storm? Had he successfully accessed its power?

He picked up his weapon. It looked unchanged. It was frigid even through his gloves. He slid it into his scabbard and slung it over his shoulder. He climbed over the boulders to the opening. In the light, the boulders seemed different, like they had been turned over.

A trampled path cut through the drift. He stepped through into a sea of titanium white. He brought his hand up to shield the light. His eyes needed a moment to adjust.

Once he was clear of the cold stone of the cleft, the bright sun and warm mountain air thawed his chilled bones. The sky was kinder to his eyes than the snow field. The gray and brown peaks towered ahead of him. They wore new costumes of snow; only the sheerest stretches revealed gray or brown. The vertical lines of the monolith held snow in between the creases of the colorful striations.

He didn't need his fur coat. Once his Akkeidii eyes adjusted, he saw a well-established foot path leading down from the mouth of the cleft to the hollow below.

A voice called out of the white. Aenguz looked down into the brilliant sea of white. A figure was stomping up the trail, waving and calling out, "Ho! Ho!"

Aenguz looked closer. It was Mandavu striding toward him. He leaned into a gallop.

In the white basin below, he could see a wide circle cut into the snow around a single corallel tent. A dark-haired figure stood and waved with both arms. A thin sound of joy came from that figure.

Mandavu laughed as he crossed the final distance. He looked Aenguz up and down and grabbed his shoulders. He inspected him again, and then he gave Aenguz a bear hug and nearly lifted him off his feet. On the steep incline, the two were almost eye to eye.

"We knew if you were alive, you would come back. Kachota was right: you are one tough Sidor."

Aenguz was confused. The pieces of what he'd experienced were not connecting for him.

"How are you? Are you injured?"

Mandavu's question confused him. "I am fine." What could be wrong?

"No more going off alone without me. Let's get down to Lokah." Mandavu took the coat from Aenguz, almost as if he meant to soothe the part of himself that wished to carry him.

At the bottom of the hollow, Lokah clapped Aenguz's shoulders. "You appear out of nowhere." He chuckled. "Are you alright? Where were you? What happened?"

Why were they the only two? Where were the others? His confusion troubled him. "Where is everyone else?"

"They left, for Legerohn's sake."

"So soon?"

Mandavu and Lokah looked at each other. They were confused.

"Three days ago."

"Three days ago?" But it was the next morning!

"Five days have passed since you went up to the cleft."

"Five days?"

"Where were you?"

"Nowhere. I was in the cleft all night. It is tomorrow. It is the next morning."

They both looked at him with that same quizzical look they had back on the Rursh Keleg, when he appeared out of the Ganzir. They were familiar with encountering things they could not understand from Aenguz, but it still troubled them.

No further answer was forthcoming, so they brushed it off and moved on to his immediate care. "Are you hungry? Let's get you some food," Mandavu chimed. "Are you thirsty?"

Mandavu guided Aenguz to a seat they had carved into the snow. Lokah went to the sled and pulled out some provender for Aenguz. Mandavu filled a pot with snow and set his weapon to melt it down to cold water. He did another for hot water.

Aenguz needed answers, so he ate while Lokah spoke. "Once our lights faded, we stood watch with Stroud as long as we were able. We only hoped you at least found the safety of the cleft. Anything else was impossible to tell. Finally, the cold became too much for us, and we decided to return to our tents. Just then, a wall of light cut a line in the storm. The mountain shook, like a thunderhead exploding. Then it was gone. It drew everyone from the tents. We could only tell them about it. It was gone by then. We only hoped you had not died in the process.

"We returned to our tents with no hope, not knowing if you had succeeded or failed. We planned to wait for you in the morning. But when we woke, the wind was gone, and the sky was clear like the first day when we arrived."

Mandavu continued, "I climbed up through the snow to the cleft each day, but you were nowhere to be found. I turned over rocks in case you were buried in an avalanche, but there was no sign of you. Only the ashes of the stump fire."

"We know all too well now that you come back from places that no one should. The fall off the cliff on the edge of the City of the Shotah, and your return on the Rursh Keleg. Your disappearance into the Well of Sorrows. We resolved to wait for you, for any sign. We would not leave," Lokah said in absolute terms.

"Saissha did not want to leave either," Mandavu interjected. "But Legerohn was getting worse. The mountain sickness got worse for him after the storm. They waited as long as they dared, but the health of the Prince was failing."

"Is he still alive?" Aenguz asked.

"Yes. He was alive when they left."

Although it was not a complete answer, Aenguz was relieved that they had taken him toward safety.

"We assured them that we would be able to survive here in the mountains alone for as long as need be," Mandavu said, as if to reiterate his oath as Aenguz's First.

"They left us a tent and supplies and transferred most everything else to the other two sleds. And they continued on. We promised to follow them."

Aenguz could see and hear in their stoic tones what they really meant. They were both ready to die in the mountains, waiting for him. He could imagine how difficult the discussions must have been to leave him, and the decisions to finally part. There would be no profit from expounding on it.

"Good. It is good that they left to get Legerohn to safety. And I am grateful to not be alone up here." He smiled a thank you to both of them as he took another bite.

"Where were you?" Mandavu asked again.

"I do not know." Aenguz swallowed as he unshouldered his scabbard and passed it over to Lokah. The stigma of the riddle of what had happened was as heavy as the blade.

Lokah took it carefully from Aenguz with unease and frustration. There was power in the Dagba Stone, but it was elusive, unruly, and cataclysmic. He stowed it away with he and Mandavu's weapons on the sled.

The food helped. The ice water was welcome. His hunger and thirst did not match with a single night. He let that mystery rest beside the others concerning the Dagba Stone and his weapon.

"Let's go find them," he said finally. He was anxious to catch up with the embassy.

They broke camp. They lowered the hoop and tent pole in the tall section of the corallel tent and pulled up the stakes on the lateen arm of the bedding section.

There was plenty of room on the sled, and their few items were secured quickly. Mandavu and Lokah were anxious too.

Mandavu pointed out the indentation in the snow that led up to the pass he and Saissha had searched the day they arrived in the hollow. Wind had softened it with blown snow, but from the west end of the camp, Aenguz could now see it leading up in a winding channel to the fold between the peaks.

The three Akkeidii shouldered the harness straps and hauled the sled through the snow after the embassy. They settled into a rhythm that bore them up the sweeping path out of the basin. At the crest of the high pass, another bank of brown mountains revealed itself, and they still saw the path the others took. It led generally south and west. It was the only direction the snow-speckled peaks allowed.

They followed it down and up and around as the sun sank behind the mountains. They set a camp before all the light was gone, eating a brief meal while they talked about how far the others might have gotten and how long before they might catch up to the embassy.

Mandavu mused about Kachota being in Inverlieth. What it might be like in Legerohn's home, and how he fared as an ambassador.

"New clothes always fit oddly on first wearing."

"Mond and Stokke will help him."

"He will represent the Akkeidii well."

When dawn came, they shared a morn meal, broke the tent, stowed it on the sled, and continued on. They helped one another and maneuvered the sled around sheer rock faces and bouldered slopes. They learned one another's tendencies and silences. They had climbed separately with warriors from their own clans, but the methods and means for climbing together were still all Akkeidii.

With his weapon stowed away, Aenguz was able to forget the burden caused by the stone. He was relieved to feel more like an Akkeidii and less like the Stone Finder and the Last Emissary.

For another day and night, they marched on. Mandavu spied tracks in the snow. He counted the boot prints, but he seemed to be searching for the smallest ones. It made him anxious to catch up to the embassy. They shortened their nights and were content to break camp by *montmorillionite* light early in the morning.

On the fourth day, in the afternoon, they came to a ridge line that dropped off steeply to a wide valley. The skirt of a brown mountain extended to a field of snow with teeth of shattered rock poking through. It ran on an angle from the right down to their left. From the ridge line, they could see no more peaks. The horizon was hidden by a hazy sky in the far distance. The Lower Lands were not far.

Mandavu spotted the embassy and pointed to a spot roughly half-way down the angled slope. "There they are!"

They trailed around the two sleds. From a distance, they looked tiny. Two scouts were far ahead, charting out the way. The rest of the company followed them.

Someone in the company saw the Akkeidii - three silhouettes on the ledge. An elated cheer rose up from the party. The two scouts turned and waved their arms at the three warriors.

Aenguz waved his hands to say, "No!" But it only excited them more.

"Fools," Mandavu spat. "Be quiet!"

"They don't know any better," Lokah answered.

Tense panic gripped them. Lokah and Mandavu were taut. Aenguz held still and hoped they wouldn't awaken the mountain.

Then, a horrible rent filled the air, as if the sky were being torn down. The sound was so loud that it seemed to take the air with it. The wind, high and low, and the rustle of snow all were gaveled into silence. A deep grating like a vast sheet of lake ice, driven by the wind that grinds onto the shore and excoriates the frozen earth as far as the eye can see, came down, unrelenting, unforgiving, unstoppable.

A shelf of snow high up in the brown mountain to their right tore free with a crack like the raw thunder of a hundred storms. New snow from the recent storm weighed on the old snow that had clung to the mountainside for an age. A vast span broke loose. It rent free in an unforgivable and terrible collapse. The white face slowly began an agonizing and disastrous slide down the mountain.

"We have to get to them!" Panic chilled him.

"We'll never make it," Lokah said.

"Come on." Aenguz turned and hauled at the sled.

For a moment, Mandavu and Lokah were paralyzed.

"Pull!"

They joined him and pulled the sled to the edge.

"We can't make it."

"We have to, or the embassy is lost!"

"We'll die too!"

"Then we'll die."

He climbed on the sled and motioned frantically for them to do the same. Lokah double-checked the ropes that held their weapons as Mandavu positioned the sled. He gave a final push, and as Lokah settled into place, the sled tipped over the edge, and they plummeted down the steep slope.

Adrenaline flooded him like the avalanche coming to meet them. They careened wildly down the slope. The sled warped and cracked under the strain. Aenguz leaned to one side to guide the sled toward the company below.

The members of the embassy were gripped in their own terror. They began hauling and pushing the sleds down the slope, away from the pluming wall of ice, snow, and rock. The cataclysmic roar and rumble effaced their shouts and cries. The two scouts turned their path to try to intercept the embassy.

The sled bounced wildly on the uneven slope. Visible and hidden rocks battered the Akkeidii. They were flung into the air and to the side. Feet and legs dangled and crashed into the snow, but they did not let go. It would mean certain death if they did.

The basin leveled, and they arced their sled until it came to a stop a long distance from the fleeing company. Lokah hopped off and pulled at their weapons. There was no time to undo the knots. He whipped out his blade, left the scabbard, and cut the ropes. They took up their weapons and made a mad dash for the fleeing company.

They screamed at them to stop, but the roar of the tsunami of ice, snow, and rock was too loud. The heavy sleds made the fleeing embassy slow. Mandavu drifted at an angle toward the two scouts that ran back, but they were simply too far. Aenguz commanded him back.

Aenguz yelled for the embassy to stop over and over until their heads turned and they finally stopped.

The three Akkeidii reached them. "Get together!" Aenguz roared and motioned with a hug to draw them all in. The Stair Guard hauled the sleds together. The Prince rested on top of one of them. His head lolled, and his languid eyes acknowledged Aenguz. Chimere fell to his knees and gripped the blankets covering his lord as if to protect him with his own body.

"Lokah, Mandavu, set the wall!" Aenguz's shout barely reached above the din.

Mandavu froze and stared at the two figures running toward them. They were too far away. They wouldn't make it. Saissha wouldn't make it. He froze.

"Mandavu! Set the wall!" Aenguz shouted. "Mandavu!" He drew his attention.

A hand reached up and touched Mandavu's arm. It was Saissha. They had assumed Saissha was out scouting the way ahead. Mandavu sagged in relief. He waved at her to get closer to the sled. Then he stood next to Lokah, who was already lost in a fugue. Mandavu held his mace out before him, drew up his considerable strength, and echoed the words Lokah had already begun.

"Tighter, closer!" Aenguz shouted at the top of his lungs. He motioned for everyone to gather in tight. He looked to the two men running toward them. Einki and his second were racing frantically through the snow.

"Aenguz!" Saissha shouted. Her high-pitched plea for the two men cut through the loud rumble and crush of the avalanche.

The front edge of a violent cloud of roiling snow and rocky churn brushed Aenguz and blurred his vision. It hinted at that unforgiving wall of ice to come.

His own desperation rattled Saissha. Her own realization and horror shocked him. He turned away and placed his hands on Lokah and Mandavu's backs and added his words to the ones they chanted.

> "Montmorillionite *guiding force,*
> *Set a bulwark against the wars.*
> *Rampart, wall, turret of stone,*
> *Make a safe space for us alone.*"

They continued on with more words of lore to shape and gird the barrier around them. Couplets continued rhythmically from them. Soon, Aenguz could not hear them. Only the metal could.

Then a wall of cloud, like the front edge of an explosion, consumed them. White tore at the three Akkeidii and whipped their hair. The others were lost in it. With his last glimpse, Aenguz saw Saissha reach over to cover the Prince's face. Stroud stood over her as if he had the power to repel the storm.

A land-borne tsunami crashed into them.

A grinding explosion of sound crushing rock and snow threatened to pulverize and efface them.

But the Akkeidiis' lore and trance held.

Terror stripped the company of any semblance of humanity. Horrible screams rose up from all except Legerohn and the Akkeidii. Abject fear unmade them.

Powder, snow, and ice swirled by, paused, and then settled to the ground. Aenguz's frosted hair dropped and fell limp against his face. The wall was set.

But the roar of the massive avalanche remained, a typhoon of rock and ice. A darkness colored in blue, brown, and white swallowed them. It seemed like the storm's final effort to win out over the trespass and defeat the embassy.

Aenguz wanted to cover his ears and protect against the deafening roar, but he kept his hand on his kinsmen. He could not hear Lokah and Mandavu's voices, but their words and vibrations of lore rose and fell on their breaths through their backs.

A tsunami ground around and past the invisible wall. A gigantic mill of old snow, ice, and crushed rock scoured around the wall of lore.

It gave a sensation of burrowing into the earth at an impossible speed. Light flickered and flashed overhead and glinted on the living wall of pulverizing destruction, a thin barrier and pocket of calm between them and cataclysm.

The grinding tumult slowed by a degree, but gave no hint of stopping. Too much snow had been dislodged. Mandavu and Lokah held the lore-summoned power beyond any reasonable measure. And Aenguz would not let go. All of their lives and the life of the embassy, Corundum, and creation depended on their strength and their focus.

The sliding river of ice and rock slowed again and mercifully came to a stop. Mandavu and Lokah dropped, as if all their strength had been carried away by the avalanche. Snow poured in around the whole company, but it did not bury them. The detritus of snow and rock cracked and snapped.

Aenguz held his breath over his two friends so as not to disturb the avalanche. The rock- and snow-laden air quieted. An opening above his head in the stayed grave confirmed for him that they were all alive.

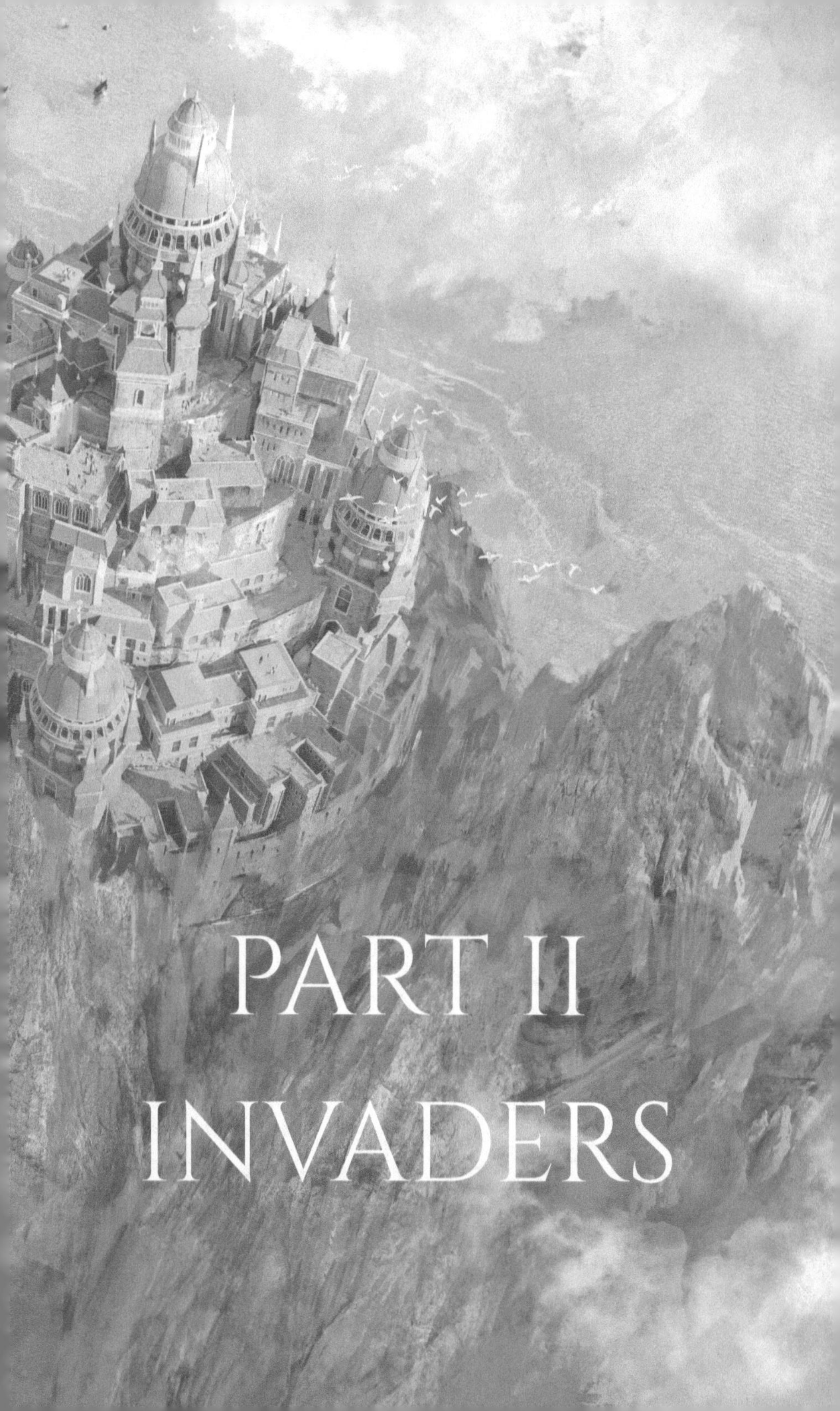

PART II

INVADERS

15

HEAVIER BURDENS

Hunks of slushed snow and ice plopped onto the embassy. Creaks and groans like frozen timber being twisted and bent tremored through the hole. Aenguz studied the lore-forged walls as pieces and parts dropped around him.

"Let's go! We have to get out of here!" Aenguz shouted urgently. He hadn't fully taken stock of everyone, but there was no aura of death in the hole. Mandavu and Lokah bent over on hands and knees. Shattered ice covered their backs. Their weapons rested in the snow. Saissha and Chimere pulled away from Legerohn. The Prince flexed his face and brushed the snow away.

Stroud stood and stared at the snow wall. His impassive gaze held a tinge of awe, as if he had witnessed a mystery.

"Go, go, go!" Aenguz barked again. "You. You!" he shouted to two of the Stair Guard. "Get up! Get the sleds out of here. Go now!" Aenguz's tone called their duty back to them. They climbed to their feet and rallied the other men around them.

"Stroud," Aenguz continued, "get Saissha out of here."

The Azari did not hesitate. He moved with an unusual speed to her side. Saissha looked back to Mandavu and Lokah.

"Go, I have them."

Stroud pulled her from the sled and warded her as she climbed up the leeward side of the hole.

Aenguz met Chimere's eyes. "Stay with him."

"I will, Sidor."

Aenguz directed some Stair Guard to take Legerohn and Chimere up.

"You, and you. Come here," Aenguz barked at two other Stair Guard. "Come here, help me." He got them on all fours beside Mandavu and directed them to slide under his chest. Aenguz heaved with them as they climbed to their feet. Mandavu was not completely unconscious. His legs moved as if they were guided by loose strings.

Aenguz knelt by Lokah and tried to reach him. "Lokah, Lokah." But the Kriel could only mumble.

Stroud was suddenly at his side.

"Where is-" Aenguz started.

"The Counsel Lord is safe."

"Help me."

The pair lifted Lokah, but before they turned, Aenguz leaned him into Stroud long enough to gather up their weapons and then took Lokah's shoulder.

The tail end of the first sled was tipping out of the hole. Aenguz and Stroud bore Lokah and followed the second sled out of the tenuous pocket. The walls groaned and collapsed. Snow and rocks knocked the three of them over and started to bury them. Hands reached in and grabbed Aenguz, pulling them all out.

Aenguz scanned the embassy and did a quick count. They stood on a broken field of snow and stone. They were dwarfed by a vast swath of devastation. Rocks and detritus were scattered like flotsam on a white sea. Light sparkled like feather-light gems here and there across the plain.

"Which way do we go?" the Stair Guard at the head of the Prince's sled asked.

The entire geography had changed. Aenguz scanned the last landmarks he recalled. The brown mountain looked stripped. It was unrecognizable. He thought he found the ridge they had ridden their sled down from, but he couldn't be sure. "Stroud, I think you were headed that way." He pointed in the opposite direction from the ridge they had come from.

"Yes, that was the way we were headed," Stroud answered him.

"Can we search for the Step Mark?" one of the Stair Guard asked.

Saissha scanned the avalanche and looked to Aenguz for an answer. There was simply no way to tell where they might be. "Preserve the embassy. Make for the ridge."

Aenguz saw the horror in her face as she gave the command. The weight of her words and the severe responsibility behind them stunned her and altered her expression. Tears filled her eyes, but she wiped them away and trudged through the snow at the head of the line.

The embassy hobbled over the uneven terrain as if they were crawling over the face of chaos. At one point, the ground shifted under their feet. A vast plate slid and bore them away from their goal. But it did not swallow them. The ridgeline they trekked toward was their only North Star.

Finally, once they reached the relative safety of solid rock, they all collapsed to the ground like felled trees. Saissha gave a gentle command for the Stair Guard to make camp, but there was no urgency. There was still plenty of light, and the clouds were breaking.

Aenguz used the last of his adrenaline to check on Mandavu and Lokah. They were spent but awake. The two Stair Guard that had let

Mandavu down sat beside him to catch their breath. Aenguz thanked them both and squeezed their shoulders. Mandavu groaned out a murky thank you.

"Just rest," Aenguz breathed to him.

Lokah reached for his *montmorillionite* that Aenguz bore and began a low chant from The Lay of *Montmorillionite*.

"You can rest now, loremaster. Good work," Aenguz consoled him.

Lokah looked up and nodded gratefully.

Stroud stood with them, as if he had the energy to carry Lokah the rest of the way on his own.

"Thank you for your help."

Stroud looked at Aenguz as if there were no other choice. His thank you seemed irrelevant to him.

Chimere was untying the Prince. Legerohn scrambled to get off the sled.

Aenguz walked over to him and studied him. "How are you feeling?"

"The torture in my head has lessened. But that unsteady ground did not help." He looked around at the mountains and the snow field. It was the first time he had stood in days. "Seems I owe you another debt."

"Remember, it was my idea to come up here."

"Ah, but it was my choice to follow you."

They smiled at each other. A stilted laugh tumbled out of them.

Aenguz turned to Chimere and asked his estimation of Legerohn's condition.

"He wanted me to let him loose earlier, but I would not."

"Good. He will need more rest, but hopefully the worst is behind him. Good work."

Chimere returned a wilted smile and turned his attention back to the Prince.

Aenguz moved clear of the Stair Guard who worked woodenly at making the camp. He searched out Saissha and saw her at the edge of the ridge. She was staring out over the avalanche field, her back to the embassy. He left the others and went to her.

She did not turn back when she asked, "How do we find them?" She seemed to be asking the Spine as much as Aenguz.

The bravery of her hope stalled his bleak answer. It challenged him to be so direct with her. "They are both gone."

"But how would we search for them if they were still alive?"

Aenguz wanted to console her, wanted to take some of the burden from her. Ice and rock shifted in the distance and ground to a halt.

"If they had *montmorillionite,* we could listen for them. But it was a huge avalanche. I do not believe anyone could have survived it. Not even an Akkeidii," he stated softly.

"I am responsible for the embassy. I knew the Spine was dangerous, but I did not expect to lose anyone. I was not ready for this." A former part of herself was buried in the avalanche.

The emptiness of unexpected loss, especially with men under his command, was not new. Most of the Champions of the Challenge had fallen after they had sworn an oath to him. And there were the dead men sacrificed on the Cairngorm. "I have known a loss like this. It was my idea to go up into these mountains. I still carry the emptiness left by those who died during our escape from the Sallow. It does not go away."

She turned to him in dismay, as if he had placed a curse on her. "You are a leader. How do you bear it?"

"I have been no leader. I have done nothing but react to edicts and demands that have been forced on me." His chest tightened. The air seemed thin. He drew back out of his own recriminations and dredged up an answer from the sludge of his own grief. "You make their sacrifice matter. You give purpose and meaning to their deaths. They bore you through the mountains so that you could deliver the Mono Lord's plea. They saw the embassy through the Spine."

Her wet eyes scanned Aenguz for more.

He looked out over the field, and at all the killing fields beyond he had crossed to reach this narrow ridgeline. "It is a heavier burden than the weight of their absence."

Something in her eyes hardened and matched his own. There was nothing more to say, no answer or salvation for the dead or her hope of rescue. He left her to her vigil and her tears.

16

WHAT NEW LANDS

The stump fires dotted the camp just before sunset. Saissha returned from the edge of the ridge and went to one of the sleds. She unpacked her blue robe and pulled out her braided staff. She called everyone back to the edge of the ridge overlooking the new landscape. The sun dropped behind them, and their shadows stretched out like long black pillars over what had become a graveyard.

When they were all assembled, Saissha began,

> *"'Life and death are intertwined.*
> *Life adapts to the world,*
> *And the world adapts to life.*
> *Life protects life.*
> *Life begets life.'"*

Saissha's recitation and remembrance quivered in places, but her voice was clear and noble, as if she were sanctifying the vast space where their bodies now lay.

The Stair Guard stood at reverent attention, as if Einki had called them into formation. They looked as if they would heed a command to dig out the entire field with their bare hands to find him and the other lost Stair Guard. As it was, they were too buried under their own grief to move.

Stroud stood beside Saissha and stared out as if he were marking the spot of their passing. Legerohn and Chimere stood silently to honor their loss. Aenguz held his dead weapon out before him. Lokah and Mandavu held their *montmorillionite* before them - an Akkeidii tradition they were proud to observe for the lost Stair Guard.

Dusk faded, and starlight sealed the chaotic landscape in a silver sheen. Saissha's ceremony ended with the last light, and then the embassy returned to the remnants of their own needs.

The next day, they took their time waking and eating. The Spine was behind them, and the end of their mountain crossing lay ahead. The promise of flat green land, tall trees, and an easier passage helped to cushion their raw grief.

The bivouacs were quickly stowed, and the Stair Guard took up the two sleds solemnly, as if they were pall bearers.

Mandavu and Lokah were still recovering, so they walked with Legerohn and Chimere. Aenguz and Saissha trekked on ahead as they wended their way downward.

By midday, Aenguz and Saissha reached a great bow of rock. They could go no further, and they waited for the others to join them. The ledge lay beyond and below out of view. The first glimpse of the Lower Lands lay before Aenguz. The tips of great pines cut a thin border between them and the foothills. Lush, rolling prairies, waves of green, and dots of tree clusters fanned out into the distance. It looked verdant and inviting. It reminded him of the moment he had reached the cliff at the head of the lower stair of Forhnthulen at what had seemed like the end of their long journey. He had looked back across the Lands while he waited for the others to climb up. He had realized in that moment that he was likely the first Akkeidii to stand there since Grieg Sidor the Venturer.

Now, looking westward, he realized that no Akkeidii had looked out from this point. No Akkeidii had ever crossed the Spine. It would have been a legendary accomplishment all on its own, on par with what Grieg Sidor the Venturer had done, but for the fact that it was done partly in service to Lord Morgrom - in service to his role as the Last Emissary.

The plan was simple: Get to Earthmight. Deliver the message. Get the One Army and lead it through the Cleve. And do it as quickly as possible. He knew Earthmight was to the north, but how far was it? How long would it take to get there? They had spent too much time trapped in the Spine, and the summer was already beginning to wane.

Once the others arrived, they discussed how to get down. Saissha offered to climb down over the edge, being the smallest, but they were wary of the risks now. She had climbed in far more perilous situations in the Spine, but now the veil of the unknown made them all cautious. Mandavu deemed it too dangerous and would not concede to letting her go. The Counsel Lord would not be placed carelessly in harm's way. Aenguz offered to climb down, but Mandavu forbade it for the same reasons. Aenguz deferred to his First, the one charged with protecting his life.

The Stair Guard turned back to their duty and took on the responsibility. They selected one from their number, the smallest among them, and lashed a line around him. He walked out and down and then lay down and crawled out on his stomach out of sight to see if there was a way down. He pulled another loose length of rope with him. Lokah went over the different signals the Akkeidii used on the free line to let the others know when to let his line out or to pull him back.

Five Stair Guard held the line and slowly let their companion down and out of sight. Three Stair Guard held the second line. They were overly protective of their companion. They knew now that anyone could be lost.

Saissha, the Akkeidii, the Moresi, and Stroud stood on the edge of the bow and waited, trying to forestall their ineffectiveness. They could only watch and hope.

The soldier disappeared, and only the ripple of the second line gave evidence of his descent. After a short time, the line jerked, and they pulled him back up.

"There is a ledge far below. I can see it. You will have to lower me down farther to reach it. The cliff cuts in. I will have to swing to it. I could not see its entire length, but I may be able to walk it and see more." It would take more rope, but they agreed and lowered him back down. Eventually, the line went slack, and the Stair Guard held a loose rope. They let it out until they came to the end of the line. Then they pulled their scout back up.

He confirmed that the ledge led down into the tree line. A steep rock-fall would have to be crossed, but then they could reach the forest.

The Stair Guard and Akkeidii discussed the plans to get the sleds down to the ledge, and how and when every last man and woman would get down. They let half their number down, and then the sleds were lowered. Everyone held the line and inched the sled down to the waiting Stair Guard. Then they released the second sled.

Then, one by one, the embassy climbed down the line until they were all on the narrow ledge. The Stair Guard had moved the sleds down out of the way, and now they could head for the trees.

They reached the rock-fall that spilled into the trees, and they had to once again navigate the sleds. The Stair Guard were tired, so Mandavu waved Aenguz on ahead, as he was afraid Aenguz might get hurt if the Stair Guard or sled tumbled forward. He sent Saissha on ahead with him while he and Lokah helped the soldiers. Stroud did not object.

Legerohn stayed with Chimere, whose lame foot made the climbing difficult. They trailed behind the sleds.

Aenguz and Saissha climbed over the tumbled boulders down into the trees. He helped the Counsel Lord down off the last boulder, and for the first time since they left Corundum, his boots crunched on the brown needles of a forest floor.

Saissha gleamed. She looked back up the slope with a smile as wide as the mountain. "I have climbed on and at the feet of the mountains around Corundum for most of my life. I never thought to see the other side of the Spine. I never believed, like some did, that the world ended beyond. And now I am here." She turned to Aenguz. "I couldn't have done it without your help. I had to learn what I learned on my own, but you all were born in the mountains. I am glad to be here, and I would be happy to explore this side too."

"Maybe another time," Aenguz joked.

"Yes, another time." She laughed in delight. The small joy helped offset their fading grief somewhat.

The sleds were wending their way down slowly. Mandavu peered down to see them both safely at the bottom. Aenguz waved back.

The pair drew down a short way into the forest. A gurgling rivulet caught their ears, and they made their way among the pillars of pine toward it. The others would be thirsty too.

Birds flitted in the trees. Squirrels and other small creatures scratched about. The shade was welcome, and the forest seemed as familiar as any in the Mashu.

They heard a sound that was not a creature or a bird. It was rhythmic - a heavy panting - a slight, sweet cry. Aenguz pulled Saissha behind him. His weapon was lashed to the sled. He only had his bare hands. They inched closer.

There were two sounds, a breathy grunt and a rhythmic moan. Long-vined shrubs thick with small red berries like kisses warded the clearing. Sun-speckled shadow filled the glade.

A wide cloth was laid out in the middle with some satchels and food laid about. A couple was locked in carnal coupling, naked and heaving, their clothes tossed next to their food. Their breaths were heavy and rising. Their heads were nearly one, cheek to cheek, hair tousled into hair. The man lay on top of her, his legs spread knees up beside her. His hands pressed into the mat. Her legs were wrapped around his waist. Her toes contorted and flexed. She clutched his back as if she were a forest nymph trying to escape from the ground, and he was her captor, keeping her in. They rocked together, each trying harder for a more desperate purchase on the other. A sheen of moisture glistened on them both. Their hips pulsed into each other. He moaned into her hair. She cried a staccato gasp through his into the sky. She pulled her chest tighter into his. Her breasts shook.

Aenguz was caught up in the heat of their rocking. Saissha's face tinged red. His own face warmed, and a contortion of embarrassment and surprise mirrored on her face.

They drew closer, caught in the thrum of their moment. The berry-laden vines stirred. The woman turned her ear and her eyes toward the sound. The man pulsed hard as if he had found the charm to hold the nymph there forever.

"Do you hear that?" she uttered.

The man pressed his forehead into her hair and then into the ground. He groaned. "What?"

Aenguz and Saissha felt a tinge of shame and straightened against the vines.

The woman saw them and shrieked. The man startled and looked around. He pulled away from his desire, naked, dripping and wet. They were young, not much younger than Aenguz or Saissha.

He scrambled to his feet. "Stay back!" he yelled.

The couple scrabbled for their clothes.

Aenguz and Saisha stepped through the brush to try to reassure them. Aenguz smoothed the air. Their eyes locked on his mottled hand, and their panic escalated. They hopped into their clothes. The woman pulled her dress on backwards.

"We are not going to hurt you," Saissha said.

"Be still. We are not here to harm you." Aenguz held his hands out.

Their clothes were in disarray on them.

Suddenly, Mandavu and Lokah burst into the glade, *montmorillionite* weapons drawn. Stroud was with them. The couple saw them, and they were lost to all terror. They ran out of the glade screaming.

17

GO BACK TO HELL

The embassy gathered in the glade. By the time the sleds were stowed, the story of what Aenguz and Saissha had encountered had reached everyone. Good-natured laughter and disbelief bounced through the company. Relief replaced the nascent stress that permeated the whole company in the face of their varying fears about what they might encounter in the Lower Lands.

Saissha asked for a tent to be erected, so that she might change and freshen up. While she waited, she gathered up the clothes and satchels left by the frightened lovers. She left them with a soldier to bear before she entered the tent. She told the Stair Guard to clean up and don their burgundy cloaks. They were representing Corundum and their brethren in the Stair Guard. They would likely encounter other people from the Lower Lands, and she reasoned that they ought to make a better impression than the first one she and Aenguz had made.

The Akkeidii and Moresi did the same thing, washing the grime off of their faces at the brook and putting on fresh clothes. They looked like they were a part of the Stair Guard.

Stroud stood in the center of the glade and scanned slowly from side to side. His tunic was marked with the dust and grime of the mountain.

When Saissha came out of the tent, the company quieted. She wore her new blue Counsel Lord's robe, and she bore the braided staff. Her hair, damp but combed smooth, was pulled back behind her ears. Her face was clean, the smudges and stains from the Spine washed away. She seemed aware of how she might look, and she took the polite silence as confirmation of her appearance.

They broke down the tent, stowing it back on the sled. She looked everyone over, and they stood as if they were standing at attention for inspection. "We are the embassy of Corundum. We are friends and allies with the people of the Lands. Comport yourselves well." She smiled approvingly, and with that, they made their way out of the glade.

There was a slight but clear path at the farther end of the clearing. Saissha led the way. Stroud walked behind her, and Mandavu walked behind him. Aenguz followed, and Lokah hiked behind him. Legerohn and Chimere walked behind the Akkeidii, and the freshly coifed Stair Guard bore the sleds through the trees in a tight formation.

The forest opened to a wider clearing, and they could see the soft, rolling green of the land far below. Other footpaths joined the clearing like the one they were on. A vibrant stream poured out of the forest somewhere to their left.

They walked through another short stretch of forest. Aenguz could hear voices intermixed with the water. As the forest opened, they saw a fitted stone bridge. On the other side, men were gathered.

They held hoes and large pitchforks and other farm tools. More were running up the hill to join them. They were startled when they saw the company, and they grew louder to bolster their courage.

As the party approached, they stomped up to the top of the bridge. Their eyes were wild and angry, the shouts a mottle of threats and curses.

Saissha halted the company. She looked back, confusion contorting her clean face.

Aenguz looked at Mandavu and Lokah.

Mandavu said, "What are they going to do? Farm us to death?"

"Lay your weapons down," Aenguz commanded to the Akkeiddi.

Mandavu and Lokah let their weapons down on the grass.

Saissha walked toward the bridge. Stroud was at her side. Mandavu tensed. He was poised to move.

"Hail, friends! We have come from Corundum, offering tidings from the Upper Lands."

They shouted back for her to stop and then said, "Go back to hell! Leave! You are not welcome here. Go!"

"We are not your enemies." She tried again. "We are making our way to Earthmight to speak with the One King."

The growing mob kept looking over their shoulders as if they were expecting others to arrive.

"They look terrified," Legerohn said.

They continued to shout at the company, "Go back!" and "Return to your hell! Leave our lands!"

"Well, we're not going back," Mandavu said drolly.

"The Free People will see to you," they threatened across the distance.

"Do you see a weapon among them?" Aenguz asked.

"No," Lokah answered. "Only farming tools."

"We could cut them down in no time."

"We as squires could cut them down."

A stone flew at the Counsel Lord. Stroud moved in a blink and caught the stone. The men startled at the Azari's speed, but then more rocks came over the bridge at Saissha. Stroud moved with impossible speed; he seemed to close the distance from rock to rock without taking a step. Saissha tried to appeal to them, safe behind Stroud's shield.

"By Grieg!" Mandavu breathed at Stroud's inhuman quickness.

"What power is that?" Lokah asked of no one in particular.

"Some power of the Azari," Aenguz answered, not really knowing what that meant.

Safe behind Stroud's protection, Mandavu walked up and guided Saissha back away from the fusillade. Stroud covered their slow retreat. No projectile reached them.

"Well, what do we do now? We can't go back," Mandavu said.

"We hold here until they see we are not a threat, and that we are not retreating," Aenguz offered, not sure how else to convince them.

Saissha ordered the Stair Guard to keep their swords sheathed. "Stand ready," was her only other command to them.

Then the ground shook. A galloping force rumbled through the ground. Over the rise, behind the angry farmers, three riders appeared. They rode on the animals Aenguz recalled from the sculpture on the walls in the infirmary - Kikey had called them the great horses. Their hooves clomped and climbed. Muscles flexed and pulsed beneath their smooth coats. Each had their own coloring. One horse was a rich chocolate brown with a black mane, a white patch running down the length of its nose. Another horse was mottled with white and tan, its blond mane weaving and waving at its neck. The third horse was as black as pitch. The rider, dressed in an off-white singlet with short black hair, rode behind the other two. The two armed riders were women, wearing round helmets and fitted leather shirts. Straps crossed their chests and ringed their waists. Aenguz could only make out the handles and hilts of their weapons. They both had a short double-curved bow in their hands. Their leggings appeared to be made of soft doe skin, and their boots were made of what looked like rabbit fur.

Mandavu and Lokah drew their weapons up from the grass.

Aenguz fought the urge to draw his own weapon. The riders and the horses sent a chill through his body. His rising heartbeat tinged his nerves. He wanted to arm himself, but he didn't want to reveal the stone.

Awe struck the whole company. These three riders were fearsome. The farmers grew bolder in their presence, and they gave way before them.

Mandavu and Lokah positioned themselves in front of Aenguz.

Saissha called out again to them that they were friends of the Lands on a mission to Earthmight to meet with the One King, but her words were ignored.

The riders drew up their bows and set arrows to string.

"What do we do?" a Stair Guard called out.

"Nothing," Saissha said.

"Stroud," Aenguz called out. "Come back." The Azari was an easy target.

Legerohn appealed to the mob, but none listened.

Then, the rider on the spotted horse called the men to be silent. They listened to Legerohn, but they were unmoved.

"Take cover behind the sleds," Mandavu said over his shoulder to Aenguz and the Stair Guard. "Take Saissha and Legerohn with you."

Chimere limped up beside Lokah, sword drawn.

The Stair Guard formed up around the sleds.

"What do we do?" another soldier called.

"Stay yourselves," Saissha answered. "Our first act in the Lower Lands will not be killing." But the situation was about to break.

"Stroud!" Aenguz yelled. "Come back!"

Stroud ignored Aenguz and walked to the bridge.

The rider on the black horse shifted. He galloped forward to the foot of the bridge and slid off the beast's back with ease. He strode up the bridge.

Stroud walked forward calmly. They met at the peak and stood eye to eye. Stroud was half a head taller, but otherwise they looked similar. Flat faces. Narrow slits for eyes. Black hair cut short. There was less gray in the other's hair, but otherwise Stroud could have been standing in front of an imperfect mirror.

They spoke, but Aenguz could not hear their words.

"What is he doing?" Mandavu breathed.

The rider he spoke with nodded tersely to Stroud, turned, walked down, and spoke to the riders and the angry men.

The two women lowered their bows. The men lowered their ersatz weapons. Their anger was replaced with a defeated consternation.

Stroud came back to the company.

"He is Azari. His name is Rehl. There are Azari here in the Lower Lands. I see through their eyes - all of their eyes." He did not focus on any person in the company. His eyes were cast down, and he took them in in his peripheral alone. "Azari eyes are spread across the Lands and throughout Earthmight.

"I have seen the One King. He is surrounded by Azari. I see Earthmight. I stand on its stone floors. I see the mouth of the Cleve."

"How do you..." Saissha trailed off.

"I am Azari. I possess the One Sight. *We* possess the One Sight. We are the Eyes of the World. Right now, all Azari see you. All Azari can see the words on your lips. Azari with the One King relay what I see and what you say."

Saissha, Aenguz, and the others looked to one another, searching for an answer. "Does he know why we are here? What have you said?"

Stroud continued, "I conveyed only who we are and where we came from, and that we bear dour tidings from the Upper Lands."

They looked at one another again. Shock gripped them all. Stroud's new vision left them in awe.

"We are summoned to Earthmight. We are to go down to the Vale below. It is called Lihkit. We will follow Rehl down to the Vale and camp there. We will hear more from the One King, and then we will depart for Earthmight." Stroud stilled as if he were listening to some hidden music.

"When is that?" Aenguz asked.

"The One King will speak to the Lihkittens and us tomorrow." That was all Stroud would say.

18

LIHKIT VALE

Suddenly, Earthmight and the One King were close, but they were also far away. The Cleve too was close, but then, it was also leagues away. Aenguz started to reel. He clutched Lokah's shoulder as the ground started to turn. Nausea upended his stomach.

"What is it?" Lokah asked. Concern clenched his eyes.

"I… I do not know. I feel like I am in the Divine Oculum. Far things are near. Impossible things are real."

"Mandavu," Lokah called.

Mandavu looked back, confused, and then studied Aenguz. "What is it, lord?"

"I need a moment." Aenguz gasped as he strained to master himself. The Azari's One Sight defied reason. His own expectations of how long their task might take in the Lower Lands shifted and became unmoored.

Rehl and the two riders rode over the bridge. Aenguz watched them. The horses also toppled his tenuous equilibrium. Rehl paused, and the two women rode by.

Aenguz watched them pass. He spied one of the riders. Her hazel eyes oriented him even though she was scowling at him. Suspicion and hate radiated from them. A coating of freckles covered her cheeks like camouflage. A stray curl of hair trailed out from under her helmet and danced around her ear. In a few thundering strides, the pair disappeared into the woods.

The leaders of the embassy stepped back and looked to Stroud for an answer.

"They go to verify my words," Stroud said.

"What are they looking for?" Saissha asked.

"Proof that we are the only ones."

"Do the Azari not believe you?"

"Yes, but there was an attack. Invaders appeared in the mountains at a vale in the north."

The leaders looked at one another, worried that their embassy had been kept too long in the Spine, worried that they were too late. But the One King and ostensibly the One Army were as close as Stroud.

Stroud continued, "They are the Free People. They ride and tend the great horses of the Lower Lands. They follow their own laws and their own Queen."

Rehl seemed impatient to lead the embassy.

"Can you move?" Mandavu breathed to Aenguz.

"Yes, I am fine. It is passing."

Saissha motioned for the company to follow. The Stair Guard lifted the sleds, and the embassy followed Rehl over the bridge.

Once the path cleared the forest farther down, Aenguz caught his first view of Lihkit Vale. A collection of fitted blond stone buildings rested at the base of the foothills. The river ran roughly beside the vale and then out into the rich land.

Undulating rows of green and tan waved out in a plain of fertile rivers. There appeared to be no blight, no empty patches. The weaving rows were full and alive. They stretched out into the distance as far as he could see. The river wound like a seam between two different crops. An archipelago of trees followed it roughly out into the distance to some final solitary trees. The verdancy of the land struck all of them. Everything was vibrant, green, and alive.

A smaller stream emptied out to the right of the vale and was lost to an overgrown channel that blended in with the weaving rows of crops. A wide path of mostly grass at the edge of the vale curved out into the distance and was lost in between the waves of crops.

A shallow amphitheater to the left was cut into the rise just before the weaving crop land. Opposite it was a small semi-circular quarter wall. It marked a flat area that was mostly dirt, with only a few patches of grass where the ground met the wall.

The mounted Azari led the embassy around the outskirts of Lihkit to the lesser stream on the north end of the vale.

Lihkittens gathered at the edge of their vale in between the homes to watch as they passed. Curious and suspicious eyes crawled over them. The men who had met the company in the clearing by the bridge held their "weapons" still and seemed to brag, as if they had subdued the company themselves. All Aenguz could see in the Lihkittens' eyes was fear. Why were they so frightened? What had happened here? What kind of attack? What invaders?

Rehl said, "Here," to Stroud, as if the two had been having a conversation the whole time amongst themselves and nothing more needed to be said.

Saissha thanked Rehl, but the Azari said nothing. He may have nodded tersely. Aenguz couldn't tell because of how he bobbed on the horse. He turned on his black mount and rode back into the village. The beast unnerved Aenguz.

The Stair Guard began to make camp. The sleds were positioned and the corallel tents raised.

After a time, the two women, who had gone up to verify the embassy's story, descended down through Lihkit to the field on the south end with the semi-circular stone wall. They glanced at the embassy as they galloped past. They rode to a simple shed made of the same stone and also timbered pine. They dismounted, and teen girls ran out from the vale to meet them. The two riders spoke to them, and the girls took the horses. They pulled the contoured seats off their backs and drew the horses by hand.

Rehl trotted over to the riders, dismounted, and handed his black horse to the girls. He listened to the pair and then spoke back to them, his head inclined downward. Then, Rehl walked to the road leading into Lihkit and stood there as if he were waiting for someone.

The bright summer sun blasted the blond stone homes behind the company. Saissha stood with the Stair Guard once the tents were raised, and they watched the sun drift slowly to the horizon. Their wonder for the moment overrode their fear about their unknowns and uncertainties and what the next day and the words of the One King might hold. Insects hovered and darted placidly above the fields in the gentle air. The horizon glowed red as if dusk might last forever. They lit their stump fires and ate a meal, aware of the curious eyes that were still on them.

"Should we set a watch?" Saissha asked.

"We will," Mandavu said flatly.

"It is all new here. There has been an attack," Aenguz said with a hint of exacerbation. "There may be other things we should be wary of."

She agreed and Mandavu nodded. She welcomed the help of men around her. With the Stair Guard leaderless, it fell to her to command them.

"If you will it, I will order the Stair Guard."

Saissha thanked Mandavu for his offer and accepted. The two of them spoke to the Stair Guard.

Three watches of three Stair Guard each would take turns throughout the night. It suited the Stair Guard too, because with one less tent, they would otherwise be crowded in their corallel tents. Mandavu gave the command, but he deferred to her to affirm it.

With the orders given, the rest of the embassy could go to sleep. Mandavu took the first watch, and Lokah went into the tent. The last thing Aenguz saw before he went into his tent was Stroud walking over to Rehl. He planted his feet with his back to Rehl. He looked up into Lihkit. The Azari too, were keeping their own kind of vigil.

They were protected, but something left him not feeling completely safe. There were too many questions, but the steady surge of the stream took him off to sleep.

———◆———

WHEN HE WOKE, A greater share of sleep still clung to him. His eyes tested the dark. Mandavu was to his right on the other side of the tent pole. The giant Makan breathed in an unconscious rhythm. Lokah must be on watch, he thought. It was still early, still night.

He reached out in the dark tent for his weapon. His fingers brushed across the leather. He fingered the detailed bands, exploring the flourishes and feeling the details of the contours. Whose scabbard was this? The fact that Mere Gurudev had given it to him was enough. But she had said that it belonged to one of his kinsmen. The weight of his weapon was present, along with its inertness. The imbalance of it struck an off chord in him. Just the knowledge of the lodged stone and its immuring impact on the lore of his *montmorillionite* torqued his understanding.

That moment in the crevice where the stone had rested came back to him. It had been lost and hidden for uncounted ages, so long that myth and the Counsel Lords' lies had all but taken it. That, along with the impossibility of finding it, the impossibility of reaching it, and the impossibility of ignoring it, had simply overwhelmed him.

A subtle and deep power had radiated from the lost stone within the alcove. The fine grass, the friable minute purple and yellow flowers, the inchoate warm glow from the contoured Dagba Stone. It held an answer, a power. He had unexpectedly awakened the stone in the pocket where it lay. It was a potent talisman, able to rend mountains, redirect rivers, and dispel entire storms. But now it held nothing. It was dead weight. Both objects were powerless. Neither could be used against the Flayer.

The dream and cataclysm that had subsumed him once he hooked the stone was like an opening to another plane, as far removed from the Lands of the Earth as the farthest precincts of the White Earth. The universe exploding and contracting. Creation manifesting and transforming. Time retreating and exulting. Meaning and revelation rebuffing each other, reconciling, resolving. Impressions of power so great that just the distant recollection of them seemed great enough to destroy him all over again. All of these impressions and forces lay at the boundaries of his wide mind. They were larger and louder in silence, and just within the boundaries of his mind was the fire of Morgrom's message. The undelivered part continued to etch grooves in his mind, like the tool that had marked the silver bands on his gifted sheath.

Five seasons will not pass before Earthmight is under siege and the One King's army is lost.

He regained his eyes and sat up. The need to orient himself was strong. A familiar routine, a familiar action. He pulled on his gifted boots and gifted shirt.

Aenguz unbuttoned the flap and looked at the Dagba Stone threaded in on the hook and the spike at the head of his weapon. The smooth contours, the wisps of black, the intonation of red through the stone… He closed and buttoned the flap and made a silent promise as much to his weapon as to himself. *I will find a way to separate you. I will get you back.*

As he stood, Mandavu called, his back still turned, "Lokah?"

"Aye," Lokah answered from outside. Aenguz had not yet fully adjusted to the protection his two friends had taken on and into the fabric of their lives. They were in a strange land now. He uttered a silent thank you to them both and left the tent.

Lokah stood before the tent, his back to the entrance. His weapon rested tip-down in the ground before him. "It is not morning yet."

"I am awake," Aenguz told Lokah. He saw two of the three Stair Guard at either end of their encampment. "Go, get some sleep."

Aenguz noticed Lokah's focus out in front of him.

Stroud and Rehl stood in the same spot on the road back-to-back. Summer starlight silhouetted the Azari. They could have been statues placed there in the middle of the road, a monument erected suddenly by the Lihkittens. "They have not moved all night." They mirrored each other in their simple tunics and cloth-covered feet.

"What do you make of their eyes and their shared One Sight?" Aenguz asked. The questions raised by Stroud in the wake of the revelation yesterday were too mysterious for him. Their power made him curious and suspicious.

"It unnerves me," Lokah responded. "How many eyes are on us when Stroud is with us? If they can see what we say, what privacy do our words have? Or our thoughts?"

It was clear he had been pondering the Azari and their abilities during his watch.

"And their movement," Lokah continued, "Stroud's quickness was… I've never seen anything like it. Have you?"

"No." These questions raised new ones for Aenguz. "I do not know if Stroud is beholden to his people or the One King in a way that does not serve the Counsel Lord or the embassy."

Lokah turned to Aenguz before heading into the tent. "Be aware when the eyes of the Azari are on you."

Aenguz nodded, affirming both of their uncertainties.

Aenguz stretched his arms and practiced a weaponless *salaage*. The movements grounded him somewhat, but without his *montmorillionite*, the steps and forms felt empty. He would need a weapon at some point. The Stair Guard swords were fine weapons, but they were not Akkeidii, not familiar.

The aura of night faded. The first promise of dawn drank the lesser stars. Though still in shadow, the ocean of fields rustled and seethed placidly. Such uninterrupted crops. The lands around Lihkit were rich and healthy.

The light articulated the foothill reaches of the Spine. The blanket of mountain pines stretched out in both directions. Here and there, pockets of openness revealed themselves. The trees knew the blight, but the fields below did not.

Across the road, Aenguz saw the three horses standing still inside the space created by the partial wall. They too stood like the Azari, though even from here, they seemed to be sleeping. Roe deer bucks slept standing up. How similar were those two animals?

Aenguz glimpsed a movement as a woman emerged from the simple shack. She wore a loose shirt. At tantalizing moments, the thin fabric would cling and highlight her firm curves. Her hair was a tousled mess of tight curls. She walked to the three horses. She moved to each of them - the brown, the black, and the spotted. One at a time, she caressed their chests and whispered up to them. She pressed against her mount and laid her head on the base of its neck.

A tingle moved through him. He held still and urged the sun to hurry. A hint of her smooth, strong legs, the freckled sheen of her bare arms, the firm and almost sensual stroking she gave the horses... A warm flush filled his face and cradled his head.

She turned toward him, seeming to feel his eyes on her. He was too caught up in the rush and flood of feeling to look away. Embarrassment at his intrusion gave him a different kind of heat. Her glare was plain in the growing dawn. She went back to the shack. The other rider was there. They touched each other's arms tenderly, in a kind of hug, and then disappeared within.

Dawn came, and the Lands glowed. Lihkittens woke, and their day began. Legerohn and Chimere left their tent and gave Saissha her privacy. The embassy stirred, and the Stair Guard began preparations for morn meal.

Stroud and Rehl parted as the Lihkittens left their homes and headed out into the fields. The young women returned to the clearing and brought grain and water for the horses. They brushed and tended them, and then they placed the seats on their backs. Shortly after, both riders, fully armed, and Rehl mounted the horses, and they rode out of the vale. Aenguz followed the rider he had watched that morning as she bounced on her horse down the road. He wondered where they were going, wondered if he would see her again.

19

A MESSAGE FROM
THE ONE KING

The day moved quickly, with the specter of communication from the One King hanging over the mundane activities of the vale.

The Stair Guard busied themselves with repairing damage to the corallel tents, counting their supplies, washing themselves and their clothes, and fixing the sleds and the harnesses.

Chimney smoke rose from the homes as hearth fires were stoked. The day was hot, and all the men of the embassy stripped off their shirts and leggings down to their undershorts. They poured pots of water over themselves to cool off as they managed their tasks. Lihkitten women found their own chores to do at the edges of the vale, where they could spy on the half-naked strangers.

At around midday, a tremor shook the ground, and a thunder-like sound rolled down the road. Rehl and the two riders galloped at the head of a herd of horses. They charged up the road, led the way around, and churned up dust in the clearing. Scores of horses ringed along the wall and spun themselves down into a gentle canter.

The young women from Lihkit who had tended the horses were exuberant. They waited eagerly by the shed. The rider he had watched in the morning deferred to the other rider as she barked out orders. The girls scrambled to feed, water, and brush down the horses.

Aenguz watched the rider whom he had seen at dawn. She pointed out horses that needed more attention, and the girls began to separate them to be looked at. Their coats were like the living colors of the earth, all manner of soil with every shade of brown and deep, rich black. It was as if the great horses had been called out of the earth. Gray manes, white manes, blond manes. Speckled horses plucked from a storm cloud shook their heads and snorted up to the sky. Some horses were very large, while some were young and spindly. Roe deer were not so large or widely colored as these great horses.

Aenguz studied the herd and the Free People who cared for them. They were horse herders, in a way. His eyes followed the one rider he had seen earlier. She worked with strange tools on the hooves of some of the horses. Some of the Lihkitten girls were allowed to watch, but only a few were allowed to help. Aenguz watched her work as she taught the others. The herd drew some awe from the Lihkittens, but they seemed familiar with it and did not dwell like Aenguz did.

In the afternoon, a group of Lihkittens made their way down to the shallow amphitheater. They began erecting a façade. Poles were set into footings by the stage, and crossbeams like a row of garrotes were fixed at the top. Colorful draperies were hung across its length. Poles were also set into footings around the outer most ring. The heads of the poles were wrapped.

The sun raced to the horizon. The men and women of the vale hurried to finish their many tasks. The smell of roasted meat and vegetables filled the air. The horses ate from heaping troughs filled by the young women that helped the riders. The embassy ate the last of their rations from Corundum. The Stair Guard informed Saissha of the state of their supplies over dinner.

"We will not starve," was all she said. She, like everyone else, was distracted by what the One King might say.

Once the sun touched the horizon, people strolled down to the theater. Most sat near the front. Once the lines from Lihkit dropped to a trickle, the embassy walked to the outer ring with the tall poles. Aenguz scanned for the rider. The pair stood at the far edge and spoke to each other. Aenguz wondered what they might be talking about.

Just as the sun dipped below the horizon, two pairs of boys with long, thin poles with dull hooks walked to the set poles. Like acolytes, they captured black rings at the top of the hoods. They lifted off the hoods, flicked the poles, and let them drop to their waiting partners. Set in the braziers were hunks of ore. They cast a white light that flickered capriciously around the rock.

Aenguz, Lokah, and Mandavu recognized it immediately.

"That's raw *montmorillionite*," Lokah said.

The boy catching the hood said, "It's silvercryst, my lord." The salutation stumbled from him, unsure of how to address the strangers.

"How is there *montmorillionite* here?" Aenguz asked of the air. He knew neither of them would have any idea. It left him discomfited. The presence of the sacred raw ore might have grounded him, but for the mystery of its presence here.

The boys finished their circuit as the sun set. The horizon was a brilliant blaze of red and deep orange. The Lihkittens quieted their conversations and whispers. Some stole looks at the embassy at the rear of the theater. Aenguz stole one more glance at the hazel-eyed rider.

A small pedestal sat at the center, just in front of the draperies. A large woman dressed in finery he had never seen before came between the curtains. She held something in her hands. She paused for a moment and looked around at the assembled Lihkittens and the strangers. Then she stepped onto the pedestal and put the delicate cap on her head. It looked like a decorative helmet or crown, a kind of circlet ringed with a rough black stone in the middle of her forehead. Her eyes were obscured but not blocked completely. Her mouth was clear. She took long, deep breaths. Her large breasts swelled and sank as if she were about to sing or swim. The amphitheater was still. No one spoke. Even the air seemed to still.

Rehl stepped in from behind her, circled to the front, and looked beneath her mask. The woman brought her hands together, resting one atop the other. Rehl spoke quietly, his voice an octave lower than usual.

Then she spoke and repeated his words.

"'Lihkittens, my heart ached when first I heard that you might be under attack. You cannot know my relief when these travelers, who apparently survived in hell and crossed the Spine of the World, were not the same as the invaders that attacked our beloved vale, Tormont. This tells me that there are paths through the Spine. The Cleve, I assure you, is still warded, but the Spine can no longer contain the evil.'" She paused in between sentences as Rehl relayed the next words to her. The Lihkittens mumbled to one another at the mention of Tormont Vale. Heads shook at the unclear horror.

"'I have requested that these travelers come directly to Earthmight, where I might learn why our peaceful lands are under assault. There is an Azari with them, and you know the Azari to be a true people of the Remnant. Ever have they been faithful. We bless and thank the Eyes of the World,'" the woman enunciated in a clear, sharp tenor tone. Neither Rehl nor Stroud had such an inflection in any of their words. But she almost performed the words as if she delivered a heart-felt soliloquy.

"'The Free People, ever our friends and allies, your daughters have been charged to bring the travelers to Earthmight. The Queen of the

Free People has charged Metzly and Carina with delivering them. Even now, families of great horses are being assembled, as you have no doubt seen. The Queen of the Free People and I thank you for your aid. I ask too that you supply the travelers and these two for the long journey to Earthmight.'" The woman paused and steadied her breath, ready for more words from Rehl.

"'Lihkittens, many of your sons and fathers have left their home and vale to join the One Army. When Tormont Vale was attacked, I spoke to all the vales and asked all who were willing to come to Earthmight and strengthen our force as soon as possible. Now, it grieves me to ask all of you to leave your homes and come to Earthmight. I know not much time has passed since many of you were here at midyear. But I must command that you all come to Earthmight, where we might better protect you.'"

At this, the Lihkittens objected loudly. The calm in the theater was gone. Stroud scanned the theater. The woman waited before Rehl. Then she shouted, "'Lihkittens! Would you have me break the Law of Creation, the tenet I am sworn to uphold to preserve life? What if these travelers were invaders? Would your end be worse than Tormont? What would you have me do? We cannot protect all the vales.

"'The Free People are stretched along the length of the Spine, looking for any other incursion. But there are not enough to protect you all. The One Army is not big enough. There are not enough Azari to help,'" the woman said in a forceful but pleading tone. Her voice carried easily above the people. She tried to tamp them down.

"What about our crops?" someone said. "We will have a harvest unlike any we or our parents' parents have ever seen." Another railed, "My grandmother is too weak to make the journey! Why can she not live out the rest of her days in the home of her birth?"

"'Lihkittens!'" she bellowed. "'Life begets life. Life adapts to the world, and the world adapts to life. Life and death are intertwined. Life *must* preserve life,'" she repeated as the One King recited the tenets of the Law of Creation through her.

"'Make your preparations. Come to the Last Stronghold, where we may protect you and keep you safe. What will come of your crops if you are dead? Do not hold to hope that we can protect you if you stay. There are not enough of us. Tomorrow, I will speak to all the vales. I will command them to come as well. Leave your homes, bring your family, forget the fields, bring your silvercryst and your plows. The stores in Earthmight can sustain you. Come and let us keep you safe in the shadow of the One King's Keep.'"

Rehl dropped his head and turned and looked at the audience. The woman stepped off the pedestal. She removed her headdress. Her face glistened with sweat. Her skin was as pale as the moon.

The relative order in the amphitheater decayed. The One King's command to abandon their homes upended them. "How can we leave Lihkit?" a man said. "How can we leave our animals?" another voice cried out. "What about our grandparents? How are they to survive the long journey to Earthmight? Will they ever return?" a fraught woman pleaded.

Rehl walked forward into the growing maelstrom. He stood still, cast his gaze down, and took in all their anger and fear.

Lihkittens demanded that the One Army be sent to protect them. Hadn't their sons and husbands already gone to join the One Army? Why couldn't they return now to defend their homes?

Stroud stared down at Rehl. Aenguz studied Stroud and wondered what the One King might be thinking about the reactions that Rehl was taking in.

Brazen men came up close to Rehl's face and demanded an answer from him, but he just stood there and did nothing.

The embassy pulled away from the growing chaos and drifted back to their camp beside the small stream. Their eyes bore quiet questions as they crossed the road to their camp.

The anxious Stair Guard circled around their leaders. Saissha, Aenguz, and Legerohn stood in the center in a small circle. Stroud, Mandavu, Lokah, and Chimere created a natural barrier around the three of them. The Stair Guard looked for any explanation for what they had just witnessed.

Saissha peeked around the men that surrounded her to look at Rehl. "Does the One King see this?" she asked.

"Yes," Stroud said. "Hannoch and Sarokin are closest to the One King. They share what Rehl sees."

"What is he going to do?"

"The One King has spoken. He has no more words for the Lihkittens."

"What happened at Tormont?" Aenguz asked. "Where is it from here?"

"Tormont Vale lies in the far north - north of the Cleve. There was an attack. Invaders escaped through the mountains and fell on the vale. Most were slain."

"Who were the attackers?"

"Monsters from the Upper Lands."

"When was this?"

Stroud paused, then answered, "A fortnight ago."

"Have the events we witnessed in the Divine Oculum already come to pass in the Upper Lands?" Legerohn fretted.

"What do they think the Upper Lands are?" Saissha asked of them.

"They think the Upper Lands are a hell. They know of the Ganzir and the Blasted Flats. Corundum, Inverlieth, and even the Mashu are all but a myth to them."

"Does he trust that we are who we say we are?" Saissha asked. Stroud paused.

Aenguz studied the Azari. "Does the One King watch us now?"

Stroud's eyes shifted to Aenguz. He seemed to be wrestling with a challenge to a tenet of his own cryptic faith. "Hannoch and Sarokin, the eyes of the One King, relay everything we see."

The invasion of their close circle shocked and froze them. Saissha's face went slack. Legerohn recoiled from Stroud. They all grew silent. Some of the Stair Guard shuddered at the Azari's strange powers. Some shifted further behind those in front of them. Stroud was suddenly a stranger in their midst.

"Stroud, leave us," Saissha commanded. Her tone was firm and tinged with fear.

"Yes, Counsel Lord," Stroud said. He left their circle and returned through the darkness to the edge of the roiling theater.

For a long moment, no one dared speak. Their shock and questions consumed them.

She looked at the men around her. "We will continue our journey to Earthmight. We must be mindful of our words around Stroud."

"Agreed," Aenguz and Legerohn answered.

"The One King wants to see us with his own eyes. He wants to see us for himself. We have information from the Upper Lands that he does not yet know. I would like to see his reaction to our tidings without any prior pondering. From what Stroud has said, he has not taken it upon himself to deliver the message of the embassy or the Last Emissary. Keep that knowledge to ourselves," Aenguz said to Saissha and Legerohn. Then he looked out and met the eyes of his Akkeidii, Chimere, and the Stair Guard.

"If he cannot defend his own people, how can he help Corundum, or Inverlieth?" Legerohn asked. "Or your home, my friend?"

Like many of their questions, this one - this most important one - did not have an answer.

"We will have to see this One Army for ourselves. We will have to see if it is capable of meeting Morgrom's forces." Aenguz hid his own worry for his home and his people.

Aenguz asked leave of Saissha to have Mandavu order the Stair Guard. They had a long journey ahead, and they should get as much rest as possible. They all needed sleep to digest the edicts of the One King. Aenguz worried about Stroud and the trustworthiness of the Azari.

Saissha acquiesced, and Mandavu ordered the Stair Guard to set the watch.

20

FORTH TO EARTHMIGHT

At dawn, most of the camp was still asleep. The Stair Guard were just beginning to stir. Aenguz met Lokah outside the tent. Rehl and Stroud were walking away from each other as if they were counting off steps in an impossible duel.

"Do they talk to each other?" Aenguz asked.

"I think their lips move, but it is too dark to be sure."

"Do they face each other?"

"Not during my watch."

Aenguz thanked Lokah and sent him in to get some sleep.

Aenguz walked away from their camp and watched the herd. The number of horses appeared to have doubled overnight. The scents of choking musk, horsehair, and manure filled the air. Tans and grays, spots and blacks, browns and yellows mingled in a palette of earthy colors. Whinnies erupted here and there. The herd seemed like one large living organism.

The smell more than the color reminded him of the roe deer herd. Their coats were not so varied, but their communal awareness and security in one another's presence was familiar and palpable. He was a young boy again, spending time with his grandfather.

He looked for the rider he had seen yesterday and found both of them among the horses, already dressed. They both moved among the herd and caressed the horse's chests as they strolled casually among the new arrivals. He was slightly crestfallen that the rider he seen the morning before was not in her simple shift. Aenguz followed the curve of her hips and the smooth lines of her tight leggings. A single cord kept her nest of curls mostly under control.

"Amazing creatures," Legerohn said.

The Prince startled him. "Yes, they inspire awe. I used to ride roe deer when I was a boy. I cannot imagine how we will ride these."

"In Inverlieth, there are large stags that will bear riders. I have ridden them. My men ride them when they patrol the borders of our forest."

They returned to the camp and shared a small morn meal. Others woke and refreshed themselves, then joined them in their familiar morning eating rituals.

The sun cleared the mountains, and Lihkit Vale was awash in its glow as the morning shadows shrank. The vale was full of life. It wasn't clear if they had resolved their objections to the One King's call. The activity looked much like it had the day before, except there was no procession out to the fields. The bustle remained in the vale among the stone houses and buildings.

Stroud appeared with the two riders. They walked with the Azari. The embassy stood stiff with curiosity and trepidation.

"This is Metzly and Carina. They are *ciracums* of the Free People. They will help select the horses for you and prepare you for the journey to Earthmight. They will guide you. Today you will find a horse and learn to ride it. Tomorrow we will depart Lihkit." Stroud stepped over to the embassy.

Carina.

Metzly spoke as if she were perturbed with her task. "These are *novas*." She gestured to the three Lihkitten girls behind her who stood before several other younger girls. "You will listen to them and do as they say. The great horses must choose you. If they do not, you will walk." She glowered at them, hoping for a reaction. None came from the embassy. They had crossed the Spine. Her tone dropped into a clear threat. "Do not think to harm the great horses in any way, or you will follow the train on foot."

"Thank you," Saissha began, but Metzly turned around immediately and walked back to the herd. Carina turned on her heel with her, and the three *novas* followed behind them. Saissha looked at the embassy and shrugged. Aenguz kept his face forward, but his eyes followed Carina.

The embassy crossed the distance to the horses through an atmosphere thick with the scent of manure, straw, and horse musk. Metzly directed them to a space just before the stone and timber shack.

She looked over the group. "You." She pointed at a random Stair Guard. She ordered one of the *novas* to take him. The Stair Guard looked startled, but he followed after the young woman.

She led him into the herd. Metzly chose two other Stair Guard at random and directed the two other *novas* to take them. They followed into the herd at different angles. Big dark eyes burned into the members of the embassy. Snorts and violent head shakes sounded here and there. The three Stair Guard looked terrified. They recoiled at every turn through the forest of raw strength and power. The *novas* glided through in adoration or something near to ecstasy.

Aenguz followed the pairs as they moved through the tremulous herd. The women reached out and touched a horse on its shoulder and murmured something up to its face. Some sign or signal caused them to continue on through to another horse. Aenguz craned his head to follow their circuit and not miss anything of their strange rites.

One pair stopped at a horse - a white horse with splotches of red painted on it. It looked like it had waded through red clay and blobs had splattered on it. The horses parted just enough for him to glimpse what she did next. After she spoke to the red-clay-spotted horse, she turned her back to it and worked her hands like she had a length of rope. She made as if she were intently doing something with the invisible rope, but her hands were clearly empty. Then she turned back to the horse and held her hands up to show the invisible rope. The horse held still. She reached up around its nose and head as if she were affixing it. The horse bent its ears down to allow the invisible line over. Her hands seemed to work at small buckles or cinches. When she was done, the horse pulled its head up, flexed the muscles around its face, and turned its ears forward and backward.

Then the *nova* held the invisible line, took the mystified Stair Guard's hand in hers, and led the horse back to the waiting embassy.

She led the horse to a large two-step wooden box. She halted the horse and the Stair Guard. "Here. Hold this." She held out the invisible line and pressed it into his hands. She called to the other waiting girls, and two of them came up and hauled up the heavy leather seat with two flopping leather straps. They climbed the steps, and with the *nova's* help, guided the seat onto the horse's back. Together they adjusted the seat. It held two swells of leather. They cinched it to the painted horse, and then the *nova* waited.

Carina walked over and studied the saddle. The younger girls waited with bated breath. Carina examined every inch of the saddle and even the invisible harness at the horse's head. She was focused, but when her inspection was complete, she said, "This is good. You have fitted this horse well." She let a smile creep through her stern demeanor. The girls pulled back, pleased with themselves.

Then the *nova* came back and led the Stair Guard to the box. She stepped up with him. "Swing your leg over." The Stair Guard climbed tentatively over the horse. He fell forward onto the horse's neck. The *nova* pulled him back. Then she climbed onto the saddle behind him. She rocked and jerked her legs, and the horse stepped into motion. She rested her hands on the Stair Guard's shoulders, and together they steered the horse out from the herd toward the road leading out of the vale.

The next *novas* brought their chosen Stair Guard. They repeated this process, and they too followed the path of the first horse at a slow gait out away from the herd.

Carina looked over the embassy and chose Saissha next. "You." She walked the Counsel Lord into the herd and led back a gray horse with faded spots of black. The girls brought the saddle, and Carina led Saissha up. "Set your hands here," Carina added to help Saissha, and then she climbed on behind her and the two rode slowly out after the others.

Metzly chose another Stair Guard, led him into the herd, and back to the box. The horse was fitted, the two climbed on, and she took him out.

After a time, the first *nova* and Stair Guard returned. She brought the horse back to the box, and they dismounted. The soldier's complexion had shifted to one of complete joy. He tried shaping words, but his laughter and elation overwhelmed him. He climbed off and stepped down.

Other girls came up and took off the two-person saddle and replaced it with a single-seated saddle. This time, the *nova* explained to the soldier what the girls were doing and what to look out for. He was shown how to tighten the straps and fit the saddle.

"Now you will ride alone." Then she directed him back up the steps.

He climbed over onto the horse, and with the invisible line, took the horse out again down the road. His smile outsized his face.

This process went on throughout the morning. It was different than the tending Aenguz had learned from his grandfather, but familiar in a way. Each animal was cared for and counted.

Aenguz hoped Carina would choose him to find a horse. He wanted to hear her voice up close, wanted to look closely into her eyes. They seemed to shimmer, a brown ringed in gold that at first he thought was green, when she wasn't looking at him. But when her eyes fell on him, the brown flashed gold and sparkled.

One by one, members of the embassy were chosen and taken through the process of selecting, riding with help, and then riding alone.

Stroud followed the *nova* out, but once at the box, he assured her and waved off the dual saddle. The Azari straddled the horse bareback and pulled the beast away at a trot.

Metzly looked Mandavu up and down and took the giant out into the herd. "You are a big one. Come with me."

One of the *novas* selected Aenguz. He tried to shrink back and let her pass to someone else - Chimere or Lokah maybe - but she guided him in. They walked through the different horses. He was not so afraid as the soldiers were, but he was still in awe of the size and power of the horses. They continued past horse after horse. Other pairs came and went, but Aenguz and the *nova* kept searching. It seemed they had been through every horse except for the young horses that were too small to ride.

Flummoxed, the *nova* brought Aenguz back to the line. "You will wait here. I will speak with the *ciracums*." She took another soldier and left Aenguz after giving him an odd look.

One by one, the members of the embassy were chosen until only Aenguz and Chimere remained. At the end, Metzly took Aenguz through the herd one more time, and Carina took Chimere, but they could find no horse for them.

The Stair Guard brought up the subject of the sleds as the embassy walked back to the camp.

Supplies had been gathered at the camp and at the shack all day. Lihkittens brought baskets, sacks, and satchels of food and water.

Carina and Metzly talked with the Stair Guard about the sleds. They found two long poles and threaded them through the harnesses on the sleds and then through looped leathers Carina had made. In this way, two horses could bear the sleds. The Stair Guard were happy to help. Although they were relieved of having to carry the sleds, they quickly developed a kinship with the horses for bearing them as proudly as they did. While the horses seemed to accept them in their way, the Stair Guard seemed to also accept them into their ranks. Corundum's past and its walls held memory and honor for the great horses in their minds.

Aenguz watched the effort of raising the sleds from a distance. When Lokah saw Carina working with leather and the tools, he went over to her and asked some questions. She gave him some straps of leather after working on a couple of the ends. Aenguz was ashamed of the glint of jealousy that rose in him. He met Lokah upon his return.

"I need something to bear my sword," Lokah said. "I lost the scabbard the people of Corundum gave me in the mountains. If I had tools and leather and time, I could fashion a proper scabbard."

The thought of their impetuous slide down the mountainside to save the embassy made them both laugh.

"I still cannot believe that worked."

Then the recollection of the avalanche and the loss of the sled and Einki came to them, and their laughter stilled into remembrance and respect.

The Lihkittens had set out long tables at the rear of the theater.

Food had been set out during the afternoon. Once all of the horses were unsaddled, watered, and fed, the embassy, Metzly, Carina, and the Lihkittens joined together in a farewell meal. Stroud and Rehl watched them from a distance, while they scanned the horizon.

They did not talk about the One King's words or the order to leave their homes. They spoke mainly about the horses. How they would come in the spring, and scores would be fitted with plows to ride out shoulder to shoulder in long lines to plow the soil. Or in the fall at harvest time to help haul the bounty back to the vale. Some wondered if there would be horses available this season, but they did not dwell on the dreads that plagued them. Instead, they talked about the personalities and colors of certain horses. Metzly and Carina would share the names of the horses and their relationship to one another in their intricate extended families. They often rode, herded, and grazed together as large, interconnected families.

Aenguz worried about why he hadn't been chosen by a horse. What did it mean? Eventually, his concern rose to the surface, and he uttered under his breath to Mandavu and Lokah, "Will I have to walk all the way to Earthmight?"

"We will all walk," Mandavu said matter-of-factly. "You are the Lord of the Akkeidii. You will not walk alone."

Lokah agreed. "It will not be harder than our last hike." His droll tone recalled the long walk on the Rursh Keleg. His dry humor had kept their spirits from collapsing while they marched to Corundum.

But Aenguz was not with them. He had crossed through the Ganzir within the Oasis. He could walk it, but it was more the time that it would take that gnawed at him.

Their low laughter ended, and Lokah added, "Maybe we can ride on the sleds." They all laughed, but the cloud still hung over him.

———◆———

THE NEXT DAY, IN the early light of dawn, the embassy made ready to leave. The corallel tents were lowered and the sleds packed. The Stair Guard hauled them over to the stirring herd. The four horses, two and two, were fitted with their harnesses and the poles slid through the straps. The Stair Guard lifted the sleds into place. They swayed with the flex of the wood and the leather, but the horses managed the weight easily.

Aenguz agonized about being horseless. Anger made him surly. He was glad no one bothered him in that moment. He could have snapped at anyone.

Chimere was brooding. He seemed to be testing the weight in his ankle. Aenguz gravitated to him. He could protect the soulful Moresi as one of the outcast pair. It gave a different place for his own angst to go. They watched together as the preparations were made.

Carina, Metzly, and the *novas* worked to saddle the horses. The great horses were brought single file before the mounting box, and one by one, each member of the embassy came up when their horse was brought around.

Mandavu saw Saissha to the box and watched her mount. He stood near the Prince as he climbed on his horse. Lokah stayed by Aenguz, with straps of loose leather covering his weapon.

The Stair Guard flirted with the *novas* as they took the invisible lines and mounted the horses that had chosen them. They were excited to ride, but they had no small attention for the young women.

As the last of them mounted, Mandavu returned to stand with Aenguz, Lokah, and Chimere. They were the last four to be unhorsed. When the huge horse that Mandavu had ridden yesterday lumbered into place, Mandavu did not budge. The *nova* called him over, but he merely said, "I will walk."

"Aye, I will too," Lokah added.

Metzly turned her mount to them. "You cannot walk all the way to Earthmight."

"We are Akkeidii. We can walk further than you think," Mandavu said finally.

Carina was guiding the growing line of riders toward the road. Metzly shouted to her to halt the line. The other riderless horses were already walking out of the vale. The horses with riders wanted to continue. Keeping the line intact was a challenging affair.

Carina rode over to Metzly, and the two of them met the Akkeidii and Chimere.

"You two will ride with us," Metzly said to Aenguz and Chimere. Their horses had the dual-seated saddles. "You two get on your horses," She commanded Mandavu and Lokah.

Mandavu and Lokah looked to Aenguz.

"Go and take your mounts."

Metzly barked at Chimere, "Follow me." Chimere was shaking and distraught. "Calm yourself."

Relief washed over Aenguz.

The worried Moresi followed Metzly over to the box. She positioned her horse and urged him up. He gingerly placed his leg over and sat down behind her. The horse riled and jostled. Metzly shouted at Chimere to calm down, and then with a softer voice, settled her horse.

Carina led Aenguz to the box. He climbed up and grabbed Carina's shoulder to balance himself and swung his leg over. He settled in behind her. His legs rested against her hips. Only her two-headed axe was between them. Her hair smelled of sandalwood and leather. She shrugged his hands off of her shoulders and snapped her head at him.

Then Metzly rode to the front of the line with Chimere and led the entourage out of the vale. All of the horses and foals that had gathered, including the riderless ones, walked with the riders. Nearly three score horses took the road out of Lihkit Vale.

Before Carina left, a *nova* handed her the invisible lines for two laden horses - her gear and Metzly's, along with other supplies the Free People might use to care for the horses. Bands of leather hung like collars around both their necks. They were sturdy horses.

Carina and Aenguz rocked lazily out of the vale at the end of the line, with the two pairs of bearer horses at the rear.

Aenguz looked back at the *novas* and the Lihkittens. The *novas* looked on with a mixture of pride and yearning. They wanted to ride, but the charge to bring the embassy to Earthmight was too important. The Lihkittens who came to watch the departure from the edge of the vale looked on as if they were witnessing their future, viewing them-selves in a few days' time in a reluctant line to abandon their homes.

21

CIRACUM

The mounted embassy from Corundum followed the road out of Lihkit Vale past the brimming fields and islands of trees. A lazy brook followed the grassy, trampled road at times, but it came and went with easy turns and curves along the wide pathway.

Aenguz rode with Carina at the rear with the foals and mares. Carina also led the two horses, bearing her and Metzly's gear, at the end of invisible tethers.

Saissha rode far ahead at the front of the line behind Metzly and Chimere. Stroud and Legerohn rode on either side of her. The Stair Guard flanked the leaders of the embassy and the horses who bore the sleds.

Mandavu and Lokah rode between the leaders and the sleds that swung between the horses on the long poles.

Riderless horses walked beside and around the column up and down the line. The road was packed with them. The warm air was dense with musk. They trotted together in loose-knit groups.

Around midday, the fields ended and gave way to open prairie.

Tall brown and green grasses swept across the gentle terrain, and small yellow and orange blossoms from the previous season dotted the soft plain. A faint trace of an intersection appeared in the trampled earth, and the column veered onto the vague path that turned north and west. Soon, however, any trace of a natural road disappeared.

As they settled into a steady gait, Aenguz said, "Thank you for bearing me. Why did a horse not choose me?"

"Not all horses bear riders." She thought for a second and then added, "Or they sense something about you that they do not like."

Shame flooded him. He looked at his scarred hand and wondered if that gave them pause, or if it was something else - the mark of the message, or the stain of being the Last Emissary.

"Thank you again for helping me."

"I am commanded to see you all to Earthmight by my Queen," Carina replied as she rocked with the horse's gentle, steady stride.

Shortly after their terse exchange, Metzly signaled back, and the line slowed to a stop.

Carina halted her horse. "We are stopping here to rest." The column had come to a halt.

He had only gotten on the back of the horse that morning with the help of a box. Now he wasn't sure how to get off. The ground seemed far away.

Carina sensed his hesitation. "Get off."

Aenguz fumbled at her back. He grabbed her shoulder and handled her waist. "Sorry." He grabbed her thigh and swung his leg over. His foot got stuck, and he hopped and then fell to the ground. The horse shuffled away from him. Carina reined the horse in with thin air. Then she swung her leg over deftly and hopped to the ground. She looked at Aenguz with mild disdain as he climbed to his feet.

Everyone dismounted. The sleds were lowered, and the horses moved into the grass to graze. The soldiers produced some food from the sled and passed it around to everyone.

Carina left to talk with Metzly.

Mandavu and Lokah joined Aenguz. They found a place to sit, where they ate and drank with the Stair Guard who warded the sleds. "I did not know my legs could be so sore in such a way," Lokah said.

They groaned as they laughed.

After the midday meal, they each found their horse and climbed on. Metzly and Carina showed them how to pull themselves onto their horses without the step box. They showed them a couple of options, from grabbing the horse's mane and pulling themselves up to springing up and landing on their stomach before scissoring their legs over the animal's back. Then they dismounted easily and waited for the others to try.

Their frustration was plain, but they were true to their charge and their duty. Aenguz stood by the horse and waited for Carina to return. She looked cross, as if her task or the novice riders frustrated her. She barely looked at Aenguz and took a couple of quick steps, leaping onto the horse's back and landing on her stomach. Then just as quickly, she kicked out her leg and swung confidently into the seat.

Aenguz set his foot in the foot loop, grabbed the pommel, and pulled himself up. He nearly flung himself over the other side. The horse staggered, and Carina grabbed him to keep him from falling. He pulled on her arm and fell part way onto her back. But Aenguz righted himself and swore, "Great Grieg!" He had been on a roe deer before; he should be able to navigate a horse, he thought to himself. He wanted to impress Carina, but he wasn't sure why.

The column continued on through the afternoon. Layers of clouds broke up the sky. Shafts of light poked through and shined on the beautiful prairie.

Before sunset, the column stopped to make camp. Metzly had chosen a spot by a wide, shallow brook with a smattering of trees. The soft rush calmed the space.

The sleds were lowered. Then the horses were unsaddled and unharnessed. The Stair Guard policed their gear. The horses sauntered off to drink at the brook and graze on the lush grass dotting the shore. As their riders made camp and they finished drinking, the horses meandered into a loose cordon around the company.

The Stair Guard raised the corallel tents, waddling around on sore legs and hips. They set some small stump fires to cook the evening meal as the sun set.

They gathered to eat the meal cooked in the kettles they had brought from Corundum and the vegetables and meat they were given in Lihkit. As they ate, Mandavu asked, "Do you think Kachota and Mond have reached Inverlieth yet?"

Legerohn worked to swallow a mouthful of the stew. "If they left right after us, then yes, they should be close to Inverlieth by now."

"Good," Mandavu said.

After the meal, Carina and Metzly went off a short distance from the company and bedded out in the open in a clear patch of grass. In the gloam, it seemed that they bedded down together.

———— ◆ ————

THE NEXT DAY, BY the time Aenguz woke, half of the horses were already saddled. The Stair Guard finished the work, and then they all mounted.

Aenguz waited for Carina at the end of the line. He was the last to mount. She rode up and down the line, making sure the Stair Guard had readied the horses correctly. When she came back, he swore he could hear his heart. He pulled himself up more easily this time - still not gracefully, but better than the day before. Mandavu and Lokah waited. Metzly watched from the front. With him on the back of Carina's horse, they were able to start their march.

Metzly urged the line into a gentle canter. Aenguz bounced with Carina. He reached out to her shoulders to steady himself, and she shrugged his hands away.

Perturbed, Aenguz asked, "If a horse would bear me, I would not be on your back. Why not find another horse for me?"

"None of these horses chose you, and we do not have a saddle for you anyway."

"So, no horse will bear me or Chimere?"

"These horses here will not. There may be other horses that will."

"Would you rather I walked?"

Her silence seemed to say yes.

"My sisters search the Lands and the Spine for more invaders, and we leave them to peril while we bear you to Earthmight, away from the danger."

What about the One Army? He thought. Then he said, "We have come to ask for help from the One Army."

"Pfft," she sounded. "There was no One Army to protect Tormont Vale when it was attacked. By the time anyone knew something was wrong, the nearest soldiers warding the Cleve were sent...too late. I have not been back since the attack. The lone Azari who rides with our Queen relayed what they saw. I do not know about my family - my mother, my father, or my sister. The Spine is no longer safe, and I am here with you."

"I am sorry. I did not know."

"How could you know? Just ward your hope against the One Army."

Metzly halted the column well before sunset. The entire company, except for Metzly, Carina, and Stroud, seemed sore. The canter had taken a toll on all of them. The Stair Guard were slow to raise the tents, but they enjoyed riding. They often trotted up the line, then drifted back to their original positions at a leisurely pace. However, they were still new to riding, and their bodies made sure they knew it.

They continued for three more days this way. The rhythm of routine, gathering and saddling the horses, making camp, eating, stretching sore muscles, refreshing themselves, breaking down and stowing the tents, familiar but foreign on the undulating prairie. The Spine was gone, the danger behind them. The small forests were calm and peaceful. Birds played in the sky.

Over the course of the days, some horses split off from the column, and others joined. In the distance, horses were grazing or playing in the open prairie. They grew curious and drifted toward the column. Families of horses were excited to join the column, as if they were participating in some kind of game. They enjoyed the herd and the rhythm of riding. Overall, their numbers seemed to grow.

Aenguz's mounting and dismounting had improved. He wanted to know more about Carina, but he mainly wanted to look in her eyes and watch the color change in different lights. One time she caught him staring overly long.

"Is there something wrong with my face?"

"No, no, um, I was… Nothing."

Being close to her warmed him. A thrum mounted whenever he was near her. Her angst toward him was not wholly reflected in her eyes. The occasional brushes and touches were more infrequent, but more treasured. He was drawn to her, simple as that.

As they made their way through the hot days, her sweat and scent made him dizzy. He asked questions about the Free People, or about the horses around them, and details about her care for them, just to hear her voice. "We tend their hooves and fit them with metal to ward them. We hold the mares when it comes time for birthing. I am proud to be a *ciracum*."

The sound of her voice sent a thrill down his neck, but he was also curious about her and her life. "What was your home like?"

"Tormont is on the front range of the northern mountains. The stone used to build Earthmight was quarried from those mountains. It is a great source of pride for my people there."

She talked at length about the light on the mountains. It set a different timbre to her voice.

"I miss the mountains around my hearth valley. I understand what you mean about the light. It has been a long time since I have seen them," Aenguz said.

"How long have you been gone from your home?"

"Since spring." He thought about Selene and their farewell. Shame twisted him like a damp rag. She seemed so far away, and she might assume that he was dead. In truth, he might never see the Mashu again. So much had happened since that time that he might tell her, but the only thing that mattered was that Ruinwasters were coming. Morgrom was coming for the One Army. He turned the question back on Carina. "How long have you been gone?"

"Since I became a *ciracum*."

He could tell by her tone that it had been a while.

"I wanted more than a life in Tormont. When the great horses came, all I dreamed about was all the lands beyond my home. When I rode a horse for the first time, I knew I was going to join the Free People. My mother was not happy, but she could not stop me either. Now, who knows if she is even alive?" She grew silent again and stiffened.

It had been a long time since either of them had been home.

22

VIOLATION

Aenguz and Carina chatted more and more each day, in rhythm with their riding. Carina pointed out and identified the extended families of horses that came and went along the column. She talked about the first horse she had ridden as her own when she left her vale to become a *ciracum*. While they could ride any horse that accepted them, a single horse was given to women when they became a member of the Free People to learn how to ride without the worry of learning the new propensities of different horses each day.

Aenguz told her about the families of roe deer and the herd hounds that helped to corral them. "Before I began my training as a warrior, my grandfather taught me many things about the roe deer. The great horses remind me in a way of them."

"Is that why you stopped serving them, to be a warrior?" she asked.

"I could not be a warrior and a deerherd. Once I began my training, there was no room for anything else."

"What did your grandfather think of that?"

"I think he would have liked to see me choose the deerherds' way of life."

Late in the afternoon on the sixth day since departing Lihkit, the column came to an unexpected halt. They had been following the course of a natural cliff at a distance. The top was flat. Its face was a stack of mocha- and rust-colored rock. It looked as if the land around it had dropped away to reveal a hastily made wall. After a long stretch, the wall crumbled. Islands of rock stretched out intermittently like prairie mesas in the same line as the cliff.

Aenguz and Carina saw Metzly signal back. It was an unfamiliar hand sign to Aenguz.

Carina called the nearest Stair Guard back to her and handed him the invisible lines, making sure both pack horses saw her. She and Aenguz trotted up the line between the column and the itinerant horses that marched along with them.

Metzly had dismounted and was feeling the horse's chest. Carina relaxed her legs against the horse's side and the horse strolled to a stop. "What is it?"

"Something is wrong," Metzly said. Her face scrunched as if she were stuck on a riddle.

Carina dismounted and handed Aenguz the invisible tethers. The pair began touching and feeling the chests of the horses - Saissha's mount, Legerohn's, Stroud's, and the riderless horses that were still near them. The others were turning and trotting away from the column into a wider circle.

"What is it?" Aenguz asked.

"Their hearts beat with fear," Carina answered. "The covert lies ahead. We were going to camp there. It is like a sanctuary for the great horses. This is not excitement. They are afraid." She pressed her head to her mare's chest as if to convey what she heard. Then she pulled back and pulled in large drafts of air through her nose.

Mandavu and Lokah trotted up to the group.

"What is it?" Mandavu asked.

"The horses sense something," Aenguz replied. "Where is the covert?" he asked Metzly.

"There." Metzly pointed to the furthest mesa.

Ahead, in the distance, was an island of rock. The prairie led gradually downward into a wide-open bowl. Long green grass whispered in the wind, shimmering like a lake of pale opal. A mesa like the ones they had followed was crowned with grass and broad trees. A small pool cupped the base. Ripples glinted in it placidly. Beyond the island, the ground rose into a near horizon.

"Have you ever seen them react this way?" Legerohn asked.

"No."

"We have been here many times," Carina added. Concern gave a heightened tinge to her voice.

Aenguz's intuition was sound. He could see no evidence of an issue. While he couldn't feel the horses' trepidation, he could feel Carina's and Metzly's. He chastised himself for letting his guard down; he should have been more alert. He reset himself, and his warrior training kicked in.

"Lokah, get our weapons." To the Stair Guard, he said, "Lower the sleds and arm yourselves."

Lokah spun the horse and galloped to the rear of the column.

"Chimere, get off."

The Moresi slid off Metzly's mount. He seemed both frightened and relieved.

"You will stay here," Aenguz said to Legerohn, Stroud, and Saissha. Chimere came around beside the Prince's horse.

Then to Mandavu, "Set the protection here."

"What are you doing?" Metzly bristled at Aenguz's commands.

"Protecting Corundum's hope. Protecting us. You said there is a problem." He looked at both of them. "I believe you."

She closed her mouth.

He continued to Mandavu, "Pick two to come with us."

Mandavu moved into action. He pulled his hulking draft horse around and commanded the Stair Guard. He chose two and ordered them to the head of the column. The rest he ordered to set a cordon around the Counsel Lord and the Prince of the Moresi. As the Stair Guard dismounted, their horses trotted away, the steeds' nervous energy adding to their own.

Lokah pulled out the Akkeidii's weapons from where he had stored them on the sled. He handed Mandavu the cylindrical scabbard as the First rode by. Mandavu slid the strap over his shoulder and continued in a circle around the mustering Stair Guard. He looked into the distance all around them and commanded the Stair Guard to stay wary. The clanking of swords and spears made the first sounds of the overture of battle.

Lokah rode to the head of the column and handed Aenguz his silver-banded scabbard.

Aenguz slung on his scabbard.

Carina looked quizzically at Aenguz, as if she were looking on a wholly new person.

"What enemies do you have here?" Aenguz asked Metzly.

"What enemies? The only enemies are the invaders that came across the Spine. We care for the horses. We hunt; sometimes we hunt dangerous prey, but there are only valers and people in the Lands."

"What is wrong here to your eyes?"

"We should not be alone. The covert is always warded. A sister should have met us by now. None may approach unchallenged. There are usually horses here," she answered, her voice beginning to fray on her uncertainty.

Mandavu rode up with the two riders he had chosen. He looked at

Aenguz and reported that the ring around the company was set. Already his expression had turned to a calculated seriousness.

Aenguz searched the perimeter and the mound ahead. He looked at Metzly and Carina again. His heart seemed to match the great horses. Then he nodded at Mandavu.

To the remaining Stair Guard and Stroud, he said, "Ward the Counsel Lord and the Prince. Do what Legerohn tells you."

The Stair Guard snapped to attention. Hardness marked their stances. They set a ring around the leaders of the embassy, spears out.

To Legerohn, Mandavu said, "Keep Saissha close."

"I will. Be careful."

Mandavu nodded a thank you to the Prince.

"Lokah, I want you to ride with Metzly."

Lokah climbed off of his mount and waited for her. After Metzly climbed on, he mounted behind her. Carina sprung up and joined Aenguz.

They rode toward the covert at a casual gait. Mandavu trotted at the fore. The two Stair Guard rode at the rear.

They followed the gentle slope and traced a line to the left side of the mound. Aenguz searched the hill of rock and the grasslands on either side. But for the lazy wind, the earth looked still and peaceful.

Metzly steered them to the left and into the shadow cast by the covert. Carina tensed.

They reached the edge of the mound. The craggy rock face looked like rough stacked brick. Crumbled shale formed the shoreline at the edge of the pool. A border of shrub and trees marked the near edge.

Metzly and Carina shook their heads. They were alert, but disheveled by the wrongness.

They dismounted cautiously, as if the ground might fall away utterly beneath them. They walked to a shaded opening that looked like a natural alcove. The area was at once simply a natural place, but also a rarefied space, something akin to sacred. As Aenguz's eyes adjusted from the sun, he saw that it was an entrance.

Aenguz signaled to Lokah and Mandavu. Mandavu slid out his mace and let his scabbard drop. Lokah unwrapped the straps of leather he had secured his weapon in. Aenguz pulled out his Dagba Stone-locked *montmorillionite,* dropped his scabbard, and pulled off the protective hunks of wood. Carina stared at his weapon curiously. She and Metzly pulled their two-headed axes from their backs. The Stair Guard drew their swords.

Then, they walked into the shadowy entrance of the covert. The smell of dusty earth and decaying leaves choked the opening. Then another odor - smoke and iron or copper. A putrid haze replaced the dust and leaves as they passed through the dark entrance.

A natural stacked rock wall undulated and rose on the right, while a flat masonry wall of fitted stones lined the left. The stones, vaguely square and rectangular in shape, were fitted perfectly together. The floor was formed into a similar cobble, but with smaller stones. The fitted stones harkened to the Mashu and the Stonemage-made buildings and walls there.

The ceiling was a network of tree branches and netted rope lines. It was too quiet. They made the only sounds. Aenguz could almost feel their hearts in the still space.

A room to the left looked ransacked. Supplies, tools, leather, and wood were scattered across the floor. Metzly and Carina's eyes confirmed what was obvious to them all - that this wasn't right.

The natural rock wall widened out away from the stone wall. Light flitted down onto the rock face. The stone wall to the left bore a mural of a solitary horse. It seemed to be standing at attention. The ceiling rose into a vaulted cathedral canopy made of large-armed trees and rope nets. The late afternoon sun lit the underside of the canopy and cast a dim light down below. Bits of blue sky poked through like chunks of stars.

They walked ahead slowly. Caution bristled from all of them. To Aenguz's right was an alcove in the natural wall. At its base was a small pool. A low wall, barely a step, ringed it. Hunks of driftwood were toppled and broken in the pool of some larger sculpture. It looked like the body of a horse, or parts of one. A sacred space, desecrated. It reminded him of the hollowed-out trunk of the desecrated cairn tree. His heart began to retch. The pool was stagnant and dirty. Suddenly, the smell of old meat and blood hit him.

Carina and Metzly gasped. Shock transformed them.

Mandavu clicked his tongue. Aenguz turned to the open area to their left. Metzly and Carina's axes dropped as if all their strength had left them. An oval space opened before them. It cupped the shallow alcove behind them and reached around to a soft point. Darkened doorways lined the curved stone walls. Etchings and carving of horses marked the walls in between. They seemed notable in a way and not just random horses.

A round altar-like fire pit rested at the center. Wisps of smoke sputtered from a dead fire. Before it lay a slaughtered horse. Its belly was cavernous. Old blood and intestines marked the floor. The horse's genitals had been burned and tortured. Metzly and Carina froze. The profanity in this safe and sacred space numbed them. Color drained from their faces.

Mandavu ordered the Stair Guard to check the rooms on one side of the open space while he and Lokah checked the other.

Aenguz froze. He was standing on the Cairngorm as if the moment was as near as last night. He didn't know what to do. The bodies of the Champions slain at the black pit... The feral Erebim, their half-orange heads darting about in the firelight… Fear and a grim core of anger rooted him and pushed him to the edge. He was hyper-wary of every door his friends came to and the Stair Guard explored. Somehow, he walked toward the horror. There were bodies beside the fire. Metzly and Carina were drawn too. In that moment, he had no means to call light to his weapon. Even if the stone hadn't prevented him, he couldn't call up the words to bring light.

"My lord," one of the Stair Guard called. His voice quivered. "There are more dead here."

Metzly and Carina split off as if to relieve themselves from the carnage and went to the rooms the Stair Guard had called from. Aenguz closed his nose and studied the profaned horse and bodies around the fire. An old woman with gray and white hair, her skull crushed in. Another younger woman, blood-soaked blonde hair, her face broken. Blood like the blood that fed the pit on the tip of the Lower Mashu.

Mandavu and Lokah met the Stair Guard at the farther side of the oval space. After they spoke, the Akkeidii called light to their weapons. They shook their heads back at Aenguz and walked back toward him. They were ghosts walking out of his past, indicting him for leading the others to death. They were the specters of lost Champions.

"There are seven dead," Mandavu reported. "We should search the rest of the covert."

Aenguz struggled to concentrate. They were looking to him for direction, but guilt, shame, and horror closed his mind. He uttered a yes.

Mandavu and Lokah left him. They seemed to understand that something struggled in Aenguz. They went on with the Stair Guard to search the rest of the covert.

Metzly and Carina shrieked and wailed at each of the rooms where they found dead. Aenguz lurched unsteadily over to the room where Carina had gone. She was on her knees, her shoulders shaking. A headless naked body lay on the floor. Aenguz looked on the violation and saw Ridder's body, his brother-friend's throat slashed open, blood spurting.

He was her shadow, and she was his. They were both fixed in paralyzing astonishment and shock. Metzly's wails rent the silence of death. Gasps and cries followed her from room to room.

Aenguz left Carina. The smell of blood and death turned his head upside down. He drifted past the defilement. The unwanted memory of the murders on the Cairngorm surrounded him like the oval space. The helplessness as much as the naked unrepentant violence ripped out the foundation of his own decency. Only the grim core of iron in his heart, formed by hate that disturbing night, kept him upright - hot hate for the Erebim. Unfinished vengeance hammered in his blood.

Carina and Metzly's sobs of rage and loss echoed in the killing chamber. Their cries bore him back to the present.

Mandavu, Lokah, and the two Stair Guard returned. They had found no other bodies, but every room - small sleeping chambers, mostly - had been turned over in one way or another.

"Is it safe?" Aenguz asked.

"Yes, although I would like to have the Stair Guard search the perimeter before it gets dark."

"I think we should have the others come down. What do you think?"

"We will be stronger together," Mandavu agreed.

Aenguz nodded and said, "Send a Stair Guard to call the others down. Have them search around outside. Some days have passed, but whoever did this might not be far."

"Yes, my lord," Mandavu answered. He ordered Lokah to stay with Aenguz while he gave his commands to the two Stair Guard. In a moment, they were off, relieved to leave the abattoir.

Metzly squatted on her haunches outside one of the rooms. She was rocking back and forth, keening along with the wind of her grief.

Her helmet lay on the ground, and she struck the top of her head with a stone she had found. Rivulets of blood trickled down her face and mixed with her tears. He did not understand the ritual she gave to her suffering, and there was nothing he could offer her to fix it. His helplessness drew him down.

Carina staggered backward out of the room that held the headless body. A steady low groan like a sustained "no" flowed out of her. Aenguz approached her slowly, careful not to intrude, yet hoping to offer some form of comfort.

He stood in front of her to block her view. She stared into his chest and clawed at her helmet. Her eyes fluttered. She hit him hard twice in the chest and then tipped forward and buried her head there. Tears and hard wails came out of her. He put his arms around her and let his weapon drop to the ground. He said nothing, offered nothing but his solid form.

He didn't know how long he stood there in the crucible of their grief, but after a time, Saissha, Stroud, and Legerohn were there. Chimere followed behind Legerohn with a twisted look of shock on his face.

Their voices broke the spell, and Carina pulled away and drifted toward Metzly. Abject shock and horror filled the newcomers' faces, except for Stroud. The Azari scanned everything, stared at everything. Aenguz picked up his weapon and met them by the pool.

"The One King and the Queen of the Free People are 'seeing' what has happened here." Aenguz knew that the Azari with each of them were relaying what Stroud was seeing. Saissha was mortified. She looked into a room or two and then at the slain horse before the altar fire. Legerohn's eyes widened in disbelief, but they were also hardened by familiar shock and loss.

Mandavu kept an eye on Saissha as he reported back to Aenguz about the column and the perimeter. He went to Stroud and told him what they had seen farther in the covert and where the Azari should look next.

Aenguz needed some air. It had all been too much. They thought they had moved out of danger when they left the Spine behind, but clearly, the Lower Lands were under assault. As he left the covert, he tried to separate the two horrors and leave the Cairngorm in the past. He wondered if he was too late to warn the One King, or if his warning would even have any meaning. The intruders were already here and farther than they might have thought.

The sun had sunk below the horizon when he left the entrance, and the crepuscular air didn't hold as much relief as he had hoped. He knew that Morgrom was behind this violation; he just didn't know how. How had he brought such violence so far from the east?

23

INFESTATION

Aenguz found his scabbard and sheathed his weapon. The protective pieces of wood held meaning, but he was too scattered, too dislocated to recall their purpose. The Stair Guard had brought up the sleds, and some were in the process of pulling off the corallel tents. Others stood guard while their comrades worked. One soldier held his hand out in a loose fist, as if he held all the invisible tethers on their horses. That an invisible line could hold command over such powerful creatures was still an odd mystery to him.

The light of dusk added a shroud to the area around the covert. It seemed like he could still smell death in the air. A brisk wind would be welcome. Stair Guard rode in the distance in a wide arc around the covert.

A soldier galloped in out of the west on a blond pony. He slid off its back, breathless, and said, "I have found a clear trail." He peered warily into the entrance and headed inside. Mandavu, no doubt, ordered them to report any signs of invaders immediately. Aenguz looked to the west to see if he could see anything, but there was nothing obvious from this distance.

Aenguz drifted over to the horses to soothe them, and also maybe to draw some measure of peace from them. They looked nervous. They held their heads high as if they were searching the horizon. Their ears flipped and turned at distant sounds, their nostrils animated.

Metzly was behind him. She snatched the invisible line out of the air and jumped onto her horse.

"Wait! Metzly!" Aenguz shouted.

She kicked her mount until the horse was at a full gallop. She raced off into the west toward the dying light. The jittery horses bucked and scrambled from the Stair Guard.

The Stair Guard grabbed at the air.

Aenguz reached out to try to help him.

Carina ran out. She raced to her horse, leapt onto the saddle stomach-first and sprang her leg over.

The horses bolted away from her.

"Carina, wait!" Aenguz raced over to her.

He grabbed the pommel to hold the horse still, but she ignored him and wheeled her horse away from the others. He ran alongside. "Stop! Carina! Stop!"

In a desperate move, he flung himself up onto the horse's back. He lay across its rump, bouncing and flailing. His words were punched out of his chest. "Grieg damn! Wait! Stop!"

Through a fluke of the rhythm and bounce, he found his seat, and one foot found the stirrup. But he had never ridden at such a pace. He flung both arms around her waist and hung on as if he might be thrown at any minute. He tried again to get her to stop and shouted in her ear, but it was no use. She raced after Metzly, but with two riders, her horse could only go so fast. He tried to look back, but the fear of being flung from the horse was too great.

They galloped up out of the shallow bowl. If there was a trail, he was too afraid of falling to see it, but he could see Metzly and her horse pulling away into the distance. There were small swells in the land, but not enough to hide her completely. If there was a trail, she was able to see it. She seemed to be racing against the slow-fading light.

Carina drove on harder. She seemed incensed by Aenguz's extra weight, but he wouldn't let go. He made another attempt to convince her to stop and wait for the others, but when tears trailed back and touched his face, he knew it was pointless.

Stars began to grace the sky. Upon checking for pursuit, Aenguz could see the waxing moon in the faded rose sky. With each stretch of gallop, the light seeped out of the air. The glow on the horizon burned out like a dying fire.

The plain levelled, and the night light cast a pale silver sheen on the earth. Metzly had become a wild dot ahead of them, but Carina pressed on. Both horses' stamina and energy were incredible. Froth peeled out of the horse's mouth and streaked its neck. Its heaving drowned out the wind of their flight, and soon its pace began to slow. Aenguz couldn't imagine that Carina would drive a horse so hard, but she didn't relent and growled at the horse, or at the additional weight behind her.

He scanned around the dark foreign land for any trace of Metzly. Then he thought he saw a hump on the ground ahead. Carina urged the horse on toward it.

It was a horse on its side - Metzly's horse. And she was trapped underneath it. He could hear her shrieks. Then he saw a pair of shafts poking out of her horse toward the night sky.

Intuition and warrior training made him react. He grabbed Carina by the forearms and pulled her and the horse hard to the right. She fought him, but the horse and rider turned too hard, and he pulled her off the horse. They collapsed to the ground as something cut through the air.

She hissed and fought Aenguz. He held her close, throwing his leg over her, and said firm and tight, "Look! Listen!"

She relented enough to turn back toward where Metzly and her horse lay. The shafts weaved in the still air as if a night wind blew them. Metzly writhed in unbearable pain.

They climbed on their stomachs through the grass to Metzly. Another sharp wisp cut through the air above their heads. To their right, their mount jogged in the distance parallel to the pair. A long shaft stuck out of the mare's saddle. Carina scolded the horse in an unknown tongue. It hesitated, confused. Another bolt whipped over its neck. Her horse turned away from them, and then it ran into the night.

They reached the cover of Metzly's horse. The stallion panted out its breath. Metzly wailed in agony. Her leg was trapped under the felled horse. No shafts were in her. Carina tried to pull her free. Metzly wailed even louder.

Another bolt hit the horse. It shifted, and she screamed again. She tried to push on the horse to move it.

"Leave her be." There was no way the two of them could budge so much weight. Besides, any movement sent Metzly into a delirium of pain.

Aenguz had only a vague idea of the direction their attackers were aiming from. They were pinned down, and his thought was for the others who would surely be following them. They would be riding into a trap. He freed his weapon. Carina pulled her axe free, but she cursed that her bow was on her horse now lost somewhere in the night.

Aenguz chanted words of lore to coax light from his weapon.

"Grieg dammit!"

"What are you doing?" Carina asked. She looked at his Dagba Stone-locked weapon quizzically.

The archers already knew where he, Carina, and Metzly were, so there was no need for stealth. He spun around, drew in a deep breath, and shouted back into the night at the top of his lungs, "Archers to the south! Archers to the south!" He could only hope that whoever was coming after them was close enough to hear, or that they could hear on the back of a galloping horse.

A bolt hit the horse's haunch. Carina popped up and screamed at the archers. Aenguz pulled her back down.

"Stay down!"

Aenguz looked at the shafts. Disbelief collided with hard experience. "I know these shafts."

Metzly's wails were unbearable. Any movement squeezed out an even worse pleading wail. Carina was beside herself trying to help her.

Aenguz looked back along the path they had come for any sign.

"Where are you, Mandavu?"

He thought he saw a light - *montmorillionite* light. But he couldn't raise his head high enough to be sure.

Aenguz rolled back, and another shaft skimmed through the night above them. Carina glanced at Aenguz in worry, and then she turned her attention to Metzly to try to soothe her.

Then he felt something. They both felt something - thumping in the ground. Aenguz brought his weapon up and nodded for Carina to do the same.

Aenguz turned back, and trotting out of the night at the only speed his draft horse knew was Mandavu. Stroud was beside him and pulled ahead at the last distance, jumping down and rushing over to them. Mandavu hopped down and strode quickly toward them.

"Get down!" Aenguz waved them down.

"The archers are dead," Mandavu said. "Remember, no going off alone without me. We have an agreement," he said, half scolding, half wryly. He called light to his mace and waved it in the air.

Stroud kneeled beside Metzly and Carina to survey the source of her pain.

"Help us!" Aenguz barked.

The three of them pushed and lifted the near-dead horse, and Carina pulled Metzly free, falling back into the grass. Metzly's leg turned out at an impossible angle from her hip.

"Her hip is out of joint," Stroud said flatly. The Azari set one knee down beside her, grabbed her thigh, hugged it, pulled, and twisted. Metzly gave out her worst shriek yet and passed out. Stroud stood and said flatly, "Her leg is broken too."

Two more horses came out of the night - mounted Stair Guard.

Then, perpendicular from their position, Lokah rode up.

"Erebim."

The three Akkeidii exchanged looks.

The Stair Guard grew chill. The Battle of Corundum was still a poignant memory for them.

"I think they were as surprised to see Akkeidii and *montmorilli-onite* as I was to see them. Their shock did not last long," Lokah said.

"Erebim?" Carina asked.

"Your invaders," Aenguz answered. "How did they get here?" he asked Mandavu and Lokah. Neither had any clue. "How about the others?"

"Safe in the covert. Legerohn and Saissha are warded by the rest of the Stair Guard," Mandavu answered.

Aenguz nodded, approving.

"There must be more," Lokah continued. "Those two were sentries." He swung his head back the way he had come. He explained the small hill and the smell of smoke and spore. "They had nested there for some time. There was a trail that led out from their post."

Mandavu listened closely to Lokah and then waited on Aenguz's words.

Aenguz took final stock of their situation and their complement. He still heaved from exertion and stress. They could leave now, but it was clear they couldn't move Metzly. And the prospect of being pursued in the dark with Erebim shooting darts in their backs didn't make sense. There were also questions. The chief one: how many more were there? His calculations were quick. His own bitterness toward the Erebim was stoked sufficiently. "Let's go." Aenguz moved to climb onto Mandavu's horse.

"I would rather have my boots on the ground."

Aenguz considered quickly and agreed. His adrenaline was flowing. He was still assembling his thoughts.

They were trained as infantry. Riding horses into a fight after they had only just learned to ride was beyond foolhardy. They would be slow and therefore easy targets.

Carina stood, axe in hand, to go with them.

"Stay here with Metzly."

"These *Erebim* will learn the price for murdering Free People. You stay." Carina may have had a drive for retribution, but her ride had been more about catching up with Metzly than fighting. They had no plan except to satisfy their rage. Now, with what had happened to Metzly, she had tipped into the same place that Aenguz was.

"Carina." Aenguz stopped. It was her people who had been killed. He had to admit that there was a different protective energy in him that asked her to stay.

Carina had done what she could to make Metzly comfortable, but Stroud had already done the only thing that truly helped. Metzly lay unconscious, somewhat at peace. At least her wailing had stopped. Nothing else could be done for her.

He looked back to Mandavu. "Leave one Stair Guard here."

Mandavu replied, "Yes, my lord." He climbed down. He called to a soldier, "Stay on your horse." The other one dismounted and came over to him. He drew his sword and waited for the next move. His nerves left him jittery.

Lokah slid off his horse. Blood covered the lower part of his sword. He still breathed heavily, but Aenguz could see he was readying for a fight. Stroud stood with them. He looked as he always did, except for some hint of bloodshed that colored his slits.

Then their party, fueled by old vengeance and new, ran toward the hill.

They encountered four Erebim almost immediately. Their half-orange heads looked burnt in the moonlight. They wore some armor, but they were not fully armed like he had seen before. Black spines ran back over the middle of their heads. They waddled as they ran on their short, powerful legs. They saw the party coming at them. They cocked their atlatls and fitted in the long quills.

In two instants, Stroud somehow closed the distance to them. He was on the Erebim with elbows and knees. He slammed into one and then the next in such quick succession that the quills dropped uselessly to the ground. Aenguz only saw frozen moments of the Azari making contact, and then in a flash, he was on the next one.

The Erebim were dazed and disoriented when the others fell on them. Carina was out ahead of them by a handful of strides. Stroud's quickness did not stall her like it did the others. She fell on the nearest Erebim, bringing her axe down in brutal blow after blow. The Erebim crumpled in shock and terror.

The Akkeidii came up after her. The Erebim were still dazed from

Stroud's blows. Aenguz's weapon was awkward and off balance, but still deadly. He blasted the Erebim with a hard swing and cut into it. The black creature bowled over. He stepped over it, stared down, and drove the spike down into its head. Weapon and Dagba Stone were covered in blood.

Lokah and Mandavu cut down the other two quickly. Mandavu's mace crushed bone and armor. Lokah's sword hacked through neck and torso. The Erebim's head rolled lifeless, and then it fell.

They stared at Stroud in amazement after their killing strokes. The Stair Guard was ready, but shocked and relieved at how quickly the Erebim were dispatched. Courage rallied up in him as he began to understand the power of those he was fighting with and how fearsome and merciless they were.

They left the dead Erebim and circled to the near edge where the mound met the flat. The prairie beyond was silver and calm. Only the flicker of orange light beyond the boundary gave a hint of something in the night.

They slowed as they rounded the edge. The smell of fresh-cut timber was mixed with smoke from fires. The backside of the mound was concave. Most of the trees had already been cleared.

Their steps were deliberate. An acrid smell came with the smoke. They peeked over some hacked stumps and saw butchered horses piled about, some raw and some charred. Blood covered the trampled ground.

Something strange in this place, but familiar in his memory, caught Aenguz's eye beyond the Erebim further back against the slope. But his attention was drawn to the two score or more half-orange Erebim heads that scrambled in the firelight. Some turned and barked and charged at the vengeful party. Their atlatls were useless in the close quarters. They hauled up their dull axes and their wide swords.

Aenguz lunged out.

Carina was with him. Lokah and Mandavu flanked them. The Stair Guard ran at their back.

Stroud was gone from their side and instantly among the Erebim, delivering blows as if they were standing still.

The company fell in behind him and finished Stroud's work after he dazed and battered them with his knees and elbows. Some he killed instantly. Others tried to regain their feet, but the Akkeidii's weapons and Carina's axe finished them quickly.

Aenguz lost track of Carina as more Erebim regrouped to repel the attackers.

Mandavu and Lokah maintained a bulwark around Aenguz that kept him from being overrun.

The Erebim would spring and tackle their attackers, and in frightening moments, Aenguz found himself on the ground. But blades found the Erebim's back before its teeth could do their work. Mandavu was always close. Others wrestled with the fearsome Erebim. Stroud went from hitting them to pulling them off of the others.

Only the sound of Carina's mad cry told him that she was still alive and still fighting.

Stroud thwarted and battered as many as he could, but he could not meet all of them. The Stair Guard swung and parried, growing more and more confident with each stroke. Erebim were everywhere.

The melee was intense, but quick. Soon the Erebim's numbers were reduced by more than half. Their sudden losses stripped their courage. But there was something else depleting their number. Then Aenguz saw why. The familiar shape in the background, framed by some lichen-covered rock, was a fane like the one on the One Bridge and the World Stair in the City of the Sho-tah.

The remaining Erebim ran toward it, into the space between the three legs, and vanished.

Their fierce fight was quick and brutal and just as suddenly over. Aenguz stood in wary awe of a *verrandulum*.

24

QUEEN OF THE FREE PEOPLE

One by one, the others joined Aenguz before the *verrandulum*. Stroud was there first, and he stared at the ancient living artifact of the One Race as if to capture every detail of the writhing cloud material.

Carina looked to be on the edge of shock as she took in the slaughter of so many great horses. It took a moment before her eyes settled back on Aenguz, the others, and the *verrandulum*. Its roiling cloud-like construction and ephemeral glow camouflaged it against the stripped hillside. Three delicate legs held the scalloped roof.

Mandavu helped the Stair Guard up off the ground. Blood streamed out of his nose, and his mouth was filled with blood. Except for some other slashes, he was in one piece.

"Not so pretty in the face," Mandavu joked as he helped him up.

"Bay-Den," he replied through his clogged nose.

"What?"

"Br-Br-N-Dan. My name is Braydehn," he enunciated through

blood, as if to check the bones in his face and also confirm that he was alive.

"You did well, Braydehn. We will fix your nose later."

Lokah surveyed the dead Erebim and made sure there weren't any feigning death.

Then they all joined Aenguz and Stroud at the silver-white fane.

"What is it? Did they vanish in there?" Braydehn asked as he wiped blood from his nose and mouth.

"It is a *verrandulum*," Aenguz answered grimly.

The question still hung in the air.

"These were old gateways before the Last Battle. But they all but vanished in the wake of that war," Aenguz said distractedly. "Morgrom warned me about them. He said, '*Do not hazard the* verrandulum. *You cannot hope to navigate them.*'"

"How do you know what this is?" Carina asked.

"There is one in the Mashu at the apex of the One Bridge, but it only appears during a full moon." Aenguz searched out the waxing moon, but it was days away from being full. "It should not even be visible now."

"Somehow, we crossed it," Lokah said, recalling their frantic race against the dawn over the One Bridge as captives of the Erebim.

"Carina, did you know this was here?"

She shook her head. "The Erebim disappeared into it?"

"Yes," Stroud answered.

"Where did they go?" she asked.

No one had an answer.

"Stroud, do the Azari see this?"

"Yes. The One King and the Queen of the Free People are being told all that has happened here. The Queen's retinue is on its way. The

One King has commanded the Monomander to send a contingent of soldiers."

"The Monomander?" Aenguz asked.

"He commands the One Army."

"What do we do?" Lokah asked Aenguz.

"We ward this portal until sunrise and hope no more Erebim come through. And we hope, too, that the sun dispels it in the morning."

Mandavu sent Braydehn back to his companion to tell him what had transpired and to send him back to the covert. They would need reinforcements, but Saissha, Legerohn, and Chimere were to remain at the covert. It was still too dangerous by the hollow. Braydehn was to stay with Metzly.

They circled the fane and spent the rest of the night waiting for any Erebim to come through. Aenguz searched the ground to find any evidence of a hardened black pit beneath the carnage. There didn't seem to be any sign of the ritual he had seen on the Cairngorm or in the City of the Sho-tah.

The presence of this gateway changed their thoughts about warding the Spine against invaders, and also the defense of the Cleve. They asked questions in the night but didn't pursue random threads. They opted instead to stay frosty in case more Erebim appeared.

When the first light of dawn came, the *verrandulum* faded and vanished. They let out a collective sigh, as if they had been holding their breaths for hours.

Aenguz, Lokah, Mandavu, and Stroud inspected the camp as dawn broke. Carina scanned with them for a bit and then stated that she was going back to check on Metzly.

Stroud stood in a clear patch near the center and rotated slowly, surveying everything within the fell glade for all of the Azari.

It seemed to be a hunting or satellite camp. The great horses were hunted freely, and discarded horse parts littered the area. Several lean-tos made from smaller trees and brush were scattered around - more than was needed for the Erebim they'd encountered. There were many tracks leading out of the hollow into the prairie. They could not be sure that these Erebim accounted for all that were here or that had disappeared.

A new form of war.

Aenguz heard Morgrom's words from the message. If the *verrandulum* was not governed by the full moon and it appeared by night each night, then who could say what his forces might achieve?

Aenguz saw all that he cared to see. He left the hollow to find Carina. They should move Metzly nearer to the hill.

Braydehn stood by Metzly and the fallen horse. Carina was on her knees at the dead horse's hooves. She worked at a hoof with a tool and removed something from it. Then she moved onto the next. She pocketed whatever it was in a pouch at her waist. As Aenguz approached, she unbuckled the strap and let the saddle fall off.

Aenguz walked around to help her with the saddle. She bristled initially and then accepted the help. They brought it over to Metzly so that she would have something to rest her head on.

Aenguz spied Carina's mount in the distance, too afraid to come any further. A long shaft stuck in the saddle and drooped to the side.

Carina comforted Metzly and then went to get her horse. She walked out slowly and soothed the frightened beast. Then she climbed up and rode the mare back to them.

Mandavu, Lokah, and Stroud came over to Metzly. The Akkeidii complimented her toughness for enduring a dislocated hip and broken leg. She was not out of the woods yet - her eyes were more delirious than focused - but with careful attention and some further healing, she would survive.

By midday, the Stair Guard from the covert returned with six other soldiers. They brought food and water, and the company ate and drank near Metzly. She was awake and able to take water. Carina ministered to her throughout the day.

Braydehn showed the other Stair Guard the hollow and told them all about the skirmish the night before. They were ashen when they finally filed back out. Their traveling embassy had come into a war.

Mandavu sent them on a wide circle around the mound. They did not want to be surprised by any other Erebim that might be about. But at sundown, everyone would be at the *verrandulum*.

They lumbered through the camp as the sun touched the horizon. They positioned themselves around the *verrandulum* and readied themselves for a fight. Everyone's nerves were on edge. Aenguz and Mandavu tried to steady them and bolster their courage. Dusk fell, and the gruesome encampment grew dark.

The night crawled by slowly with the company hanging on their every nerve. Every stray noise from the night startled them. The moon watched quietly with them.

But the heightened night passed without incident. When light came to the sky, the spindled legs of the *verrandulum* faded with the light. Relief seeped out of everyone. Waiting was even more draining than an attack.

They returned to their open-air camp beneath the trees by Metzly. The fresh Stair Guard had too much adrenaline to rest. They kept a watch around the camp while the others ate, drank, and rested.

Metzly drifted in and out of sleep. Carina gave her water when she woke.

Aenguz, Mandavu, and Lokah half-napped.

Aenguz watched in the distance as puffed mountains of cloud moved across the sky. The thick air was humid. Char still tinged the prairie air. Cicadas peeled throughout the trees.

Lokah sat beside Aenguz. He sensed Aenguz's introspective mood. "What are you thinking?"

Aenguz pulled back from his pensive hole. "The *verrandulum* have changed, and I am not certain why or how. Only the full moon would even bring them to light. Now it seems they come each night. It may have started around the time I touched the Dagba Stone." He turned the stone over on the ground in front of him.

"You wonder what it means for the Mashu and the One Bridge?" Lokah asked of the air. He continued to stare with Aenguz out at the clouds.

"In the Divine Oculum, I saw distant flashes like stars flashing and dying out. I knew the light. It was *montmorillionite*."

Lokah turned to him. "You think the Mashu is under attack," he stated.

"Mono Lord Lana said they could not determine the time for the images that we saw. But the Erebim have used the road that led to the One Bridge. If the One Bridge was solid, I would think they would take that path onto the Lower Mashu and into that *verrandulum*." He looked at the inert stone and wondered how far the power of the Keystone of Creation reached. What other woes had he unleashed by defying the Counsel Lords' warnings? The rules that governed the earth had changed - and changed recently.

The earth rumbled. The ground shuddered. The pair stood and brought their weapons up. Suddenly, the thundering quake surrounded them.

All of a sudden, scores of riders surged from around the back side of the mound at a full gallop. Scores of other riderless horses came too. Some bore loads, others were bare and free. The herd charged and arced around the opening to the hollow and the company. Riders, dressed like Carina and Metzly, charged up and leveled short spears at the men. The Stair Guard bristled. They looked to one another and the Akkeidii for some direction. Riders near the opening gazed into the carnage in the Erebim camp. Shock erupted from them. Their horses reeled.

Carina walked out to the riders with her arms open. Metzly turned her head and may have smiled.

One rider, with a tall plume on her round helmet, rode through a cordon of Free People toward Carina. She rode a great gray horse that looked like the color of the storm clouds that brushed the horizon. She dismounted easily. The nearest riders around her dismounted with her. They wore fine wool vests. One took the invisible tether from the woman.

She pulled off her helmet and revealed coiffed blonde hair. An elaborate network of braids ringed her head like a cap. Her eyes were determined and severe. She was middle-aged and in the full flower of beauty and womanhood. Her face gleamed with sweat. Her faint red cheeks glowed. Thin straps of leather necklaces hung close to her neck, bearing different objects.

She strode straight to Carina, looking as if she were some incensed horse lord. At the last moment, she flung her arms around Carina and hugged her with all her might. She pulled back, looked her over again, and pulled her in once more.

"Oh, Carina, daughter." The woman allowed herself a smile finally, and her whole face warmed.

"My Queen," Carina uttered with gratitude and relief. She looked at the members of the embassy. "This is the Queen of the Free People, Warder of the Great Horses of the Lands, Sorolokova."

Words conspired to come from the Queen, but her mounting relief held them in. All she could say was, "And Metzly?"

Carina led the Queen over to Metzly. Sorolokova kneeled and gazed down into her face. "How are you, daughter?"

"My Queen, seeing you fills my heart." Metzly's face twinged slightly.

The Queen reassured her and called out for medicines. Other Free People quickly pulled supplies to set Metzly's leg and hip from the packs on their horses. They rushed over and began to tend to Metzly. A few riders hugged Carina as the Queen stood.

Aenguz and the Akkeidii were pushed back up the slope.

Carina addressed Sorolokova. "My Queen, these are the travelers that we are taking to Earthmight. They saved both of us. They fought and killed many invaders." She inclined her head toward the Erebim camp. Stair Guard filed out and joined the Akkeidii.

Sorolokova looked over the men. Behind her, a man in a plain tunic rode up and dismounted.

Stroud stepped forward, acknowledged the Queen with a tight bow, and then faced the Azari.

"Stroud," the Azari said. His hair was more white than black. Crow's feet marked the corners of his eyes, and lines rounded the corners of his ears.

"Telakot," Stroud answered. They said nothing else to each other.

Sorolokova spoke in a deep, rich voice built for song. "I have heard what has happened here." She inclined her head toward Telakot. "I thank you for aiding these Free People. You have made a friend of the Free People. I will see with my own eyes what terrors you faced." Then to the women nearest her, "Once Metzly is secured, bear her to the covert."

"Yes, our Queen," they replied and moved to make preparations to bear her.

"This is Aenguz. He is the Lord of the Akkeidii. This is Mandavu, and this is Lokah Akkeidii. These other soldiers are Stair Guard. This one warded Metzly, and this one fought the invaders with us two nights ago."

Sorolokova greeted and thanked them all again and said, "Mane and hoof."

"Mane and hoof," was echoed by all the riders, including Carina. Even Metzly answered with her frail voice.

The Queen motioned for Carina to show her the hollow. Free People surrounded them. Aenguz walked to the edge and watched as Carina explained everything to the Queen.

Telakot dismounted and stood and watched, tracking the Queen. Stroud had surveyed the space thoroughly. Telakot had seen it as if he too had been there.

Carina told the story of their ride there. She only spoke briefly about the horrors of the covert. The Queen saw how difficult it was and waved her onto the parts of the story she did not know, and the parts of the battle that Stroud could not relay, engaged as he had been in the fight.

The Queen steeled herself against the carnage and the felled Erebim. The Free People walking with them looked around as if they stood on another world.

Carina stopped before the spot where the *verrandulum* had appeared. Aenguz saw her describe with her hands the shape and height of the ethereal artifice.

The Queen touched Carina's shoulder. Carina continued on as they walked back out of the killing ground.

As they got closer, Aenguz could hear the Queen again. "You brave girl. You have honored the name of the Free People. You have honored me." Then Sorolokova spoke and commanded silence. "When Metzly is ready to be borne, we will make for the covert. Burn the bodies in the spot where they came from." To a woman near her, she said, "Thirty will remain to ward this space tonight."

The woman nodded and answered, "Yes, my Queen."

Carina whispered something to Sorolokova. The Queen looked at Aenguz and nodded to Carina. Then Sorolokova was lost in the coterie of her immediate retinue.

25

CONCLAVE

The surge and pulse of the great horses and the Free People filled the prairie around the embassy. Aenguz watched Sorolokova as she called out orders and sent riders to and fro. She answered questions with certainty, and her firm tone cut through the din. Her voice imbued the riders with her energy. They moved into action quickly with each command. A contingent of riders were sent off in haste toward the covert. Other riders moved the assembly of pack horses and riderless horses into a semi-organized herd away from the mouth of the mound.

Aenguz, Lokah, Mandavu, Braydehn, and the other Stair Guard drew together. Those who had been around Metzly were shooed away. Aenguz wanted to remind the Queen that they were still there. He didn't want to trigger the incensed riders, though, or give them cause to mistake them for invaders in their anger and haste.

Telakot appeared to be the only man among the Free People. He had no doubt told the Queen about all of them. He had relayed everything he knew and saw about the embassy through Stroud to the Queen. Telakot rode beside her, very nearly attached, and scanned everything

Sorolokova saw like a second set of eyes. The One King saw everything - or heard from his Azari, rather - and undoubtedly knew about what had happened in the covert.

Amongst all the Free People, Aenguz had lost Carina. He climbed the short rise to look into the Erebim camp to find her. A close chaos filled the hollow. Riders lashed lines to dead Erebim and dragged them by horse to a spot. Women sorted through Erebim weapons, looking for some to use and some for trophies. Aenguz searched the riders and found Carina. She stood and indicated where the *verrandulum* would appear.

The Queen dismounted and stepped through the dead. She helped draw corpses to the grisly pile. She was rough with the Erebim, as if she were merely clearing timber. When other women came to take the duty from her, she waved them off. The Queen referred to everyone as "daughter" or "sister."

Initially, Aenguz had understood the Queen's address to Carina and Metzly to mean that they were her children, but now he saw that it was a term used among all the Free People. They were all one enormous family, like the great horses, and Sorolokova was mother to them all.

Carina worked alongside her sisters, gathering the horse shanks and parts and piling them into a separate stack. The lean-tos were taken down and used for fires, both for the horse carcasses and the Erebim bodies.

Aenguz left them to their grizzly work - the hard work of war. They needed a way to expend their thwarted rage and fresh grief. And they needed a way to comprehend what had happened in their lands so far from the Spine.

A litter was fashioned for Metzly. Poles were slung between two horses with loose leather straps in between. Metzly was wrapped in yellow and rust-colored patterned blankets and lifted gently into it. Metzly groaned and clenched her teeth, but she nodded gratefully at the careful sisters. Whatever medicines they had given her lessened her pain. The delirium had left her semi-conscious for the past two days. Now, at least she could finally rest and perhaps sleep.

Horses were marshaled for the embassy. Saddles were placed on new mounts drawn from the herd - all except for the horse that Carina and Aenguz rode. That mount had been fitted again with the same saddle he and Carina had used. The riders and the men of the company climbed onto their horses. Carina appeared at last. She hopped onto the horse's back, landing on her stomach and then kicking her leg over.

Being around her own people gave her a different kind of energy. She seemed taller, surer of herself, confident. She wheeled the horse around and brought it up beside Aenguz. She reached her hand down to pull him up. She took his proffered left hand. The purple-and-gray warped flesh didn't faze her. His heart vibrated when he touched her. He hauled himself up and settled in behind her. He was as grateful as he had been the day they left Lihkit. With that, the caravan returning to the covert with Metzly was ready to depart. The sun was dropping to the horizon when they set off.

As their column settled into a rhythm, Aenguz took one last look back and saw two columns of smoke rising up from behind the trees.

The slow sunset at their backs lit their way. A dozen riders rode at the fore, with Metzly's litter in their midst. Stroud rode with them. Carina and Aenguz rode behind the last of those riders. Mandavu rode behind them on a large black draft horse. Long tufts of black hair covered its hooves. It pranced more than walked. Lokah rode on a blond mustang. It was a young horse with boundless energy. He struggled to keep a flank with Aenguz and Carina.

The Stair Guard rode at the rear in pairs behind them. Braydehn rode at the head. He had become a kind of hero for them. They chatted constantly about the wonder of what they all had just experienced. The

Free People were intoxicating to them. As much as they enjoyed riding the horses, the beauty and mystery of the Free People captivated them. They were astonished at the strange new world they found themselves in.

The dimming eastern sky was dominated by the waxing moon. The brightest stars joined the moon in the faded orange sky. It would be full in a few days. Aenguz wondered if a full moon would have any further impact on the *verrandulum* - some other capability of the *verrandulum* he did not know. And would the Erebim return? Or any other of Morgrom's allies? Were there Urnings or Ruinwasters in the Lower Lands? Evidently, Morgrom knew how to navigate the portals.

At dusk, the Queen's train raced past the caravan with an earthborne thunder. The riders waved and trilled in high voices to one another as they passed. Telakot rode behind the Queen like a tangible spirit in his bone-white tunic.

Night settled on the rolling plain. After a time, a rider met the caravan. She spoke to the riders at the head, and then she rode back and spoke to Carina in their enigmatic tongue. Then she returned to the head of the column.

Aenguz asked what she had said.

"The rest of your people are camped outside the covert. You are not allowed there. I am to take you there and then return to the covert."

Something in her voice was unsettled.

"What is wrong? You seem worried."

"The Queen is fair-minded, and these are extraordinary times."

The caravan split. The riders led Metzly on, and Carina rode up and led the company to the left.

In the distance, Aenguz could make out the silhouette of the mound. It rested like an island in a sea of undulating earth. Hundreds of horses milled and grazed in the wide area around the covert. Their coats shimmered in the pale moonlight. More arrived out of the night. Small groups and families of horses materialized and joined the herd. So many horses… They made the Queen's retinue seem paltry. Carina skirted the edge of the herd to a depression north and west of the covert. She led them over a small rise. There, beside a small creek, were the corallel tents.

The Stair Guard saw them first and alerted the others. Saissha, Legerohn, and Chimere stood out from the firelight. The company rode down the final distance and dismounted. Stump fires punctuated the space around the tents. As they dismounted, Carina called the Stair Guard who remained to unsaddle the horses. They came up cheerfully to help. Once free of their riders and saddles, the horses turned and trotted off to join the others in the wide space around the covert.

Saissha flung her arms around Mandavu. Her head barely reached his chest. Then she wiped away some tears and hugged Lokah. She met each of the Stair Guard as they set their horses free. She inspected Braydehn's bruised face and welcomed him back. Their comrades presented him like a returning hero. They clapped shoulders and hugged one another.

Aenguz lingered with Carina. Finally, he climbed off the back of the horse. The horse shifted a bit, and he tipped into her as he dismounted. She held her hand to catch him, though he didn't need it. Her hazel eyes glinted like crystal. "Thank you. You saved my life and Metzly's. We would have both probably died if it weren't for you." She looked at the others in the camp and then back at Aenguz. Then she turned away with a drawn look to join her sisters in the covert.

Legerohn clapped shoulders and greeted the soldiers and the Akkeidii. Chimere mirrored his Tahnka. Legerohn found Aenguz.

"You run toward danger like others run away from it," Legerohn said with a laugh as he greeted Aenguz.

Aenguz hugged his friend and took Chimere's hand. "It was

Erebim," he said squarely into Legerohn's eyes. The Prince nodded as he pondered.

The Stair Guard gathered together and began to share their stories with one another. Braydehn had deep black lines under his eyes. His nose was bent, and his face was still swollen. Each member of the company greeted him, lauded him.

The Akkeidii and Moresi gathered with Saissha around the stump fires. A stew of roast vegetables and wild turkey awaited them. Stroud looked on all of them as if he were counting them, then he turned and walked to the edge of their camp to the rise overlooking the great horse herd and the covert.

In between bites, they told one another each of their tales. Aenguz told them how he got caught up with Carina, and how they had found Metzly trapped under the horse. Then, Mandavu and Lokah took over the story and told Legerohn and Saissha what had happened. Mandavu picked up with his slow chase and how he sent Lokah on ahead to catch up with Aenguz and Carina. Lokah explained how he had heard Aenguz's warning and turned to find the Erebim that had ambushed Aenguz, Carina, and Metzly.

They talked about the battle. The tone dropped when they told them about the *verrandulum*. Aenguz withheld his speculation about the portal, as he didn't have any confirmation for his thoughts.

Saissha explained how they handled the dead in the covert. They weren't sure how to deal with the bodies, but they knew they needed to give them some dignity. They found coverings and arranged them in the open area. It was hard, grim work. Then they left the covert. It was a sacred space, and Saissha reasoned that any further disruption, however well intended, might be considered profane.

"Eventually," Saissha continued, "a rider returned and assured us that you were alright. But when they relayed what happened, we were very worried. Then there was nothing until the Queen of the Free People arrived. She barely acknowledged us. They all went into the covert. There were such horrible cries. When they came out, we were relocated to the camp here. I am glad the Prince was here. His diplomacy was welcome in that moment." They each traded stories and filled in the myriad details of their experiences.

Aenguz excused himself and walked to the ridge between their camp and the distant covert. Stroud stood on the rise like a statue and stared at the island mound.

The strong scent of so many horses, grass, and thick musk made it hard to pull in a clear breath. But the smell and the ebb and flow of so many horses brought Aenguz back to his childhood. The great horses were vastly larger in number and size than the roe deer, but his memories still found a connection to them. In his own way, he understood the fealty and love the Free People had for these horses.

Aenguz came up behind Stroud, but the Azari held out his hand behind him and halted Aenguz.

"Aenguz?" Stroud stated more than asked.

"Yes."

"Stay back. None may watch but the Azari. The Queen speaks. The One King listens through Hannoch and Sarokin."

Aenguz wondered about Stroud and his allegiances. He had not had an opportunity to ask how Stroud was handling being reunited with his own people again. He had thought himself to be the last, and now he was connected in a way Aenguz could scarcely understand. How did it feel for Stroud? How did it feel for the Azari? He had been invaluable in their fight against the Erebim. And with this small act here, keeping Aenguz out of his periphery but not shooing him away, Aenguz sensed that there was some conflict in him, something that he was still processing. There were more questions, but right now, all he wondered about was what was happening in the covert, what was happening with Carina.

"They work to clean and sanctify the covert. The Queen has gathered the Free People to hear Metzly and Carina's story. Carina has told of how they came upon the covert and how they found it. Now the Queen is determining what to do about Carina and Metzly's transgression."

"Their transgression?"

"They brought strangers into the covert. Strangers and men."

"They knew something was wrong. They did not know if the Erebim were still there. We could not let them leave to go alone."

"These are the laws of the Free People." He looked forward as if he could see directly through the earth into the inner sanctum of the covert. He would pause for long moments, and Aenguz chomped his teeth while he waited. Then Stroud would continue with his paraphrasing. "The crimes of the Erebim have a greater weight than the trespass. Metzly and Carina's heroism counts for much." Stroud grew silent again. The herd mingled and snorted. "Metzly will remain in the covert to heal. Carina..." Stroud paused. Aenguz ached for the next words. "...will ride with the Queen. She has fought against the Erebim. She saw to Metzly. They will not be punished. The Free People are happy with the Queen's decision on the matter."

Stroud was silent again. He filtered and curated according to his own will. Then without preamble, he said, "The Queen now speaks with the One King."

"'What of your strategy now, Thelen? Invaders appear out of the air, and the Free People patrol the length of the Spine to no effect.'

"'Sorolokova, Hannoch and Sarokin have told me all that the Azari have seen.'" Stroud altered the timber in his voice as he relayed the One King's words.

"'I did not agree on having an Azari ride with us.'

"'I must know that you are safe. I must see what you see.'

"'I have the Free People to protect me. When will your army come to aid us down here? We who bear the brunt of this war.'

"'I have ordered the Monomander to send a contingent right away. They are south of Llangollen. They will arrive as soon as they can.'

"'We cannot watch the entire Spine and all of our coverts.'

"'We are building up the One Army as fast as we can. But I will still need your help. Now that it is clear that invaders can appear anywhere through these *verrandulum*, we must search for them throughout the Lower Lands.'

"'More? You ask more of us? What else might we bear for you? The Free People bear everything. The Heart of the World bears the cost.'

"'The Cleve is warded.'

"'Has there been a whiff of trouble from the Cleve?'

"'It is or was the only path to the hells of the Upper Lands.'

"'What about the Azari? Send them to search. We cannot do it all.'

"'I have discussed it with them. More will be sent.'"

Stroud stopped as if he were considering the One King's words.

"'There is another matter,'" he continued in the Queen's tone. "'I understand that you are keeping horses at your training grounds.'

"'We are preparing them for war. We are fitting them with protective armor. We do not have time to gather new horses every day or make new armor for different horses.'

"'Do you understand that it is play to them? The Heart of the World does not know what you intend for them.'

"'They have as much a stake in this war as we do. We cannot defend ourselves without them.'

"'We watch the Spine. Now we are to scour the land. We convey this embassy to you. We are to bear people and wagons back to the Last Stronghold. Many will not go; they wait for the harvest. You keep freedom from the great horses for the benefit of the One Army. And the great horses are being hunted out here. Where is the One Army? What have your strategies yielded but mistake after mistake?'

"'We are doing everything to marshal the One Army.'

"'Do it faster.'

"'Perhaps the embassy bears aid for us. How soon can they depart?'

"'They will depart tomorrow.'"

Stroud went silent. Then he said simply, "Telakot is dismissed."

As Aenguz walked back to camp, he tried to process what he had heard about the state of the One Army. Even though they had made it over the Spine and several days toward Earthmight, the help they sought seemed even farther away.

26

APPROACH TO EARTHMIGHT

Aenguz held Stroud's secret of the conversation he had overheard through him and the fact that the embassy would be departing the next day. He wanted to talk with Mandavu and Lokah about what he had heard and seen, but he didn't know how to relate what he knew without giving up what Stroud had "shown" him. He would find another time.

At dawn, eight riders appeared in the camp with a coterie of great horses. Lokah poked his head into the tent to tell Aenguz and Mandavu. Aenguz wondered if Carina was with them.

The Stair Guard were roused, and they began the work of breaking camp and getting some small food to everyone. Pride motivated them before the Free People, and they ushered the leaders of the embassy aside while they worked. Even Chimere's help was waved off by them.

Saissha informed the embassy that they were leaving. Stroud had informed her once the riders arrived. It set the preparations in motion. Everyone was a little surprised, except for Aenguz.

Roula announced herself as the rider charged with taking the embassy to the Last Stronghold. She was a member of the Queen's own guard. She had been given strict orders to deliver the embassy as quickly as possible to Earthmight. She was terse, but respectful. She explained that there would be long days of riding ahead.

Aenguz scanned the eight riders, but Carina was not among them. He wanted to break the prohibition against looking into the covert and go back to the rise to see if he could catch one last glimpse of her. The possibility that he might not see her again left him suddenly crestfallen. He deferred to the others to take their mounts first, on the chance that an opportunity still might come.

They tried among the horses to find a mount for Chimere, but as the sun rose, Roula sent one of her riders back to the covert for one of the double saddles.

Legerohn reassured Chimere. The young Moresi's shame was plain on him like his persistent limp.

None of the riders took Aenguz through the small herd to find a horse. He wondered and worried if he too would have to ride with another woman.

One by one, the members of the embassy mounted.

On the rise, with the sun at her back, was Carina. A tall brown horse with white socks for feet stood beside her. Aenguz hurried up to her. Carina wore a finely spun wool vest, same as the riders that had surrounded the Queen. As he came up, he saw that the left eye on the horse was sealed shut. The horse only had a saddle for one rider. She wasn't coming with them.

Carina's hazel eyes were dim, as if joy had been blanched from them. "I ride with the Queen now."

It meant she wouldn't be coming with them to Earthmight. He wouldn't be riding with her again.

She turned her attention to the horse. "This is Draymondon. He was the first horse I learned to ride on when I came to live with the Free People. He was my first horse." Her voice quaked slightly. "We have hard riding ahead, and he is old. He will not be able to keep up." Sad sparks glinted from her eyes as her tears welled.

Aenguz ached for her.

"His eye got injured and infected. I thought he might die, but he is a sturdy horse. If he accepts you, you can ride him to Earthmight. If not, will you see him there? They will care for him there."

"Of course."

She drew the old gentle horse to him. She took Aenguz's hand in hers and placed it on Draymondon's heart. She pressed her head into the horse's shoulder and waited. Some ineffable power exuded through her. Draymondon turned his one good eye toward the pair and nosed them both brusquely.

Carina exhaled. Tears coursed down her face. "He will bear you."

Relief washed through both of them.

Aenguz didn't want to disappoint her. He wanted to hug her. The urge was stronger than he had anticipated.

She handed the invisible lines to Aenguz and held his hands in hers. They stood close. Draymondon shifted and fixed on them with his big black eye.

"Ride him from time to time while you are at Earthmight. I want his last days to be joyful. He will bear you well. Look after him for me while you are able." She dropped the empty lines as if the last of her strength fled. She leaned into Aenguz and gave a restrained hug. Aenguz held the line and wrapped his thick arms around her while she wept.

A call from the riders broke the spell of their embrace. Carina pushed back and motioned Aenguz on.

He climbed on Draymondon's back and felt the curve and girth of

Carina's horse. It was the first time he had been on a horse alone. The exhilaration was acute, but Carina's absence before him on the saddle dampened the feeling.

He rode down the hill. As he settled into the line, he looked back at Carina. She took one last look at them, turned, and went back down the hill toward the covert and her new responsibilities.

With that, Roula called the line into motion.

Gone was the slow march they had taken from Lihkit. Now the rhythm was one of canters and gallops, depending on the terrain. Walking was infrequent. It was done primarily for the horses' benefit. The riders were expected to maintain the pace set by Roula, despite their pain.

Draymondon galloped along with a powerful dignity and a small degree of playfulness. He trailed at the rear, happy to follow the other horses ahead of him. Lokah and Mandavu rode with Aenguz at the rear. The sleds trailed behind the line. No itinerant horses followed along with them, only the embassy from Corundum and the eight riders assigned to take them.

Thankfully, they had the earlier days of riding from Lihkit; otherwise, the pain from riding would have been insufferable. Breaks were never long enough.

They rode from dawn to dusk. As soon as the tents were stowed and the horses saddled, they were off again. Even the morn meals were hurried. There was no time for *salaage* practice in the morning, though Lokah always seemed to find time before dawn to practice the five forms with his sword.

The Stair Guard were pressed to make camp and dinner before the sun set. Roula's riders took care of the horses with a regimented efficiency. They were unsaddled quickly, watered and fed, and then drawn together so that they too might rest. The Stair Guard tried to work with them, but only in small ways would the riders allow the soldiers to help them. There was a chilly distance between them.

The eight Free People bedded apart from the embassy, near to the horses. They tented together in three small tents that were little more than tarps that barely reached off the ground. They ate their own food, kept their own company.

Days wore on. They rode in the heat. They rode in the rain. They rode in the wind.

Early on, Roula questioned the need to make a full camp each day. It took time away from their progress, she reasoned. Why could they not sleep more like they did? After a few days of questioning, a compromise was struck. They would pitch only one corallel tent for Saissha. She was a Counsel Lord and would be afforded this one small grace. She was bearing an urgent request to the One King. The Stair Guard would look after the Counsel Lord's needs in this way. She was a dignitary and would be afforded the amenities of such, as meager as they were. In the end, it was Legerohn who brokered the solution between Roula, the Stair Guard, and Saissha. The rest of the company would sleep under low lean-tos. Aenguz was fine with the arrangement, and Saissha was willing to sleep like the rest, but it was a point of pride for the Stair Guard that she have a pitched tent on the rolling plain.

They passed by ranches and farmsteads, clusters of stone buildings nestled amid fields. The roofs were just visible in the distance, rising over the lush, green crops. People paused from their chores to wave at the riders, and the Free People waved back as they galloped onward.

The open spaces between the ranches steadily decreased. The land changed from open grasslands and prairies with small forests here and there to wavy manicured fields, vast vineyards, and sprawling orchards. There seemed to be no evidence of blight, except the stumps in the orchards and the varying heights at the tops of the fields, as if some plants had been dormant and then suddenly brought to life. They passed vales and saw more people. They waved at them, and some waved them toward their vale. However, the company avoided them, opting for a more solitary course through back farm roads that weaved among the fields and vineyards. They camped on those roads almost as if they were trespassers.

The days were hot, but the evenings were growing cooler. Chilled fogs began to greet the dawn. One day, early in the morning, the familiar hoof falls changed to clops, and the column slowed to a walk.

As Draymondon reached the cobblestone, Aenguz saw the white pillar that marked the edge of the road. Unfamiliar letters and images were carved in relief on it. One of the riders uttered, "We are within the precincts of the One King's Keep."

On the distant horizon, there was a mote of white crumple that looked like a sheer pile of tumbled stones stacked to a tip. Aenguz dismissed it as an oddity of the landscape and continued to search for any sign of Earthmight.

Cattle ranged freely to the right and left. Across the range to the left, Aenguz could make out a dotted line of horse-drawn wagons on a road running roughly parallel to the company.

They saw more people now. Curious eyes studied them as they passed. Smiles for the Free People were replaced with dour expressions when they saw the embassy.

The crumple was larger now, and it sat on a two-faced block. The right side was a brilliant white. The sun beamed on it. The left side was in a graduated shade as if the face were curved. There was a gothic cut in the middle. Aenguz assumed that it was Earthmight, but it did not conform to any standard he might have held. It was not like any of the fortresses in the Hearth Valleys of the Mashu.

Earthmight was slow to grow. Its size and distance created the illusion. More people were on the road walking and riding. They gawked at the embassy openly. The road to the left was nearer now, and it was clotted with traffic moving in both directions.

The crumple took on form. The space beyond it was as empty as if it sat at the end of the world. Shadows cut the detail in the keep like cuneiform on white stone. Windows, balconies, and domes ringed it in a wide conical rise. It leaned out from them on top of a shoulder of rock that was butted up against the will of the ocean beyond. The white block beneath the spire rose and rose until it blocked off the lower tiers. On the far right, a natural crag ran up to the lowest tiers and butted against the vast wall. The gray was merely shaded. It ran in a gentle curve to the open vastness, and at the center was the massive gothic portal.

To the embassy's right was a field of tents and encampments. Some looked well established. Others were being set up. The company was led to an open space just off the road at the rear of the ring of encampments that filled the space all the way up to the wall.

The fortress of Earthmight towered over the growing tent city. The bustle stalled in the cluster of tents around them and then halted. Women, young and old, stared at the embassy from Corundum. Mothers and daughters, small children, and grandmothers gathered at the edges of their small villages to look at the riders and the embassy. There were young boys and elderly men, but none that might be considered of fighting age.

Attendants awaited the company and marked the space where the embassy was to make camp. They too were mostly women. They wore narrow beige aprons over their clothes. On the front was an articulated shape, a rendition of Earthmight. On the backs of the aprons were scores of ashen-gray handprints. Palm prints in the center and fingers splayed out to the sides ran down from neck to foot. Beyond the scores of curious eyes, Aenguz could see other attendants moving in and out amid the implied roads between groups of tents.

Effusive welcomes poured out of the attendants. "We are keep stewards of Earthmight. Welcome. Here is your space. Be welcome here at the One King's Keep."

The Stair Guard let down the two sleds and positioned them at the center of the area as the embassy dismounted.

Saissha and Legerohn greeted the keep stewards in return. Saissha identified them all as the embassy from Corundum, and the stewards said they knew who they were. The attendants talked about water and food and assured them that any questions they had about their needs would be answered by any steward. The embassy was welcome here, and the Head Steward would arrive presently. Saissha and Legerohn thanked them with facile dignity.

The eight riders dismounted and unsaddled the company's horses, stacking the saddles by the sleds. After unsaddling Draymondon, a rider moved to take the invisible lines for him. Aenguz would not let go. "He goes to the stables here. I will see to it."

Roula called off the rider, and then she spoke to Saissha. "You are delivered safely to Earthmight. May your coming bring a boon to the Lower Lands." Saissha thanked her on behalf of the embassy.

The riders led the horses back the way they had come. Draymondon pulled his head to go with them, but Aenguz laid a hand on his neck and assured him as he would a roe deer. "You have a place here in the stables. Be calm. I will see you there." He would honor Carina's last request of him.

27

ACROSS THE CHASM

Earthmight towered over the embassy. The sheer wall and the thick spire seemed to scowl down at them. Balconies and windows filled with people curious to get a glimpse of the embassy. So many eyes discomfited Aenguz. It left him self-conscious, and he drew in closer around the sleds.

The keep stewards held back and gave them their space. They stared in wide-eyed wonder from up close.

After so many days with the horses, to suddenly be without them left them disconcerted. Aenguz was grateful that Draymondon gave him an anchor against the loss.

Saissha ordered the Stair Guard, "Make our camp. Ask the stewards about water and food."

The Stair Guard appeared self-conscious at first, moving slowly into tasks they had done dozens of times and in some cases in the most extreme conditions. This situation seemed even more extreme and exposed.

A tall man with a cap of bright white hair walked off the road and approached the embassy. He wore a narrow apron with a silver silhouette of Earthmight on the chest. An Azari was with him.

"The Chief Steward is here," Stroud said with his back to the white-haired man. He turned first and greeted the Azari. The Azari nodded and said, "Stroud," with a slight air of reverence.

"Welcome, welcome to Earthmight, the One King's Keep!" the man bellowed and flung his arms out wide. "My apologies for my delay. There are many matters to attend to supporting the One Army, and now that the One King has drawn the people of the vales to Earthmight, there is a great deal to do, and a great many to welcome." Then his tone dropped a bit, and clear hints of exhaustion complicated his eyes. "And it will likely be longer than our midyear celebrations were this summer." His generous smile returned instantly, and he continued, "I am Sutton, Chief Keep Steward of Earthmight." He cocked his head and gave a slight bow. "The One King awaits your arrival in the upper Spire. If you are ready and able, I am here to take you to him. The keep stewards here will see to all of your needs." He swept his hand to the four keep stewards who had shown them to their spot.

He looked at Saissha. "You must be Counsel Lord Saissha, the ambassador of the embassy from Corundum." Awe made saucers of his eyes. "A Counsel Lord at Earthmight..." He straightened more before her. "And you must be Prince Legerohn of the Moresi." Then he glanced at the three Akkeidii. He pulled back from Mandavu, and then he took in Lokah. His eyes trailed to Aenguz's left hand. "And you, you are Lord Aenguz of the Akkeidii."

The leaders were taken aback by his awareness of their names. Stroud's mien affirmed to Aenguz how he had learned them.

Saissha looked to Aenguz and Legerohn to see if they had any objections. "Is there any reason not to fulfill the purpose of the embassy now?"

"No," Aenguz and the Prince answered simultaneously. They half smiled at each other. Both were eager to deliver their messages and return home. They were already delayed longer than they had expected due to the incursion of the Erebim. They decided that the Akkeidii and the Moresi would go with Saissha. The Stair Guard would remain to make their camp. Though nothing was said, they understood that Stroud would come with them. The seven of them would represent the needs of Corundum and all the peoples of the Upper Lands. Aenguz would soon act again as the Last Emissary and bear dire words for the One King - the threat from Lord Morgrom, his minions, and the Ruinwasters.

Saissha retrieved her staff from the sled. Chimere asked for a sword for his prince, but Legerohn waved it off. The Akkeidii all had their *montmorillionite*. Aenguz still bore his scabbard under his burgundy cloak. Lokah's wrapped sword rested on top of the second sled. He pulled it off. Mandavu already bore his sheathed mace at his back.

When they were all ready, they followed the Chief Keep Steward to their audience with the One King.

Aenguz motioned at invisible tethers and drew Draymondon to him.

"Where are the stables?" Aenguz asked.

"Just within the gate," Sutton answered cheerfully. "I will show you."

Mandavu and Lokah walked close to Aenguz. Aenguz's First bent his head down. "This is a finer welcome than we received from the Stair Guard on the Rursh Keleg."

"Or at Corundum," Lokah added with a tinge of guarded disbelief.

"It is a formidable keep," Mandavu said as he looked up at the tall, flat wall.

The Stair Guard had rebuffed them, and the Counsel Lords had imprisoned them. What if this was another ploy? Aenguz turned to Lokah. Under his breath, his loremaster said, "It would make a formidable prison."

Aenguz wondered if they might be walking into a trap again. His intuition was piqued, but it gave him a sense of a different kind of danger.

Megalithic foundation stones made up the base. Polygonal joinery fit the roughly rectangular blocks into a kind of puzzle assembled by giants. The blocks were easily twenty men long and four or five men high. They reduced in size halfway up the Plateau, but they were still larger than a man. The joinery looked like Stonemages' skill, but the size was larger than anything in the Mashu. The wall met the rough basalt or black granite of the mountain far to the right that the Spire was built on. The lowest reaches of the Spire began near the top of the Plateau.

Aenguz scanned the wall for any doors or windows. The few in the block wall were thin and high. The lowest balconies on the Spire were met by sheer rock. And all the eyes of the tent city and the Azari could see the keep.

Sutton spoke to the Azari beside him and ordered the entrance of Earthmight to be cleared. He talked about the challenges of making room for so many people from the vales and farmsteads. Since the One King's command, people had been arriving every day. Whole sections of the vast keep were in the process of being organized, families relocated. There had been plenty of space before, but now accommodations had to be adjusted.

The tent city ended about thirty yards from the wall. It left a clear sward of green that stretched to the black mountain. Children ran in the open space closer to the line of tents. A single Azari stood in the green boundary. Sutton said it was a safety precaution for the people. "If anything fell off of the Plateau, it could seriously harm or even kill someone. No one has ever been killed in Earthmight," he said with clear pride.

He told them about the two main sections of Earthmight. The "Plateau," as he referred to it, was the wedge-shaped block at the base of the tower. And the Spire that sat above on the imposing shoulder of rock was the other part of Earthmight. Inside the Plateau was where the storehouses, granaries, cisterns, and workspaces for Earthmight were housed.

They were approaching the mouth of the keep, the great door he had seen on the ride up. Sutton halted before the main intersection. A commotion of horses and wagons was being gradually cleared and redirected so that the embassy might pass.

"Is this the only entrance to Earthmight?" Aenguz asked.

"Yes," he answered. "But it is wide, and there is no gate. Earthmight is open to all."

"We will be eager to return to our camp once we have spoken to the One King."

"You are welcome to stay in the Spire. Rooms have been prepared. I hope that you will stay with us."

Saissha demurred. She seemed to understand Aenguz's caution. Mono Lord Lana would have told her about what had been done to hold Aenguz and the others before the Well of Sorrows was sealed.

Legerohn stiffened. "We have been together with our companions since we left Corundum. We are not yet ready to be separated from them. Even being separated from the great horses is difficult for us."

Sutton was briefly crestfallen, but his alacrity brightened in him again instantly. "It is, after all, your home too. You may come and go as you please."

Aenguz looked at Stroud. The Azari was as impassive as the towering corner wall before them.

Sutton continued, "None could be more welcome here. Your forebears built Earthmight. It belongs as much to you as it does to those who dwell here now. You are not only guests of the One King, you are the most honored guests Earthmight has ever known."

The leaders of the embassy looked to one another as if there were some answer or understanding to be found among them. Sutton continued on. When he turned, Aenguz whispered to Mandavu and then to Lokah.

A breeze blew the smell of the sea into the company. It was strange to Aenguz's nose. The road opened to a wide round at the front of the keep. A cliff rose to the left at a steep slope, mirroring the façade of the keep's entrance wall. They formed a gateway to the vastness beyond.

"The Sunfall Sea!" Sutton introduced it as if he were responsible for it. The road led down a long gradual slope to the shore. A curved black wall ran out into the water, and long boats floated inside the protective jetty. The round area was empty, but all around it, people were packed shoulder to shoulder to gape at the embassy. Stewards with their narrow aprons stood apart to hold the people back and keep the space clear. There were Azari positioned at the four corners of the round too. The road to the left was backed up with wagons and horses. The air was a mixture of salt, manure, dead fish, and musk. It was a busy intersection, but for the embassy, it had been cleared and brought to a halt.

Sutton told them about Llangollen, the city to the south, where goods and people came to and from every day. "But since the One King's command, the old have been coming here for care and safety. Men were arriving every day to join the One Army and make ready. All of the efforts in Earthmight have been set toward preparing for war."

They walked to the towering gothic opening at the center of the gently curved outer wall of the Plateau. Here, Sutton's pride and welcome radiated. The intricacy and size of the opening took the breath away from the entire embassy. For Sutton, there was not only a new audience, but *the* audience for such an introduction.

The jamb pedestals at the foot of the arch looked familiar to Aenguz. They were shaped like small renditions of squatting Hyrrokkin. They ran in rows on both sides of the wide opening. They might have easily been confused for a roughhewn stone base for the pillars, but Aenguz knew their shape. Sutton confirmed it by explaining the role of the Hyrrokkin in the construction of Earthmight. "A meditation in stone against the will of the Sunfall Sea." His reverence was pure, and he held a respectful honor for the stone thralls.

Hexagonal columns rose out of the squatting figures' heads. Ornate colonnettes were fitted in between. Figures were cut into the jamb columns. Sutton explained that these were the architects from the Remnant who had selected not only the site for Earthmight but also the design of the keep. The archivolts overhead held sculptures of scores of artisans, stewards, farmers, bakers, brewers, and all manner of craftsmen and craftswomen engaged in their skill.

The peaked tympanum held a mural of Earthmight with Akkeidii, Moresi, Azari, Straathgardians, and others Sutton named of the Remnant that Aenguz did not know. The panoply of all the souls that had come together to build the Last Stronghold were rendered in black basalt and white marble.

Sutton pointed out that there were no doors on the portal, except in cases of war, but they had never been used. "Earthmight is open for all," he repeated.

Aenguz saw no doors of any kind. They all examined the details of the massive opening, their eyes and heads shifting in revolving turns. They might have spent hours there, had their mission not been so urgent.

Sutton drew them into the tunnel that led into the keep. Aenguz noted a channel just inside the tunnel that looked like it might be made for a door or a fitted slab. Draymondon's hooves clopped on the stone. He wasn't impressed with the façade. He looked ahead with his one eye as if he had been through the portal many times. His calm dampened Aenguz's worry.

When he had entered Corundum, he had no knowledge of the Well of Sorrows. But that knowledge had set in motion actions that had nearly killed him, and it had changed the world around Corundum. What unknowns did Earthmight hold that might actually take his life here? The stonework was soothing and discomfiting simultaneously. It was both familiar in a way and out of place.

The wide tunnel was only momentarily dark. Aenguz guessed that fifteen men could walk easily shoulder to shoulder. Sutton said that it was wide enough for three Hyrrokkin to walk side by side, but no one had seen a Hyrrokkin to confirm or deny that comparison.

The passage led upward at a gradual incline. Stone half-shells were spaced evenly high up along the corridor. Bright light flickered capriciously up to the flat ceiling. This light, too, was something that Aenguz was familiar with.

Lokah asked, "Is that *montmorillionite* in there?"

Sutton confirmed that the braziers held large hunks of raw *silvercryst*.

Raw *montmorillionite* here? It raised more questions. But it also confirmed Akkeidii Stonemage craft. The light flickered like trapped lightning, but the combined rhythm worked together to shine in a consistent pulse.

They reached a level landing, and Sutton proudly pointed out the stables ahead. Another steward waited there with two younger stewards beside her. "My lord," Sutton addressed Aenguz directly again. "This is Tanna, the Chief Animal Steward of Earthmight." Her smock bore a simple animal monogram over her chest. "Your horse will be taken care of here." Stalls led into the distance on either side. Straw, carts, and animals filled the open area. Another horse was being led by stewards halfway down the long stable.

Aenguz stroked Draymondon's neck. "I will see you soon." Then he handed the invisible tether to Tanna. She took the ethereal lines and passed them back to the young girl behind her. She led Draymondon away into the thick atmosphere of the stable.

Sutton led them back up the switchback. He explained that there were ramps on either side of the main ramp. They came back together to the center incline, then they led back up toward the keep. Each landing led to the different levels of the Plateau. The landings met the head of the corridors that led into the body of the Plateau.

Sutton continued talking about the grain stores, cisterns, and warehouses on each level, and the different workshops and craft areas within. Back and forth, up and up they went. Flickering light lit the way. Cold stone filled the air. The wider center ramps always led up into the keep.

Then there was fresh salt air. Light cut down halfway up the tunnel ahead.

Sutton led the leaders of the embassy of Corundum out onto the flat surface of Earthmight.

The Spire rose up in front of them in relief against the blue sky. Sea wind whipped their hair and tossed their cloaks. Saissha's robe fluttered. People lined the road that led to the base of the Spire. They formed a human wall on either side. Keep stewards and Azari held the line. Unintelligible murmurs from the crowd got tossed about in the wind.

But for the spectators, the top of the Plateau reminded Aenguz of the glaciers in the White Deeps north of the Hearth Valleys in the Mashu. The feeling drew Aenguz back to the memory of the last adventure with his father in the White Deeps. "It makes me think of walking on the glaciers at home," he said to Mandavu and Lokah. They agreed, but they were both tense.

The Spire rose up in a cluster of buildings and tiers. Wide balconies gave way to smaller and smaller ones. Arches and windows climbed up in a kind of permanent stone-pillared scaffolding. The Spire leaned and shifted at the middle tier, as if it were setting its will against the power of the Sunfall Sea.

Sutton continued his effusive monologue, sometimes drifting into soliloquy about Earthmight, the Plateau, and the Spire - the builders, the design, and the noble charge of the various stewards who devoted their lives to maintaining some aspect of the keep, many of whom were anxious to meet all of them. At the end of the road, Sutton explained about the amphitheater below and the bridge that crossed over it and another less ornate gothic opening beyond.

The people on either side of them ended abruptly. The wind, the white flat, and the mountain-like Spire sparked a feeling of vertigo in Aenguz. He had to check his steps. Then the road led onto a bridge. The Spire looked like it was about to come down on them. People filled the wide balconies and agoras above him. Their attention was strangulating. The Plateau fell away down to a stage far below. An angled wall like half a funnel ran to a tall façade that dropped down to a stage. Opposite the wide stage was a steep row of seats that ran from the bottom all the way to the base of the Spire. The lower balconies were shaped and angled and looked like an extension of the theater. They made up part of the lower tier of the Spire. Dark stone was left exposed around the base in places as natural accents. A smattering of children stared up at the bridge and the company.

The sudden height threw Aenguz into a spin. He grabbed Lokah's arm. The Kriel loremaster froze. He turned to Aenguz, thinking he saw what Aenguz saw. Set in the natural stone tympanum of the doorway was a skull fitted with a *montmorillionite* helmet. Sutton explained the sculpture and did not notice the stalled Akkeidii behind him. He reveled in the prospect of sharing something that must be so meaningful to the Akkeidii. "This is one of your forefathers, Hernus Kriel." Silver wings rose on the sides. A plume of impossibly fine fibers marked the top of the helm. The skull was enclosed in the helmet as if a permanent symbiotic bond had been achieved between bone and *montmorillionite*. The hollow eyes looked down on the bridge, down on Aenguz.

The bridge was suddenly the ice bridge on the glacier in the White Deeps. The final hunt with his father, the chasm, the fall, the beast, his father's final plummet and fight to save Aenguz's life… His own stunned stillness from the fall… His inability to rise and help… The manifested expression of *suraskanskeld* above looking down on him, judging him… The reminder of his attempt and his failure at the forge that set in motion his own blasphemous and tortuous path… It was too much. Vertigo took his balance. Aenguz fell.

"What is it?" Mandavu was at his side. The world flipped. Aenguz clung to the ground as if he might slide down to the theater floor below.

Lokah knelt beside him.

Sutton panicked and rushed to Aenguz.

Saissha, Legerohn, and Chimere bolted to him and blocked the Chief Steward.

"What is wrong with him?" Saissha asked desperately. Fear of losing a key member of the embassy cast dread into her tone.

Legerohn bent down to Aenguz's face. "My friend, my friend, what is it? How can we help?"

"Get me off the bridge," Aenguz was able to mutter.

"Lift him," Legerohn commanded.

Sutton nudged his way through.

"He is fine," Mandavu barked. "Lead on, steward. He is over-whelmed by the skill of our forefathers."

They dragged him forward under the helmeted skull. Aenguz

pulled his feet out of the mire of his trauma. Lokah stared overhead as if Hernus Kriel was judging them.

If he fell now, at least he had seen the embassy to Earthmight. The One King was waiting for them, and Saissha could make her appeal. He would have kept his promise to the Mono Lord, and save for their two deaths, had gotten them there in one piece. His father might have been proud, if he were alive.

28

IN THE AUDIENCE
OF THE ONE KING

Inside the entrance, Aenguz regained himself as a new wave of awe overwhelmed him. He was steady enough to stand on his own. A wide rotunda of rose marble greeted the embassy. Before them, opposite the entrance, was a round tier of steps that led up to a round landing. Another rise of steps cupped the dais and led back to six portals that disappeared into the keep. On both sides of the rotunda, curved ramps led up around the stairs and out of sight. Denizens of Earthmight lined the outer edges of the ramps and the outer edges of the upper stairs. Four Azari were spaced about, two on the floor and two on the dais. There were other stewards with symbols and images Aenguz did not recognize among the people. All eyes were on the embassy, but it seemed as if all eyes were on him.

Sutton continued his talk about the entrance and the series of stairs and ramps that led around and up into the Spire. He led the company up a passage to the right. As they passed, the denizens moved on, and the rotunda churned back into life with people coming and going and pouring into and out of the Spire.

Sutton led the embassy through a maze that passed by open arched balconies that looked out to the wide spread of the tent city and undulating fields of green and tan. They passed large chambers filled with people busy at one thing or another. Sutton told them about the work they did to supply the growing One Army.

The air in some places was filled with the scent of baking bread and roasting meat, while in others, it carried the smell of cloth and cotton. They navigated a winding path up the ramped walkways, where stewards pushed carts, then climbed stairs to higher levels.

Here there were rows of doors on either side. These were the apartments and suites for families and other denizens. Sutton relished leading the embassy around to an open landing that looked out from another vantage point from the height. Here they could see the rocky cliff face that ran along the shore to the north. Green ran up to it, and horses and cattle grazed there placidly. The edge of the Sunfall Sea tantalized mysteriously on the edge. White waves rippled in and out of sight into the distance.

Up and up they went, and around and around. Sutton steered them to an arched balcony where they could look out over the full expanse of the sea. Rooftops feathered on top of one another below. Aenguz had never witnessed anything so vast or so awesome. It was like the sky laid out on an earth-sized table. Pointed birds with pink wings and green tail feathers banked in loose flocks around the keep. Down below, he could see dots of long boats inside the curved jetty. The whole company was silent. Even Sutton stilled to let them take in the view.

He led them up further. They saw the roof of the Plateau below. The road leading in and out of the Spire was teeming. People dotted the surface, engaged in some processing or managing of one thing or another.

Sutton led them to an ornate portal. An Azari stepped aside and acknowledged Stroud. The corridors were empty here and the turns tighter. Doors to more apartments lined either side. Open lookouts appeared here and there. Azari were always in sight. Sutton explained that these upper reaches were for the One King, guests, and all the other Chief Stewards.

They ringed the upper quadrant of the Spire one final time before Sutton stopped at a pair of large carved doors. Panels were filled with scenes of people at craftwork or dialogue. Sutton was about to explain more about the door, but he restrained himself. He beamed. His pride as Earthmight's Chief Steward radiated from him. Saissha and Legerohn thanked him. Chimere also thanked the steward.

He reminded them again that they were welcome in the keep and announced, as the doors opened, "The One King awaits."

The doors swung open by some hidden means. Sutton backed out of the way.

Inside the chamber was a forest of Carrara marble columns. They were shaped like cottonwood trunks. They widened at the base and reached into the smooth white marble floor. Aenguz could see slats of blue beyond the petrified forest columns. Above, the columns expanded in thick branches into an interconnected series of vaults. Stone leaves filled the ceiling.

Stroud led the company forward, and they moved in and through the faux trees. The sensation of being in a sculpted forest made of stone awed them all. Legerohn seemed to be on the edge of ecstasy. Chimere seemed disoriented or in a state of shock.

Stroud led them out of the marble forest. To the left against the wall was a wide two-stepped dais. There stood the One King. Two Azari with jet-black hair stood at his back. They stared unblinking at the embassy. A wide throne was behind the Azari. The seat was made of a black hexagonal slab, and the back rose to an oblique point. The throne was dark and plain, but it was solid and heavy and wide enough for three men to sit easily on it. To the right was a natural opening in the black rock that looked out to the clear blue sky.

The One King was nearly as tall as the Azari. He had the first creases of middle age. The lines seemed new on him as if worry and concern had conspired to age him. His bald head was smooth but for a ring of short gray-brown hair that connected his ears behind his head. He wore a circlet of white gold. The band was intricately formed of tiny hands raised up in praise or supplication. A polished oval of obsidian, almost egg-shaped, was mounted at his forehead. It looked like an imperfect unblinking pupil. His breastplate was made of ornate sheaves of metal, and a white cape draped casually over his back and down to the floor. Metal greaves and shin guards covered his extremities. Simple banded rings without jewels ornamented his fingers, and his hands hung loose and comfortable at his sides. He was calm and unconcerned, but also curious about the people standing before him.

"Welcome to Earthmight, honored embassy from Corundum. Welcome to your home - the home your forefathers built. None could be more welcome here. I am Thelen. I am the steward and One King to this keep and to the peoples of the Lower Lands. What pass have you found in the Spine? What news do you bring from the desolation of the Upper Lands? You have seen and fought the invaders that have brought war to us. My thanks on behalf of the people and the Free People and the great horses for defeating them. What can you tell us of these invaders and the passes through the mountains?"

Saissha stepped forward with pride and purpose. Though she was small, she towered over the embassy. She held her braided staff before her. It seemed more rooted and stronger than any of the shaped stone pillars in the hall. "Lord One King, I am Saissha, Counsel Lord of

Corundum, daughter of Nathalia and Girmai. I have come on behalf of Corundum, and I have brought a gift from the Mono Lord." Saissha reached into her robe and produced a small pouch. She walked up to the One King and handed the pouch to him. The two Azari followed her every move. "These are some of the last seeds from the Vaults of Corundum."

Thelen accepted the pouch solemnly. He moved his hand so the Azari could inspect it. Then he passed it off to one of them.

Aenguz marveled at Saissha. She had secreted that prize all the way from Corundum. She had to have worked all the time to keep the seeds safe, even in the coldest reaches of the Spine. She still held surprises.

"Thank you for this gift. I will see that the Chief Garden Steward wards and cultivates these seeds. The Mono Lord has been generous with this gift, and though the blight seems to have been lifted from our lands, we will cherish this gift."

Saissha nodded and returned to her companions. Then she said, "I have come with the Prince of the Moresi and the Lord of the Akkeidii. They came with me so that you might know the plight of the Upper Lands. I have come so that you might know the need of Corundum. Sadly, we bear dark news from the Upper Lands. And we come to make a plea of you."

Thelen held still and readied himself. The obsidian orb dominated his face.

"Corundum came under attack. We prevailed, but the Stair Guard were severely depleted. Waters flow again around the citadel, and the Glaize is dispelled, but the Vaults of Corundum have been destroyed. They are no more. The Woe Sower is alive, and his servants move abroad to assault the Remnant and the peoples of the Upper Lands."

"And the peoples of the Lower Lands, it would seem," Thelen added.

"The Mono Lord bids me to ask aid of the One Army to protect what remains of Corundum and the people there." Saissha let out a breath in relief.

Thelen considered her words. Then he asked, "Where are the armies of the Moresi and the Akkeidii? Why did they not help in the defense of Corundum? Why did you come through the Spine and not through the Cleve?"

Legerohn stepped forward like a king in his own right. "Thelen, One King, I am Legerohn, Prince of the Moresi, Ruler of Inverlieth. I am heartened by all the evidence of Moresi craftsmanship in Earthmight. We have known of our work here, and it is but for the darkness of the Dimmerdross that we have not returned to the Lower Lands and to Earthmight." Legerohn drew in a breath and rooted himself like the stone trees around him. "Before winter left our lands, I set out with fifty Moresi warriors to the One Forest. The Rings of Life that run through root and bow and also the bones of the Moresi told us that the One Forest was under assault. I set the defense of Inverlieth, and we departed for the One Forest to aid the Chosen Freeholder." He seemed to commiserate with the One King. A kind of compassion exuded through him and his firm speech. "Only four Moresi survived that charge.

"Chimere is here with me, and two others - Mond, my First, and Stokke - have returned to Inverlieth in my stead to maintain the defense of our home while we traveled here to seek your aid. So, I understand the defense of home and the duties of leadership, and the responsibilities we hold to the people we serve.

"When we were at our lowest point, when we were decimated by Erebim and Sallow, when all was lost, we were saved by the Lord of the Akkeidii." Legerohn turned and looked at Aenguz with gratitude. His lips pressed together as he met his eyes. "He saved us. And he saved our mission and gave us back our purpose. That purpose, with the remaining

Moresi, brought us to Corundum. We moved with haste against time to warn Corundum of the coming threat and help the Counsel Lords, friends of the Lands, protectors of the Law of Creation and the Lands of the Earth. We reached Corundum in time to aid in its defense. You know the outcome from Counsel Lord Saissha.

"We needed your help, and time was still against us. The Dimmerdross still stood as a barrier to the Cleve. So, we attempted the Spine, with the aid of these Akkeidii, to cross the perilous mountains." He held the room with his tenor. "I nearly perished in the Spine of the World to help bring you this plea. Two members of our embassy did die - two of the Stair Guard who are sworn to protect the Stair of Forhnthulen. We all knew the risk when we attempted to cross. Corundum's need - our need - the urgency dictated the course. It was Aenguz with the Akkeidii who believed they could cross those mountains. And we did. And it was to fight Division, Woe Sower, and the First Treacher. My final orders to my First were to await the One Army's arrival - to join with the One Army and give battle for the sake of the Lands of the Earth and all of creation."

Thelen's eyes wilted. His heart seemed exposed outside of his folded breastplate. He nodded unconsciously on the verge of emotions that outstripped him. But he mastered himself and gathered his words. "We, the people, are saddened by your loss and your sacrifice, and that of the embassy that attempted so much to come here. 'Life and Death are intertwined.' Your loss is our loss." He touched his fingers to his circlet, clasped his hands over his heart, and then lowered them and opened his palms to the Prince.

Legerohn stepped back and intimated for Aenguz to step forward and speak. "I am Aenguz, son of Sairik. I am the Lord of the Akkeidii, Polemarch of the Warriors, and I have sent word to the Mashu to marshal for war." Aenguz looked at Mandavu. Mandavu beamed stoically with pride at Kachota's charge. "The Akkeidii will join the One Army, but the Mashu is distant."

Aenguz became grave. "I am also the Last Emissary of the Divider. I have been given a message and a warning for you and Earthmight and the One Army. We had hoped to get ahead of the timeline the Flayer warned of to give you the best advantage against him." Aenguz took a moment to steady himself. "Of the words the Woe Sower said to me, for you, he said, *'Five seasons will not pass before Earthmight is under siege and the One King's army is lost. You will know the grieving of the Lower Lands. But war is not the worst thing you should fear. Despair will unwind the fabric of your souls. All will be divided against all.'*"

Thelen looked stricken. He stared at Aenguz as if he were some kind of ghoul. Horror quaked his face. His eyes shook. He looked at the whole embassy as if they were inexorable bearers of doom.

"We departed the Mashu as prisoners in spring," Aenguz continued. "We are on the threshold of autumn. If we move against him before his plans can come to fruition, we can counter the threat with the combined armies on the Upper Lands. We can nullify this threat before it takes root. Our sacrifice has given us the chance to do what Lord Morgrom does not expect. He could not have foreseen that we would have crossed the Spine, foregoing the barrier of the Dimmerdross and the Cleve. Will you join us in defense of our homes and the Lands of the Earth?"

Thelen looked gaunt. His armor seemed small on his frame. The obsidian orb glinted black. "We are under attack here. We are at war now. We thought invaders had only come through the mountains. Now we see that they can appear anywhere. I am charged with preserving life - and life here is under threat. That is why I have called the people here to the safest place on Earth, where I can protect them."

"What you have seen so far is only the smallest expression of the Flayer's power. The force that assembles beyond the Cleve is vast. The

Tsurah and Sallow fight with Erebim. Urnings roam the night, and Ruinwasters are free in the Lands of the Earth. I have seen them. What you have experienced is a sortie, a trifle."

Thelen looked to the two Azari. "Hannoch, Sarokin, is this true? When will this happen?" Hannoch and Sarokin looked at Stroud.

"These were the words brought by the Lord of the Akkeidii, Aenguz Sidor, to the Counsel Lords at Corundum," Stroud answered as if he were sharing the most benign information.

"What else did he say?"

"That the limit of their days upon the Lands of the Earth are before them," Stroud added matter-of-factly.

Saissha added, "We have seen what the Divider intends to do in the Divine Oculum. If we act, we can disrupt his plans."

Thelen seemed to search for something to cling to, something to moor himself to. "We have lived in peace here for ages. We have not lived with the hells of the Upper Lands that you have. The Woe Sorrower was defeated. I would call you mad if I had not 'seen' what has come to our lands. We are already under siege. We cannot abandon the defense of Earthmight. It is our only defense, and the Cleve is barred."

"Lord King," Saissha continued, "Corundum needs the One Army. We barely survived the Battle of Corundum. We will not survive another. You must come. Surely, your oath to protect life extends to Corundum."

"I cannot abandon Earthmight."

"Lord King..." Aenguz's tone hardened. "If you wait, you play into Lord Morgrom's hands. Would you have the Ruinwaster-led hordes destroy all of your lands slowly over time here, instead of meeting them in the Upper Lands with two well-trained armies by your side? With the Cleve at your back as an avenue to fall back on? Straathgard may yet join us as well. But alone and separate, we will fall."

"How can I forego the lives here that I have known? The people of the vales, the people of Llangollen, my home, the people here at Earthmight, the stewards? I cannot abandon them for an unknown terror." He came to his conclusion unsteadily. He was at the end of his rope.

"Thelen, you cannot win the battle from here. You - we - must attack it at the source. What you are experiencing is only the forward assault. I do not know Morgrom's strategy, but I do know war strategy. We need to assemble our forces and surround his forces. He will not be expecting it. He believes in division. We believe in uniting."

The One King struggled as if he were wrestling inside himself.

The embassy from Corundum hung on a precipice. The fate of the Lands hung in the balance.

Saissha pleaded on behalf of the families of Corundum. They would not survive without help. Legerohn said that he had commended forces to the protection of Corundum. As they were a people dedicated to the life of the Lands, it was his responsibility.

But the One King was silent. Some resolve had found a place in him.

Aenguz had not expected to be rebuffed by the One King. But he knew that his own reasoning was sound. In their eyes, this was the war. They were living it. *Verrandulum* could appear anywhere. Their fight was here. The Upper Lands were a hell to them. How could they leave?

"Lord King, I hear your concern and your duty to the Law of Creation. We have our duties to attend to as well. And I know the threat and power of the Woe Sower's words. Already, we are delayed. We must begin our trek and reach our home before winter strikes. We will cross the Cleve and attempt the Dimmerdross to reach Inverlieth on our own. Then we will join our forces there. Then maybe you will see the power of our combined armies and join us in battle."

"You cannot."

The One King's words didn't make sense to Aenguz.

"You cannot leave here," Thelen repeated.

29

WELCOME HOME

Aenguz clicked his tongue at Mandavu.

Mandavu flipped his scabbard over his shoulder and slid his mace free in a snap.

Saissha shrieked.

Wind whipped Aenguz's hair.

Lokah flinched and brought his wrapped sword up.

Aenguz placed his hand on him to still him.

Two Azari were at Mandavu's back. Their hands were locked on his shoulders.

Legerohn cried out, "Mandavu!" He pushed Saissha behind him.

Chimere stumbled and fell.

Aenguz's hair tossed again.

Two more Azari were before Mandavu in a blink. They gripped his wrists and his elbows.

Hannoch and Sarokin were suddenly before Thelen as if they had always been standing before the One King. Thelen was safely hidden behind them.

Stroud faced Mandavu. He placed himself between Mandavu and the One King.

Mandavu flexed his prodigious strength. His muscles bulged. The lines in his neck grew taut. Redness grew in his cheeks and filled his forehead. A low, steady growl seeped from him as he strained against the power of four Azari.

In the stone forest, Aenguz saw at least a dozen Azari standing next to the trees, waiting.

They were surrounded.

Stroud spoke. "Stop."

Mandavu's strained roar intensified.

"Stop," he said firmly.

The impassive Azari strained against him.

"Stop!"

"I," Mandavu gritted through his teeth, "do not take orders from you."

Aenguz counted the Azari, questioned Stroud's allegiance, and assessed Thelen's fear or lack of it.

"Mandavu," Aenguz spoke calmly.

"Yes, lord." He squeezed out the words. "Have you seen enough?"

"I have. You may relent."

With that, Mandavu released, and the cords in his forearms faded. His neck and shoulders relaxed. The creases in his shirt smoothed.

The impassive Azari looked to one another as if they had missed something.

Tension held in the chamber like something else might snap. Aenguz tried to glean more from Stroud, but he seemed only vaguely surprised.

Stroud calmly commanded the Azari to release Mandavu. He had an undertone of authority in his voice. He turned to Aenguz as if he were taking stock of him for the first time.

The four Azari released Mandavu, but they did not move far. They looked at Aenguz as if he had changed suddenly before them. The Azari who had appeared behind the pillars were suddenly gone. Hannoch and Sarokin returned to their positions behind the One King in an odd kind of pivot.

Thelen studied Aenguz and Mandavu. He revealed more fully the confusion the Azari barely showed.

Aenguz spoke confidently, as if he were more powerful than the One King. "So, we are to be your prisoners here."

"You misunderstand me. You are guests here. You are in your home in the Lower Lands. You can live freely anywhere. But you are welcome to live here in Earthmight with us.

"But you cannot hazard the Cleve. It would mean your death. I am sworn to protect life. I will not allow you to enter the Cleve."

"What if we wish to attempt it?"

"No one who has entered the Cleve has ever returned."

Aenguz looked at Legerohn. He released Saissha. Chimere climbed to his feet.

"There was a time," Thelen started, "after the Azari came, after the Last Battle, after they lost their women and children to the Cleve, when each year they would send one in to find them, to see if perhaps they were beyond the old highway. But after a generation they were convinced by the One King at that time to halt their futility. They have more cause than any to unravel the mystery of the Cleve. But it broke the One King's heart to see them lose one of their own each year. The agreement to stop came with one condition: they set a Sentinel there to watch the Cleve and wait for their women and children."

Aenguz said to Stroud, "It was through the eyes of the Sentinel that you saw the Cleve?"

"Yes."

"What if we wish to attempt the Cleve regardless?"

"I am bound to protect all life. If you told me that you meant to walk across the Sunfall Sea, I would prevent it. I could not let you willingly kill yourself. It would be as if I allowed it. There is a garrison there that wards the Cleve. They would prevent you from entering. The Cleve is another reason why I will not risk the One Army there."

Legerohn looked at the One King and Aenguz. He could not say or add anything.

Aenguz and Thelen were at an impasse. Then Thelen said, "You are free to go anywhere here. But if you must leave us, then you may search for a pass through the mountains, a safe pass, over the Spine."

"We lost two Stair Guard in those mountains. We nearly lost Prince Legerohn."

"Without the Akkeidii, we would have all died," Saissha added.

"Can you not return the way you came?"

The entire company demurred. There was no way back, and no way to bring Legerohn safely over the mountains again. There was no confidence in that moment that they could survive another crossing. More than that, they could not return to Corundum without aid.

"Your enemy is our enemy. We are allies. Can you not help us to fight them, as you have asked help of us? Can you and your Stair Guard not join us in the fight against the invaders and the battle you say is to come?" Thelen suggested.

Aenguz deferred to Saissha. She was riddled with consternation. She calculated quickly. "The Stair Guard are here for my protection alone. They are here to see to the safety of the embassy. That charge was given by the Mono Lord and the Stair Mark."

"You have no need of protection here. No one has ever been killed by another's hand here in Earthmight. I hope you will come to change your mind. Every man is needed." Then to all of them, he said, "I understand that this is hard news for you. It is only in the service of life that I deliver it. I would see the bond between the Upper and Lower Lands restored. Be welcome here. Please accept our hospitality. The Stewards wish to share what Earthmight has to offer, what your forefathers have wrought here, and what we have sustained. This is the Last Stronghold. If we are to meet the forces of the Woe Sower, then there can be no safer place."

Stroud led the despondent embassy down and out of Earthmight after departing from the One King. They all sagged like they had been fitted with heavy chains. They shuffled down as surely as if they were prisoners being led to a dungeon. Stroud led them on a different but more direct path than the one Sutton had led them up. Stroud had the benefit of all the Azari's eyes to guide him.

Aenguz gave a terse command to Mandavu and Lokah for silence. He did not want their consternation to be heard. The One King's edicts were maddening. Assemble the One Army, but offer no aid. All the freedom, but no release from the Lower Lands. Protection and shelter, but willful ignorance of the enemy and what Morgrom could do.

The lower corridors and pathways teemed with the denizens of Earthmight. They still stared as the company passed. The embassy blended in with lines of people as they crossed the Plateau to the ramps that led all the way down to the packed intersection at the gateless mouth of Earthmight.

Stroud led them to their encampment. The corallel tents were raised, and they stood apart from the other canvases in the tent city. The shadow from the Plateau moved across the growing tarped metropolis.

The Stair Guard were busy organizing the camp. They had water and firewood. They were anxious to learn what the embassy had seen and heard from the One King. Mandavu barked at them to keep a watch. The embassy needed to speak. They had not processed themselves the fact that they were prisoners. How were they going to tell the Stair Guard that they were never going home?

PART III

DEFENSE

30

A REALM OF SILENCE

"Grieg the Sanctor!" Mandavu cursed as he bent into the open flap on the corallel tent.

The leaders of the embassy filed in and circled the center pole in the tall section of the tent. They all began to fret and talk over one another.

Stroud stood at the door and faced them.

Mandavu cursed the One King and called him a fool. He railed at the prospect of crossing the Spine as the leaders of the embassy settled down. Lokah whispered couplets from the Lay, as if to steady himself or to find an answer.

Aenguz sat quietly with his back to the long lateen end of the tent. They were trapped. He had led all of them into a trap. Despite his noble intentions, the One King had ostensibly barred them from returning home. How could he have been so stupid? How could he have known? What would his father think of his son, the leader? Winds of anger and self-recrimination buffeted him. He recalled something his father had taught him about how anger, like winds, would fade. He had reminded Aenguz that the anger came from him. As a warrior, *he* was master of those emotions. They did not come from outside of him. If he was going to be a leader, he would have to understand that and embody the kind of control necessary to let the winds pass.

After the first heat of his anger was spent, Mandavu noticed that Aenguz had not spoken. He closed his mouth, embarrassed. Frustration turned his face a different shade of red.

By degrees, they all quieted. All eyes fell on Aenguz.

When Aenguz saw that they were all ready to listen, and the winds inside him died down, he looked up at Stroud. "Stroud, leave us."

Stroud might have flinched at the command. The pause was infinitesimal, but it was there. He turned and left the tent.

"Everything we say and do is seen by the Azari," Aenguz reminded them. He looked at each of them to see if they understood. Saissha, Legerohn, and Chimere all nodded in turn.

Lokah and Mandavu straightened and held perfectly still. They would not utter a single word until Aenguz asked something of them.

"What can we do?" Legerohn uttered dejectedly. "I must return to Inverlieth. We all must return home."

"We have no aid for Corundum, no One Army to come for them. They will think we were lost in the Spine," Saissha said half to the others and half to herself. Her words floated as if she were a castaway in a strange dream. "How can we live here and never leave? It will be as if we died."

"We will appeal to the One King again," Aenguz said. "He cares for his people here. How can we gainsay him? They have never known war. They face a threat they have no experience in facing. His faith is in his fortress, but he does not understand the threat. We do. Legerohn, you and I must prevail upon the One King. We are responsible for our people, like he is. We will have to find another opportunity to appeal to him as leaders of our people. We have oaths to uphold as well."

"Yes. We must," Legerohn answered. But he too was lost in his own dire thoughts.

"What do I tell the Stair Guard?" Saissha asked.

"The One King wants them to join the One Army. He wants all of us to help in the defense of Earthmight. If they are taken into its service, they will be lost to you. We should all find other ways to help in the defense of Earthmight. But not by joining the One Army." If they became members of the One Army, they would be beholden in service to it.

"Tell them that the Cleve is unsafe. Tell them that they must find a way back over the Spine for us. Let them search for a pass that can lead us back over. Tell them the One Army is still yet assembling, but that we wish to return sooner. Get them away from here, or they will be lost."

Saissha nodded at what Aenguz was saying, but a myriad of contemplations kept her eyes unfixed. "I cannot believe this is happening."

"I dread going back over the Spine." Legerohn's voice shook. The Prince seemed to be sinking. "I may not survive."

"I know, my friend. Chimere, go to the infirmaries here. Search for some medicines that will ease his crossing. And see if there is some way you can help there."

"With all these people coming in, another healer would be of help. Tahnka?"

Legerohn gave Chimere leave to go.

After Chimere left, Legerohn asked, "What are we going to do?"

"You are the Prince of the Moresi. Find Sutton and tell him you are tired of sleeping in a tent. Tell him that you would like an apartment befitting a Prince. Scout out where he houses you. Make certain we overlook the land and not the sea. And insist that we all stay near one another. In a few days, we will join you, reluctantly. You are a dignitary here. Be a dignitary. The stewards want to show you the work of our forefathers. Let them show you."

A wry smile slipped across his face. "You still have surprises in you, my friend. Very well." The Prince got up and left the tent.

Saissha stood to collect herself. She straightened her robe, drew fortitude from her braided staff, and followed the Prince. She needed time to figure out how to tell the Stair Guard.

Aenguz could sense that Lokah and Mandavu ached to speak and ask questions, but they sat still and waited on him.

"Stair Guard!" Aenguz called out.

Braydehn poked his head into the tent. The dark lines under his eyes made him look tired, but he also looked curious. His nose seemed to pull his face to the side.

"Yes, my lord."

"I take counsel with my First and my loremaster. We are not to be disturbed."

"Yes, my lord."

Aenguz unshouldered his scabbard and laid it across his lap. He drew out his weapon. Mandavu followed suit. Lokah unwrapped the leathers from his sword. Aenguz looked at his weapon. The Dagba Stone was a useless lump of stone attached to its head.

"We need a Realm of Silence," Aenguz whispered.

He held his weapon to his left. Lokah placed a hand on it and reached his sword over to Mandavu. Mandavu grabbed the blade. His skin was protected by the lore in his veins. He leaned the mace over to Aenguz. Aenguz grabbed it. It formed a network between them.

> *Silence in the earth, metal's home,*
> *No light, no sound there to be known,*
> *When secret counsel is needed,*
> *Recall its realm, and 'tis heeded.*

Then Aenguz called for Braydehn again.

He poked his head in. "Yes, my lord."

"See that we are not disturbed."

"It is done, my lord." Confusion complicated his face.

When the flap closed, Aenguz cursed, "Grieg damn!" Another power lost. Another failure. Why did he keep trying? There was only one power left to try, but he didn't want to die to prove it.

Lokah's lips moved. Some idea brightened his eyes. He cocked his head and said, "Try your arm. You still have *morillion* in your veins."

Aenguz laid down his inert weapon. And their hands changed so that his arm acted as his weapon. They repeated the lines from the Lay.

> *Silence in the earth, metal's home,*
> *No light, no sound there to be known,*
> *When secret counsel is needed,*
> *Recall its realm, and 'tis heeded.*

"Braydehn. Braydehn!" Aenguz called. Then, with a shout, "Stair Guard!"

No one came.

"Now we may speak."

"I beg forgiveness, my lord. I have failed you. I was not given leave to speak," Mandavu said with more vulnerability than Aenguz had ever seen in him.

"You voice all of our frustrations. What did you learn?"

"That the One King is indeed surrounded by Azari."

"Can we trust the Azari? Can we trust Stroud?" Lokah asked.

"I am not sure. I need to learn more about the Azari and what Stroud knows about his people here. I do not know if he stands with us or them."

"How are we going to get home?" Mandavu pleaded. "As long as the One King prevents us, and the Azari see us, we will not get out of the shadow of Earthmight."

"Listen, this is a war within the war, but we cannot fight our way free. We will get back to the Upper Lands one way or another, with the One Army or without. They are still our allies, but they are also our foes, but they do not know it. They do not know what they do. They are a greater force. And against a greater force, only guile will serve."

"What do you wish of us?" Mandavu asked, as if he were prepared to sacrifice anything for Aenguz.

"Mandavu, I need you to find out about the One Army: their complement, their readiness, their numbers. Glean what you are able. You are a guest here. You are free to move around. These people have not prepared for war like we have trained for. Gauge them against what you know of the Akkeidii. But do not let them know what you are doing."

Mandavu nodded and said, "It will be done, lord."

"Also, I need to know what this garrison at the Cleve is like. Find a way to learn the same of the force there. Is there a way to get around it? I do not know a warrior alive that could sit with idle hands for so long."

"Yes, lord." He seemed satisfied to have tasks to direct himself toward.

"The Sentinel there is another matter. I will ask Stroud about him. Leave that to me."

Aenguz turned to Lokah. "Find the armory. Find out how the One Army is equipped. There must be more bodies than supplies. How are they arming them?

"The vales have brought their metal here. They have brought *montmorillionite*. Find out what they are doing with it."

"I will, my lord."

"And Lokah, find a way to get the Dagba Stone off of my weapon. I will happily leave it here, but I will not leave my weapon. I do not believe we can bear the stone across the length of the Lands and survive. It will be protected by the Azari here. But my weapon comes with me."

"Yes, my lord. I understand." His uncertainty about how to do what Aenguz asked was apparent, but he still exuded the certainty of a soldier receiving a direct order. "Why did you not tell them about the Dagba Stone?"

"In that moment, I did not think about it. I was too shocked at being barred from leaving. And now, the One King may take it from me, and my weapon with it. I will not let that happen." He looked at them to see if they understood his utter command.

Lokah and Mandavu shuddered. The thought that the Dagba Stone might be taken was one thing. Aenguz had found it, but it was of no use. But having his weapon taken too would change their calculations considerably. They could not allow it to happen. And they would die to prevent it or die trying if they had to fight to take it back.

They all knew what Aenguz's words meant. He said, as if in answer to it, "Find me a suitable weapon in its stead."

"I will find you something. Or I will make it myself."

"Good. Now listen…" Even though they were in a realm of complete silence, Aenguz leaned in and drew them close to him. "And this is the most important thing. Let nothing you do or say belie your true purpose. The eyes of the Azari are on you. The One King can see everything you do or say. When you speak, hide your true intent. When you need to speak to one another, always speak in silence. And when we speak, none may hear us. Do you understand?"

They both echoed, "Yes, my lord."

"What about the Prince and Saissha?"

"I will find a way to talk to the Prince. I do not want to put him in a situation he cannot hold. I will handle Legerohn. Saissha will be fine. We can draw her in when the time is right. For now, it is enough that they all know that we plan to go home. What they cannot know, or share, is how we will do it."

"How will we do it?"

"With guile."

"What will you do?"

"I am a dignitary. I will act like a dignitary." The three Akkeidii smiled a warrior's grin, as if they had been gifted a new weapon.

31

THE ONE ARMY

The next morning, Saissha assembled the Stair Guard. She could not bring herself to address them the night before. She needed time to think and time to consider how she might ask what she intended of them. She looked like she hadn't slept.

The embassy from Corundum gathered while the canvassed city around them came to life. People from the vales and farmsteads prepared morn meals and tried to take comfort in their new surroundings, though many of their men were gone. Keep stewards helped direct people toward fresh water or led elderly family members toward the keep.

Soldiers from Earthmight sauntered down the road past the expanding encampment. A few men from the new arrivals, without arms or armor, left their people and joined in groups that flowed toward the assembly in the distance.

Carts moved on paths between the tents. Grain stewards bore warm loaves of barrio bread to everyone. They handed a few loaves to the Stair Guard. Saissha thanked them and waited for them to pass.

Legerohn and Aenguz stood beside her. Mandavu stood next to Aenguz, and Lokah flanked him. Chimere was beside his Tahnka. Stroud positioned himself to the side of the embassy's leaders and faced Saissha.

The Stair Guard were anxious. They gathered around her and quieted. They sought to glean anything from her demeanor before she spoke.

"You have achieved the goal of the embassy from Corundum. Our mission here is a success." The soldiers seemed to exhale as if they had been holding their breath since Lihkit. Their stances eased. Many of the thirteen remaining Stair Guard smiled. "We have met with the One King and made our plea for aid for Corundum. As you know, and have seen, war has already come to the Lower Lands, and the One Army is assembling to give battle to the Divider's servants. The Cleve is currently barred. They have not yet found a way through. We, however, must get word back to Corundum sooner. So, I bid you, I command you to return to the Spine to find a new path over the mountains." Her words were frangible. They were more plea than command.

The soldiers' smiles dissipated. Uncertainty and frustration made them stoic.

"You will take the sleds and supplies and march east. There, you will make a camp and search for passes into the Spine. The Akkeidii will teach you what to look for and how best to search out passes."

"The Akkeidii are not coming with us?" a stocky Stair Guard asked.

"We…" She gestured to the leaders of the embassy, while at the same time she tried to draw courage from them. "…will remain to help prepare the One Army to join us in the defense of the Upper Lands."

Their set stances frayed. They began to mill.

"You will send a messenger back every ten days to report on your progress and refresh your supplies as needed. You may take the sleds with you."

Braydehn spoke up. "We are charged with your protection. Should some of us stay here to protect you?"

"The Counsel Lord will be warded," Mandavu said firmly.

Another soldier asked, "What if we do not find a pass?"

"If we must return to Lihkit Vale, then we will. My hope is that we will find something closer to Earthmight. Head east and begin your search there." She was trying to protect them, but she was stripping them of their purpose and giving them one they didn't believe in - one they couldn't possibly perform. If they stayed, they would be taken up into the One Army, and they would never be able to leave. She couldn't share this truth. Aenguz could hear that it tore at her.

"Reach out to the stewards, gather any supplies you need. You will depart once you are ready."

"Yes, Counsel Lord," they replied timidly.

"Is that how you address a Counsel Lord?" Mandavu called at them.

"Yes, Counsel Lord!" they repeated with vigor.

The Stair Guard fell out and mumbled to one another as they tore at their loaves.

The leaders of the embassy turned toward one another.

"You did what had to be done," Legerohn said, trying to assuage her fraught gaze.

Aenguz put a hand on her shoulder. "He is right. They would cease to be Stair Guard if they stayed."

"Shall we go to the keep?" Legerohn asked, trying to change the subject and move on to their other challenges.

Aenguz eased her gently toward the road.

Mandavu turned from them and grabbed a saddle.

"Where are you going?" Saissha asked.

"I may not be too welcome in the keep," Mandavu answered. He threw a saddle up over his shoulder and turned away. He left the leaders of the embassy as they headed toward Earthmight.

———◆———

MANDAVU DID NOT LIKE lying to Saissha, but it was a small lie. She would assume that he felt some shame in his attempted assault on the One King yesterday. He didn't need to go into why he was staying away from the keep. Besides, Stroud was still watching. The Azari were a riddle he hadn't solved yet. They were formidable. He would find a way to overcome them when the time came.

For the time being, he had to trust that they would keep Saissha and Aenguz safe. They would help him maintain his oath by protecting the Lord of the Akkeidii. And they would also help him maintain his own personal oath he had sworn to protect Saissha. The One King and Stroud had said that no one had ever been killed in Earthmight. He had to trust them. What was he going to do? Shadow Aenguz and Saissha everywhere they went among allies? Aenguz had ordered him to discover the state of the One Army and that was what he was going to do.

He walked with the line of men and soldiers toward the mustering point of the One Army. Men from the vales mixed with soldiers from the keep. The soldiers talked with one another, but many of the other men did not know them or others from the other vales. They looked nervous and sheepish. No one talked to him. He was headed toward the camp just like they were.

It was comforting to walk with soldiers, except for the fact that Kachota was not with him. His brother's absence was omnipresent. Lokah had become a friend, even a brother-friend, but he was not Kachota. He hoped his brother would find safe passage back to the Mashu. The delay caused by the Cleve and the One King's edict might work in their favor. If Kachota could relay what had happened and the clan lords were convinced, then the Akkeidii might reach Inverlieth by the time the Cleve was cleared and the One Army persuaded to join the fight in the Upper Lands. His father would not be hard to convince once he knew his eldest son was alive. When he saw his father and his brother again, it might be at the head of the train of the One Army. He began to think about that day, even though the One King had forbidden the Cleve to them. Still, he missed his brother.

The pavilions of the One Army rose on an elevated flat to his left. The soldiers and men turned off the road and headed for them. There was a larger tent, presumably a command pavilion, and some similar smaller tents. There were long barracks. Men stepped out of those and formed into lines before heading off into the wider field. There were mess tents with large cook fires and rows of tables where many ate.

Men were busy setting poles for additional shelters, while others loaded and unloaded wagons or refitted confiscated ones. The scene resembled a construction camp more than a war camp. Carpenters and smiths worked in open spaces littered with wood shavings, seemingly building frames for stacked cots. The smiths appeared to be handling small metalwork, their tents open on all sides to let the wind pass through.

The new men were directed to a line of desks, where they were met by soldiers who asked questions. They scribbled down something and passed the recruits through. They were then hustled through a tent, and when they came out, they were laden with clothes and a sword. They looked more scared when they came out.

Mandavu spied a large fenced-in area filled with horses. He split off from the line of men and soldiers and headed toward the corral of great horses. The surge and smell were familiar. Like that morning in Lihkit, he mimicked what he had learned from Metzly and the *novas*. He climbed through the fence with his saddle.

Brown, black, and blond horses milled and teemed in the corral. They moved around him, their dark black eyes studying him. A large tan draft horse stood before him. Mandavu pantomimed what he had seen in Lihkit. He felt somewhat foolish performing the ritual, but he slid the invisible harness over the horse's head. Then he threw the saddle over its back and cinched it. Then he climbed up.

Three soldiers rode through the herd toward him as he navigated the invisible lines.

"You there! The horses are for the One Army."

"The great horses are free. And the horse chose to bear me."

"We need horses and men to battle the invaders. Dismount and come with us."

Mandavu held his tongue. He wanted to see what they would do next. The soldiers looked at one another and drew in closer.

"You will dismount and leave the horse."

"I was welcomed by the One King. I am from the embassy of Corundum. I am a guest here."

They looked at one another.

"The war takes precedence."

An Azari rode up and spoke to the soldiers. "He is from Corundum in the Upper Lands. He is a dignitary; he is not from the Lower Lands. He is not for the war yet."

The soldiers turned, and Mandavu rode behind them out of the corral.

Mandavu circled the edge of the construction and intake area. In a field beyond, he saw squads of men marching in unison back and forth. Beyond that, more long tents with troughs lining them bordered a large oval. Another rectangular corral held scores of great horses.

In an open field, soldiers rode and swung at straw men planted in rows. The horses wore heavy leathers, and straps were wrapped around their heads. Men pulled and tugged at the leather lines to direct the turns and stops.

Other men lined up to strike wooden totems. The chaos of shouts and galloping and tools and wagons filled the wide space. Mandavu saw scores of arrows trace into the sky in the distance.

It was so different than the training he had been taught as an Akkeidii. But the Akkeidii were ready to assemble at a moment's notice. They focused on fighting and forming into lines and smashing into others as they would an enemy. They practiced the five forms and trained with spears and shields and Akkeidii steel swords. They practiced with their *montmorillionite*. They ate together, slept together, trained together. Considerations for comfort were scoffed at, as if it might soften them. What comforts could they hope for out on the battlefield? Why practice having those things now? There would be no comforts during a war. The Akkeidii reasoned that the sooner they defeated their enemies, the sooner they could drink around a warm fire.

He rode on and came upon a caravan. Wagons were being filled with food and supplies. Mounted horses wore protective leathers, a kind of soft armor. They were about to leave. The head of the column pointed south.

He counted forty men in the caravan. Then he counted the mounted riders. Soon he realized he would need more time. More men were coming every day, and many were leaving on the task of meeting the invaders to the south. There were perhaps a few thousand men here, but he couldn't be sure he'd seen all of them. The field stretched on into the distance.

"Looks like we have some riding to do. I hope you're up for it." He patted the horse's neck. He would need more time to get a reliable number. And all of these men were at different levels of expertise. Any number would have to be qualified between those with experience and those who had never handled a sword.

It would take some time, but he didn't have another choice. And he still didn't have an answer for the garrison at the Cleve. He would need that information too. But he had an idea of how he might get that.

32

SMITHY

As Mandavu headed away from the keep, Aenguz and the others left the Stair Guard and headed down the road toward Earthmight.

Stroud did not follow them to the One King's Keep. He took a seemingly innocuous position on the road and stared down at the ground, opening the breadth of his peripheral vision to all the Azari.

Sunlight blazed on the complicated chiaroscuro web of polygonal joinery on the face of the Plateau. The road filled gradually with soldiers filing out toward the training grounds. Keep stewards flowed up and down the road. Some bore aged family members toward the keep; others poured into the tent city to help the people there. Grain stewards rolled empty carts back to the keep after passing out all of the barrio bread. There was an undercurrent of fear and uncertainty in them, which they tried to bury underneath their duties.

"Will you try and talk with the One King today?" Aenguz asked Legerohn.

"Not today. He is set on his strategy. In truth, I did not expect to find the One King at odds with the passage between the Upper and Lower Lands. I have not yet thought of a way to counter his thoughts and fears since they are also my own." Legerohn smiled wryly at Aenguz. His eyebrows raised and drew lines on his forehead.

"If I could somehow get word to Mond and my forces, and I knew that the One Army would attempt the Cleve, I would tell them to march on the Dimmerdross. Then I would be able to offer something to the One King. My heart tells me we could wipe away the barrier."

If Akkeidii forces were nearer, Aenguz would do the same. They'd take on the wood, even if it meant burning it down. It was something Legerohn simply could not do. Aenguz had to rely on Kachota and his ability to persuade the clan lords to bring the Akkeidii army to him. But Kachota was weeks away from the Mashu. What could he do without men? He had seen the Ruinwaster-led army in the Divine Oculum. They would need all three armies aligned together.

Aenguz empathized with Legerohn. "There is an answer to be found in the Cleve. If the Divider has set the barrier, then there is a riddle at the heart of it. He must fear what the uniting of the Upper and Lower Lands might do to his plans." Morgrom's plans confounded Aenguz. The Cleve was part of it, and the *verrandulum* too, but he needed some time to contemplate what Morgrom intended. And he needed time to come up with something to counter it. Hopefully, the Divider was unaware that they were even there.

The Plateau blocked the Spire. The round intersection before the gate was a bustle of activity. The road from the south was packed with wagons and horses. Horse-drawn wagons bearing fish were being hauled up the road from the shore below. Stewards directed traffic as a steady line of people issued out from the massive gate.

The blue stretched out to the horizon like an uncreated earth. The vastness of the Sunfall Sea was its own barrier. It was as impenetrable as the Spine. But Aenguz had seen the Sallow's barges. Perhaps this was the avenue of attack.

Saissha signaled a keep steward and asked for Sutton. With the aid of a nearby Azari, a steward was called to lead them.

A sturdy woman, a keep steward, arrived and led them into the flow through the gate and up the *montmorillionite*-lit ramp way.

At the first landing, the company parted ways. Legerohn, Saissha, and Chimere walked up into the keep, and Lokah asked the keep steward for help to see the smithy and the armory.

Aenguz watched his loremaster disappear into the Plateau. He hoped Lokah would have good luck unraveling the puzzles he had given him.

———◆———

LOKAH FOLLOWED THE KEEP steward around the main entrance of the stables to another corridor that led straight ahead into the depths of the Plateau. He bore his weapon, but the leather straps wrapped around it were coming apart. The keen edges of *montmorillionite* were cutting through. He would have to make himself a proper Akkeidii scabbard for his weapon.

He listened while the steward explained what was above and on either side of them. She pointed to the wall to her left and told him about the giant cisterns in the plateau that held water for the keep. Lokah could feel an ominous pressure through the angular ribbed black stone. It reminded him of the footings at Galangall Wash.

Lokah took note of the things beyond the walls, but he was more attuned to navigating the halls. Corundum had been a maze, and on the day he rushed to stop the Counsel Lords from sealing the Well of Sorrows, he was lost in the keep. Only by holding that small boy by the scruff of his neck and frightening him into giving directions had he reached the top of the keep. He wouldn't let himself get into that position again. But Aenguz was relying on him for far more than navigating Earthmight.

The steward explained about the grain stores to their right. Crops were collected to not only feed Earthmight, but also any vales that experienced greater bouts of blight. Grain stewards managed that charge.

Aenguz placed a greater responsibility on him. He was a loremaster now to the Lord of the Akkeidii. It had been a small ceremony in the sanctum. It was nothing like how he had expected it would be back in the Mashu - surrounded by his clan, granted the title by the Kriel Clan Lord, the other ascended Kriel loremasters, his father and his mother, his uncle-fathers, and his brother-friends all around him. That was how he had imagined it. But nothing had gone the way he had expected.

He had to find a way to unlink the Dagba Stone. The One King's edict holding them in the Lower Lands was nothing next to the prospect of leaving the stone and Aenguz's weapon behind. He could not return to the Mashu without it. There would be no explanation that would be accepted.

The keep steward went on about the process of supplying the smithy. Raw ore was carted in, along with salvaged metal from plows and other tools from the vales, all re-purposed to forge weapons for the One Army.

She led him down a long hall until he could hear metal clanging, and the smell of soot and smoke filled the corridor. Men came in from the other direction and turned into doorways to their right, Lokah's left. The steward led Lokah into the storehouse where the ore and other formed metals were piled for the smithy beyond. Men were picking through surrendered plows and loading them into a small, heavy cart. He searched for the glow from the collected *montmorillionite*, but he could see nothing.

They walked through to the further wide portal. The chamber

opened up before him. Hot air hit him, and the familiar smells of molten metal and carbon assaulted him. It was similar to an Akkeidii forge for steel and other metals. There was no *montmorillionite* that he could see, or an Akkeidii forge, but the space was filled with men working at the common forges shaping molten metal and feeding fires. She waved over one of the metal craftsmen and deferred to him.

"This is Gregoire. He is in charge of the smith works."

He was a clean-shaven middle-aged man. Sweat and ashen smudges marked his face. He was slightly perturbed at the interruption, but seemed to collect himself as he came over.

"This is Lokah, one of the Akkeidii from the delegation from the Upper Lands."

He looked Lokah over. He took in Lokah's size and the *montmoril- lionite* at his side. It was enough to reconcile his preconceived notions.

"I am Gregoire, the smith steward. Have you come here to help?"

"He is a dignitary, Gregoire," she replied.

"I am unfamiliar with your processes here, but perhaps, once I attend to my lord's needs, I might be able to assist you in the work here."

"What are your lord's needs?"

"He requires a weapon. If I cannot find a suitable one, then I will have to forge one."

That seemed to satisfy Gregoire. The keep steward left Lokah with him, and she turned to head back to the tunnel where they had come from.

Gregoire walked Lokah through the long high-ceilinged chamber. Forges lined the wall to his left. They were set into the nooks between the edges of hexagonal columns that made up the strong wall. Chimneys and hoods were set above the fires and the forges to draw heat and smoke out and away from the smithy.

Gregoire oscillated between pride in the space he oversaw and the challenges of coordinating all of the demands of the Monomander and the One Army. Forms were ready to take molten metal. Squat anvils like fists were set in rows along with worktables. Every spot was filled with a smith or a craftsman working on some piece of metal for some purpose to serve the army. Young boys darted about at the bark of commands to help, move ore, or feed a fire. They weaved around Lokah and Gregoire. They stopped and started their paths so as not to interrupt the hectic dance.

They walked to the far end of the smithy. A rough rock wall bordered the hexagonal wall at the end - the base of the Spire. It was an overflow area. Broken carts, strange contraptions, and discarded tools with their metal removed were piled into the tight nook between the pillar wall and the raw rock.

"If I cleared some space, may I work here?"

Gregoire looked at the mess as if he couldn't understand the appeal. "If you keep the space clean and avoid getting in the way, then you can work here. But late at night there are fewer people here. If you are to do anything, come after midnight. You would likely find a forge and an anvil free. But you will have to do everything yourself. We are behind on all of our work."

"I will be able to manage. How do you know what to make, and where do you store your finished weapons?"

"We deliver everything to the One Army once it is ready."

That would make counting difficult. It would take time to catalog the weapons. He didn't want to let Aenguz down. Aenguz had named him as his loremaster, but more than that, they had bonded in their travels and trials together. They had spent time poring over the Lay, and they shared a deep passion for the sacred metal. Aenguz experienced things with *montmorillionite* that Lokah could barely conceive of. His own experience searching the liquid pool of *montmorillionite* for proof of life had left him with feelings and impressions about the metal that he had difficulty deciphering.

Seeing Hernus Kriel's skull encased in a helm of *montmorillionite* added a layer of expectation beyond what he already felt from Aenguz. His clan's forefather - Grieg Sidor's best friend - had been here. It looked down on him and seemed to be considering if he was worthy, if he had the capability to reach the depths necessary for commitment and loyalty. The *surasanskeld* lore that fused the metal to the bone was lost now, along with any answers it might hold for his current problems. And Hernus Kriel had not forged his own death mask; Grieg Sidor had done that. Two heroes.

Like Aenguz, he had the wisdom and skill for deep lore. Lokah would have to sink deep into his own understanding if he was to live up to Hernus Kriel's expectations, and Aenguz's.

Gregoire broke Lokah's reverie. "Is there anything else? I have work to do."

Lokah contemplated, and then he asked, "One more thing - where are the leatherworks?

33

DRAYMONDON

Aenguz watched Lokah disappear, and then he turned into the stables. The air was rife with manure, musk, and blood. The smell might throw others off, but for Aenguz, the smell reminded him of the roe deer stables. It also hearkened back to the memories of the pens inside the Sallow's *cog*. They didn't care well for the animals they had taken. He had seen that they were all freed.

Stewards had aprons with silhouettes of animal heads on the front and handprints fanned out from top to bottom along the back. They hurried about from stall to stall and were busy with cleaning and sweeping and shoveling straw or manure. Other people, mostly young girls and older women, stayed with the animals to comfort them. Livestock lowed or slept in the open pens in the vast stable.

Aenguz weaved carefully through the busy stable. He stopped one steward and asked where Draymondon was. The young girl directed him to the back of the stable. He passed a handful of tables, dodging the people and the stewards. A ewe was in labor, and steward midwives were locked in and focused on delivering the lamb.

The commotion lessened a bit, but most of the stalls were filled. Some of the animals - old steers and old horses - kneeled on the ground in a kind of repose. An occasional steward was there, sweeping or cleaning the stall. He recalled cleaning stalls similarly in the Sidor Deerherd shelter. His grandfather had insisted he do it. He had hoped Aenguz might become a Deerherd.

At the last distance, before the stable turned back into a corridor, Aenguz found Draymondon. A steward was brushing his coat. She was a young woman wrapped in a light black shawl. Her apron tailed out from underneath it. She pulled a brush in long strokes over Draymondon's rear.

"My lord," she started.

Aenguz came up to Draymondon's face so that his one eye could see him. He took his face in his hands and stroked the long nose. "Would you like to go for a ride?"

Draymondon blinked.

"I am going to take him out."

"Yes, my lord."

"Thank you for taking care of him."

"I am an animal steward, my lord."

"Tell me, what do those handprints on the back of your apron mean?"

"When we finally accept the path of stewardship, we are given these aprons. All of the animal stewards mark the apron with their hands. It tells us that they are all behind me. They all support me. We all support one another."

Aenguz nodded at the sign of unity.

He took the saddle from the knob on the wall and fitted it onto Dray's back. Then he slid the invisible bridle on.

He led Carina's horse through the stable and down the ramp in line with the outflow of people, horses, and wagons. Draymondon held his head high, and though the hair and whiskers around his mouth were white and gray, the years seemed to fall off of him.

Aenguz led him away from the cataract at the gate and mounted him. He pulled his hands out and tapped his side like Carina had shown him to ride out toward the tent city, but Draymondon turned toward the road that led down to the Sunfall Sea. Aenguz felt foolish trying to right the horse, and his face flushed red and grew hot. What would Carina think of him?

Draymondon walked down the road, navigating easily around the horses that hauled wagons of fish up from the shore. Aenguz kept trying to turn him around, but eventually he let the old horse have his way.

The Sunfall Sea filled the horizon, a blue plain glittering with gems. The shadow of Earthmight blotted out the gleam of the water to the right on the further side of the curved wall that ran out into the water.

The breakwater formed a perfect curve of hexagonal pylons, with the tallest ones lining the outer ring and the rows gradually descending toward the open harbor. Long boats were moored to it, and others were rowing out from the protected space. At the shore, the breakwater split. Half led to the road that led up to the gate. The outer half rose up and up to join the seaward wall of Earthmight. It was an imposing wall of hexagonal columns. It ran all the way up to the top of the Plateau. It covered the base of the Spire and wrapped around it out of sight. Rough fists of rock like accusations marked the shore before the wall. Heavy surf rolled in and churned against the rock and the hard basalt. It was a completely different fortress from the sea.

Draymondon crossed the road and trotted onto the shore. A natural cliff rose to his left, leaving a strip of shoreline that weaved southward into the distance. A handful of long boats were drawn up nearby on the smooth-rocked shore. Gentle waves lapped at the soft rocks. Men pulled out nets into the sun. Eyes followed Aenguz and Draymondon briefly, curiously, and then they returned to their work.

Trains of children were led down the shore by stewards. At intervals, they worked at setting stone in deliberate artful patterns on the shore. Spirals, circles, and shapes were fashioned with similar and varied rocks. They were paired with gradations in color that ebbed and flowed. The stewards guided the children to work together, to navigate decisions and opinions.

Farther down, older children built larger and more complex and ambitious installations on the shore. They worked well and deliberately together.

Draymondon flicked his tail and held his head high as they passed the teams of children. Some of them were newer. Their clothes did not have the same uniform look as the clothes of the children from Earthmight. And also, they were timid of the sea. The sound of crashing waves seemed to startle them. The stewards and the children from the keep worked to welcome and integrate them.

They walked on until the shore became more sand than rock. The steady surf counted the moments to the earth's end. Time was running out for Earthmight and the One Army.

Draymondon walked south down the empty beach in flat surf. Sea wind blew through his mane and whipped Aenguz's hair. Aenguz was patient with the old horse that Carina had given to him to watch over. And it gave him time to think.

He had to convince the One King to lead the One Army to the Upper Lands and meet Morgrom there. He did not want to squander the advantage he had in coming through the Spine and warning Thelen. They would have to move quickly, though.

He had promised *a new form of war*. Were the *verrandulum* part of his new tactic? The Erebim were problematic enough, but there would not be enough of them to lay siege to Earthmight. Not unless there were more *verrandulum*. If their real intent was to find gateways for the Ruinwasters, then Urnings might also be in the Lower Lands.

A fear crept up on him like a slow and deadly python. What if they were already here? What if one or both of the Ruinwasters that could inhabit bodies were already here? What if the reason Thelen did not want to attempt the Cleve was because he was a Ruinwaster? How could he even tell if the One King was possessed?

Mere Gurudev worried about the *verrandulum* falling into Morgrom's hands. She had said, *"Morgrom could undo the universe. Destruction and desecration would supplant creation and life forever."* She shuddered at that more than when she told him about Tycho Ruinwaster. *"If Tycho was freed, the Earth would already be in ruin."* Indeed, the Ganzir and the Blasted Flats were evidence of his annihilating power.

On the earth, they would all need forms to inhabit. *"They are all just spirits of malice and woe,"* she had said.

"Shivic leads Oblivion's armies. He gives Oblivion's minions a general and a tactician." Since the earth was not in ruin, Tycho was not yet free, and since he had seen Morgrom's armies in the Divine Oculum, Shivic might already be free. Aenguz had been a witness to two summonings. Were others now free from the Black Earth?

The Chosen Freeholder had told him about Mezekiah. *"His work breaks the walls between worlds. The separations between the White and the Black Earth would be eradicated were he freed to work his ill."* Aenguz could only guess what that might look like. But she had said Mezekiah could also facilitate the release of the other Ruinwasters.

It was the other two that concerned him, that seemed more insidious. They were *"brothers."*

Arkarua and Ophiactii.

Aenguz recalled how Mere's face sneered when she spoke of them. "*These two are murderers, traitors, and possessors. They sow dissent and mistrust. They were the First Emissaries. They divided the last of the Remnant from one another. Always they seek to be together. When they meet and join, they are almost as powerful as Tycho.*"

He remembered her final words to him when he asked how he would know which ones were free. "*Only the Earth knows,*" she said. "*Their coming presages the Earth's doom.*"

The cliffs undulated into the distance as if they had been shorn off by some titan's blade. Draymondon slowed as if he sensed Aenguz's gloom. He sniffed the air and slapped the water.

Another fear gripped him. What if one of the Azari was possessed? Would they all be compromised if one was inhabited? Could he trust Stroud at all? If either Thelen or the Azari were possessed, they would be helpless against any onslaught. The Azari as enemies would be impossible to defeat. And if the One King did not agree to attack the source of Morgrom's power, then they would just be chasing *verrandulum* forever, like wildfires on dry, rugged terrain.

Morgrom couldn't know that he was here. He might or might not know that the Dagba Stone was no longer in Corundum. He could not know that his chosen Last Emissary was working against him. With the warning delivered, Aenguz felt a small relief. But now he was engaged in a battle against a god. And the allies he hoped to find were not emboldened or courageous enough to fight back.

As Draymondon turned back toward Earthmight, Aenguz began to process what it might mean if this was going to be his new home. If Lokah couldn't free the stone, and if he couldn't find a way to persuade the One King to let him attempt the Cleve, then he would be forced to fight and die here. It didn't feel like a noble sacrifice, but rather a complete failure of leadership.

34

THE FIRST LINK

It rained the day the Stair Guard left. Saissha, Aenguz, Legerohn, and the other leaders of the embassy stood in the cold gray morning while the corallel tents were stowed on the sleds.

Aenguz gave up the tent he, Lokah, and Mandavu shared. They might as well spread out while they camped at the foot of the Spine, he reasoned. They had taken over the tent Saissha and Legerohn had shared with Chimere. The three of them had already taken up quarters in Earthmight.

Stroud was not there. Another Azari kept watch over the departure.

Chimere gathered together a bundle of bandages, healing herbs, and poultices for the Stair Guard. He also helped assemble the supplies for them. It was a holdover from when he helped corral food in the refectory at Corundum, when the others were scouring for a way to find Aenguz after he had disappeared into the Well of Sorrows. He tracked down the different keep stewards and pressed them for the things the Stair Guard would need.

Gathering enough horses took the most time. After Mandavu's

"procurement" of the blond draft horse, the soldiers that managed the great horses for the One Army would not release any to them.

Fortunately, there were *novas* among the people from the vales, and they helped the Stair Guard retrieve enough horses, far from the tent city, for the expedition to the Spine.

In the short time they spent together, the Stair Guard grew attached to the determined young women that sought to ride one day with the Free People. Lokah and Mandavu reported about the nighttime escapes by some of the Stair Guard to rendezvous with the *novas* they had become enamored with.

So, it was with an additional layer of sadness that the soldiers from Corundum climbed onto their horses for the last time in the tent city.

Saissha named a leader among them, a man by the name of Nedenthal. Braydehn was an option for them, but the men liked the idea of having a hero among them. If he became their leader, he might move too far away from the comradery that held them together as a team more than any leader could. As it was, Nedenthal was respected, and he listened to his men. He reminded them all of Einki in a way, and it was perhaps for that likeness that they were welcoming of Saissha's choice for them.

Saissha said some words and wished them good fortune in finding a path over the Spine. She reminded them of her charge to have a messenger return every ten days. With travel time, they might see a Stair Guard once or twice again before the first snows fell. Though she kept a brave face, Aenguz could see the worry beneath it. Legerohn stood to her left, both men steadying her like a pair of buttresses.

Mandavu rode out with them. He had navigated around the fields where the One Army trained, and he knew of a road that led eastward.

Some *novas* stood at the edges of the nearest tents and watched the young men as they rode off as if they too were going to war.

With their tents gone, it was time for Aenguz, Lokah, and Mandavu to take up quarters in the Spire. Keep stewards stood nearby to take up the few bags of clothes and supplies the Akkeidii had.

Aenguz wondered if this was a kind of surrender or defeat. Although they had *montmorillionite* to keep them warm, the mornings were getting colder. The willing and ready hospitality of Sutton and the keep stewards was too tempting not to accept. In a way, it seemed to Aenguz that they were taking a large step toward accepting the reality of the One King's edict and welcome. This was to be their new home. If the Stair Guard didn't find a way up into the mountains, the embassy would become part of the defense against whatever siege Morgrom had in mind.

They climbed the ramps and crossed the Plateau. Lokah checked with Aenguz before they crossed the bridge over the amphitheater. Legerohn and Saissha paused too. Aenguz kept his eyes forward, avoiding the depths below and the judging eyes of Hernus Kriel ahead.

Sutton met them at the mouth of the Spire. He led them through the entrance and up into the keep. They climbed to the upper tier, where apartments and suites were set aside for dignitaries. Sutton assured them as they walked that if they needed any clothes, they had only to ask. They would be more than happy to provide them with whatever they needed.

Aenguz knew that he could come and go from Earthmight, but farther up in the keep, he just felt less and less sure. Azari were everywhere, but there was no sign of Stroud. They could speak to him through the Azari, but Aenguz wanted to talk to him alone - wanted to talk to him as he had the night of the conclave in the covert, privately and unwatched.

They came to a corridor, and Legerohn and Saissha showed him their rooms. Aenguz saw that they looked out east over the tent city and the One Army's training fields beyond. They came to three open doors, and the Akkeidii looked in. Aenguz did not cross the threshold at first. He inspected the door for a lock, confirming that it could be opened and closed easily. The lock was on the inside. Aenguz chose a room. But then he and Lokah agreed on a room in the middle, with Lokah and Mandavu on either side. The keep stewards moved to place their few belongings.

Aenguz stood in the hallway. It felt like giving in. Legerohn and Saissha stood by to reassure him.

"Lord Aenguz, there is one thing our lord king requests," Sutton asked with a sudden placating timidity. "He asks that the Dagba Stone be kept in a more secure place - a place overseen by the Azari, where it may be warded."

Aenguz froze. Adrenaline seeped into his heart. Lokah gripped his weapon and let a strap unwrap. Azari watched on both ends of the hall, but they did not move.

Sutton continued, "The One King merely wishes to keep it safe and preserve your privacy. Otherwise, an Azari would have to stand in your apartment."

Aenguz looked at Legerohn and Saissha as if he had been betrayed. "They learned of the Dagba Stone from us," Saissha said. "And they merely wish to protect it. It is yours.

"You are the Stone Bearer," Saissha added. "The One King just wants to keep it safe. It is the chief weapon against the Divider."

Aenguz turned to walk back down the hall.

Lokah mirrored him.

"My lord, my lord, wait! Here, look." Sutton showed him a room that was little more than a closet across the hall from their suites. It was cut into the gut rock, as were the shelves for bowls and linens and other accoutrements. A storage room. A small stone table sat in the middle. "Please, your weapon is yours; he just means to keep it safe here when you are not here. Azari will remain in the hall to ward it when you are asleep or away."

Aenguz's blood boiled. He had hoped to keep the Dagba Stone a secret. But he had to admit that they would find out eventually. He had planned to tell the One King once he was able to talk with him again. He could not watch it all the time, and he had always intended to leave the stone at Earthmight once Lokah found a way to separate it from his *montmorillionite*. The fused weapon already kept him at Earthmight, for the time being, at least. Where it was housed, as long as it was near to him, didn't matter too much.

"It is mine to take, or Lokah's, or Mandavu's, any time we wish?"

"Yes, yes of course. It is just safer here. The Azari can watch in the corridor. The weapon should be kept secure, but it is yours."

Aenguz considered Sutton. Saissha pleaded silently with Aenguz. Legerohn kept his calm and tried to reassure his friend.

Aenguz went over to the small storeroom. He inspected the door. There didn't seem to be a lock, but the door bothered him.

"Lokah, there is no need for this."

Almost as if he had read Aenguz's mind, Lokah unwrapped part of his sword, pressed the flat head into the hinges, and cut through the lesser metal. The door dropped to the floor, and Lokah positioned it in the hallway.

Sutton's eyes widened, but he said nothing.

Aenguz unslung his scabbard, laying it on the table, and Lokah laid his sword across it, whispering words of lore and anchoring it to the tabletop.

An Azari took a position at the farther end of the hall. He stepped into place as if he planned to stand there forever.

The tension in the hallway lessened somewhat. Aenguz didn't say anything to Saissha or Legerohn. He looked at them once and retired to his room. Even with his door open, it seemed like he had willingly walked into a cell.

35

STROUD

Aenguz stepped into the hall the next morning. Flickering raw *montmorillionite* light strobed the bare closet. The broken door was gone, as were the loose items that were on the shelves. It was becoming another sanctum for the sacred artifact. There was no line of people, only the Azari at the far end of the curved hall to his right. Another Azari was at his back, facing the hall leading to the One King's precincts. The Azari looked older than Stroud. His tunic looked more worn, and his hair was the color of muddy salt. He didn't look at Aenguz, just cast his eyes down to the farther end of the hall.

Lokah's wrapped sword lay over the top of Aenguz's scabbard on the stone table. It was not upright yet, as it had been in Corundum. Would that be necessary here? Would people want to see it? No one was lined up to see the Dagba Stone or touch it, but would that eventually come to pass?

They didn't need a chain of people to watch the stone. The Azari alone provided the greatest security for the Keystone of Creation.

Aenguz was at once drawn to his weapon and relieved to be free of it. The push and pull held him still in the hallway. He did not want to give anything away as to his desire toward his weapon, or any hint about what he might want to do with it. As it was, Lokah hadn't found an answer yet to remove the stone.

As he stood there contemplating his immurement and the different walls that were coming up around him, Mandavu met him in the hall. He wore a loose shirt, seeming to be in the middle of getting dressed. As he walked up, Aenguz noticed that his door stood open. Mandavu had been waiting on him. In spite of the Azari, his First still kept an eye on him.

"How have you found your quarters?"

"A welcome break from the tent and the hard earth."

"Where is Lokah?"

"He is in his room." Mandavu pointed to the room nearer the poised Azari. "We split the watch, then he heads off to somewhere in the keep at night. He is fast asleep now."

Aenguz nodded.

"Where are you going?" Mandavu asked as he rolled his shoulders.

"I am going to find Stroud. I have not seen him for days."

"Why not ask that one?" Mandavu inclined his head toward the salt-haired Azari.

Aenguz chastised himself. The Azari's power was omnipresent and difficult to always keep in mind. "Yes, of course."

"Let me finish getting dressed, and I will join you."

"There is no need. I am safe enough. You can explore the keep."

"The stewards are all anxious to show their handiwork. Sutton assured me yesterday when he brought me up here."

"Yes. They do want to share what they oversee here."

"I think I will go find something to eat."

"Just ask a steward."

Mandavu smiled. "Right."

Aenguz went to the Azari. "Where is Stroud?"

The old Azari dropped his head and lowered his voice an octave as he spoke. "I am on the corner of the Plateau overlooking the Sunfall Sea, Message Bearer."

The old Azari raised his head and looked back down the hall.

An Azari was always present in the periphery as Aenguz wended his way down through the Spire. The hallways and stairs filled as Earthmight came to life. Keep stewards were everywhere, and garden stewards too. The handprints on the back of their aprons were vibrant green.

Aenguz passed by balconies that looked out over the sea, then over the Plateau, and then over the tent city. He passed a refectory halfway down and took a slab of warm and nutty barrio bread. He slathered some butter on it and stood as he ate. The dining hall was filled, mostly with women. Mothers fed and corralled their children. The din was loud and lively with an urgency that belied the threat of war that permeated the keep.

Aenguz exited the doorway into the rose granite entrance. Streams of people were pouring up and down the circular stairs. Eyes fixed on him briefly, but there were so many new faces, and the people were so focused on their tasks that they paid him little mind.

He passed under Hernus Kriel and kept his eyes ahead on the vast flat beyond. The plateau was teeming with people, tents and carts. Keep stewards and grain stewards were directing traffic, leading wagons and drovers.

Aenguz wondered how the Azari and the One King could possibly protect so many people. And how many Azari were there?

Aenguz knew that if the One King was going to be convinced to take on the Flayer's Ruinwaster-led hordes, the Azari would be an essential component in convincing him. Perhaps Stroud could be enlisted with Legerohn and himself to make their case.

A cold wind blew over the Plateau. Aenguz made his way through the throng to the corner edge. Long boats bobbed up and down behind the breakwater like leaves on the ocean. They looked like toys in the water. Clouds pulled off the ocean and diffused the sky. Stroud's tunic ruffled in the wind. His short black hair tousled tightly in the sea breeze.

"Stroud," Aenguz called over the wind.

"Emissary," Stroud replied. He did not turn.

"What do you keep watch over?"

"All eyes keep watch around Earthmight, so that we might not be approached unawares."

The Azari were interchangeable. They each saw and stood where the others stood. He was watching over the entrance to the closet across from his room right this instant. How strange it must be to have been alone and then suddenly a part of all of his Remnant. Aenguz itched to know.

"How has it been, being among your people again?"

"It is one thing to see out of the eyes of so many, but it is another to learn what they have seen and experienced over so long a time. I have only heard from a small number of Azari."

"How many are left from those who came to the Lower Lands?"

"As many as remain."

His answer seemed oddly cryptic, but Aenguz let it go. There was so much he didn't understand.

"Are there enough to help fight in this war? I have seen you fight. You and the Azari are strong allies."

"The One Sight is a powerful gift. But it is not without its limits. It is not without its drawbacks. We are not impervious, though we are bound to Time in a way we did not foresee. Like many of Oblivion's assaults, his attack on us was imperfect."

"What do you mean?"

"We did not descend fully out of the Oneness that defined the One Race, as the Akkeidii did, or the Moresi. We are bound to Time. We flow with it, *fixed*. We are half in and half out of the world.

"The One Sight is all that remains from our former lives. We no longer share in the One Mind or the One Heart. We are not unlike the great horses, although they are born and will die. They are more fully within the Law of Creation than we are."

Aenguz reeled at Stroud's words. The scope and scale shrunk him like the heights shrunk the boats below, or even more so. The coming war was larger than anything he had known, but the things Stroud talked about and the machinations of Lord Morgrom were on a scale that dropped him into a chasm of meaninglessness. Being charged as the Last Emissary had brought him partway into that realm. And finding the Dagba Stone placed him squarely in the fulcrum between Creation and Time and the turning of the world. He did not feel equipped to move among such forces. He came back to the problem at hand: the war below.

"What do you think about the One King's strategy?"

"How can I gainsay it? It is the same decision the Azari made."

"What do you mean?"

"Before the Last Battle, before our lands were about to be devoured by Tycho Ruinwaster, we sought to preserve our people. We knew our lands would be lost. We knew then, as we know now, that Corundum was not a fortress, not a defensible position. The safest place was in the Lower Lands. Earthmight was not yet completed, but it was intended to be the stronghold that could stand against Oblivion. We did what seemed right to us. We sent our women and our children down to the Lower Lands by way of the road through the Cleve. An emissary convinced us of the way. An emissary led them. We did not yet know that they were treacherous.

"A number of our men led the way, but once they crossed through, the women and children were no longer with them. We did not know what happened. The emissary was confronted. He was revealed to be a Ruinwaster, the possessor Ophiactii. He was slain. Many Azari died. But he was banished back to the Black Earth - or rather, the body he inhabited was slain. But the dearest part of our people was gone. I made what I thought was the best decision for our people. Look where it led."

The loss was incomprehensible for Aenguz. Aenguz saw Stroud's impassivity as a grief so profound that it might turn the Azari to stone were he not bound to Time as he was.

"Why did you stay in the Upper Lands in Corundum?"

"I made sure all reached the Cleve safely. Oblivion's hordes threatened then, as they do now in the Divine Oculum. Then I returned to aid the Old Counsel Lords and Grieg Sidor against Oblivion."

The realization shocked Aenguz. Stroud had stood with Grieg Sidor. He knew the Venturer.

"You knew Grieg Sidor?"

"I saw him. We all saw him."

Then another realization hit Aenguz. Stroud was not just another Azari. The slight deference that all the Azari showed him came into clear focus. Stroud was their leader.

"Stroud... are you their leader?"

"It is a necessary construct for this world. A way for decisions to be made and communicated with the people and with other leaders."

Here Stroud was, standing like a random sentinel looking out over next to nothing at the edge of Earthmight and the Sunfall Sea. It appeared like the most benign post. Why was he not up with the One

King? The answer was that he didn't need to be; he was with the One King through Hannoch and Sarokin.

Another question came to Aenguz. "Why did you leave Corundum? The Mono Lord sent fifteen Stair Guard to protect Saissha."

"I did not come to protect Saissha." He turned for the first time and stared into Aenguz's eyes. "I came to protect against *you*. Mono Lord Lana needed a bulwark against you as the Last Emissary if you chose to betray the embassy. You hold the Dagba Stone. You bear Oblivion's words. You rent the Vaults of Corundum. You might well be the thing that was forewarned of by him. You might be the One King's doom."

The revelation shook him. That was why he had come, and why the Azari were always near at hand. The Plateau shifted under his feet. The Sunfall Sea spun. He would never be rid of the stigma of being the Last Emissary. And he knew that with that power in potential in the Dagba Stone, he had unknowing access and ability to destroy Earthmight and all the people around it.

"Would you kill me if you thought that I was treacherous?"

"If we saw that you would do anything in the service of Oblivion, we would stop you. If you sought to destroy anyone or anything here, we would banish you."

"Do you think I am a Ruinwaster?"

Silence. Stroud turned his eyes to the cliffs and the vast southern horizon. "There are limits to what the Azari can see."

36

CARINA

Stewards came to Aenguz's room at all hours. Their desire to share the workings and their stewardship of Earthmight with the embassy was nearly compulsive. They wanted to not only prove the worth and value of their stewardship but also welcome the embassy to their new home and their interconnected community. But the needs of the growing throng arriving at Earthmight pulled some of them away.

Saissha and Legerohn embraced their roles as ambassadors. Saissha spent time with the garden stewards. She described to them the flora that would grow from the seeds she had borne over the Spine. Mono Lord Lana had shared with her the details of each type of seed - the needs of sunlight and shade and water. It was too late in the season to plant any of them now, but in the spring, they would be ready to plant the valuable seeds from Corundum.

Legerohn followed a near unceasing line of tours through the Last Stronghold. The woodcraft was of particular interest to him, as the work of his Moresi forefathers was evidenced everywhere. The craftsmen and women who worked with wood asked him about the trees in Inverlieth and about the rare Gildelmun trees that were associated with the Moresi. Some pieces of translucent maple were polished to a gleam to emulate the sacred wood.

Each night, the members of the embassy would dine together in a hall near their quarters. They shared their experiences from the day. Chimere went on some tours, but with all the people gathering to Earthmight from the vales, his help in the infirmary was needed and welcomed. They kept many of the elderly there to provide comfort in their final years. Living in the tent city was no way to rest in their last seasons.

Chimere noted how there were many gravid women. They came to the infirmary to confirm their states. "It seems that everyone is with child. There seems to be no blight at all."

Indeed, the grain stewards and the crop stewards had their hands full with the fields and the orchards that appeared to be relieved of the dampening effects of the Woe Sower. Like the people in Lihkit, they were elated and guardedly surprised about the abundance that was coming, and coming quickly, Legerohn remarked, and Saissha affirmed.

The coming harvest and Harvest Festival gave the idle hands something to do, as all were enlisted to work in the fields. Even the Monomander was impressed upon to release some of the newer members of the One Army to help in culling what the healed earth brought forth. It mitigated the fear and apprehension about the Erebim and *verrandulum*. With the abundance of the harvest, the people were safe in retreating within Earthmight, surrounded by the One Army and the great horses, flush with stores.

Mandavu reported over a plate of baked fish that caravans went out every few days or so. They went primarily to ferret out men and or women who did not heed the One King's words to leave the vales and farms to come to Earthmight. The One Army continued to train as autumn settled in and the warm days of summer finally left. Horses were corralled and outfitted and became part of the force that would repel the appearing Erebim.

"How many horses have come into the One Army?" Aenguz asked over a plate of roasted mutton seasoned with rosemary and spiced salt.

"It is hard to say. There are two main corrals with more being built. A horse is worth four or five men," he said offhandedly. "A thousand horses, maybe more," Mandavu said in between bites.

Three or four thousand men. It was Mandavu's way of communicating the numbers subtly to Aenguz. Mandavu glanced at Aenguz with a slight flicker of uncertainty. He was still counting.

Lokah spent most of his time in the Plateau. He was helping to forge weapons and share Akkeidii knowledge of metal work. He was able to get some leather from the tannery and some tools to begin work on a proper Akkeidii scabbard for his weapon. The stone table in the closet across from their rooms was covered in scraps of leather. It also allowed him time to ruminate over the stone and how to free it.

"If it was not so busy at that entrance of the Spire, I would like to look closely at Hernus Kriel's *surasanskeld* fused helm." It was an avenue he had remarked to Aenguz that might hold an answer to freeing the stone. There was an example of lore here, though they both admitted, when they pored over the locked Dagba Stone, that it wasn't really fused, but rather fitted. Most of the time, Lokah worked down in the smithy late at night, and he yawned in between bites of barrio bread and roasted meat.

Aenguz was grateful that some of the Chief Stewards had grown so busy. The water steward, ale stewards, and healer stewards were among others that tried to get some of his time. Legerohn stepped in and filled the place for Aenguz.

The Harvest Festival was fast approaching, and with it, their window to cross the Spine was closing. The option of attempting the Cleve was becoming more necessary. Aenguz wasn't sure how to approach Thelen about attempting the Cleve. And with the delay, he worried that they might get too settled in Earthmight. They all played the part well, as if they were resigned to staying there, but it seemed that it might not be so much of a charade as the hospitality and comfort of Earthmight surrounded them.

The reprieve from the busy stewards finally gave Aenguz more time to see Draymondon. He made his way into the stables and Draymondon's stall. A steward was standing behind the tall old horse. He greeted and thanked the steward and asked how Draymondon was doing. When he came under his neck, he saw Carina.

She seemed lost in a thought so deep that she might have stood at Draymondon's side forever. Her hazel eyes were focused elsewhere. They took a moment to register him. At first, she seemed to be perturbed, as if she were pulled out of her own self-prescribed private space. She was connected with Draymondon as she stroked him, but she was not thinking about him. She wore a dark green blouse with a dark leather vest that fit tightly over her. It looked official in a way, formal to a degree. She wore her round helmet like a mask. Her curly hair was bound up tight underneath it. Her leggings were smooth and tight, and her doe skin boots came up to her knees. A short dark cloak like a shawl rested on her shoulders.

"What are you doing here? Why are you here?" Shock and joy fumbled Aenguz's words and made them sound like an accusation.

Her mind hadn't yet surfaced from the depths where it lingered. Her eyes flickered, surprise flashing briefly before settling into a different expression. She seemed both troubled and intense. She recognized him and a place he held in her memory, and she softened at his familiar face and something more. "We came last night via the shore road." Whatever tremors she wrestled with, she mastered herself and brought her attention back to Draymondon. "He looks well. He seems happy here. Have you ridden him?"

"Yes, yes, I have been pressed by the stewards to learn about the keep, but I have taken him out several times since we arrived here. I came to ride him now." Aenguz touched Dray's neck and moved closer to Carina. His heart charged and pulled him toward her.

She swallowed, her throat contracting. "I am riding the perimeter for the Queen. We could ride together."

Aenguz went to the wall, grabbed the saddle, and threw it easily over Draymondon's back. Draymondon stepped heavily, as if he was readying his old joints. Aenguz fitted the saddle. He wanted to impress Carina and show her that he remembered all that she had shown him. He was foolish and elated. His one regret was that they would not share in riding Draymondon together. He wanted to feel her against him.

Carina led the way, and Aenguz followed behind her. His eyes caressed her. She came to a stall with a gray-and-white horse that looked like it had run through a puddle of ash. Its lower half was all gray and black specks, but its mane was white as fresh snow.

She saddled the horse, and together they led them out of the stable past the busy stewards and down the ramp in line with the flow of traffic.

Clear of the roundabout, they mounted. Carina turned her horse toward the wall of the Plateau and rode north in the open space along its face. She looked out over the tent city and mentioned how empty the Lower Lands were - how the vales and farmsteads were nearly empty. "We tried to get the men to come when we came across them, but they were stubborn. They wouldn't leave their fields. The Queen said that the horses would not be coming to help with the harvest. We explained about the invaders, but they would not listen."

They shared worry about the stubborn, reluctant men.

Their talk drifted to their flight to the mound and the fight with the

Erebim. They recounted their race to catch Metzly with more humor than remembered fear.

"How is Metzly faring?"

"She is healing, but it has not kept her from keeping others in line."

They laughed at this too. Metzly's harshness had been a defense that was easy to see now. There was also a relief that she had survived and was recovering.

They passed beside the sheer raw rock that the Spire rested on. They rode onto the hard plain that bordered the rocky cliff that overlooked the Sunfall Sea.

They continued talking about that night and the days that followed. Carina had always wanted to ride with the Queen, but she hadn't expected it to happen so soon. Because of her experiences in the battle and with the embassy, she had been thrust into the role of a councilor to the Queen. It caused no small envy among the other riders. Always, they were looking for ways to prove themselves worthy to the Queen, and Carina had done it in one wild night - a night where she surely would have died if it weren't for him.

Aenguz dismissed her tempered thanks. "You were angry. I understand. The Erebim had violated a sacred place in the Mashu. They killed my brother-friend. I would have killed them then and there if I was not a prisoner."

"Why are they doing this?" she asked. "They slay the great horses wantonly. What is their plan?" It seemed to Aenguz that it was more a question the Queen had peppered her with than one she had.

"The Woe Sower has bestowed the land to the Erebim. He has given them to believe that *we* have taken lands that are rightfully theirs."

She looked at Aenguz curiously. "How do you know this?"

Aenguz didn't want to share with her his connection to Morgrom, but he had a hard time withholding from her. "I was chosen as the Last

Emissary. I was given a message to the Remnant and the Peoples of the Earth. It fell out of my control." Shame flushed him, and he stopped. He didn't want to give her any reason not to like him.

Carina swerved her mount. Her hazel eyes became intense. She pulled back and stared at him all the way.

"You have seen the Woe Sower? What are you?"

"I am the son of Sairik, an Akkeidii Warrior of the Sidor Clan. I am not allied with the Flayer, as we name him in the Mashu. I just came into his presence." The long story was just too big to retell. He prayed that she wouldn't hate him or shun him in that moment.

She regained her previous air. She seemed to recall what she knew of him from all those days of riding together. Another question formed in her.

"What is the hell of the Upper Lands like?" she asked, as if he had specific knowledge of the ruined places in the Upper Lands.

"There are desecrated places," he started. What seemed like a self-indictment followed. "The Blasted Flats east of my home. The Ganzir. The lands around Carrowen Celd are all desolate and Ruinwasted. But it is not all like that. My home is beautiful." Thinking about the Mashu only reminded him that he might not ever see it again. Also, much of what he had seen on his journey to Corundum had been blanched and blighted by titanic forces that could turn vast stretches of hale earth into scorched plains. It drew a cloud over him, and words fled.

They turned east, away from the high cliffs to a gentle forest. The Spire greeted the day behind them like a benediction. The tent city was spread out before it.

The pair came to the northwestern edge of the training grounds the One Army had established. They cut a course in the open space between the makeshift barracks and the ever-growing tent city.

"How long will you be at Earthmight?"

"It depends on the Queen and the One King. She is not contented with the support he provides."

Aenguz knew more, having listened in via Stroud that night at the covert. But he was careful not to let on more than he knew. He shared Sorolokova's discontent, but for different reasons.

"But we will likely be here until the Harvest Festival. The One King gives the Free People food and grain to fill the coverts. Now that he finally sends his army out to help, maybe we can regain our lives." Then, she asked, "How long are you here for?"

"Forever. We cannot leave. The One King has forbidden us to enter the Cleve."

She looked at him with such hard discernment, he thought he might fall off of Draymondon's back. "You are going to stay here forever? Why not climb over the Spine, like you did to come here?"

"There may not be a way to cross. Corundum was already high up in the Spine and afforded easier access to the reaches. But I would not hazard it again from here, even if there were a way. We lost two men on the way over, and it would most likely kill Legerohn. He is susceptible to mountain sickness. I will not risk his life."

"What about your family? And your home?"

"I will never see either again." The embassy was trapped. The One Army was nascent. His life was not his own. "I am responsible for so much as lord of my people. My life has not been my own since my father died." It was the first time he truly understood that. He was realizing it and revealing it to her all at once. "I wanted to be like him. When he died, I thought I would never be like him or become what he wanted me to be. Now, I am beginning to understand all the duties and responsibilities he had. I think I understand why he was gone so often when I was a boy. He cared so much for others, for our people."

Aenguz couldn't meet her eyes. His guile put him in a position to withhold so much from her. He ached to tell her what he aimed at, but he couldn't. He didn't even know if he could succeed.

They crossed the road that led to the keep and then turned west along the fields and the tall stalks that formed a wall. There were people working amidst the wavy rows.

They finished their circuit in silence. They led their horses to the roundabout and back up to the stable. They parted to house their horses. Aenguz unsaddled Draymondon and then stroked his nose.

Carina came into the stall. She looked into Aenguz's eyes.

He swallowed a knot.

She was saying something about reporting back to the Queen, but the words mumbled out of her. He couldn't make them out, anyway. His heart twisted and pulsed. He stepped to her, driven by a tsunami of an urge. He wrapped his arms around her and brought his mouth to hers. She welcomed it and kissed him back. She pressed into him. Their mouths opened, their tongues probing and circling. It was as if they were feeling each other in the dark. Carina let out a soft moan. A tremor shook her. Aenguz's hands moved all along her back from her shoulders to the top of her legs. He couldn't pull her hard enough into him. Her helmet dropped to the floor.

After an age, they pulled away, breathless and astounded. Hot inertia grabbed them, and they came together again and kissed. Then Carina pulled away. She picked up her helmet, left the stall, and disappeared into the keep.

37

RENDEZVOUS

Thoughts of Carina's lips and mouth kept Aenguz from sleep. His first thought when he woke was of finding her - finding her alone.

He reached the private dining hall the embassy shared with the intention of leaving for the stables as soon as he finished his morn meal. There were more stewards there than usual.

The Chief Grain Steward, Monguerra, was with Legerohn. His brown eyes were big saucers, kind and attentive. Aenguz drifted by the pair and urged them to continue. Monguerra was explaining to Legerohn about the old grains that had survived the blight. Einkorn, he explained, was a staple of all of the breads in Earthmight. But with the people from the vale bringing in other grains, he was able to mix and experiment. "There will be some new breads for the Harvest Festival." He motioned to the grain steward with him. A woman with long gray hair, that was tousled as if she had just woken up, arranged the loaves before the Prince and Monguerra. Aenguz took the opportunity to continue to the platters on the long table against the wall.

Saissha and Mandavu were surrounded by a gaggle of garment

stewards. They had bolts of deep red cloth laid out on the table before them. Saissha smiled graciously as they explained about the profusion of red berries that had come this year that they used to make the dye that colored the fabric. They would make a dress for her. She demurred, "I am a Counsel Lord. My robe is enough for me." But they kept pressing her: "It is for the Harvest Festival."

Mandavu ate standing up beside her. He and Saissha's plates were half eaten before them. Two of the stewards were measuring Mandavu's frame. They were flustered that he wouldn't hold still. He looked to Aenguz like he was ready to spirit Saissha away from the cluster of stewards. Mandavu tried to motion Aenguz over to them, but Aenguz navigated away to eat.

He stood, eating at the buffet. He cut a slab of barrio bread a loaf with hunks of cheese and green hot peppers inside. He spread rich butter on the warm bread and slapped thin strips of salted pork on top. He chewed quickly, more out of urgency than hunger.

He skirted Mandavu and Saissha as he ate. Just then, a tall, thin woman met him. Long straight golden hair framed her face and shoulders. Interlocking waves of blue marked the curve of her chest on her Steward's apron.

"Lord Aenguz, I have not yet shown you the waters of Earthmight."

Aenguz nodded, his mouth too full to respond.

"I am Yasdriine, the Chief Water Steward of Earthmight. You have not seen how we see to the water that is the source of life here in Earthmight. You have not seen the cisterns after a rain."

Aenguz nodded as he cleared his mouth. He held some curiosity, but there was only one thing and one person on his mind.

Just then, Lokah appeared in the doorway. Sleep clotted his eyes. He yawned long as he surveyed the focused commotion in the dining room.

Aenguz walked over and drew Yasdriine toward Lokah. "Yes, of course, I will see the cisterns, but Lokah…" He swung his arm around Lokah's shoulder. "…knows about water in the earth. He called to it once when we were outside the One Forest. He would love to see the cisterns with you."

Lokah blinked at Aenguz. "Well, I was going to get something to eat and go to-"

"That is perfect. He will be ready to join you as soon as he eats."

"But Lord Aenguz, I was hoping to show you."

"Yes, yes, I will see the water. But I have matters to attend to concerning the great horses." He slid Lokah in front of him and turned out of the dining hall.

He gobbled down his loaded barrio bread as he walked down the Spire. The halls were crowded. Keep stewards, grain stewards, and other stewards with their own unique logos on their aprons smiled at him and addressed him as either "Lord Aenguz" or "My lord."

Other denizens were flowing down the curved ramps and wide stairs of the Spire. The thrum of industry and purpose was in their gait and their eyes.

At the rose marble entryway, he followed in the flow of people who walked down a ramp below the bridge that led across the amphitheater. The ramp wended to a covered pathway beneath the bridge that connected into the Plateau. A colonnade of gothic openings framed the bridgeway. In the Plateau, a pair of ramps split in either direction, to the left and right. They switched back down to the bottom of the Plateau. Narrow windows dotted the corridors all the way down. He looked out on the amphitheater. The seats floated by as he descended. The separation kept his vertigo at bay. Near the bottom, he followed an animal steward when she turned into the tunnel at the center of the Plateau.

Stewards filled the long corridor, and *montmorillionite* light lit the ceiling. He smelled the stables before he saw the commotion of animals and animal stewards.

He went to Draymondon's stall. There was no one there. No steward. No Carina.

He saddled the one-eyed horse and talked to Dray to distract himself. He passed over the spot where he and Carina had kissed, and a gentle headiness swirled him. He took the invisible lines from the invisible harness he had fitted over his nose and led the old horse out.

The wide corridor was packed tight. Aenguz was protective of the one-eyed horse. He got clear of the throng at the roundabout and mounted Draymondon on the grassy sward before the Plateau.

There, with two other Free People, was Carina. She saw him and turned back to the riders, bidding them farewell. She rode her spotted mare to him.

"Are you ready to ride?" Her hazel eyes gleamed. She wore a soft leather coat over her fine wool vest. Her helmet was tied to her saddle, and her tight curls were fashioned into tight braids. A few stray curls poked out here and there.

Aenguz's face glowed and warmed. Dray pranced over to her and swapped steps in place before her. Carina let the smallest smile slip, and then she took off at a run along the fading green. Draymondon took off right after her. Aenguz urged him on, but he didn't need to. Draymondon followed his first rider in a joyful gallop as fast as he could go. Carina stayed ahead of them.

They rode the same circuit around the expanding tent city. There were more fires to battle the chill and more men to join the One Army.

They rode a careful arc around the training grounds and corrals. Scores of Free People tended the growing herd of kept great horses. They helped as soldiers of the One Army fit heavy leathers on the horses.

They finished the circuit quickly. Carina led the way up into the stables and brought her horse into Draymondon's stall. They didn't speak much on their ride, but it was clear that Carina wanted to get back.

They unsaddled their horses quickly. Stewards brought water and grain for the horses. When the stewards left, Carina drifted to the corner of the stall just inside the door.

Her eyes smoldered. Aenguz was drawn to her, just like Draymondon had been outside. He let the heat of his desire override him. He bent to kiss her, then he squeezed her and lifted her until her toes cleared the straw.

He walked her back into the corner. Her leg snaked around his, and she settled into a spot on his thigh. She began to rock into him. Aenguz pressed her into the wall and matched her rhythm. Their kiss was deep and unrestrained. Mouths tongued and gaped and kissed. Their faces were wet with saliva.

Aenguz held her to the wall. He reached into her leather coat and squeezed her breasts through the wool vest. Carina fumbled at the buttons. Her face was all yearning and pleading. Aenguz felt her through her shirt. She moaned then, and he lost himself. They rode one another to a sudden grinding climax.

Her leg relaxed, and he let her down. Soft kisses followed her to the ground. Carina looked up into his eyes and breathed, "Tomorrow?"

The next day, they rode their circuit quickly. When they returned to the stall, the horses conspired to give the pair their privacy. They crowded at the door and snorted and huffed, recovering from their hard ride.

When they were abroad together, they comported themselves as colleagues. But in the relative privacy of their stall, they surrendered to their intimacy. Their clothes dropped quickly. Hands worked on each other's loops and belts. He pinched her hard nipples and then pulled her in close. Her hands gripped his thick shoulders and taut backside.

Their eyes were as hungry as their mouths. They hugged and squeezed each other in a hot, carnal embrace. Once they climaxed, they collapsed together in the fresh straw, spent and sweaty.

Carina dressed quickly. Aenguz studied her every line. She bent down to kiss him and then stole away into the Plateau.

38

INNOCENCE LOST

Rain washed the night. In the bespeckled storm, glints of raw *montmorillionite* light caught the sleet and rain and made it look like the stars were falling in droves out of the night sky. Aenguz lay in bed in night-clothes, dreaming of Carina beside him.

The Harvest Festival a few days before still reverberated for him. But it was Carina who dominated his thoughts.

Aenguz had fought to keep his eye on Sorolokova when she had come with her retinue to greet the embassy. The Queen's riders, all with similar but unique dresses, had flanked her in wings of scarlet. Her braids had been undone, and her lush blonde hair had spilled onto the dress. All of the riders' hair had been free of their tight braids, but Sorolokova's hair had been resplendent.

She had greeted Aenguz formally as the Lord of the Akkeidii and reaffirmed her appreciation to him and the others for what they had done to fight the Erebim and secure the covert. She had called him a "horse-friend" before moving away. The wave of perfume had lingered after they had left.

Aenguz had pivoted in the crowded hall to watch Carina's back.

Her hair had been free and styled, and her curls had danced on the dimples in her shoulder blades.

Legerohn had tried to distract him from staring, but it was the arrival of the One King that ultimately had broken the spell. He had worn a formal tunic and his obsidian circlet. He hadn't worn armor. With Hannoch and Sarokin behind him, he had looked like a king of the Azari more than the war-time leader of the people.

He had been gracious and kind as he had drifted across the room. He had thanked and applauded the stewards for all of their fine work. He had gone to the balcony that overlooked the Plateau and, with the aid of the Azari, had spoken to the whole host assembled there to celebrate the harvest. Stroud had recited word for word Thelen's speech for the embassy, but Aenguz had only half listened to it. He had positioned himself to spy Carina through the throng and waited for her to find him. When their eyes had met, she had smiled so seductively that a thrill had run through his body.

She had come to his suite after the festival in the red dress she and all of Queen Sorolokova's retinue had worn. The back had been open perilously low. The long skirt had had fitted layers like a cascade of roses accentuating the shape of her thighs. Her arms had been covered by smooth red fabric, with a ruffle flirting at each wrist. It had been a tantalizing mix of exposed flesh and sultry curves.

They had been careful of their privacy before, but after the festival, when she had appeared at his door, she had said with her presence and her eyes that he was hers. He had looked at the Azari that stared blankly down the hall for only a moment before taking her in his arms and drawing her into his room.

He had kissed her hungrily, as if his long-burning desire during the festival had left him famished, fumbling urgently with the long sleeves while he had kissed her neck and her breasts.

They had somehow made it to the bed, and he had almost lost himself while she had squirreled her way out of the form-fitting skirt. His shirt had vanished, and his leggings had come off quickly.

They had rolled together on the bed, free of the horses, the bed of straw, and any prying eyes. With those things gone, they could forestall their urgency and savor each other and the lust they shared. They had rolled and grappled, each shifting to a new position the other craved. Aenguz had let her push him down so she could mount him. She had urged him to guide her when his own passion needed leverage and pressure for its expression.

Her aching voice and throaty gasps had shot pulses of electricity through him. They had rocked and heaved, grinding to a climax that had astounded both of them.

He had pulled her back to him and curled around her while they had floated in the glow of their release.

"I have to leave with the Queen tomorrow." She had been forlorn.

"For how long?"

"I do not know, exactly… a few days."

He had hugged her close and pressed his face to her cheek.

"I will wait for you here, and we will leave the stables behind."

She had smiled at this and nestled closer to him.

He thought of that night as he waited for her to return. A knock at the door startled him, and his heart leapt. He hurried to open it, but it was Yasdriine, the Chief Water Steward. Her golden hair was smooth and clean, falling comfortably down her back. Her narrow water steward smock was cinched tight at the waist.

She looked at him intently, seeming to gauge him, to gauge his response to her, and said, "My Lord Aenguz, I hope you will forgive this intrusion, but you promised you would let me show you the cisterns during the rain."

He had dodged her once using Lokah, and one other time several days ago. Now he didn't have a response for her. He excused himself to put on some leggings and a shirt. He grabbed a light coat and followed her into the corridor.

The back-to-back Azari were to his right. The salt-haired Azari's eyes were cast down the hall. They did not look directly at Yasdriine or Aenguz.

She talked about the network of gutters and grates and channels that captured water and the sand traps that filtered it for the apartments in Earthmight. They circled down the Spire in the rainy and sleet-soaked night. "During storms like this, the system could overflow, so the rainwater is channeled into the cisterns in the Plateau."

She led Aenguz over the covered bridge to the switchbacks beyond. They passed few people. Most were in for the night. Those they did see were mostly stewards and Azari.

The corridor under the Plateau was quiet. Raw *montmorillionite* braziers lit the way. They passed only one steward and no Azari.

They came to a fork in the corridor. To the left, sacks of einkorn were stacked on carts where stewards had carried them or would carry them in the morning. Aenguz was looking to his left when Yasdriine stopped. He walked fully into her. She turned and blushed. She pushed herself gently back from him and smiled seductively. "I know that still pools of water may not be very interesting, but you might be surprised by how deep they are. Without the cisterns, we would not be able to keep the gardens watered or provide water for everyone throughout Earthmight. When it rains, the whole system comes alive."

She led him to the right.

A rush and echo bounced off the walls in the distance. They passed the first cistern. The surface churned and rippled. A flat waterfall poured into it from the farther edge.

The sound grew louder. She climbed a short stair. The second cistern churned and roiled as another short waterfall poured into it. Water surged and pulsed over the lip. Hunks of *montmorillionite* were set on the farther wall and cast light like small flickering moons on the waving surface.

Yasdriine climbed the final set of stairs. Aenguz was drawn up. The roar of water surrounded them. They were alone. She stood close to him, touching him so that he could hear her.

"When it rains," she breathed, "Earthmight is filled."

Overhead, a river of water poured in a wide cascade into the center of the last cistern. Waves surged outward from the downflow, the surface rippling and undulating.

"Is this not impressive?" She stayed close to him. Her eyes pulled his away from the awesome rush.

His heart grew louder than the drowning pour. The open space felt constricted.

Her lips parted. She welcomed him to hold her with a look.

He pulled back from her, then a splash interrupted the epic pour. They both turned to the water.

The *montmorillionite*-lit surface was broken by a bobbing shape. He could make out a narrow smock and a tangle of hair. The sound reminded Aenguz of the splash outside the *cog* when the dead fisherman was discarded by the Sallow.

Disbelief twisted her eyes. Aenguz put the shape together as the form turned in the water.

It was a body. Dead.

A steward. A young woman.

The two bent out over the edge of the cistern to confirm what they saw. The body cartwheeled slowly sideways as it bobbed. Yasdriine was distraught.

The waves carried the body to the far wall where they could not reach. They raced to the nearest edge, but the body was too far away.

Yasdriine jumped in. She swam to the body and dragged her toward the edge and Aenguz.

He reached down and pulled the body up and out. He laid her down on the causeway, and then he pulled up Yasdriine.

A dead girl lay next to them. Her throat was split and splayed open. Red seeped into the ribbed tube of her esophagus. Her eyes were a milky gray. Her mouth was open with the horror of an unfulfilled scream. Red water pooled in the morbid cup of her wound. The shock of her final moment, her dead eyes, her pallid skin, and her open throat screamed up at them.

Yasdriine found two boys, grain stewards. Aenguz lifted the dead girl by the legs, and the boys each took an arm. They were white with shock, as if they had taken blows to the head. They all rushed as if she could still be revived. Yasdriine hurried on ahead, her wet shoes slapping on the cold stone. But the girl was dead, and soon, they slowed.

Yasdriine led the way down the corridor. When they encountered the Azari, the sentinel's eyes shifted and fixed on them. He turned in that odd Azari way and followed them. They went down the ramps that led to the lowest quarter of the keep. It was grim within the seaward side wall of Earthmight. The polygonal fitted stones were replaced suddenly by titanic walls of black-edged columns.

They came to a flat hexagonal landing. Stairs led to the right and the left. Aenguz could hear the rain and the violent surf. To the right was a dim chamber formed out of edged black basalt, as if a whole section of the internal sea wall had been removed. Squat basalt pedestals filled the center of the oblong room. Three bodies were wrapped on the three tables nearest the door. At the farther end of the darkened chamber were two square portals. Both were shrouded in obdurate darkness.

The one at the right showed a few worn steps before disappearing into the black. The portal on the left dropped into nothingness. The crash of the sea and the angry rain echoed from it, as if a behemoth snored beyond in the dark.

Yasdriine directed Aenguz and the boys to a tabletop. They set the girl down, and Yasdriine moved her dead limbs into a settled position.

She ordered the two stewards to stand near the door, but she would not let them leave. They cowered there like pale ghosts. Their own shock mirrored the dead girl's.

39

MORS IN KEEP

Forlorn drops hit the floor in the black chamber. They counted out the moments of horror. Aenguz and Yasdriine dripped too, soaked from their efforts to retrieve the girl's body. She lay on the black stone table with her eyes and mouth agape. The long gash at her throat from top to bottom echoed the shock and horror of her last moments. Her cold lips were calm and pale. An ashen sheen colored them, the same cold gray as her eyes. Yasdriine reached over and gently closed them.

The Azari stood in the entrance at the top of the short stair. He stared at her body and Aenguz and Yasdriine, but he did not say anything, and he did not enter the room. The shock did not touch him in any obvious way. His arcane observance to the duty of the One Sight overrode his shock, if he even felt it. What horrors might all the Azari have witnessed over all their time since the Last Battle? But there was something ephemeral in his gaze. Perhaps it was the knowledge that not only did all the eyes of the Azari see them, but that all of their attention was also focused on them too, and not just with a peripheral awareness.

Two more Azari arrived. Then four. They walked past the first and scanned the room, Aenguz, Yasdriine, the two grain stewards, and then the body. They didn't speak a word.

Stroud appeared with the embassy. Saissha was behind him and Mandavu was behind her. She stepped down into the chamber cautiously. Her blue robe was uncinched. Her braided staff was poised as if she meant to call power from it.

Mandavu wore a loose shirt. He searched out Aenguz. He scanned the room as if he were checking for a threat. His brow tightened as he worked to put the pieces together.

Lokah was behind him. He looked at Aenguz too, and then scanned the room much like Mandavu had done. The Prince and Chimere were behind him. Legerohn's shoulders dropped as if some hope he held had failed. Chimere's eyes held fear and surprise.

They circled around the body. One by one they asked, "What happened?" The same question in a chorus rose from them. They asked Aenguz, Yasdriine, and the Azari, as if they were the last to arrive at a macabre parlor game.

The Azari and Stroud tightened perceptibly as one. The One King was at the top of the stairs. Hannock and Sarokin were behind him. Their black-haired heads sat like ravens over his shoulders.

Thelen looked aged, worn down by stress. His armor was gone, replaced by an ornate night shift. His eyes shimmered like damp coals, and he panted, his chest rising and falling as he looked down. He took each step carefully, as if he might lose his balance. Hannoch and Sarokin matched his gait and warded him as if he might topple like an elderly man.

"What happened here?"

The embassy parted to let the One King through.

"She spilled out from the falls into the cistern."

"You two were down there?" Thelen averted his eyes from the girl and focused on Yasdriine.

"I took Lord Aenguz to see the cisterns."

"Why so late?"

"With the rain, the waterfalls…" She trailed off.

Sutton reached the doorway with his Azari behind him. He was out of breath. He was so stricken that he might have been possessed. His face was lined with shock and disbelief. His eyes looked to be housed in loose fists. He wore a long night-shirt under his steward's apron. It hung cockeyed on his tall frame. He looked like a doppelganger of himself to Aenguz, and not the welcoming soul he remembered.

"You found her like this?"

"As we watched the waterfall, she came out and fell into the outer cistern. She was dead. We could not reach her. I jumped in, and Lord Aenguz helped me get her out." Yasdriine's voice wavered like she might cry.

"Who is she?" Thelen asked.

Silence and stillness returned to the death chamber.

Then a timorous voice said, "It is - was - Illia, my king." The other boy nodded unsteadily, as if his own head might fall off.

Sorolokova reached the chamber. Carina and two other riders were with her. Carina scanned the room like the rest. Aenguz met her eyes. She saw the girl, then she looked at the two drenched figures. A sheen of concern approaching accusation colored her complexion.

Sorolokova demanded to know what happened. She began to echo Thelen's questions. She held her perch on the stairs. Telakot was behind her. Sutton echoed them too. They both demanded answers from everyone, anyone. A chorus of "I don't know" met their queries. Their voices echoed off the hard walls and made everything loud and chaotic.

Finally, the One King spoke calmly to Hannoch. Then all of the Azari, including Stroud, said, "Quiet!" in unison.

Everyone quieted. The room stilled.

"Illia," he said to himself. "Who are her parents?"

Sarokin answered, "Her mother is a grain steward. Her father is an archer in the One Army. He trains those new to the bow."

Thelen considered for a moment. "Summon Monguerra and the Monomander. Have them come here. Do not summon her parents yet."

"Illia," Sutton quaked. "She's…she's Elin and Dalmeida's daughter." His words slurred. His breathing was ragged. His Azari held his arm to steady the Chief Keep Steward.

"How could she fall into the drains?" Thelen continued.

"The grates are removed in the lower levels when it rains. It prevents the water from backing up."

"Is there anything that could have caught on her throat like this?"

Yasdriine shook her head. "I do not believe so. The channels are nothing more than enclosed gutters."

Thelen turned to Hannoch. "Did any Azari hear her?" His face ticked as if he had slapped himself. Her throat was gone. What could they hear?

Everyone looked at the rough gash in her throat. The column of her esophagus was laid bare, as if the answer was splayed there.

"Has anyone ever fallen into the channels?"

"Not since I have been a water steward," Yasdriine replied.

Thelen looked to his Azari.

"We know of none," Hannoch replied.

Deliberateness hung in the air.

"Who or what could have done this?" Thelen's eyes were back on her throat.

"What about an animal?" Aenguz asked. "Could an animal be loose in Earthmight?"

Thelen looked at Sutton and Yasdriine. Then he spoke to Sarokin. "Wake Tanna. Ask her if an animal has escaped the stables. An animal that could...attack...like this."

Sutton wheezed. He couldn't catch his breath.

Aenguz regretted the question. The wound was too localized. An animal would have left other marks. It was a killing stroke - a deliberate, silencing killing stroke. He looked at Lokah and Mandavu. They had been trained to take out sentries by attacking the voice pipe. The cut was too crude, but the method was familiar.

Lokah and Mandavu seemed to affirm his thoughts, but they might not know if Aenguz was dancing around a truth he could not share in the room. They stared at him. Their eyes told him that they shared his thoughts.

Sarokin tilted his head down and dropped his voice an octave and said, "'There is no animal loose in Earthmight. Why? What has happened? The stables are closed at night. What animal is loose?'"

Thelen cut off Sarokin with a wave of his hand.

The One King's Azari lifted his head.

"Why? Why would anyone do this to this girl?"

"Oh, no, no..." Sutton was loud and hysterical. "A killing in Earthmight. A murder!" The word "murder" curdled in his mouth. Revulsion torqued his frame; Sutton keened. His Azari held his other arm, but the Chief Keep Steward wilted to the floor as if his bones had lost their strength.

Thelen looked at the embassy. Grave anger came over him. "Why would you do this?"

"We did not do this. None of us could do this," Saissha stated unequivocally.

"You are the only new people in Earthmight. There has never been a murder here, ever. How am I to believe it is not one of you?"

Aenguz looked at his companions. The situation was slipping from them. "Do any of you know this girl? Have any of you seen her before?"

Each member from Corundum shook their heads.

Chimere offered tentatively, "I may have seen her in the infirmary, but there are so many new girls, I cannot be certain."

Thelen straightened as if he were ready to shoulder the weight of Earthmight.

"You will go to your chambers and remain there. Take them." The Azari moved to each member of the embassy in an instant.

Sorolokova flinched at the sudden movement. Carina and her riders moved in close to the Queen.

"Lord One King, why would we kill anyone? We came here to help," Aenguz pleaded.

"Yes, what reason would we have? Let us investigate what happened," Saissha said. Authority swelled her frame.

"What if you are responsible?" Thelen countered.

"Let the Azari stay with me."

"Chimere and I will find where she fell. He may have seen her. We will discover what happened."

Thelen seemed unconvinced.

A horrible thought reached Aenguz. There was only one thing that might be responsible for such an act. But his reasoning would cast more suspicion. He wrenched over the line of reasoning he was about to voice. "I know it is not us. And you must know that it is not us. It cannot be anyone who already resides in Earthmight." He looked up at Carina and Sorolokova. "I would not impugn the Free People, but they too have arrived anew recently."

"You dare to insinuate -" Sorolokova started.

"The Free People are beyond reproach, Message Bringer," Thelen cut her off. He raised his hand to invoke the Azari.

"No, I do not accuse the Free People. No, listen to me. It may not be one of us. It may be, I fear, a Ruinwaster. A Ruinwaster may have come to Earthmight. One of the possessors. One of the brothers, Ophiactii or Arkarua."

All the Azari turned and stared at Aenguz. Their unified gaze pierced him. Aenguz felt accused by their eyes and judged as a criminal.

Thelen's eyes spun on the new horror, a new revulsion knotting his face.

Sorolokova, Carina, and the other riders suddenly had twisted looks on their faces as if sulfur had permeated the room. They looked at one another.

"Why do you think this?" the One King asked. Suspicion saturated his tone. "How am I to believe you?"

Aenguz chose his words carefully. "Only a Ruinwaster would be capable of this. Who else or what else could so wantonly take an innocent life? 'Five seasons will not pass before Earthmight is under siege and the One Army is lost. You will know the grieving of the Lower Lands.'" The words chilled the death chamber. "Let us investigate. There may well be a greater threat here than Illia's murder."

"How do you-" Thelen started to ask Aenguz. Then, he asked Sarokin, "Is this true? Could this be true?"

"Of the five Ruinwasters, these two would be capable of this type of deceit," Sarokin stated.

"How do you know this?" Thelen continued.

"I learned this from the Chosen Freeholder of the Ganzir."

Thelen ruminated as Illia's body howled for justice.

"Ambassador Saissha, you and your healer may investigate her death. Sarokin, you will follow her. Report to me everything you find. The rest of you will return to your quarters until an answer is found."

Thelen flicked his hand. The Azari stood back from Saissha and Chimere.

Sarokin stepped to the side as if he was moving out of formation. He walked to Saissha. Stroud pivoted away from Saissha and walked in behind the One King and replaced Sarokin.

Aenguz and the remainder of the embassy were guided out of the death chamber. The Queen of the Free People scowled at Aenguz as he passed. Carina did not look at him.

40

INVESTIGATION

Aenguz, Legerohn, Mandavu, and Lokah walked the long way back up the Spire to their suites. Earthmight was cold and dark. Even with the light from the *montmorillionite* braziers, the halls seemed dimmer.

Four Azari followed them. When Aenguz looked back, he saw them all staring back. The Azari they passed on the curved hallways and the tops of stairs did not look into the distance. Their eyes followed them. Their heads turned.

He cursed the One King and his power. Step by step, the cordon closed in around them. With the Azari at his command, there seemed to be no way clear of Earthmight, to say nothing of the Lower Lands. His accusation was such an affront that Aenguz could barely hold himself still. They were not the enemy. Morgrom was; the Ruinwaster was.

They shuffled down the corridor that led to their rooms. Aenguz led them to his quarters. Before turning in, Aenguz looked into the closet. His weapon was on the stone table. Lokah's blade lay across it. The Dagba Stone was still there like a dead weight. Scraps and swaths of leather were scattered on the table. Wood-handled tools lay amid the unfinished leathers.

They filed into Aenguz's suite. Lokah closed the door behind the Prince. They sat around the small table in the sitting room. Wind and brittle rain scraped the windows and the stones on the balcony.

"Do any of you know anything about that girl?" Aenguz whispered. "Have any of you seen her before?"

"There are so many people and so many stewards. I am not sure I would remember her even if I had." Legerohn sighed plaintively.

"Where were you tonight?" Aenguz whispered.

"I was in my quarters, fast asleep," Legerohn answered.

Aenguz looked at Lokah.

"I was in the smithy. An Azari found me and pointed me to the death chamber. I met you in the hall just before we arrived." He spoke in a low tone and intimated toward Mandavu and Legerohn.

"Where were you?"

"I..." Mandavu paused.

Aenguz and the others leaned in.

"I was with Saissha." His face flushed.

Under different circumstances, they might have smiled, but the situation kept their expressions subdued.

Mandavu looked sheepish. It seemed for a moment like he might apologize, but then he just sat with his words.

"Do you really believe a Ruinwaster is here?" Legerohn asked.

"What else could it be? We are not the killers, and the only other people who have had contact with the *verrandulum* or the Erebim are the Free People."

"The Queen did not react well to your accusation," Legerohn said. His gentle push toward diplomacy for Aenguz was drowned out in their sudden quiet cabal.

"What about the Azari?" Lokah breathed. "The Queen's Azari has been by the *verrandulum* and the Erebim."

"I did not see any signs of the black pit there, but there may be other *verrandulum* that have been discovered elsewhere. Who knows?"

Telakot. He was always with Sorolokova. It was a fear he didn't want to bring to the surface. He didn't want to believe that it might be true. But Stroud's behavior and his alignment with Thelen and Hannoch forced him to acknowledge the possibility. "I do not know what it would mean if an Azari was compromised. Would they even know if one of their own was possessed?"

They had no answers for him. And Aenguz could not ask Stroud.

"If it could be hidden from them," Aenguz continued, "and if one could be taken, then it would be like, like a blindness in them. A truth could be hidden. And a lie could become truth."

"The One King relies heavily on them. Their counsel could sway his decisions. Earthmight would be vulnerable to anything." Foreboding saturated Legerohn's words.

Their eyes all said what they suspected. Aenguz couldn't say it, wouldn't say what they were thinking. Legerohn wasn't referring to all the Azari; He was referring to Stroud.

"We do not know. We do not know," Aenguz repeated. He tried to cling to the uncertainty and hoped that it might be enough to redeem their suspicion. But in a deep corner of his heart, he acknowledged that it was a thin hope.

Stroud had accused him of being a Ruinwaster. Perhaps that was part of the deception, part of the stratagem. Now he was next to Thelen.

"What do we do?" Mandavu sounded worried, almost afraid. His courage was undercut by the mystery.

"We wait. We wait for Saissha to prove to the One King that we are not guilty of this crime."

They departed to their separate rooms.

———◆———

STEWARDS BROUGHT FOOD TO them in the morning. They were not free to go to the dining room. Back-to-back Azari warded both ends of the hall. Food was brought again in the evening.

Aenguz paced around his suite and up and down the hall. He ignored the Azari that watched him. He needed to get back to the Upper Lands, but he couldn't even get off their floor.

He never got the chance to appeal to the One King to let the embassy attempt the Cleve. There was no plea that he would hear while they were prisoners. The Dagba Stone was still locked to his weapon. Lokah was no closer to removing it. The Harvest Festival had passed, and winter was coming. Attempting the mountains, even if there was a pass, would be impossible until spring. Spring, the fifth season from Morgrom's dire warning. Earthmight would be under siege by then.

Lokah worked in the storeroom on his scabbard and the stone. Aenguz walked by his focused loremaster. Aenguz was too wrapped up in his own thoughts and his own failures as their leader to be of any help to Lokah.

Another day passed. The rain stopped, and a cold front settled on Earthmight. Aenguz wanted to see Carina. He wanted to explain his reasoning and his accusation of the Free People. He did not think she or the Queen were Ruinwasters, but maybe one of their number was. They were trusted allies to Thelen. What better person than a rider of the Free People to sow division? He played over what he would say to her if he ever saw her again.

He joined Mandavu in his suite. Mandavu stood out on the balcony, wrapped in the large steward-made coat. He looked out at the One Army. Smoke trailed up from campfires and cook fires in scores of places. Tents and pavilions ran to the horizon. Crowded oval corrals seethed like open sores on the earth. Mandavu looked down on the force that he was charged to count, but his mind was elsewhere. He looked as disconnected as an Azari.

"How many do you see?" Aenguz asked.

"There are close to seven thousand men and around four thousand horses. Most of the men have never been in a fight of any kind. And only five to seven hundred horses have armor."

Aenguz pondered. "It is not enough men, is it?"

"No."

Scores of arrows arced across the sky at static targets. Men and horses weaved on muddy paths between the tents and the open arenas.

"If they number one to one with the Erebim, Tsurah, and Sallow, they will fall," Mandavu said with a grim finality. "They will not come to help us, and they are not enough to stop a Ruinwaster-led army."

"What about the Monomander, Biniam?"

"He is good at outfitting and feeding an army. Weapons arrive every day, and they have all the wagons they could need. He was the Chief Keep Steward. Sutton was his second. The One King named him the Monomander. There has not been one as far back as anyone can recall. He has never led in a war."

They would be like herd animals led to the slaughter. Corundum's aid and Mono Lord Lana's hope was as frangible as snow.

"What about the garrison?"

"I do not know anything about the garrison yet."

They came in from the cold, took off their coats, and stood by the fire.

Aenguz looked up at his First. "Saissha?"

"We wanted to keep it a secret. I am sorry I did not tell you."

"You do not have to tell me the matters of your heart. Do you-?"

"I love her," he cut Aenguz off before he could finish. "I have loved her since we entered the Spine."

"You have not seen her at all."

"No. We have not spoken since yon yester-night."

Aenguz looked into the fire. He could see how her move to investigate Illia's murder wore on Mandavu. Aenguz understood his pain. He hadn't seen Carina. He had accused her Queen and the Free People. He had been caught wet with Yasdriine, with a dead body. What must she think?

He looked at Mandavu. "I have been with Carina."

Mandavu's eyes widened, and then compassion settled into him. "Do you-?"

There was a commotion outside the suite. They rushed to the door.

Saissha, Chimere, and Sarokin were standing just outside the storeroom. Two other Azari were with them. Lokah stood defiantly at the table. Legerohn came out of his room to meet them.

"I told you - I was in the smithy. Aenguz commanded a weapon of me. I am only able to work at night."

"Were you in the tannery?" Saissha was firm and direct.

"Yes. I have leatherwork to do."

"Did you take any tools from there?"

"Yes." Lokah gestured to the table.

"Saissha!" Mandavu raised his voice.

Saissha whipped up her hand and silenced Mandavu as if she had slapped him.

"Did you walk near the infirmary?"

"I sometimes walk near the infirmary to get there. The halls are crowded."

Saissha turned to Sarokin. "Search the room."

Sarokin walked into the storeroom. The two Azari positioned themselves beside Saissha and Chimere.

Legerohn came forward. "Saissha, you cannot believe that Lokah is responsible for this. He has been as loyal and true as any of us."

Sarokin studied the tabletop. He shifted the undone scabbard and patches of dark leather.

"There is blood here."

"That is my blood. I cut my hands sometimes on Aenguz's weapon."

Sarokin found some tools. He inspected a skiver and an edge beveler. He rooted around more and pulled out an angled knife and a mini round knife. He turned to the two Azari and said, "Search him."

They stepped slowly toward Lokah.

Mandavu stepped forward. "Saissha, you know Lokah!"

"Stand back," she commanded him without meeting his eyes. Hers trembled.

The Azari each held an arm and searched his pockets and his shirt. They pulled out an edge skiver.

"Take him to a cell," Sarokin ordered the Azari.

"I did not kill that girl!" Lokah nearly shrieked.

They hauled Lokah out of the room. The remnants of the embassy backed away. Sarokin led the two Azari, holding Lokah, down the hall.

"Saissha, Lokah could not have done this!" Aenguz pleaded.

She snapped back at Aenguz, "Do you know that *silvercryst* is missing from the ore stores?"

Aenguz was confounded. He did not know what she was saying.

"Aenguz, I did not kill anyone!" Lokah shouted as they reached the back-to-back Azari.

"Where are you taking him?" Aenguz demanded.

"He is being held until he can be questioned further," Sarokin replied.

"Saissha, you have to know that Lokah could not have done this!" Aenguz pressed her. "This is a mistake."

"He might not be Lokah," she answered. "You said so yourself."

Sarokin put the leather tools into Saissha's hands.

"Where?!" Aenguz shouted.

"To the cells," she said and turned away.

Mandavu grabbed her arm. "Saissha!"

"I must go and test these blades. They may or may not be the weapons that killed Illia. Let me go." She snatched her arm away.

His arm dropped like it had been severed.

They walked past the twin Azari at the end of the hall.

A rage like a wind-fed fire rushed up in Aenguz. The forbidding Azari. The lack of control. The lack of the power to do anything. His friend being taken away, accused of murder.

"Follow him," Aenguz commanded Mandavu. "I want to know where he is being held."

Mandavu responded instantly as if he had been unleashed. His inertia reverberated off the walls. When he reached the two Azari, the one facing away spun, and both grappled with him. He pushed forward with them as if they were just sandbags lashed to his frame.

Mandavu roared and pushed through them. One of the Azari holding Lokah was suddenly gone from Lokah's side. He was instantly with the others. They forced Mandavu onto all fours. He continued crawling forward.

Saissha watched Mandavu in horror as Sarokin led Lokah and the single Azari out of sight. She looked like she might sob.

"Let him go. I know where he was the night of the murder."

The Azari released him. He climbed to his feet and snarled at them. But Saissha had already turned and followed Sarokin out of sight.

41

ALL WILL BE DIVIDED AGAINST ALL

"He is somewhere beyond the death chamber, through the dark door to the left. There must be cells beyond. I could not see. An Azari stands watch at the entrance. I could not get any closer." Mandavu recounted the space like a tactician. He smoldered as he spoke.

Aenguz and Legerohn listened intently. The fire popped. It gave all of them a start.

"I should have had my weapon." Mandavu turned his head to the top of his scabbard over his shoulder as if to say, *"But I have it now."*

Aenguz seethed. Being stuck in his room had only intensified his fury as he waited for Mandavu's return. Legerohn was somewhat helpful, but his words didn't change the facts of their predicament - did not change the fact that Lokah was imprisoned, accused of murder. Or that he too was imprisoned at the top of the Spire under constant scrutiny. And they were no closer to getting home. And the One Army was not enough. They were not coming to Corundum's aid. The embassy was divided. It tipped him over the edge. Lokah was alone. That fear was something that he knew. It ran gelid in his own veins, more than being accused of a crime he didn't commit or even being imprisoned. He shot up out of his chair. "I am getting him out of there."

Mandavu rose with him.

Aenguz flung open the door and crossed to the closet. With words of lore, he removed the anchor of Lokah's sword and handed it to Mandavu. Mandavu unslung his mace and took Lokah's blade from Aenguz. He hefted the weight of Lokah's *montmorillionite* and uttered words of lore. Mace in one hand, sword in the other, he was ready for any order that Aenguz might give. Blood was in his eyes.

Aenguz took his weapon. Although the lore in the sacred metal was quiet and the balance off center, the feel of the *montmorillionite* and the weight of his weapon twinged unused muscle memories in him. But it also felt new, like something wholly different. Years of training and months of heightened intuition collided in him.

Legerohn looked frantic. "My friend, you must calm yourself. This is not the way!" Legerohn spoke quickly, as if he knew the time on his friend's rage was running out. He tried to calm them, urged them toward peace.

"Stand back," Mandavu said to the Prince.

Legerohn backed away from Mandavu as if he feared to make a target of himself for the giant Makan.

Aenguz turned to his left toward the seasoned, salt-haired Azari. Mandavu turned the other way. Confusion flashed across his eyes, but he adjusted instantly and got behind Aenguz.

"Aenguz, no," Legerohn pleaded desperately.

Aenguz walked up to the old Azari and into his line of sight.

"I want to see the One King right now." His jaw flexed. It was the only thing holding his rage in check.

The stern, old Azari stared into his eyes and through them.

"Lord?" Mandavu asked over Aenguz's shoulder. He was begging to be released.

The Azari's eyes shifted once to Aenguz's First standing behind him and the *montmorillionite* weapons in his hands. Then he looked back at Aenguz.

"I want to see Thelen *now!*" His own eyes hardened. The corners of his eyes flexed and twitched.

The younger Azari behind the older one pivoted and faced the two Akkeidii.

Aenguz raised his weapon like a scepter and held it to the sentinel's chest.

The Azari stood unfazed.

Aenguz's chest pumped. He took a deep breath and shouted through the implacable Azari as if the sound of his voice would carry through along with the power of the One Sight. "Stroud! I want to see Thelen, right now! I am the Lord of the Akkeidii. We will not be imprisoned. And I will see Lokah freed."

Aenguz peered through the old salt's eyes at all of the Azari and demanded Stroud's attention.

The old Azari dropped his head. His voice dropped. "Follow him."

The young Azari stepped to the side, turned around, and walked up the hall.

Aenguz strode after him. The granite shadow of Mandavu followed behind.

They ringed the upper reaches of the Spire. They walked past the carved wooden doors where they had first come to meet the One King. They came to a smaller wooden door beyond it, as ornate as the last. Figures were captured in different poses of craftwork. Their complexions were joyful, hands were clasped. Smiles were carved on every face. The door was ajar.

The young Azari pushed the door open. Thick, smooth columns vaulted in even rows in the chamber.

Aenguz saw Azari tunics ahead.

Thelen was there. He wore his obsidian crown and fine silver armor. The ring of hair around his bald head was wild. Stroud and Hannoch were behind him. Stroud stared at Aenguz. Hannoch was whispering in Thelen's ear. Two Azari were in front of the One King. A dozen Azari held a wide circle around the One King, the four other Azari, and a long table.

The large, long table was the centerpiece of the space. It was covered with a light white cloth. It was not flat; the long side was pointed and contoured from something poking up underneath. Other smaller points tented at spots along the long table.

The young Azari leading Aenguz and Mandavu turned from them and joined the other Azari, closing the circle around them.

Thelen took a few steps away from the table. All four Azari moved in step with him. Then he stood still to meet Aenguz as if he were impervious.

The scene unnerved Aenguz. It stalled him. Only the feel of his weapon and Mandavu's hard presence kept him steady.

"I want Lokah released. He did not kill Illia. He is with me. He is under my charge. Release him and let the embassy go."

"It remains to be seen. Sarokin and Ambassador Saissha are in the abattoir now with the tools he took."

"What will you do to him if you believe he killed her?"

"Well, he cannot stay free. It would be too dangerous. He could kill again. I am sworn to protect life by my oath as the One King and the tenets of the Law of Creation."

Aenguz cut off Thelen. "He did not kill Illia." Frustration fanned his rage again.

"We have not used the cells in an age for such a thing, but he would remain there until his death. His natural death."

Aenguz flexed his grip. His knuckles turned white. "Let him go. Let us go, and we will quit the Lower Lands."

Aenguz's demand to leave startled the One King. Thelen's eyes narrowed and then relaxed. "I am not keeping you here."

"You said we could not enter the Cleve."

"Yes, but it is not my edict. I am a steward to the people. I hold to the agreement of *their* will. The One King who negotiated with the Azari to stop their futile attempts turned the matter to the people. It is they who agree to bar the Cleve."

The people? How could the people hold such a proscription?

"You never meant to stay here, did you? Could you really find no happiness here?" the One King asked.

"War will soon be upon the Lands of the Earth. Corundum is defenseless. Inverlieth stands in the path of ruin." Exacerbation scraped Aenguz's tone.

"You talk about a war we have not seen." He turned his head slightly toward Stroud. "The war is here. The war is now."

Thelen walked slowly closer to Aenguz. The cordon of Azari mirrored his steps.

The One King looked disheveled. His eyes were swollen and the lines around them were deep. His cheeks were sunken like the water had drained out of his body. He fixed his obsidian eye on Aenguz. "Have you come to destroy us?"

Aenguz was taken aback. What had Stroud told him?

"No one has ever murdered another person here. Do you know what that means for Earthmight? Do you know what that means for me?" Thelen was wracked. "I called the people from the vales to come here so we could protect them. Now what can I say to them? How can they believe anything I say?" He seemed to be continuing a dialog with himself that he had been wrestling with since Illia's murder.

"I asked Sorolokova to ward the Spine, and it left one of her coverts defenseless. The great horses are hunted in scores. Their migrations are interrupted by the invaders." Thelen was distraught.

"What is it like for you and your people in the hell of the Upper Lands? Do you kill one another wantonly? Is there no safe place in your homes from this - this kind of violence against your own?" He seemed genuinely perplexed, as if a new form of reason had been introduced to him without explanation.

Feuds were not uncommon in the Mashu. While Aenguz's father had done much to stem the warring between the Akkeidii clans, killing was a fact of life. Even Mandavu would have killed Aenguz if the Challenge had not been interrupted by the marauding Erebim. What kind of naive world had the One King lived in?

"I do not understand why anyone would do such a thing. I ask again, have you come to destroy the peace here?"

"There will be no peace on the Earth while Morgrom lives. The whole of creation is under threat. I came to warn you about what would happen. I came for Corundum and the Mono Lord. I came for Inverlieth, for the Mashu. I came here for the One Army to join in the war above," Aenguz litigated to the sovereign of the Lower Lands.

"Because you are the Woe Sower's Last Emissary." Cynicism dripped from Thelen's words.

Uncapped magma rose in him. His teeth ground together like a vise.

"Perhaps you are something more. Perhaps you are the doom that he foretells."

Aenguz's anger overwhelmed him. "'Hear me, my victory will come in a new form of war. Its ways and movements will be beyond your ken. All will be divided against all.' That is what the Woe Sower promised. That is what I came here to tell you. That is why we came over the Spine, so that we might get ahead of his plans. So that he will not know that we are here, and we can move first."

Thelen considered Aenguz. He walked to the covered table. The four Azari pivoted. Their eyes never left Aenguz.

"So, the Woe Sower does not know that you are here."

Aenguz nodded exasperatedly.

"Three days ago, a company from the One Army reached a vale south of here. Heideren Vale. It is on the shores of the Sunfall Sea."

Aenguz eased his grip. The Dagba Stone sagged.

"You know that I have commanded that all the people come here to be safe until we wipe out all of the Erebim invaders. But not everyone would come."

Aenguz nodded. "I know."

"When the men come upon the vales, they search all the homes. The vales can feel too still. Sometimes they search the surrounding lands, but Heideren is on the shores of the sea." Thelen looked over the blank cloth as if he were reading a map. "Smoke trailed from the center of the town, a sign that someone was there. They knew my edict, but still they kept a fire during the day.

"As the men came into the center of the vale, they found bodies. Six men. All were dead. Erebim tracks were everywhere." His throat tightened. His jaw shifted side to side. "All of their arms - *their left arms only* - were burned. The soldiers could tell that they had been held in the fire and burned while they were still alive." Thelen looked back at Aenguz, and then his eyes dropped to his gray, mottled hand.

Aenguz's head shifted side to side. The cordon around him seemed to tighten, though no one moved. His anger morphed into panic. His breathing grew shallow. The air seemed to attenuate.

Thelen continued, "They made their camp and dug graves for all the men they found. A gloom fell over them. And when night came, and the sun hid beneath the Sunfall Sea, they saw this." He lifted a part of the covering. A blue strip with lines of white met a yellow strip. It looked like the edge of the ocean. There was a small white icon. It had three thin legs and a scalloped top. "Did you know these *verrandulum* could appear on the water as well as on the land? Do you know what that might mean? Do you know why they did this to six of them?"

"I do not know why. I do not know what it means." Confusion added to his vortex.

"There are six of you here from your embassy." He looked down at the small spot on the map as if he could see the bodies there. "How could they do such a thing?" Revulsion twisted his face as if a rank odor rose from the table.

Aenguz swirled with the information. Six of them. He did not include Stroud in his estimation. Perhaps he was already lost to the embassy. How did Morgrom know that he was there? When did he know? What kind of message was he sending? How far could he see? Stroud's accusation on the Plateau haunted him. Was he himself somehow a Ruinwaster? Was he more than just the Last Emissary? Was he like Ophiactii or Arkarua who had doomed Stroud's women and children in the Cleve? Had one of them come through that *verrandulum*?

"If Lokah is not the killer, then one of you is. And what of the *silvercryst*? Why have you taken it? What have you done with it?"

Aenguz was subsumed. His thoughts were rent. Nothing held together. "I do not know about the *silvercryst*. I do not know what happened to it."

Thelen waited a long moment for Aenguz to speak again. But Aenguz had no answers. There were too many questions.

The One King moved back from the table and away from Aenguz. He gathered himself beneath his bright armor.

"Illia is to be interred tomorrow. Her parents have requested that you be there. Yasdriine shared how you both retrieved her body and carried her to safety. I will not gainsay their final wish for their daughter. Death stewards will come and lead you there. Please, leave your weapons. I do not want to see anyone hurt. I am sending more Azari out into the lands to search for invaders. There will be fewer here in the keep."

The One King said nothing more. Stroud turned a small gesture with his head, and the Azari that had brought them stood before Aenguz.

Aenguz hobbled after him out of the hall as if he had been condemned.

42

SEPULTURA IN THE SUNFALL SEA

The next morning, apprehension seeped into Aenguz while he waited for the death steward. Anxiety around their end-of-life rituals and the expectations of Illia's parents drained his appetite. The platter from the keep steward sat untouched.

His nerves were scraped raw. Every slight noise, from the fire to the stewards that shuffled by, startled him. He was trying to collect himself and master his unease when a green-tailed bird slammed into his window. His legs shot out. The chair skittered across the stone floor. His heart pumped dense silt. The bird lay dazed on the balcony for a long moment. At first, he was sure it was dead. Its wings were splayed awkwardly, and the body was turned cockeyed, its head craned at a disturbing angle. He went back and forth over what to do with the bird. Then a twitch, a weak flap. The head righted. Mandavu startled him again when he came to check on his lord. When Aenguz looked back, the bird was gone.

He replayed the One King's words and his not-so-subtle accusations, but the picture of Illia kept coming to the forefront. Her vacant face and ripped open throat, a shocked but placid stare, and the horrible gash that stole her life, her breath, and her voice personified utter silence more than her death. She had looked so young, but death had somehow made her old. The glint of life was gone from her. The pale, wet skin and tangled hair seemed unnatural, unholy.

So, when the death steward arrived at his open door, he jolted again and nearly swore at him.

The death steward was a wiry old man. His iron-gray hair was coifed. It matched the cold gray clouds that pressed down on the land around Earthmight. His thin apron was black. His bony arms and legs poked out from a torso-less body. The face of a skull was splayed over his chest. It was stretched and imperfect, as if a skull had been rolled in chalk and cupped into the fine black fabric. He bore what looked to be a black cerement before him.

"Lord Aenguz, I am Willion. I am a death steward. I have come to take you to Illia's death ceremony. This capelet is worn by the grievers to honor her life and her passing to the White Earth." Empathy and reverence imbued his tone. Though Aenguz towered over him, he felt small, like a child trying to hold still, on his best behavior.

Willion walked forward as if each step were sacred. He unfolded the capelet and placed it over Aenguz's shoulders. His gentle touch sent thrills of electricity through Aenguz's neck and head.

"We do not acknowledge or address others as we walk to the death chambers. It is a time for contemplation and respect. We hold ourselves quiet to honor the dead." He did not scold or talk down to Aenguz. It felt like he was performing a rite to be initiated into a cryptic order.

He turned to lead Aenguz out into the hall.

Unlike the other stewards' aprons, Willion's narrow apron had only a single white skeletal handprint on the back. It seemed to impel the death steward like a macabre push.

Mandavu stood in the hall. The black capelet did not fit him. He looked like a father wearing a toddler's cape.

Legerohn looked like a dark king in his capelet. He held his hands together before him, fingers interlocked. His dark face was cupped in shadow under the black hood.

Willion led them past the Azari down the hall. There was only one keeping watch at each end of the hallway.

He led them down through the Spire. When they passed stewards, the aproned servants made fists with their hands, touched knuckles together, and brought them over their heart. They bowed their heads until the solemn train passed.

They walked down the curved ramps and stairs. People stood aside, made way, and quieted. Lines of children were whispered at to be quiet as the procession passed.

Willion led them down the steps of the rose marble entry way and to the underside of the bridge leading to the Plateau. They zigged their way down past the parting throngs.

Out the window, near the bottom of the amphitheater, Aenguz saw Monguerra. He wore a capelet. His hood was down. The Chief Grain Steward was ordering about rows of standing grain stewards. Their wheat-crested aprons fluttered in the wind over their winter coats. They wore black scarves around their necks, and they stamped their feet against the cold. They were sullen. Many wept.

As Willion led them down the final distance to the landing between the death chambers, Monguerra appeared through a door by the stage and hurried up behind Aenguz. A plaintive choral dirge followed him in with the cold wind.

They came to the hexagonal landing between the two black

chambers. White sage smoke and the fetor of dead fish choked the space. Aenguz looked over the wrapped bodies and found a lone Azari standing in the darkened door to the left. It was Sarokin. Lokah was somewhere beyond there.

Two death stewards appeared in the second doorway. They carried a body wrapped in a shroud down the steps on a litter. He was wondering where the stairs led when Mandavu turned left.

The death chamber to the left was built into Earthmight's seawall. Huge, ribbed columns walled the room. The ceiling was an uneven pattern of hexagons. The white sage and bycatch made a sickening soup of the atmosphere.

Hooded mourners stood in small groups and exchanged occasional tentative whispers. He saw Saissha. Her face was white. Her eyelids bobbed as if to close. She rocked like she might fall over. Chimere was with her. His dark skin was pallid. He made eye contact with the train and gave a look of apology through the slurry of his own sleepiness.

Yasdriine looked up at Aenguz until something akin to shame made her look away.

Elin and Dalmeida stood near the center of the outer wall. Elin was flanked by an older couple. They looked drained. Dalmeida was cupped by a half dozen soldiers. They wore formal regalia of leathers and armor and long gray cloaks. They seemed to ward their comrade against a wall of grief.

Illia lay wrapped in cerecloth on a sturdy wooden table, its legs positioned at the center rather than the ends. Two spindled wheels flanked the middle, their lathed spokes and the table's surface carved with clean patterns resembling interlocking bones. Two death stewards stood on either side, their fists pressed together at their chests.

Willion led the way through the loose assembly of mourners. Most held to themselves. The prospect that death could come to one so young and vulnerable left them sad and pensive.

Willion approached Elin and Dalmeida. "I grieve for your loss. Life and death are intertwined. Too soon to the White Earth. There you will meet again." He stepped aside to reveal Legerohn.

The Prince of the Moresi came next.

> "'Too *short* is the time of life,
> Too *sharp* is the pain of separating,
> Too *deep* is the grief of loss.'

She holds you still in her mind's eye, as you hold her in yours. May that comfort you until the time when you shall meet again."

The couple thanked the Prince. Dalmeida pulled Elin into him.

Willion introduced Mandavu. The giant Makan towered over the couple. "I grieve for your loss." He turned quickly after Legerohn.

Aenguz's heart raced. He was suddenly nervous. Willion introduced Aenguz. "Aenguz the Sidor, Lord of the Akkeidii."

Before he could speak, Elin said, "Thank you for saving Illia from the water vats. Yasdriine told us how you carried her-" Her voice broke. Dalmeida pulled her in closer. He scowled at Aenguz. He had no intention of speaking. The eyes of the soldiers behind him were grim.

"I speak for the Akkeidii. We grieve your loss. The White Earth is brighter now because of Illia."

Elin broke down into tears at his words. Aenguz was grateful when Willion drew him away.

He led them to Saissha and Chimere. Chimere whispered for Legerohn's forgiveness, but the Prince told him not to worry. Mandavu looked over at Saissha. He worried about her. She gave him a faint smile.

Willion told them to be quiet with a firm glare.

Thelen arrived at the top of the landing. Stroud and Hannoch were at his side. They remained on the landing as Thelen descended. His capelet shimmered like dark opal. The hem was contoured and accented with intricate embroidery. The grain stewards' choral dirge flowed in behind him.

Thelen crossed the chamber like a supplicant. He reached his hands to Elin and Dalmeida's shoulders slowly, as if grief made his arms heavy. He recited lines from the Law of Creation about the nature of life and death. Then he said, "The whole of Earthmight grieves with you and for Illia." He leaned in and hugged them to him. Elin shook. Dalmeida grasped the One King. They held there together for an age. The One King shared in their grief.

The death stewards began their threnody. It slowly canceled out the grain stewards' dirge. There were no words, or none that Aenguz could understand. Willion inhaled and added his voice to his peers'.

Thelen pulled away from them but still stood near them.

Stewards walked over to Illia's parents. They drew them away from their little girl.

Another steward by the wall near the table pulled a thick cord. A slat slid up. It was made of charred wood and blended in with the black basalt.

The fetid odor of dead fish rushed in and canceled out the white sage. Waves crashed below without rhythm. The Sunfall Sea was disquiet. The threnody grew louder to counter the waves.

Elin's sobs pierced through the death stewards' dour song. Then the dirge stopped abruptly.

The two death stewards at the sides of the table turned the spindled wheels. The tabletop angled down. Illia's body slid off into a channel in the basalt wall. There was a moment of sliding, and then a deep plop and splash made its way back before another wave eradicated it.

The stewards waited a long moment, and then they turned the

wheels back as if they were righting a listing ship. The black slat came down and closed out the sea.

Dalmeida carried Elin out of the chamber. Thelen followed them with her parents and the soldiers in tow. The grain stewards' sad choral dirge returned.

As the mourners began to file out, Aenguz and Mandavu cornered Saissha. Mandavu was fraught about her. Up close, she looked even worse. There was blood on her blue robe.

"Is that blood? What happened?!" he asked her, as if he wanted to exact some revenge.

Saissha waved it off. "It is animal blood."

A few of the mourners turned. The leaders of the embassy held still until the room cleared.

"Why do you have animal blood on you?" Mandavu ached for her to make sense to him.

"None of the tools made the wound in her throat."

"What happened to you?" Aenguz fretted for her.

She started to speak when another yawn came.

Chimere said, "The Azari never sleep. When she began her search, Sarokin would not let her stop. When we needed to rest, Sarokin insisted we continue."

"We followed Illia's steps the day of her murder. We spoke briefly with her parents. We spoke to the other stewards who knew her and some of her friends," Saissha added. "We searched the grates with Yasdriine for where she might have gone in."

Chimere tried to carry her burden. "We tried to find where she was murdered. Sarokin recounted all that the Azari knew and had seen. He repeated their words as if he had questioned all the Azari who had seen her in person. But Saissha wanted to see where they were. Sarokin led us."

"He questioned us about all of you." Saissha looked at all of them with bleary eyes. "Where you were the night of her murder."

"That is how we came to Lokah. The man in charge of the smithy told us that Lokah was there, but that he was not always watching him. He would sometimes be there and sometimes not be there." Chimere seemed to apologize to Aenguz with every word.

"It led us to the tannery and the tools he took." She took in deep breaths to try to shake her somnolence. "But none of the tools caused the wound. Sarokin admitted as much."

"But he forced Saissha to cut on the animals again and again until he was satisfied," Chimere said with empathy for her.

Mandavu bristled.

"Then the One King knows that Lokah did not do it, like I said. Like we knew," Aenguz vindicated.

"Yes."

"I want to see him. I want him released now."

"The people in Earthmight believe Lokah killed Illia. Rumors have spread throughout Earthmight. He thought it better to wait until tomorrow, after Illia's burial, to release him," Saissha answered.

"I want to see him. Let's go," Aenguz said to Mandavu.

"Aenguz," the Prince started, "Saissha and Chimere are exhausted. Let me take them back to their quarters."

Relief brightened Saissha faintly, but then she added, "There is one problem. Since Lokah did not do it, and we did not do it, there is still a murderer free in Earthmight. And the Azari and One King still think it is one of us."

They all looked at one another. Aenguz thought about the story of the six men with the burned arms. He kept the story to himself.

"I am going to keep searching, but I need to sleep."

"Let me take her out of here, Aenguz," Legerohn said firmly.

Aenguz relented.

Legerohn guided Saissha and Chimere out of the death chamber.

Aenguz regretted pressing her so hard, but she handled it well. There was some other force out there able to kill, but he couldn't tackle that now. He wanted to see Lokah. He patted Chimere on the shoulder to thank him as they parted.

Aenguz and Mandavu entered the other chamber and passed by the other wrapped bodies that waited for their loved ones and their internment. They pulled their hoods back.

Aenguz walked right up into Sarokin's face. "Move! I want to see Lokah! Grieg damn!"

"He will not be released until tomorrow."

"He is innocent!"

Sarokin did not budge.

"Mandavu, I want to see Lokah," Aenguz started.

Sarokin glanced at the giant Makan and then stepped aside.

Aenguz looked back and saw Stroud standing on the landing.

"Lokah! Where are you?" Aenguz shouted and jogged down the hall.

"Here! Aenguz! I am here!" An arm shot out from the wall ahead.

Edged basalt walls ran out in a curve out of sight. The corridor bent to the right like a dark angular mine shaft. The cells on either side were open. The first two held bundles of cerecloth and shrouds that were stacked in along with other accoutrements.

Aenguz ran to the closed cell and Lokah's outstretched arm. The gap was only wide enough for it.

Aenguz clutched Lokah's arm. It was cold. Then he reached through the narrow opening and grabbed his neck. "We have been held in the Spire. I am sorry it took so long to get to you."

"I knew you would come. Mandavu was here."

Mandavu reached through the crease and palmed Lokah's head. His arm wouldn't reach any further.

"Let me out," Lokah pleaded. He was relieved to see them, and he was ready to go.

"Tomorrow. We will come and get you tomorrow."

"Why? Why not now?" His arm dropped.

"Everyone in Earthmight thinks you killed Illia."

"I did not kill her!"

"I know."

"Saissha knows too," Mandavu added.

"We were at Illia's burial ceremony at the Sunfall Sea. The One King thinks it would be callous and unseemly to have you freed on this day. But we will be here first thing in the morning."

Lokah nodded and stepped back enough for Aenguz to see in. A simple black cell stretched out before him, with a bench running along the back wall. A small, deep-set window angled upward toward the sky, too narrow for a head to fit through. Water trickled down the wall to a small hole in the floor in the corner. A heel of barrio bread rested on the bench.

"I am sad for her parents. I cannot imagine the pain they are going through."

"It is also the first murder in Earthmight," Aenguz added.

"There is still a murderer loose in the keep," Mandavu said.

Lokah's brow furrowed.

"The One King thinks it is one of us. One of the embassy."

"What are we going to do?" he asked.

"We are going to get you out of here. Then we are going to get out of Earthmight."

43

THE FORGE

Aenguz lay awake, waiting for dawn. At first light, he would get Lokah out of the cell. Then he would get the embassy out of Earthmight. He would leave his weapon. It was the only way. He simply could not risk having it fall into Morgrom's hands.

They would make for the Cleve and test the garrison. If they were rebuffed, then they would tackle the Spine. If there was no good option, then they would return to Lihkit. But Legerohn would have to stay. Chimere would stay with him. They could return to Earthmight.

But what if Thelen would not let them go? On the one hand, he might welcome having them all leave Earthmight, but could he be persuaded to allow them to pass the garrison or attempt the Cleve? If he was telling the truth, it was the people of Earthmight forbidding the way. How long would it take to change all their minds? There wasn't enough time to talk to everyone.

Morgrom knew he was there. The Flayer had sent him a message - had sent them all a message. Was it to cast fear into the embassy? Was it to cast fear into the One King and the fortress of Earthmight? It was unclear if anyone besides the One King, the soldiers who found them, and the Azari knew what had been done to those men and their arms. Perhaps he meant to draw attention onto the embassy and away from the killer - a killer who was still loose in Earthmight.

Could Saissha be convinced to surrender the search and leave? She was tenacious. Would she insist on staying to exonerate the embassy? Could she be convinced to abandon the search? She might want to remove all doubt from the embassy by finding the killer.

How could he return to the Mashu without his *montmorillionite*? How could he explain the exigency of a choice like that to the clan lords? He would be exiled and named Hearthless. Legerohn would welcome him in Inverlieth. He would give him a home... until Inverlieth itself burned.

The clouds in the east shed their black.

Mandavu met him in the hall.

"Let's get Lokah," Aenguz said.

Aenguz's First nodded determinedly.

As they walked past Saissha's door, Aenguz asked, "Have you talked with her?"

"She has been asleep since yesterday." He was worried about her, but he also grumbled about Sarokin for keeping her awake for so long.

As they passed Legerohn's door, Mandavu asked, "Should we wake Legerohn?"

"No. I want him here in case she or Chimere wakes up. Let them all sleep." And they would need rest for their journey to the Spine, Aenguz concluded.

There was no Azari at the near end of the hall, only the old, stolid Azari that barred their way to the One King behind them. Their numbers must be reduced. Only the watch over the Dagba Stone needed to be maintained.

They walked down the Spire. A few keep stewards passed by. Most of the denizens of Earthmight were asleep. A child mewled. Land and sea and cliff flashed by the windows. The reek of dead fish grew stronger. They passed through a long chamber that looked out onto the Plateau. The smell drew them to the window. Below, beyond the outer edge of the Plateau, was the wall that ran into the sea. Dead fish filled the inside of the breakwater. The long boats were pressed up against it. White bellies weaved and sloshed against the wall and all along the shore. Red water lapped at the stones.

"By Grieg," Mandavu uttered.

The fish kill stretched into the distance.

"What is the Flayer doing?" Mandavu asked.

Fishermen dotted the breakwater and shore. They looked forlorn. Their hands went up and dropped. Even from a distance, they looked dazed.

Aenguz stopped a young keep steward. "What happened?"

"I do not know, my lord. The fish just keep dying. They say it is worse in Llangollen. Many are leaving to come here." The boy looked sallow.

Birds drifted on the breeze and dropped down to pick at the carcasses.

They made their way down to the death chambers. They walked past the wrapped bodies. Sarokin was gone. Another Azari was in his place.

There was no confrontation. The Azari led the way to Lokah's cell. He bent down to the corner of the door opposite the narrow gap and removed a brick-sized block of stone. A stone grate covered a channel along the floor at the edge. The Azari pushed in on the wedge, and the heavy basalt door turned out on hidden hinges.

Lokah was at the opening. They welcomed him out.

"Let's get out of here." Aenguz smiled.

They led Lokah up to his room. Stewards and soldiers stared at them as they passed. They excoriated Lokah with their glares.

The Prince was awake when they arrived. He held Lokah in his hands and welcomed him. The Prince nearly cried, he was so pleased.

Mandavu went to retrieve a platter of food from the dining hall.

Lokah went to the storeroom. He fingered some of the leathers and his unfinished scabbard. He touched his weapon, uttered words of lore, and hefted it up. Aenguz envied the thrum of power that must be flowing through his veins, but he was happy for his loremaster.

Lokah set it back down like an anchor over Aenguz's weapon.

"Any progress?" he asked.

"No," Aenguz answered. He didn't want to burden his loremaster with his decision to leave his weapon at the moment.

"I have been thinking more on the Lay," Lokah said cautiously, but his eyes were heavy.

"Later. Get some food. Get some sleep."

Aenguz left Lokah in his room. He wondered how he was going to tell his friend that he had decided to leave his weapon behind.

Late in the afternoon, after Lokah had eaten and slept, he came into Aenguz's room. Mandavu was with him. Aenguz asked him to see if the others were awake. Only Legerohn was. Aenguz decided to start with them. They could talk with Saissha later.

The fire was fed, and the four men sat around the table. Aenguz told them of his intention to leave Earthmight as soon as they were able. They began to pepper Aenguz with all the questions he had turned over in his own mind. "What would the One King allow us to do? What would Saissha say?"

"What about your metal?" Lokah asked.

"I am going to leave it here."

Mandavu and Lokah were stricken.

Legerohn asked incredulously, "Can you do that?"

"There is no way to remove the stone, and it may be safer here than abroad in the Lands of the Earth. Morgrom is coming here regardless, so we would not be saving them by taking it away, like we did to protect Corundum."

Legerohn mulled over Aenguz's words. He saw the look in Lokah and Mandavu's eyes.

"There may be a way. Something we have not tried," Lokah said.

Aenguz cocked his head.

Lokah held his tongue.

"What? What is it?" Aenguz asked. The promise of hope notched his denuding desperation.

Lokah looked at Aenguz and then at Legerohn, but said nothing.

"You can trust Legerohn, Lokah."

"Well..." He leaned in close. "...it is not something we can do here."

"Go on."

"I need all of your help."

They bent in together like conspirators.

"Legerohn, can you distract the Azari?"

"Yes, I think I can."

"We will need to get the weapon out of the room without the Azari knowing."

"They said it was mine to take." Aenguz grew suddenly defensive, as if his weapon might be taken away from him right then and there.

"I do not want to get stopped here. Once we are among people, they may be less inclined to stop us." Lokah told them his plan.

"Where will you take it?" Legerohn asked.

"To a place where we might be able to remove it. It will be safer for you here. Do not follow us."

"If Saissha wakes, tell her of our plan to leave. If anyone can convince her, it is you."

"You may overestimate my power of persuasion or underestimate her persistence."

Aenguz gave him a wry smile. "She wants to return to Corundum as much as we want to return to our homes."

Legerohn strolled out of Aenguz's suite. He turned to the right. He began talking to the old Azari.

Mandavu and Lokah left and stood just outside the door. They chatted about getting dinner until Lokah nodded. Mandavu kept his back to the Azari.

Aenguz slid in between them, and they casually drifted to the storeroom. Mandavu stayed outside and continued his ramble about what might be in the dining hall as if Lokah were still there.

Lokah released his sword and moved it off Aenguz's weapon.

"Here, keep it close to your chest. Mandavu, stay behind Aenguz. I will walk in front of you. All eyes should be on me. The Azari may not notice that you have the weapon until we are among more people."

Aenguz clutched his weapon close. A growing fear that it might be taken away snatched at his heart.

A nagging question came to him. "Why did you doubt the Prince?"

"We did not have a realm of silence, and you commanded us to not speak openly without it."

Aenguz chewed on Lokah's answer for an instant. He would speak to Legerohn. There had been scant opportunity, but he needed to bring him in closer to his thoughts. "I trust the Prince."

He followed Lokah out, and Mandavu walked in step behind him. Legerohn prattled on until they were out of sight.

They passed the dining hall and left the upper levels of the Spire. People stared at Lokah with suspicion or thinly veiled disdain.

The denizens of Earthmight were crowding into the larger refectories. Their eyes moved to Lokah and the hulking presence of Mandavu. They only glanced at Aenguz.

Azari were dotted at junctures and confluences in the keep, but none moved to stop them.

They moved sometimes with and sometimes against the flow, but people parted ahead of Lokah as if he were contagious.

Lokah avoided the rose marble entrance. Instead, he led them on a course by the infirmary on the seaward side of the keep. The corridor led to the covered bridge, and they flowed across with others to the ramps that led down into the Plateau. Lokah maintained a casual pace. Aenguz didn't know how he managed it. He wanted to run to keep pace with his racing heart.

As they turned down the central hall that led to the main gate, an Azari followed behind them.

Mandavu whispered about the Azari to Aenguz and Lokah.

Lokah slowed even more. He turned into the smithy.

Smoke and heat clotted the atmosphere. The clang and hammer of metal echoed off the stone walls. Soot and char blackened the white stone. Smiths' faces glowed over pools of orange. Others labored with raw ore or finished weapons to temper or sharpen. Steam rose here and there from buckets of water. Hone rods keened edges on axes and swords. Hammers beat out an uneven rhythm, announcing the inevitable doom of war. The men and women worked diligently and deliberately to arm the One Army.

A few looked up at the Akkeidii briefly, but they seemed to not be surprised by Lokah and returned to their work. He led them over to the corner where the basalt wall met the raw stone foundation of the Spire where Gregoire had allowed him to work.

The clutter had been organized in the small alcove. A wall

of broken cart frames and beams demarked the space. Inside, a makeshift workbench had been assembled. A wheeled hammer had been righted and repaired. Raw ore was piled by the bench, and spent slurry was scattered on the floor. "This was the only spot where I could work."

The Azari reached the entrance. Lokah nodded at Mandavu.

Mandavu pulled his mace out blithely, as if he were going to use it or hand it to Lokah for some innocuous reason. Aenguz kept his back to the Azari. Mandavu shifted as if he couldn't find a place to stand, as if the space were too small. It brought him close to the Azari.

He got beside him, and in a fluid move, curled his arms under the Azari's. He swung his weapon up in a snap. It was deceptively light. Then, with words of lore, he made it heavy. He uttered, "'*Anchor's might,*'" and the rest of the couplets to draw mass into his weapon. He snaked his legs around him too. With his strength and the weight-ed mace, he drew the sentinel to the floor on top of him behind the makeshift wall. The Azari struggled and kicked, but Mandavu had him. Mandavu turned his head to look at Aenguz and Lokah. "I have him," he growled, straining.

The Azari writhed, but he was immobilized. He could see up into the benign walls of the smithy.

Lokah led Aenguz past the wheeled hammer. It blocked a stairway carved into the foundation of Earthmight. The cut of the rock, the soot, and disuse hid the seam between the basalt and the schist. The remote, cluttered corner of the smithy hid the path that led up the side of the base of Earthmight. The smell of smoke faded somewhat, and the sound of hammering dimmed. Only the distant flickering light of *montmorillionite* ore pulsed on the walls. The blacksmiths and stew-ards were out of sight.

Lokah led the way up the stairs into a black pocket of rock. A ratty tarp covered what looked to be a rough boulder shaped into the schist. A small ledge ringed part of the bottom.

Aenguz joined him on the ledge. Lokah pulled back the ratty tarp. Bright chaotic light flashed out. It was an open forge - an Akkeidii forge. Hunks of raw *montmorillionite* of all shapes and sizes nearly filled to the brim, the stolen ore from the storehouse and from throughout Earthmight.

"How did you?" Aenguz started, then added, "How did you find so much and not get caught?"

"Azari eyes are not everywhere. They trust the people of Earthmight. I stumbled on the steps when I was clearing the space to work. Then, it was just a matter of time and stealth to get enough *montmorillionite*. It is prized here too, and not easily stolen. If they found me out, I might truly have been imprisoned. I had to keep it a secret."

Aenguz smiled and shook Lokah by the shoulder. "You are a cunning loremaster. *Montmorillionite* is Akkeidii metal. You did not steal it."

"You know what I realized?"

"What?"

"That if Hernus Kriel and Grieg Sidor were here, they would have stood where we are standing right now." Lokah looked around at the forge and the ledge as if he were taking it in again for the first time.

"They must have brought the metal here to the Lower Lands."

"Or mined it somewhere near here."

The discoveries of not only the Akkeidii forge and the found *montmorillionite* were such a surprise that the thought that the Venturer and his dearest friend had stood in the same spot overwhelmed Aenguz. The magnitude of that realization snapped him back and forth through time from the deep past to his hurried present. A twinge of vertigo threatened his balance.

"Grieg Sidor must have fashioned Hernus Kriel's death helm here,"

Lokah continued with an awe that he had finally voiced for the first time after keeping the thoughts a secret. "*Surasanskeld* was performed here. If the shape of your weapon can be altered, this would be the only place."

Whether it was the echo of a distant friendship or all that Lokah had done to serve, support, and befriend him, Aenguz felt a bond with his brother-friend made loremaster. It was the first time since Ridder's death that he had felt so close to someone.

Fidelity, fealty, and love made his face and eyes earnest and serious. It was as complete an acceptance and acknowledgment as if he had embraced him right there.

They then both turned their attention to the forge. Aenguz calmed and centered himself. Lokah began an inchoate chant. Aenguz joined him and whispered in unison with him. The couplets of the Lay about the birth of refined *montmorillionite* drawn from the wild ore of the earth metered out in a familiar rhythm.

They turned the rocks over and positioned them. The flickering light organized and pulsed in rhythm with their chant. The rarefied platinum shimmered and slowly released its hold on the raw rock encasing the *montmorillionite*.

There was no heat, only the compulsion and responsiveness to lore and Akkeidii blood. Bit by bit, the hunks of rock sagged as if red heat were stoked in the cold forge. Liquid metal began to pool at the bottom. The inert rock did not sink but rather floated to the top like bits and hunks of wood.

Aenguz and Lokah began pulling off those bits of rock from the melting *montmorillionite*. They tossed them to the stairs. They were cold to the touch, but they sparked and smoked when they hit the schist.

The pulsing light slowed and took on a solid, even glow. A vault of silver light shot out from the open mouth of the forge.

The two continued to skim the surface as motes of rock popped up to the smooth skin of the liquid metal. Soon, every bit of rock was gone. The sheen rippled like water. Their faces were lit by the glow.

Lokah gave Aenguz a look, saying, "It's ready."

But now they were in uncharted territory.

"What do you think will happen?"

"Your weapon has more flex than any other base metal, but it will still resist. Try bending the spike first. If that yields enough, then you should be able to draw off the stone."

"What about the stone?"

Lokah shook his head slowly. "There is nothing in The Lay of *Montmorillionite* that speaks to this. You will have to focus and guide the Lay."

The memory of the blast when he had hooked it in the caverns beneath Corundum scared him. What might it do here?

Aenguz waved Lokah back. He would not jeopardize him. And anyway, they both knew that only Aenguz could do what might be attempted. He would only risk his own life, not Lokah's.

Lokah drew away from the forge and backed down the stairs.

Aenguz held his weapon up over the edge. Nothing moved in his weapon: no lore, no power, no song. He just needed enough power from the *molten* metal to bend the spike enough to slide the stone off. But in order to do that, he would have to touch the Dagba Stone to the liquid *montmorillionite*.

He held it out over the languid pool of platinum. He set his focus and called on couplets that sung to the metal's hardness and flexibility. He hoped it would be enough.

He touched the spike to the liquid metal. It remained hard. He kept the stone clear and tried the axe. He was careful of the edge. But his caution did not give him the force he needed. He would have to submerge it. Metal and stone would have to be covered, just like his father's skull.

He was brought back to the trauma at the forge in the Sidor Hearth Valley, his profane attempt at *surasanskeld* to memorialize his father with a *montmorillionite* helm. Grieg Sidor had done it for Hernus Kriel - and he had likely done it in this very forge. His thoughts went back to the cleft in the Spine and the five lost days, and to the alcove in the bowels of Corundum. Fear at unleashing the untamed power wobbled him, but he managed to keep his focus.

He slowly let the stone down into the pool of *montmorillionite*. His eyelids fluttered closed, anticipating the blast.

None came.

He pulled his eyes open gradually and reached beneath the surface to try the hook again.

It didn't budge.

Frustration found a foothold. He tried to stop it, but he wanted to have his weapon back and leave the stone. The metal should have just responded. But his metal had "aged." It had taken on the aspect of years. The subtle attenuation in the shaft, the slight wave in the tip of the axe - the deeper curve in the dagger at the hilt... But it was more than that alone. The stone had immured the metal's power.

But he couldn't give up. He tugged and pulled at the hook. Then he tried to bend the spike. The liquid metal slid up onto his left hand and did not drop off right away. It was thick and syrupy against his skin. The *morillion* embedded in his arm tingled.

He cranked on the hook and spike, but there was no movement.

Frustration had a hold of him now. An idea came to him out of his frustration and fear - a thought as sacrilegious as what he had attempted with his father's skull. There was enough metal here to do what he wanted. He could draw out a new weapon - a duplicate. And with the remaining *montmorillionite*, he could leave the stone submerged beneath the metal. Once it hardened, it would be encased in the hardest substance in all the Lands of the Earth. Only an Akkeidii could free it. It would be safe, and he would have a weapon again, a copy, but a *montmorillionite* weapon, nonetheless. It was profane, but it might be the answer he was looking for.

He set his weapon on the edge of the forge. He began to draw another weapon from the platinum pool. He went into the creative part of the Lay that he knew by rote. Lokah might have objected if he could hear him through the cone of light and power that surrounded him.

The pool shifted, and his left hand was getting more coated in the metal. Aenguz sluiced it off and visualized the weapon he meant to make. He reached in to draw it out for the first time, as if it existed just below the surface of the platinum.

The liquid metal was caressing him more. It was clinging halfway up his forearm.

This behavior seemed odd, but his focus was intense. He tried brushing the metal back and off his arm, but it only reached further. This wasn't right. Panic dispelled his focus. He tried to pull back from the forge, but the *montmorillionite* had a lock on him. He braced and pulled, but the metal slinked up further.

His heart jumped; his lungs seethed. Pressure and thumping pounded in his panicked mind. He couldn't get it off, couldn't pull his arm free, couldn't break the spell.

And then silver light reached up into his mind and drew him down into a bright argent unconsciousness.

44

UNFATHOMABLE LORE

Aenguz woke from a liquid metal tomb. His eyes were pressed into a die. They did not open at first. Odors of blood, sweat, and dead fish told him that his lungs still worked. He was alive and in a bed.

The quiet whispers and shuffles told him he was in an infirmary. Whiffs of herbs and vinegar verified the sensation. It reminded him of the infirmary in Corundum, but for the smell of dead fish.

His eyes fluttered open. The room was not like the stall in the crystal citadel. It was small. A divider gave some privacy beyond the foot of the bed. At the thin opening, he saw the back of an Azari tunic.

Healing stewards flickered by the creases where he could see. The hum of their whispers and low conversations were just out of reach.

He was not as lost as when he awoke in Corundum. Being in an infirmary was familiar - different, but familiar. The stone and the sea air told him it was Earthmight. He had been saved from the forge, like he had been saved from the waters of Mimirmere.

He began to take stock. Hunger. Thirst. Both demanded attention. How long had he been out? He took an inventory of the pain. He was sore in places, but it was not localized. It was like the beating he had endured at the awakening of the waters beneath Corundum, like he had fallen down a flight of stairs.

He had been at the forge Lokah had found, but he was no longer there. Where was his weapon? He checked the small room. Lokah must have it. He must be alright.

He traced back in time to the last moments he recalled. The stubborn metal wouldn't give up the Dagba Stone. The liquid *montmorillionite* had crawled up his arm the way *surasanskeld* should have done to his father's skull, or how it had onto Hernus Kriel's head above the entrance to Earthmight's Spire.

His hand didn't hurt. He remembered the scorched pain after his failure at the forge with his father's skull. Sleep had been impossible. The pain alone was enough to kill him. It made him beg for death.

His left arm was wrapped in white gauze, but it felt fine. He was well acquainted with the intricacies of a molten metal burn.

He pulled at the loose gauze and moved his arm to feel the skin at the joints. No pain. The dressing seemed superfluous.

He unwrapped more, rolling his wrist.

The first glimpse of skin seemed smooth. It was not the sickly gray and purple. He pulled back more gauze.

A silver metallic sheen covered the back of his hand.

"Aaah-" He blurted out.

He freed his fingers. Silver-coated digits.

"Aaaah-" He wriggled them, and panic swelled.

"Aaaaaaah!-" Frantic, he whipped his arm out to throw the silver free.

Stroud rushed in.

"Message Bearer." He paused, unsure of what to do.

Aenguz kicked his legs and flung himself out of the bed as if to get away from his arm.

"Chimere!" Stroud shouted.

Aenguz scrambled into the corner. His wails came from an unknown place. He stuck his arm out as far away as he could.

Chimere rushed down to him and climbed in close. "Aenguz, Sidor, Emissary. You are safe, calm yourself."

"Aaaaahhhhaaaahhhh!" His eyes peeled back far enough for them to fall out.

The Moresi shouted, "Get some soporific!"

More stewards came in at the sound. Shrieks came from Aenguz that he did not recognize. One steward grabbed his arm. Aenguz flicked it, and the steward flew back against the wall and bounced down onto the bed.

"Stroud! Hold his arm!" Chimere yelled.

Stroud gripped his arm with all his Azari strength.

"Take it off! Take it off!" His reactions jolted out from the inner heart of fear.

Chimere pressed something dank into his mouth and then covered his lips. "Shhh, shhh, shhh…"

Warm sap filled his throat and soon his head. His eyes surrendered their threat of flight. His shrieks were quelled, but did not stop until his eyes closed. And then a new tomb of sleep enveloped him.

45

LIMINAL

Pulses thrummed in his head, his heart, *and in his arm*. The silver skin registered the rhythmic pressures and amplified them. Blood flowed into minute capillaries and pulsed like *montmorillionite* light.

Another pulse, deeper, slower, more subterranean, meted out an intermittent drum that beat across days. Raw veins of metal within the foundations of the earth pulsed glacially slow. The ichor of the earth pumped from the world's heart. His arm mirrored it and echoed the slow pulsation from the deep.

Aenguz pulled out of the thrums and woke into the infirmary. Stroud was a cornerstone in the room. The Azari stared at the wall, but Aenguz saw that he was within his periphery. The eyes of the Azari were on him, aware of him. Their leader would be the first to act, the first to take the responsibility of challenging Aenguz and what he had become, should he demonstrate acts of ruin.

The metal arm was surreal and benign. The silver skin was firm, even hard, but the sensation was definitely liquid. It flowed and fluttered - at least, that's what it felt like. The feelings in his fingers were sensitive to the point of sentience. His palm tickled to the touch.

It reminded him of his first caress of his weapon when he drew it out of the forge in the Sidor Hearth Valley. The perfect smoothness. The soft platinum sheen. It had pressed back into his hand, welcomed his touch. He had passed the final rite; he was fully an Akkeidii Warrior, his father's son. Pride, achievement, culmination, and the manifestation of lore had shot a trill like titillation through him.

The sensation connected him to the smooth skin of the Dagba Stone. His first touch in the sanctum in Corundum. Cupping the smooth bone-like stone in his hands. It had been smooth and hard. Its curves and arms were sensual. It gripped his weapon adoringly, and his weapon hugged it back in a desperate kind of yearning.

A sensation of attraction like gravity radiated from his arm for his weapon. He would not be separated from it, could not surrender it or be parted from it. He searched the room for it.

"Do you need a healer, Message Bearer?" Stroud asked, still staring at the wall.

"No." Hunger and thirst demanded attention, but those wants were pale, almost ephemeral. He wanted to feel his talisman, verify it.

He rolled up to a sitting position on the edge of the bed, and sudden wisps of dizziness unmoored the room. His sense of balance sloshed and tried to reorient. His equilibrium fought against the new weight in his left arm. Vertigo made him swoon and tossed his head. He gripped the bed to master the roil. Two sediments, biological and metallic, stirred and mixed. His bare feet set a base while both sediments drifted to settle.

"What happened? How long have I been here?"

"It has been a day since you first woke. It was three days before that when Lokah and Mandavu brought you here," Stroud recounted.

The hidden forge. The abortive attempt to skirt the will of *montmorillionite* and draw out a parallel weapon. Mortification at his rash act shamed him. His loss of control and frustration... He shook the feelings back into the sediment in hopes that it would carry them down.

All of the things that were keeping him from getting home had also undone him. The barriers to getting help for the Mono Lord and returning the embassy to the Upper Lands overwhelmed him. His attempts to save the earth and the course of creation subsumed him. Divisions among allies kept them from coming together. Lord Morgrom's stratagems were replete.

He had to bury those things for the time being. At the moment, he couldn't stand. And his desire for his weapon was at the forefront of his mind.

"Where is Lokah?" Lokah would know where his weapon was, if he was not hurt or worse. He would be the only one who could come close to understanding what he was experiencing, *once he was able to tell him what had happened.*

"All the members of the embassy have been told that you are awake." Stroud paused for a long moment, then continued. "They are all coming here. Do you need a healer?"

"I am parched. Can I have some water?"

Stroud opened the divider and left.

Healer stewards walked by. Odors of vinegar, lavender, and rosemary stirred in the air, but they failed to cover the fetor of dead and charred fish.

Chimere came in, and Stroud resumed his position.

"How do you feel?" Chimere asked. He walked to the table in the corner of the room and set a pitcher down. He came over to Aenguz and handed him a cup of water. The Moresi looked over Aenguz's bruises.

Aenguz noted them too, but like his hunger and thirst, they were minor compared to his primary need. If he weren't so dizzy, he would have left right then to get his weapon.

As Chimere pored over the bumps and scrapes, he remembered the stairs at the forge. He tumbled. The brow around his eye hurt. He felt at a bandage and then noticed a few others as Chimere inspected him.

Chimere avoided the left arm all together. He seemed afraid of it. "How does it feel?" he asked. His lips curved and his eyebrows squeezed.

How to describe it? "Like I am half underwater." It was the simplest terms he could think of to explain it.

"Lokah is here," Stroud said.

Lokah turned into the room. His eyes pleaded. Awkward scabs marred his face. He looked stern and grief-stricken. He bore something wrapped in leather in his hands.

He rushed over to the bed, and Chimere slid out of the way. Lokah walked down onto his knees as if he had stepped into a hole. He flung his head down onto Aenguz's thighs. "Aenguz, my lord, forgive me, forgive me! I am so sorry. Forgive me, I beg you, I did not know what would happen, I thought it had killed you!" Lokah grabbed and hugged him.

Aenguz rested his right arm across Lokah's back. "You did not do this. Rise. This is the will of *montmorillion lore*."

Lokah beat his head on Aenguz's legs.

"Rise, Lokah. This was not your fault. You could not know what would happen. I know you would never hurt me."

Lokah pulled back and climbed tentatively to his feet. He wiped his eyes, but his face was still curved into a frown. He was on the verge of tears; his eyes were wet. He obeyed Aenguz, but self-recrimination blanched him.

"I need you to help me figure out what this is." Aenguz held up his arm.

Lokah looked cautiously at the silver arm. His eyes darted up and down the length of it. "What happened at the forge? Did your weapon resist? Did the stone resist the lore?"

Aenguz was not ready to admit his sacrilege or the desperation and frustration that had led to it. And certainly not in front of the Azari.

"I lost my focus," was all he could muster. "Do you have my weapon? Is the Dagba Stone still attached?"

"Yes," he said mournfully, as if he had failed Aenguz. "It is back in the storeroom. The One King has ordered that it remain there."

Aenguz glanced at Stroud. Now it was fait accompli that the Dagba Stone and his weapon would remain in Earthmight. Being stripped of the choice left him feeling even more powerless. As difficult as it was, reaching the decision on his own had given him a small sense of control.

That was before the forge.

Now, the One King had made a decision and a command. The fear of leaving his weapon ran cold in him. There would be no argument that would sway Thelen now. And the One King was suspicious of him. What could he possibly say that would make him release his weapon?

His arm was coated in *montmorillionite* now. Perhaps this was the means to free the stone. Perhaps the will of *montmorillion* had done this so that he could remove it. He needed to try, but the vertigo was still tipping him askew in the room. He slid back onto the bed.

"Are you unwell?" Chimere asked.

"My brain feels like it is floating in water."

"Let me get you something. Many of the gravid women here experience the same thing. There are a lot of them." Chimere left as if he were grateful for a reason to help - or leave.

Aenguz's attention was drawn to the leather Lokah had cast onto the bed. "What is that?"

Lokah handed it to him. It was a scabbard with the belt straps wrapped around it. "It is forged Akkeidii steel."

He passed the scabbard to his silver hand. He gripped the handle and drew out the Akkeidii sword. The knuckle bow was wide and square with rounded corners. The grip was knurled and contoured to fit the hand. The metal was a dark gray, like faded anthracite. It shimmered between storm gray and coal in the raw *montmorillionite* light. The blade was narrow at the hilt but widened and thickened gradually. Halfway up, it widened quickly into a thick, heavy blade. It curved slightly and met the back edge, with a concave curve to complement it. It was a short sword for close-quarters fighting.

"You commanded a weapon of me," Lokah said with a muted pride.

Aenguz admired the Akkeidii blade. "This is… This is a fine example of Akkeidii metalwork. You are a gifted loremaster, Lokah."

Lokah gave a grateful but timid smile.

"I honed it on my blade and on Mandavu's mace. Outside of *montmorillionite*, it is the sharpest blade in these lands."

Aenguz slid the sword carefully back into the scabbard and laid it on the bed close to his leg. He admired the leatherwork. Lokah noticed.

"I have finished my scabbard too," Lokah said proudly.

"You have worked hard on that. I look forward to seeing it."

Chimere returned. Legerohn was behind him. Chimere held a mortar and pestle with a vial and some herbs in it. He went over to the table, emptied the contents into it, and started to work the herbs into the salve from the vial in the mortar.

Legerohn carried a pitcher. He set it down beside the mortar and left Chimere to work. He came over and laid a hand on Aenguz's shoulder.

"I find you too often in an infirmary," the Prince said brightly.

"And I may be here a bit longer, unless Chimere has an answer for my spinning head."

"This will help. It will take a day or two, but it will help," the young Moresi said over his shoulder as he worked the ingredients together.

"You should be well enough then to see the One King speak," Legerohn said.

The question was plain on Aenguz's face.

"The One King has called a gathering. He will speak to all the denizens of Earthmight at the amphitheater over morrow. All the Azari. All the stewards. The One Army. Us. Everyone."

What could he have to say? Was that how he garnered the will of the people? What was the One King intending?

"I have spoken with Saissha. She still investigates Illia's murder, but I have convinced her that we must leave. As soon as you are well enough to travel, we can begin our preparations."

Aenguz nodded. He looked at Stroud. The Azari stared at the wall. Legerohn's back was turned. Stroud heard him, but he could not see Legerohn's mouth.

Chimere came over and handed Aenguz a dollop of salve with dark flecks of green in it. "Here, take this."

He smelled the tannic paste. The bitter, sour mixture was hard to swallow.

Mandavu turned into the room and rushed to Aenguz. He rapped his knuckles on the metallic arm and smiled curiously and said, "My brother said it: 'You are one tough Sidor.'"

"Not tough enough, it seems," Aenguz demurred.

Chimere explained the dizziness to Mandavu. "It will take a day or two, but the dizziness should dissipate."

"Do you have orders?" Mandavu turned his head just enough to indicate that he knew he was hiding his words from Stroud, but he could still hear.

"Be ready," was all he dared say with the corner of Stroud's eye in view. They trusted Stroud enough to let him hear, but not enough to share with all of the Azari.

Saissha came in with Nedenthal, the newly promoted Step Mark of the embassy, behind her.

The members of the embassy were all pleased and surprised to see Aenguz. He nodded and greeted them back, but he did not smile. Saissha's face stayed locked in worry and concern.

It struck Aenguz as strange that the leader of the Stair Guard was there to gather supplies.

Saissha looked to the others to glean Aenguz's state. She sighed with relief and laid a hand on his leg, but her burden and consternation did not ease.

Nedenthal greeted Aenguz tentatively, but he looked at his metallic arm suspiciously, as if some strange parasite were attached to it.

Mandavu fretted over Saissha.

"Braydehn is missing," she said in dismay.

Consternation gripped the embassy.

Nedenthal stepped closer. "We sent him earlier than usual for supplies and more warm clothes. He should have been back already. I came to see if he made it here, or if something happened to him." The Step Mark was worried.

Saissha asked the embassy, "Have any of you seen or heard from him?"

What could have happened to him? An accident? Erebim? Aenguz wondered. He had been unconscious and in bed. He had nothing to offer.

"He is held in a cell," Stroud said.

"What?! Why?" Saissha strode up angrily to Stroud. "Why did you not tell me? Where did you find him?" she demanded.

The Azari faced her. "The Stair Guard Braydehn was found trying to approach the Cleve. The soldiers of the garrison brought him here two days ago. The One King commanded that he be immured."

"Why? For how long?" Saissha pressed Stroud.

"The Cleve is forbidden."

"Stroud, in a cell? For how long? I want him freed right now," Saissha ordered the Azari.

Stroud lowered and then raised his head. It was an indication that what he said next was not his own words, but that they were recounted from the One King. He did not lower his tone. "The Cleve is forbidden. The One King will release him on one condition. If you call the other Stair Guard back to join the One Army, then he will be released to fight alongside his comrades." He swallowed.

Saissha yelled at the One King through Stroud. "You protect life and yet hold it for ransom?!" she railed on. "Those tenets are incompatible!"

Legerohn argued alongside her. "You cannot do this!" He made a case and explained to the One King how his actions broke faith with his charge to serve and steward the people.

Mandavu swore by Grieg Sidor's name at Stroud and at the One King. One of their own was imprisoned.

They couldn't leave Earthmight without Braydehn. Saissha would not abandon him. None of them would. The plan to make for the Spine and secretly attempt the Cleve was dead in its tracks.

Aenguz's throat tightened. Braydehn was alone. No one had gone to him.

"Get down there," Aenguz ordered Mandavu and Lokah. "He thinks he is alone. No one has seen him." His words slurred out at the end.

"Aenguz should rest. The medicine needs sleep to take hold," Chimere said. He was trying to follow his duty to heal.

Saissha was torn between yelling at Stroud and going to find Braydehn. Mandavu pulled her out of the room. The rest of the embassy filed out after her.

Stroud adjusted the divider and turned back to the wall. He seemed conflicted.

Sleep was quickly overcoming Aenguz, but he had questions for Stroud.

"Are you still a member of the embassy, or are you a part of your people again?" Aenguz asked.

Stroud stood like he had no intention of answering. The medicine was taking hold.

Then, Stroud started, "I have lived without my people for an age. I have not shared the One Sight with anyone in that time. I have lived more like the people of the earth than as an Azari. I never thought to see through their eyes again. I accepted that new way of life.

"Sharing our eyes reminds me of much of who I was. Their dedication to service and to defending against Oblivion reminds me of the service I held in defending the Counsel Lords. When I left Corundum, I expected to return like you. Corundum has become my home." Stroud shifted. His complexion changed. "I thought I would see it once again. You think I am without emotion. But I understand your desire to return home better than any Azari. Even though the Lower Lands and Earthmight are not their home, it has become their home, like Corundum has for me." He seemed to consider his next words carefully.

"I thought I would see Mono Lord Lana again. I have known her for her entire life. I thought I would return to her. If I did return, I would ward her for the rest of her days. If the world gave me a choice, and if the world remained, I would ward her to the end of her life."

The stolid Azari looked depleted.

Sleep was drawing in fast.

"Are you here to protect me, or are you warding against me?" Aenguz asked.

"We do not know what you have become."

"Stroud?"

"Yes."

"Where is Carina?"

46

ABDICATE

The next day, Chimere stood by Aenguz as he took his first steps. The Moresi limped beside him and provided a steady hand as they walked through the crowded infirmary. Stroud did not follow them, but he kept them in sight.

"Will Saissha give up the Stair Guard?" Chimere asked. Worry filled his voice.

"I do not know." Aenguz had tossed and turned over her impossible dilemma. There was no way out. He needed time to think of a way to solve the compounding problems and save the embassy, maybe from itself.

"I have gathered medicines for my Tahnka," Chimere whispered as they walked away from Stroud. "They do not know of mountain sickness here, but I have gathered medicines to help with pain and nausea."

"Good, Chimere." Aenguz was grateful for him. Everyone was doing their part to help them get home, but now with Braydehn imprisoned, it seemed impossible that they would even reach the Spine or the Cleve. He couldn't see them leaving him there.

A pair of healers bore a litter to an unobtrusive doorway. The lifeless form seemed fragile and desiccated beneath the shroud.

"What is that?" he asked Chimere about the room.

"It is a room for those who die, mostly the old from Earthmight, and now the vales. The healer stewards take them there so that their family can come and see their loved ones before they are taken down to the death chamber. In the back of the room, there are stairs that lead down to it."

Mandavu and Lokah visited him and reported back on their meeting with Braydehn. "He apologized to Saissha. He wanted to go home. When it was his turn to return for supplies, he went to the Cleve," Mandavu explained. Then he tightened. "It is just a block to lock the door. We could free him easily."

"But we would not get far," Aenguz answered.

"I know," Mandavu replied dejectedly.

"It is a Stonemage design. The cell block was crafted by Stonemages," Lokah said.

"Stonemages?"

Lokah nodded.

Aenguz pondered what that might mean. He wondered about Braydehn's decision. It seemed out of character for him. He worried about his solitude. Aenguz shivered at the thought. At least now the embassy knew he was there. "Make sure you see him every day." The pair nodded and agreed. "Does he know the One King's ultimatum?"

"Saissha told him," Mandavu answered.

"He told her to leave him and not force his brothers to fight on his account."

Aenguz understood the wrack of impossible choices for Siassha and the irrevocable demands of self-sacrifice. He blamed himself for her unbearable choice - for all of it. He had promised the embassy that he would find a way out, but now they were all more trapped than ever. He wanted to try removing the stone with his new arm, but even if that worked, with Braydehn captured, they still couldn't leave.

On the day of the One King's speech, Aenguz was able to walk without fear of falling over. Healer stewards were making their way out of the infirmary to head to the amphitheater. They were mostly women. There were a few young boys and very old men who were either too young or too old to fight. Aenguz was getting dressed. Chimere was close by. Stroud urged them in an inexorably stolid tone that the speech was getting close.

Aenguz's long-sleeved shirt covered his arm, but his hand was still exposed. "Can you find a glove?" Aenguz asked as he flexed his fingers. He was embarrassed by its strangeness. It was akin to the shame he felt when he first saw his arm after the *morillion* had left it ghoulish and mottled.

"I think so. Let me go and see." Chimere stepped out. He turned back with a look of confusion and said, "Carina is here. She is coming over."

Aenguz was suddenly flummoxed. He wanted to see her, but he felt trapped in the small room. And there was no privacy. He needed to talk with her and explain so much.

"She came to see you each day when you first came here," Chimere added. He must have realized that Aenguz had no idea.

Aenguz clutched his silver fist and hid it behind him.

Chimere pulled back the divider and weaved out among the healers to give them some privacy and find a glove. Stroud did not budge.

Carina looked peaked. Her dark copper-blonde curls were unruly. She wore a long wool coat and tall black boots. She walked timorously, and her smile seemed forced. Her eyes darted to him and away like a small bird fighting against a gale.

Aenguz stepped toward her, but the moment he moved, she stopped. "I wanted to see you."

"I wanted to see you, too."

"I am sorry for all that happened. I did not plan for any of it."

"Did you plan to stay?"

She knew the truth. She knew that he was planning to leave.

"I have to return, but the One King has one of the Stair Guard imprisoned. We cannot leave without him."

"But if you did free him, you would leave." It was more a statement than a question.

He wanted to give her any other answer, to hold her, apologize, and beg for forgiveness. If she only knew… But he could only stand. His silence was answer enough.

"The One King will speak soon. We must go," Stroud interjected.

"We must all hear what the One King has to say," she said blithely, as if it couldn't matter less to her.

"Chimere, come," Stroud said.

Chimere limped slowly past Carina. He passed the white glove over to Aenguz.

Aenguz pulled his hand out and held it out long enough for her to see it. Then he slid the glove on.

Carina stared at his silver hand. She gulped. Her tongue poked out at her cheek like she was pondering a problem. Tears filled the fringes of her eyelids. She glanced at Chimere and Stroud and then fled out of the room.

"Wait!" Aenguz called, but she was gone. She blended in with the flow of healer stewards. He followed her with his eyes until she disappeared.

Stroud led Aenguz and Chimere out of the infirmary. He led them up a series of stairs carved into the schist of Earthmight. Stewards were ahead and behind.

He led them to a long gray chamber with columned arches and the balcony beyond. The chamber looked out over the corner of the Plateau that met the stone base of the Spire. Three tiers of hexagonal pylons formed the raised edge of the basalt sea wall, stretching to the far corner of the Plateau. A chilled wind swept down from the north, its force softened by the Spire. The Sunfall Sea was to his right. Long plains of alto-cumulus clouds were interspersed in the sky. Dead fish lolled inside the curved breakwater. Columns of black smoke trailed up beyond the Plateau between the cliffs and the sea. People filled the top of the Plateau. Azari were interspersed evenly among them.

Stroud led them over to the embassy. Mandavu, Lokah, Legerohn, and Saissha were there. Nedenthal was beside her. He looked at the assembled throng of Earthmight with apprehension.

Healer stewards and keep stewards were there, but they kept apart from the embassy. There was worry in the undercurrent of their low chatter. They didn't seem to know what the One King planned to say.

They greeted Aenguz and Chimere and made room for them at the edge. The balconies to the left were crowded with people - stewards and denizens of the keep. Aenguz looked down into the amphitheater at the assembly in curiosity. Below, he could make out the soldiers of the One Army. There were other armed men too - men of the garrison. Stewards sat in wedges with their compatriots behind them - keep stewards, grain stewards, water stewards, and so on. Their beige aprons with the fanned handprints on the back over their coats supported them, one and all. He saw Sorolokova at the bottom rows directly below him. He found Carina near her. Scores of Free People were around them. The rows were filled. The whole of Earthmight was gathered to hear the One King. The stage was clear.

Stroud stood at the center of the balcony and said, "The One King is about to speak."

He dropped his head and his eyes, and the people grew quiet. Aenguz noticed all the Azari dropping their heads in unison - on the Plateau, on the balconies, and in the higher tiers of the amphitheater.

The One King entered from the center door of the façade at the back of the stage. Hannoch and Sarokin were beside him. They took a wide arc away from the One King and stepped down from the edge of the stage onto the sole step that ringed the wide edge of the stage. They both turned and faced Thelen. Every soul in Earthmight was silent. Only stray ruffling and lone coughs poked at the silence. Aenguz could hear Thelen's footfalls on the stage. The One King looked all around the assembled host. His black obsidian-eyed crown seemed to take them all in. He took a few final long breaths, and then he spoke.

"My heart overflows with gratitude. Seeing all of you assembled here: stewards, soldiers of the One Army and of the garrison, artisans, craftsmen, people of the vales, members of the embassy of Corundum - all of you are servants to one another and to the Law of Creation. It fills me beyond understanding. It is in my heart to serve you. That is why I have called you here today in midwinter."

Although his words carried up to the balcony, they were distant. Stroud mirrored the One King's words an octave lower than his own voice. All of the Azari echoed what the One King said in unison.

"I have ever been a servant unto you all since becoming your king. I am the Chief Steward of the Lands. In these times, it is both a grave and joyful honor. Your faith in me has sustained me in stewarding life here. *Life protects life.*'

"War is upon us all. Invaders attack without restraint in the vilest and most heinous of ways. The people of the vales have been assaulted. *Remember Tormont Vale!*

"The great horses have been slaughtered. The secret places of the Free People have been violated. The Woe Sower has set his designs on our people and our lands and on our home here in Earthmight. The One Army assembles. All hale and able men join in our defense. *'Life and death are intertwined.'*

"Even in the midst of this invasion, the abundance of the earth reveals the abundance of creation. A harvest where all trees bear fruit, where all seeds yield full crops. The blight that made our lives such a struggle seems to be gone. More children come. *'Life begets life.'* The children that will be born will come into a fruitful world, an abundant world. *'Trees and plants bear fruit according to their kind. Seed to root. Seed to life.'* The world strives to multiply. But the Woe Sower has sent his servants to destroy life. *'Life and death are intertwined.'* Even the Sunfall Sea is under attack."

He strode to his left toward the Sunfall Sea, as if he were hurrying to its aid.

"I have tried to outthink the Woe Sower's designs, and I have failed. I have tried to protect you here, and I have failed. The war seemed far away, but it is now at Earthmight. I have failed you."

His head dropped as if the weight of the crown was suddenly too much.

"Some of you have heard of Illia's death. Elin, mother, and grain steward of the keep. And Dalmeida, first archer of the One Army. Their daughter's life has been taken."

A wave of gasps moved through the crowd. Those who knew provided a validation for those who didn't believe or who hadn't yet heard the news of her murder.

"I have failed her. I have failed in my obligations to you and to

Earthmight. I have failed the Free People and the Heart of the World. My decisions have led to ruin. I have been outmatched by the Woe Sower."

Thelen returned to the center of the stage and faced the agitated crowd. "I therefore relinquish the crown, my stewardship, and the rule you have bestowed upon me."

He removed his silver-and-black crown and laid it down on the stage.

Cries of "No!" and shock rose up in pockets from the crowd. The commotion surged and grew. Many stood and shouted that he take back the crown.

Thelen looked relieved even at a distance. He seemed small. His bald head made him look plain.

The Monomander, Biniam, calmed his men and the men of the garrison. He saw the growing chaos and took matters into his own hands. He swung up the two steps and walked over to the crown. He picked it up. A pocket of cheers and "Yes!" crested in spots over the "Nos." Biniam looked around briefly. Some conflict may have been in him, but it was brief. He walked over to Thelen and placed the crown back on his head. Thelen pulled back slightly, but he ultimately accepted the crown from his Monomander.

The assembly cheered, even those who had urged Biniam to take the crown.

"I am humbled by your faith in me. I have been too timid, too conservative. *'Life adapts to the world, and the world adapts to life.'*

"Tomorrow, I will lead the One Army south. We will fortify Llangollen. We will protect the great horses from the Erebim and ward their birthing grounds in the Shattered Lands. We will eradicate the Woe Sower's minions. We will raise a mound around each *verran-dulum* discovered.

"We will scour the lands from Earthmight to the Shattered Lands, from the Sunfall Sea to the Spine of the World. We will march, and we will not stop until every invader is eradicated, and our lands and our homes are ours again."

Loud cheers rose in the amphitheater. It was a massive release from the assembly.

As the enthusiastic cheers calmed down, Thelen raised his hand to still them, and then he continued, "We welcome the soldiers of the Stair Guard in our fight."

Thelen reached his hand up to the balcony where the embassy stood.

"What?!" Aenguz said. Shock broke the spell of the One King's words. He turned to Saissha.

"Grieg the Sanctor!" Mandavu swore.

They all turned to Saissha. "I have agreed to his terms."

"But Saissha…" Aenguz started.

"What would you have me do? Leave Braydehn here?"

"Saissha, we cannot climb the Spine without them!"

"I will not leave him here. This way he can be free, and they can live and be safe in the company of the One Army."

"They will never return home. You have banished them."

"'*Life protects life,*'" she said with such a fatalistic tone that she ended the conversation. Her decision was final. "Nedenthal will return to the other Stair Guard and call them here." She handed her staff to Nedenthal and reached her hands up to Aenguz and Mandavu as if to console them both. They bent down, and she cupped their faces. In close, she whispered to them, "When Nedenthal leaves and they let Braydehn go, we will leave." She gave them both a subtle shrewd smile.

47

NO TO THE STONE

Back in Aenguz's room, Legerohn, Mandavu, and Lokah gathered around the table. They were all sullen. Saissha had dissolved the embassy and their means to cross the Spine. Legerohn was dour. He looked as if he stood before the sharp sky-reaching peaks. He feared the passage more than all of them. His personal dilemma was not so different than Braydehn's and Saissha's. If he attempted the Spine again, he might die. If he stayed, he would accept a self-imposed exile in the Lower Lands.

He asked the question that hung in the air for all of them. "How can we cross the Spine without the Stair Guard?"

"We will have to cross through the Cleve," Aenguz answered, resigned. "My friend, we were never going to cross the Spine. That was only ever a ploy for the One King to allow us to leave Earthmight. You cannot risk those mountains again."

"What about the garrison?"

"The bulk of the garrison is here," Mandavu said.

"How do you know that?" Legerohn asked.

"Braydehn told me," he answered. "He was not trying to sneak through to the Cleve. He was doing reconnaissance on the garrison for us."

Aenguz smiled at Mandavu.

"You ordered me to find out the complement of the garrison. They captured him on their way here. Thelen has called all of them back to Earthmight to join the One Army. There are less than fifty men warding the encampment at the mouth of the Cleve. I did not expect him to be captured," he said to Aenguz, as if to take the blame for their current dilemma.

"Do not fault yourself. You gave us the information we needed. Now, it is only a squad of men and the Sentinel. Did he see the Sentinel?"

"Yes," Mandavu answered. "The lone Azari stands on a hillock north of the Cleve. Braydehn told me he is a statue. He stares at the opening, unmoving, unblinking."

Legerohn quickly understood what Aenguz was suggesting. "My friend, you cannot kill those men." He acknowledged Mandavu and Lokah. "I know they would follow your orders to their deaths, but we cannot kill them. Any doubts the One King holds toward us would be confirmed. He will think we murdered Illia. They do not need fifty men at the Cleve. One would be enough if we meant to kill."

"We have to leave, and soon. We are running out of time, and this is our opportunity." The question of his weapon was still poised like a beacon at the front of Aenguz's mind.

"If we were to cross the Cleve and return with an army before Lord Morgrom's forces arrive, we would still bear the stain of that spilled blood. They would not forget that transgression. It would reflect ill on Saissha as well."

"What can I do? I cannot convince all the people of Earthmight to lift the prohibition over the Cleve." Aenguz seethed at the compounding dilemmas. "That is not even the greater problem. He not only leaves the Cleve undefended, he is leading the One Army the wrong way. '*Five seasons will not pass before Earthmight is under siege, and the One King's army is lost.*'"

Mandavu stated the strategic flaw matter-of-factly. "The defense of their fortress would be utterly negated. They will have to fight the Flayer's forces on the plains where they trained as if they were the invading force."

"And there are not enough men in the One Army," Aenguz added. "In spring, in the fifth season, the One Army will be as far south as the Shattered Lands."

"The strength of Earthmight would be divided from the strength of the One Army," Lokah said, as if he appreciated the tactical success Morgrom had achieved. "And our armies also."

All will be divided against all.

——— ✦ ———

THELEN RODE OUT FROM Earthmight on a white destrier. His silver armor gleamed in the midwinter sun. Hannoch and Sarokin rode with him and forty other mounted soldiers. The Queen of the Free People rode behind them. Telakot was at her side. Aenguz found Carina's horse, but all the riders looked the same with their heavy leather armor, their short bows, and their two-headed axes. He couldn't be sure it was her, but he held that it was her in his heart.

Cheers followed the One King as his complement rode toward the training grounds. The edge of the tent city was lined with people, mostly women, to cheer him on. The edge of the Plateau was packed with people watching and cheering on Earthmight's defender. And all the different stewards filled the balconies and called out after the departing army. The embassy had made their way down to a balcony on the southern side of the Spire to watch the hope of the Lower Lands depart.

The wide column of great horses and men stretched to the south. The logistics train was a chaos of wagons and people in the heart of their former camp.

Biniam met the One King with his mounted Azari and his attending guard, and they both rode south along the column. A cheer from the One Army followed them and faded as they galloped to the head of the formation.

Then, like a giant caterpillar, the line undulated like a wave. The One Army marched on, with Thelen out of sight at the head, to Llangollen and the far southern lands beyond. The train of wagons carrying smiths, stewards, and all the support adjuncts trickled slowly after them.

Saissha reported back to the embassy as they walked back up through the Spire that there had been too much commotion in preparing for the One Army's departure. She and Nedenthal had been unable to get the supplies they needed, but she assured them that once the One Army was gone, they would get what they needed, not only for the Stair Guard, but also for their crossing.

They watched the line disappear from a balcony not far from their dining hall. Mandavu adjusted his count for Aenguz as they watched. There were fewer than seven thousand mounted men and infantry. It was a vast number, but Aenguz, Saissha, and Legerohn affirmed that it did not match the vast hordes they had witnessed in the Divine Oculum.

———◆———

AENGUZ WAS RUNNING OUT of time. They would be departing soon, and his weapon and the Dagba Stone would be left behind. He tried not to think that it would be lost to him, that he might never return.

He wore the Akkeidii steel sword that Lokah had given him. It assuaged some of the discomfort of being away from his weapon, but it did not replace it.

Lokah seemed to sense Aenguz's unease. He brought his newly made scabbard over to Aenguz's room. The large, long leather scabbard was tooled with intricate detail. Aenguz pored over the lines and details that flowed down the length of it. Thick straps were riveted in place, thanks to one of the Free People, he had said. It made him think of Carina, but Lokah's craftsmanship brought him back.

"This is incredible work," Aenguz breathed in amazement.

"I spent a lot of time at the entrance to the Spire to study Hernus Kriel." Lokah pulled the flap up to reveal a patch of leather that he had worked silver into to fashion a likeness of Hernus Kriel's helmeted skull. The detailed nose piece and the fine angular etching on the helmet, the delicate lines of the feathers on the wings that rose up beside it as if it were bearing the Akkeidii forefather's skull up and away into the White Earth… Lokah's skill humbled Aenguz.

Aenguz touched the tooled patch gently with his silver hand, almost to confirm that it was real. "I am amazed," was all he could say.

Lokah went on to explain the lines and symbols that connotated his line all the way up to Hernus Kriel. His name appeared at the very bottom, followed by his father's, then his grandfather's. The embossed lines were both symbol and story. Aenguz followed the pressed details and stories of his family and clan as he walked through the Kriel familial and clan history.

"I hope to show this to my father," Lokah said in a mixture of pride and sorrow.

"You will. We will find a way to get home." Aenguz tried to sound reassuring, but at the moment, it didn't seem possible.

"I am sorry I did not find a way to remove the stone."

Urgency, proximity, and the fear of loss surged up in Aenguz. "I have not tried this hand yet." He held up his *montmorillionite*-coated hand.

Lokah cocked his head. "You cannot."

"Of course I can. This may be what the *montmorillionite* intended." Aenguz got up and headed for the storeroom.

"Wait, Aenguz, lord, you cannot touch it!" Lokah circled in front of him.

The old Azari at the end of the hall focused on them.

"Move. I am going to try this."

Mandavu left his room and crossed to meet them.

"We are leaving soon. This is my last chance." Desperation sent a rush of panic through Aenguz.

Mandavu stood shoulder to shoulder with Lokah.

"Move, both of you. I am not leaving my weapon here."

The old Azari was suddenly at Lokah's other shoulder. "Hold, Message Bearer."

"I do not want the stone, but I need my weapon."

"You cannot touch it, Aenguz," Lokah started. "You know what happened in the cleft in the Spine and in the caverns of Corundum. Who knows what that power would do to Earthmight? You could topple the Spire!"

The Azari shifted into a subtle fighting pose.

Mandavu was resigned.

"I order you to let me try and remove the stone."

"We cannot let you," Mandavu said.

Aenguz swirled. Frenetic energy tightened his arms. The definition of his warrior self was calling to him. He had unbelievable strength in his arm. He could fling them aside in one sweep. Violence and reason estranged him from himself. An idea came. "Then let me take it outside. I will try it away from Earthmight."

"The One King has forbidden it. The stone cannot be removed," the old Azari said.

"We took our chance at the forge. We cannot take it again," Lokah said dejectedly, as if he took all the failure onto himself.

Mandavu placed a hand on Aenguz's left shoulder. "We will explain to the clan lords and the loremasters why your weapon had to remain. We will be the voice for the metal. You will bear no shame."

Aenguz's heart was in upheaval. The pulses thrummed. One deep pulse pushed him like a wave, but Mandavu's hand reminded him of his father and his words about letting the storm pass. The feelings were coming from within him, but he still had to master them. He breathed past his heart and drew long breaths. His shoulders dropped. They were his friends. They had only ever warded him. He gripped the hilt of his steel sword and went back to his room, as crestfallen as if the world had collapsed.

———◆———

MOONLIGHT POURED INTO AENGUZ'S suite. Nedenthal was leaving the next day. Shortly thereafter, the embassy would head for the Spine. He would have to figure out how to get to the Cleve without killing any of the men there.

They had all held up their end of the bargain. Only the stone and his weapon remained. Mandavu gave him an answer for that. But how could he explain his need to them? He could barely understand it himself. His arm cut a pathway to *montmorillionite* through an expression of *montmorillion* lore that was as cryptic as it was powerful. It was elemental and raw, unassailable. He could leave Earthmight. He wouldn't hold the embassy back, but he didn't know if he could endure how desperate he might become, didn't know if he could hide the deterioration he might endure. He had already failed them as a leader. Now a yearning stronger than any he had known was forbidding him from leaving. He would do it; he just didn't know who he would be when he left.

Saissha had made an impossible choice to save the Stair Guard, but it would force them to the Cleve.

Legerohn cautioned him against killing any of the men of the garrison. He understood his rationale, but the situation was already dire. Extreme measures might have to be taken.

Nedenthal would leave. The only gear provided was what the One Army bore. Since they were joining them, it made sense to provide those kits and gear.

Saissha kept up a good face. She agreed to what the stewards provided, even though she had no intention of releasing them to the One King. Once they freed Braydehn and gathered enough horses for the embassy, they would leave and catch up with Nedenthal. With the Stair Guard, they could perhaps threaten the remaining men of the garrison and avoid a fight altogether.

All of the impossibilities bounced off the walls of Aenguz's mind. And all of it was compounded by the One King's actions. They had come to get help, and instead the One Army was marching away, and the embassy was caught in a prison without doors or walls.

The silver moonlight slipped out of the room as Aenguz pondered in rhythm with the *montmorillionite's* thrum.

———◆———

Nedenthal left the next day. The embassy saw him off at the stables. Two young horses were loaded with gear for the Stair Guard. They were deemed too young to be conscripted. Bridles were looped around their heads.

At that last moment, Aenguz told Mandavu to saddle Draymondon and ride out with him for a time, so that the Step Mark would not be alone within the shadow of Earthmight.

Saissha wished him well and gave a blessing to him for all the Stair Guard camped at the base of the Spine. Braydehn would not be far behind. Once he was released, he would follow and find him. Then they could ride together to join the One Army.

The pair rode off in the cold morning with the two pack horses in tow. The rest of the embassy climbed the ramps to the top of the Plateau and watched the pair disappear beyond the nearly barren training fields. Only a handful of stewards kept the camp from being utterly empty.

———◆———

It was dinner-time when Mandavu returned. He assured Aenguz that Nedenthal was on his way and that Draymondon had done well.

Stroud stood in the room with all of them in his periphery. The food held no interest for the leader of the Azari.

Mandavu asked Stroud as he grabbed a plate, "Where is Saissha?"

"She is coming here," Stroud said impassively.

"She has been asking about Illia." Aenguz and Lokah offered some food to Mandavu. He accepted it with a distracted familiarity.

Chimere talked with Legerohn about the medicines he had to help his Tahnka weather the Spine. Legerohn put on a brave face, but he couldn't totally hide his concern.

Saissha stormed into the dining hall. "The people's steward! I was a fool!"

"What happened?" Mandavu got up and guided her to the table.

"He is not going to let Braydehn go."

"What?!" they all asked.

"The One King thanks me for commanding the Stair Guard to join the One Army, and once he sees them, or the Azari sees them, joining their ranks, he will let Braydehn go."

They cursed in Grieg Sidor's name. Legerohn called to Stroud, but the Azari gave no answer.

They wouldn't leave until Braydehn was freed. They were hostages. The One King was adapting.

Mandavu tried to console Saissha.

———— ◆ ————

AENGUZ ORDERED LOKAH DOWN to the cells the next day to keep company with Braydehn. His loremaster balked, but relented, as he had the most experience down there, for better or for worse.

Mandavu saw to their supplies. He and Legerohn also worked to find horses. It would take time to get ready, and they had to keep up the charade that they were leaving and that they would observe the One King's ultimatum.

Saissha went back to the work of solving Illia's murder. Something in her believed that if she found her killer, the One King might release his obduracy toward the embassy. And also, she wanted to remove all doubt from the embassy. She found Elin and questioned her about her daughter and her friends and any boys she might have been connected with. After dinner, she would search out her friends and see if there was any reason why someone might want to hurt her.

Aenguz had fallen further into despair at the news of the One King's edict. He was afraid that they would have to leave Braydehn. He would be imprisoned and alone. Who knew if the One King would keep his promise?

Only six of them remained, the last of the embassy. It might not be enough to hold off the men still at the garrison. A fight seemed inevitable, and not all of them might survive long enough to reach the Cleve. And then there was the Sentinel. Once he saw them, their ruse would be up.

* * *

THEY GATHERED ONE BY one in the dining hall for their last morn meal in Earthmight. Legerohn was talking with a grain steward about the special breads that the Chief Steward Monguerra had baked for them. "Whatever you do not finish, we will wrap and pack for you for your journey," the gray-haired woman said.

Chimere hobbled in with a stuffed satchel over his shoulder. He limped to his chair and let the bag down onto the table.

Aenguz spoke with the new Chief Keep Steward, Janelle. Sutton had not recovered from Illia's murder. He blamed himself, and it had become clear that he could no longer maintain his responsibilities.

Stroud stood in the same spot, staring at the wall. Although there were fewer Azari in the keep, it seemed his attention was more focused than ever. His responses were slower. Aenguz noticed Azari moving in the halls. They had to cover more ground.

Lokah and Mandavu came. They were both dressed for travel. They bore packs filled with clothes from the garment stewards. Mandavu moved to his chair and asked Stroud, "Where is Saissha?"

Mandavu offered barrio bread to Aenguz and Lokah. They handed him some back in return.

Stroud shifted his head slightly and held for a moment. "Counsel Lord Saissha is dead."

PART IV

DEATH

48

MORS OF A COUNSEL LORD

Mandavu sprinted through the halls. Aenguz tried to slow him, but his First was lost to shock. All they could do was follow him. Lokah, Legerohn, and Chimere raced behind them.

Mandavu blew through stewards, old men, women, anyone in his way. One Azari tried to slow him, but he picked up the stocky Azari and continued to run. The Azari managed, after a few strides, to squirrel away from Mandavu.

The Azari shifted tactics instead and moved ahead of Mandavu. Aenguz watched as they flashed ahead, stopped in front of or next to people, and moved them out of the way. It was a complicated dance that ran ahead of the wild boar that would not be stopped.

Mandavu scrambled down stairways, lunging two, three, four steps at a time. He sprinted along the inside curve of the hallways. The Azari caught unwitting people stepping out of their doors.

At the rose marble entrance, he must have fallen. Aenguz heard the screams and shouts. Mandavu was already rolling to his feet at the round dais when Aenguz arrived. Mandavu sprinted down the round stairs toward the bridge. Everyone in the grand entrance was in shock. Only the presence of the Azari kept them intact.

Mandavu ran down the center of the lower bridge. The line of sight gave people a chance to move.

The trail of the embassy caught up with him there. Legerohn begged forgiveness from the people and asked for pardon as he ran by. They fell behind as they worked to help those whom the Azari could not reach or who had fallen in the wake of their efforts to save them while moving on to others.

At the ramps, the Azari were ahead of him again, moving stewards, pushing craftswomen, and shoving carts to the side of the hall. Stroud flashed by them and coordinated other Azari.

Mandavu slowed at the hexagonal landing between the death chamber and the funeral room. He looked to his left and then to his right. He pulled back in horror and then lunged into the death chamber. Aenguz was right behind him, and Lokah was at his side. Stroud suddenly walked on wooden legs.

Death stewards were at the doorway to the right that led up. Two Azari were already there. They stared down. The death stewards stepped back as Mandavu ran up.

Saissha lay on the bottom steps, half in shadow. Blood covered the steps and stained her blue robe. Her face was impossibly pale. Her throat was ripped open, just like Illia's had been.

Mandavu scooped her up in his arms and hugged her lifeless form. His keening was a long, deep note, as if he had suffered a slow but mortal wound. It seemed foreign; it didn't sound like Mandavu. He rocked and wailed with her clutched to him.

Aenguz broke for both of them. In a day, they would have been gone. Tears and shock blinded him. Part of him wanted to demand answers of the death stewards.

Lokah sagged and shook. He tried to hold back tears as he processed the horrific scene.

Aenguz heard Legerohn wail as he came up beside him, "Oh, nooo, ohhhh…"

Chimere gasped as if he had suddenly taken poison. He reached to his Prince to comfort him, but he seemed to need his Tahnka more.

Mandavu supported Saissha's head and brushed her hair gently. He gasped and heaved like he was drowning. His wail turned to tight sobs as he took her up carefully in his arms and walked her over to the table. It looked like he was afraid to wake her. Her body folded down onto the black pedestal table. Her vacant alabaster face was a blight against the basalt.

Aenguz's rage overwhelmed him. "What happened?! Who found her? When? Why was she down here?" Aenguz left no room for the death stewards or the Azari to answer. Legerohn touched him and inclined his head to Mandavu. Aenguz's assault on the death stewards was battering his friend. He let his rage-filled interrogation stop. The remaining members of the embassy circled Saissha, their lost ambassador, with the shroud of their helplessness and woe.

49

THE END OF THE EMBASSY

White sage incense and the smoke from fish pyres dampened the atmosphere. The death stewards rocked as they sang their mournful dirge, a sore, cryptic keening. The ocean crashed below. Somber clouds pressed down on the Sunfall Sea.

All of the chief stewards were there. The dirge from all of the gathered stewards in the amphitheater beyond was loud and doleful. It was as if Earthmight itself were moaning with grief for Saissha.

Stroud stood on the landing out of respect for the people who could succumb to death through time. The Azari's bond with time could be considered an affront to those who could not escape its hold, Willion had explained to Aenguz.

Saissha's cerecloth-wrapped body lay on the spindled table. The wheels were about to turn.

Mandavu was a statue of dour stone. Something irrevocable had happened inside of him. He was an automaton now, able to follow simple commands, but any and all other signs of life were gone from him. Grief had stripped the Makan in a way that made him unrecognizable to the embassy. He stood next to the spindled table, watching over Saissha's wrapped body in his periphery. The capelet he wore was better fitted to his large frame, and it matched his sorrow. Saissha's braided counsel lord's staff was strapped to his scabbard. He bore it like an oath on his back.

The embassy ringed her like Illia's family had surrounded their daughter. They were death stewards for the embassy. Their love for her was ripped from them as surely as her voice had been torn from her.

Legerohn sang the Moresi dirge over her. It was the same song all of the Moresi had sung on the Sallow's *cog* where they had all once been prisoners. Legerohn changed the words for Saissha and for the embassy.

"So long the journey between our two lives
When will our grief find an end?
No rudder, no oar, no great horse to bear me back
Far from home, further away and further from

The light of our life is gone from us now
The gentle swaying does not soothe us
Along the troubled river to her forever home
Away from family, away from friends, away from her loves

Too short was her time in life
Too sharp is the pain
Too deep is the grief of our loss
Not even the troubled swaying gives us peace

We hold you now in our mind's eye
Your gentle face, without tears or crowded brow
We take our love for you with us on our long empty journey
Until the end of time brings us home."

The steward's threnody in the amphitheater was plaintive and discordant alongside Legerohn's Moresi dirge. The crash of the Sunfall Sea added its own somberness and disequilibrium to form the fugue.

The spindles turned. Saissha's body slipped off the table and down the channel into the depths of the sea.

50

EIRENICON

They sat in the dining hall, but no one ate. Aenguz stared at the bread on his plate as if it were a riddle.

The keep stewards were dutiful, but eventually they left the somber room. Saissha was gone. The soul of the embassy was lost.

Mandavu wanted revenge. Aenguz shared his feelings, but they had no suspects. After Saissha's death ceremony, they questioned the death stewards again and tried to understand why she was on the stairs that led from the infirmary to the death chamber.

The only clue that came was when Willion told them that sometimes the room above was used as a rendezvous for young lovers. It was a hidden place, when not in use, for those seeking a little privacy. But that didn't tell them much. Was that what Saissha had learned? Did Illia have a paramour that for some reason took her life? If so, how did that relate to Saissha's murder?

Aenguz wanted to leave before any more people died. He was as lost as the others, except for the fact that he was trying to save all of them and the course of creation. Everything weighed on him as if it were drawing him down into the lowest depths of the Sunfall Sea.

When he pulled his head up and spoke, it startled the others.

"I want all of you armed at all times. There is a killer here." He looked at Legerohn and Chimere. "Find a bow or some weapon. I do not want you walking the halls here unarmed."

Legerohn and Chimere assented.

"Stroud, call a gathering of the people. I will appeal to them to let us enter the Cleve. And if they will not, then I put it on you to warn the men of the garrison. We do not wish to kill them, but we will not be stopped. I will try this one time to persuade the people here.

"Mandavu, you and Lokah, go and tell Braydehn that we are leaving. He will wait here until the One King releases him, and then he will join the Stair Guard and the One Army."

"You are leaving him?" Legerohn asked.

"We are in danger here. The sooner we leave, the safer we will be. And it was Saissha's last wish."

"He does not know about Saissha," Mandavu reflected. Fresh sorrow came to them all.

"You two go tell him about Saissha, and make sure he has food, blankets, and whatever else you can provide him with. He will bear the message of Saissha's death to the Stair Guard, if the Azari do not tell them first.

"I will speak to the people tomorrow, and then we will leave."

After their empty meal, Aenguz was ready for any objection that Thelen might have for calling his own assembly. Aenguz walked up to Stroud and dared him to challenge him. "What does the One King say? Will he stop me?"

Stroud kept his head up. "You are the Lord of the Akkeidii. Your forefathers built Earthmight. You have every right to call an assembly."

Aenguz was hoping for more of a fight. He wanted to vent his rage at the One King and at the leader of the people who should have protected Saissha. But up close, he could see that Stroud was grieving too.

The next day at midday, the remnants of the embassy followed Aenguz and Stroud down the hall. Mandavu tapped his shoulder to prompt Lokah to bring his weapon. Their lord was addressing Earthmight, and he ordered them to be armed. Lokah retrieved his weapon and adorned scabbard and followed them.

Stroud led Aenguz through the dark corridors behind the façade to the faux door at the back of the stage. The plaintive murmurings and mumbles of grief of the assembling people pressed through the door and filled the tight entryway. For all the suspicion and uncertainty they had felt toward the embassy, Saissha was immune to it. Her dogged efforts to find the killer of the girl had become a point of awe for them. She had even suspected one of the members of her own company. Her determination to get to the truth was greater than her allegiance to her embassy. While they couldn't understand the methods she had employed to find the killer, her faith in her own determination was something that they could understand. Their grief was tangible.

His appeals to Thelen had been misplaced. He was, as he had described, the steward for the people. It was them he would have to appeal to. It was the people's minds he would have to change. If he could overcome his fear of this amphitheater chasm, if he could convince them to trust that they were not only willing to attempt the Cleve, but also capable of crossing it and bringing help, they might let them leave, and no one would have to die by their hands.

Aenguz's heart worked to push the slurry through his veins. The weight of old trauma and the pressure of speaking to so many with so much at stake squeezed his chest in an unrelenting vise.

He had to get them out of there. He had to convince the people to let them leave. Their presence had caused the murders. The needs of the earth were more than enough reason, but second only to that was the woe and despair they had brought to Earthmight. If for no other reason, they had to extricate themselves, and maybe some of the hopeful innocence of the Last Stronghold might return, might be preserved. If this was the last hope of the people of Earth, then it had to still possess some shred of the ideal of good and trust that it held when he had first arrived. Deep down, Aenguz had to believe that he could do some good and not leave the places that had welcomed him in to the depths of existential ruin. He had tried to eschew and ignore Mono Lord Lana's words. If he couldn't turn this around, he might well indeed be the ruin that Morgrom promised. He might well be the agent of earthly despair. He might well be the chief Ruinwaster. He was, after all, the Last Emissary.

"Let's go." He had to get out of his own thoughts. They would unman him.

Stroud cracked the door and led Aenguz out. The sheer walls of the theater brought him back to the place of his trauma. The icy air. The smooth walls. The reminder of the place where he had fallen and where his father had lost his life. The baneful results of his selfishness. The memory of his attempt to fool the warriors and the clan lords in the theater in the Valley of Gathering that he wasn't wounded, that he hadn't broken the law, that he was something other than he was in trying to take his father's place. The reminder of the lies. Those feelings made him feel like he was walking out spitted on a pike.

Stroud walked out ahead of him to the edge of the stage, continued down the steps, and turned to face him.

Fresh mourning and grieving still filled the theater. The seats were only half full. Heads peeked over the balconies and over the bridge. Their eyes were weary and damp.

Lokah and Mandavu were seated off center a few rows up. They were roughly at eye level with him. Mandavu was still not the same. Saissha had taken his heart down with her.

Legerohn was not far from them. He was a few rows behind them. The Prince's eyes were withdrawn. Lana had charged him with protecting Saissha. While Mandavu had taken on that charge tacitly, Legerohn had taken it on explicitly. His eyes said that he might never forgive himself. A bow lay across his lap.

He didn't see Chimere. He might be sitting with the healers he had come to know from the infirmary. Other older men who had taken on the task of guarding Earthmight to augment the Azari were also in the crowd. Seeing so many armed when so few had been armed in the keep when they arrived was odd, almost surreal. As people filed in, they looked at the old armed guards warily.

Azari dotted the theater.

Would Carina understand what he was about to do, what he was advocating? He had made promises to her in his passion. He had even thought to not leave and fight at Earthmight when no clear way to get to the Cleve had come to him. Had he not been so trapped and wretched, he might have found another way. But that was a lie. The only hope was a return through the Cleve. He had to lay himself bare and appeal to the people. Would she understand that what he was about to do didn't mean that he didn't love her?

The One King had to be watching. Hannoch or Sarokin would recount his words. Thelen did not stop him, and Stroud would not override the Azari. His presence and Aenguz's quieted the mourning well of grief.

He felt exposed and vulnerable. A thousand eyes were on him. He took a deep breath and raised his voice loudly into the theater. "I am Aenguz, son of Sairik, Lord of the Akkeidii. We came here over the

Spine from Corundum to warn the One King and you about the Woe Sower. We came to appeal for the aid of the One Army in the Upper Lands to meet his forces. We planned to return, but we were forbidden access to the Cleve and bidden to remain here. And while we wished desperately to return to our homes, we knew that the edict barring the Cleve was set out of love and in faith with the Law of Creation." He fought the tightness in his throat that sought to make him sound shrill and exacerbated.

"We have come to see why you love your home here. We have seen the dedication of the stewards to Earthmight and all the people here. We have seen the pride of the artisans who create with passion and dedication. The preparations you have made for the One Army to defend your home are driven by that sacred law. We have seen the devotion of parents to their children. We see love in Earthmight, and we have lived with it." Aenguz pushed away the thoughts of his lost loves.

"But it is clear to me that we have brought death to Earthmight. We know that many have held us responsible for Illia's death. Now..." He swallowed back the lump and avoided Mandavu's eyes, "...Saissha, Counsel Lord and ambassador of Corundum, traverser of the Spine, is dead. She sought to find Illia's murderer even among those of us who came here with her.

"While we are not responsible, our coming has coincided with their deaths. That is why I beg you to let us leave. Let us attempt the Cleve. Let us return to our own homes - homes we love no less than yours while they still stand. Only you can release us. Only your words through the Azari to the One King can do this. I beg you to let us go before more are killed."

Aenguz considered his next words and what they might do to their plight, but he could not hold the secret any longer.

"I believe the reason Saissha was not able to find the killer is because the killer is hidden among us. I believe that the killer is a Ruinwaster. And with the Dagba Stone and this arm, I believe I have the means to kill it." He couldn't help but appeal to gain his weapon before the people. Maybe they could be convinced. He walked to his left toward his companions. Stroud followed him. Aenguz pulled off his white glove and flung his hand into the air.

The assembly gasped.

Then there was a trick of the eye, or what seemed like a dark flicker to the eye. It was strange, unsettling in its unfamiliarity. Normally, an arrow's trajectory was clear, trailing across the sky from one point to another, or arcing out into the distance. But there was one perspective, one sole position that offered one unique view - the final view for the target.

The tip of the bolt was a pinprick. Then it simply expanded instantly. It did not move through space but grew instantly in size. And then it was on him, was in him. It punched him deep in the chest. Disbelief staggered Aenguz as much as the force of the bolt. Another one came in a quarter beat after. The second blast was enough. He stumbled back. The amphitheater tilted, swinging down. The facade flipped over him. The edges of the canted amphitheater darkened, and then everything turned black.

51

CHAOS

Aenguz fell backwards onto the stage. Two arrows stuck straight out of his chest like young saplings. A stunned pause baffled Lokah for an instant that seemed impossibly long. The shrieks and gasps were so ear-piercing and horrible that he knew at that moment that he would remember them for the rest of his life.

Mandavu bolted first in shock and terror. He whipped out his mace. Lokah reacted and grabbed him to protect the people around them. He fell on Mandavu and pushed him down before he could set his feet, fearing he might accidentally kill someone among the throng trying to escape. Mandavu cursed and strained while Lokah worked to stall him long enough for the space around them to clear. Lokah craned his head back to where the arrows had come from.

The Azari were already there. They grabbed the Prince to protect him. He could not find Chimere. It must be an unknown soldier. Or perhaps Dalmeida, Illia's father, seeking revenge.

He leaned and turned to try to see around the Azari to glimpse the assassin. One of the Azari ripped Legerohn's bow away. People were still falling over one another to get clear as if they were running from an explosion.

More Azari coalesced around the Prince.

Lokah couldn't see around them. He could not find the assassin.

Stroud was suddenly straddled over Lokah and Mandavu.

There were too many Azari on the Prince. Stroud seemed to give silent orders to them.

Where was the assassin?

Lokah found Legerohn's eyes. A wicked, vile sneer warped Legerohn's face. He peered at Aenguz's dead body in grim satisfaction.

The Azari looked ready to tear the Prince apart.

Lokah craned his neck up to Stroud. "Do not kill him! We need to question him."

Stroud's mien showed a profound restraint. Something akin to vengeance glassed over his slits, but he held back. "Hold him," he commanded. The Azari rooted around the Prince of the Moresi, Aenguz's assassin.

Lokah and Mandavu clawed to their feet. Mandavu found Legerohn and the cluster of Azari. Naked horror turned his face white.

They bolted down the tiers. Lokah saw Azari darting throughout the amphitheater, trying to help people. Some were tripping over one another, others fell and tumbled. Some warding Azari caught them and helped them to their feet. They ushered many away toward the doors that ringed the hollow belly of the theater. Screams and cries echoed everywhere.

They rushed up onto the stage and over to Aenguz. He and Mandavu dropped to their knees as if they couldn't bear the weight of what they were witnessing. Mandavu's mace fell. He flicked the feathered quills with his fingertips as if he were trying to prove to himself that they were real. Then he let out a howl so loud and so full of rage and anger that it startled the last fleeing people.

Lokah shouted at Aenguz to get up as if he were only wounded, but still alive. "Aeng! Aeng! Lord! Wake up! Grieg damn, wake up!"

Mandavu's soul seemed to drain out. He was pale like a visage of death. A moan like a strangled sob seeped out of him as he rocked on his knees.

The Azari with Stroud at the fore were dragging the Prince of the Moresi away. They headed to the doors that led into and under the seawall. Chimere was at their backs. He called for his Prince.

If he'd had his *montmorillionite*, if it wasn't immured by the stone, he could've blocked the bolts. The Akkeidii sword he had gifted Aenguz seemed worthless to Lokah. A thought came.

"Stroud!" he shouted. Stroud looked back as he hurried the assassin Prince out of the theater. "Check the Dagba Stone!" The tether holding Aenguz's weapon to his life was gone. His weapon would lose its shape and sink back into the earth. The stone would be free.

Stroud looked off to the side, as if he were listening for something. He looked back and said, stolid but grim, "The Dagba Stone is gone."

The world shrank around Lokah. He was a mote, and the amphitheater was an eye. If he weren't kneeling, he would have fallen. Mandavu looked at him even more lost, almost afraid. The Makan was unrecognizable. Abject futility and loss stripped them of everything that defined them.

Lokah didn't know how long he kneeled there with Mandavu. Their failure to protect their lord and friend swallowed them whole. The movement of two stewards who had set down a litter near them broke the numb spell of loss that froze him.

They were gutted. Mechanically, automatically, they placed Aenguz's body on the litter and lifted him. They walked and teetered to the edge of the stage and down the steps to the door at the floor of the theater. They walked through the corridor like lost spirits. There were distant voices and shouts further up the ramps. They turned into the death chamber. They set Aenguz's litter on the nearest slab. Lokah found some shrouds and covered Aenguz, wrapping the thin fabric around the arrows so that it could lay flat.

He covered Aenguz's face as the Azari came out from the hallway that led to the cells. Chimere was with them.

Stroud stared at Aenguz while the other Azari left. Then Stroud looked at Lokah and Mandavu with a hardness that Lokah had never seen in him before.

"The Ruinwaster is secured, but the Message Bearer is dead. Oblivion's Last Emissary is gone. The Dagba Stone is lost. The Azari will search the keep."

"Sairik's line has ended," Lokah said morosely.

"I failed to protect him," Mandavu wheezed.

"We all failed him," Lokah uttered. "The charge of the Last Emissary is over. We will bear what remains of that duty now."

52

THE EYES OF THE ONE KING

"'I believe the reason Saissha was not able to find the killer is because the killer is hidden among us. I believe that the killer is a Ruinwaster. With the Dagba Stone and this arm, I believe I have the means to kill it.'"

That last bit surprised Thelen. He had become used to Sarokin's level recitations, but even the sage Azari seemed vaguely stunned.

His command tent was all but empty. The war stewards had cleared almost everything from the pavilion where the One King kept counsel with his Azari, Biniam, and Sorolokova. Only one brazier was left to smolder to keep most of the cold at bay.

He wanted privacy to hear what Aenguz would say. Only he and the Azari knew what the Last Emissary intended to do. He could not prevent him from speaking, and even if he could, it might only set the stage for more violence.

The slow rattle of the supply train moved beyond the tent. Biniam and Sorolokova were at the head of the column. The One Army was moving slowly, and once he was done listening, he would ride to the fore. The One King's guard waited patiently for him outside. They would be a day out from Llangollen. Too slow. After they reached Llangollen, he would command more speed from Biniam.

Sarokin raised his head. "The Last Emissary is slain."

"What?!" The flatness of his tone was too discordant with the news he recounted. The shock of what he said didn't have time to fully register.

"The Last Emissary is dead," Hannoch repeated.

Their terseness frustrated him. Sometimes he was sure it was deliberate.

"What?! What happened?" Shock, dismay, and astonishment all crowded around him. The empty pavilion was suddenly claustrophobic.

"He was shot with two arrows."

"Shot?! What?! By whom?! What happened?!" He immediately regretted allowing weapons widely in the keep. But after Saissha's murder, it had seemed the only prudent thing to do. The Akkeidii had their weapons, but Illia and Saissha had not been armed. No one walked the halls of Earthmight armed, except for soldiers coming and going. Even that was strange. So much had changed since the arrival of the embassy from Corundum. Now it seemed that another member of their group was dead: Aenguz, the Lord of the Akkeidii. How could it be? It was hard to let the suspicion of the embassy go, but he had to admit that the killer was not among them.

"There is chaos in the theater," Hannoch said, as if he were describing cold porridge.

"Who shot him?!" The Azari were infuriating sometimes, but they had done so much for the people of Earthmight and the Lower Lands. Thelen had learned to adapt to their stolid inflections.

"The Azari have the assassin," Sarokin said finally.

"Who is it?"

"Prince Legerohn of the Moresi."

He wished the war stewards had left a chair. He needed to sit.

"The Kriel loremaster cautions against killing it."

"It?" Thelen tripped on the distinction. How could it be Prince Legerohn? What did they mean "it?"

"We have it. We have one of the brothers. Ophiactii or Arkarua."

"Listen to the Akkeidii, we need to question him."

"It is Oblivion's servant."

"Take him to a cell."

Both Azari went silent again - another exacerbating trait at times. Ever since he had reduced their numbers in Earthmight to augment the One Army, the delays in responses had become near maddening, although it only meant a few extra moments more than he was used to. Frustration and gratitude for the Azari had become a familiar feeling.

"The Keystone of Creation is gone," Hannoch said flatly.

"What?!" Thelen yelled.

"The Sidor Akkeidii's weapon is dissolved, and the Keystone of Creation is gone."

"How?!" He needed them to make more sense. Three deaths, three murders, and the Dagba Stone taken. "Search the Spire!" He felt denuded by being away from the keep. Even though he received most of his information via the two Azari, not being present made him feel blind. There wasn't an order he couldn't give from anywhere else, but somehow, he felt restrained, even hobbled not being within Earthmight's walls.

"The defiler is imprisoned," Hannoch said with a slight frustrated satisfaction.

But Thelen was waiting on word about the Keystone. "What about the Dagba Stone?!"

They both went silent again. The train outside lumbered by. A horse whinnied. Wagons groaned. A constant subtle tremor shook the ground.

"Where is it?"

"The search has begun," Sarokin said. Thelen knew he would say nothing more until they found it.

"The Last Emissary's body is in the death chamber. The Akkeidii are with him," Hannoch said.

"Where could the Keystone be? Who could have taken it?"

The Azari said nothing more.

The home he had known as the One King was being dismantled before his eyes. His decision to leave Earthmight had tormented him, but he never guessed that there would be so much death and desecration behind. He had hoped to take the focus away from Earthmight and take the battle to the Woe Sower.

The embassy from Corundum had been the malignancy, but they did not know it. Stroud had warned him about Aenguz. He had shared the concern when he had taken Sarokin's place. He told Thelen about his charge from the Mono Lord. But now it seemed like her worry was misguided. The Prince of the Moresi had been taken by a Ruinwaster. With Aenguz's threat toward it, he must have had no other choice than to kill him right then. The Azari had told them that the Ruinwasters dreaded their immurement in the Black Earth.

He commanded them not to share what was happening with Sorolokova or Biniam. He would tell them at the next camp. He needed his own time to think and to deliver the news. The One Army and the Free People were already on edge enough as it was in this sudden campaign. He left the tent. His white destrier was waiting for him. A battle steward held the bridled steed.

Sarokin and Hannoch climbed onto their horses, and they galloped beside the column toward the front of the line.

53

THE FINAL DEATH

All of the Chief Stewards ringed Lokah, Mandavu, and Chimere in the death chamber. Janelle, Yasdriine, Monguerra, and all the rest made a solemn arc in the dark hall. Death stewards stood at the ends of their line and at the spindled table. Willion presided over their cryptic and arcane rites.

Stroud stood on the landing between the twin death chambers and watched down on the mourners. His impassive face seemed older, wilted somehow.

The last members of the embassy from Corundum in Earthmight stood near Aenguz's cerecloth-wrapped body. Lokah and Mandavu held their *montmorillionite* weapons before them. Chimere mirrored them with his newly acquired bow.

Their death rituals were odd to Lokah. The dirge from the theater was loud. The threnody from the death stewards and the Chief stewards was sorrowful and reverent. Their observance seemed to hold honor for the slain dignitary.

The incense and char reeked, but smoke at a death ceremony was not unfamiliar. There would be no cairn. His bones would not be recovered from the ash of a pyre. If they had done those things, Lokah would have seriously pondered attempting the *surasanskeld* ritual and fitting Aenguz with a permanent *montmorillionite* helm. The intensity of his grief made it seem possible, achievable. He would mount it next to Hernus Kriel, perhaps above it. But he wouldn't decapitate Aenguz without a pyre and defile his body that way. They instead spoke to his body like they had for the dead on the Wester before they emptied the liquid metal into the river.

Mandavu apologized for his failure. He honored Sairik and made a supplication to him for forgiveness.

Lokah recounted all that Aenguz had done in the time he had known him. Lokah wore the sword he had made for his lord and given him just days before. Then, Lokah recounted how Aenguz had saved the Champions from the Sallow. How he had led them safely across the Lands all the way to Corundum. How he had saved them from an Urning. He had delivered the unwanted message as the Last Emissary. He had found the Dagba Stone. He had crossed the Spine and delivered the embassy of Corundum - Saissha's embassy - to Earthmight to warn the One King.

"And he was my friend. I was honored to be his loremaster, but I have never known a closer brother-friend. May your body find peace in the sea and your soul find rest in the White Earth. Others now will have to carry on and take up your charge."

Chimere recounted Aenguz's actions to free the Moresi from the enslaving Sallow. And he recalled his courage to free them from the Erebim and the Urning at the City of the Sho-tah. He had walked with a Chosen Freeholder in the Oasis of Ganzir. "He was always kind to me. When I couldn't do much, he made whatever I did feel important and necessary."

Willion looked for a sign.

Lokah gave a tight nod. Mandavu was blank stone.

The death stewards turned the wheels and Aenguz's body slid off into the channel. The crash of the surf took him away.

They lowered the plank and closed out the sea.

The Chief Stewards filed out. Lokah, Mandavu, and Chimere followed after them.

On the landing, Chimere turned to the other chamber. "I must see my Tahnka," he begged.

Mandavu wrapped his arm around Chimere. "Do not worry, we will see to your Tahnka."

54

CARINA'S LAMENT

In the pavilion outside of Llangollen, Thelen told Sorolokova and Biniam about Aenguz's death, Legerohn as his assassin, and the loss of the Keystone of Creation. Bleak doom surrounded them all.

"He was a friend to us after all," she uttered, almost castigating herself.

"What about the Keystone?" Biniam asked. "It would be a powerful weapon."

"The Azari still search for it."

His Monomander shook his head. He appeared trapped in a strategic conundrum that he couldn't see his way out of.

After they left, Thelen heard horses racing by his tent.

"Who was that?" Thelen asked Sarokin as a war steward helped him out of his armor.

"Three of the Queen's riders head to Earthmight."

"Why?"

"One of the Queen's guard was an intimate of the Lord of the Akkeidii."

————◆————

SOUTH OF LLANGOLLEN, SAROKIN guided Thelen out ahead of the line.

"He said what?" Thelen asked.

"'We will see to your Tahnka,'" Hannoch replied.

"Have Stroud keep a watch. If they kill him, we will not have the chance to question him. Keep the death stewards out of the death chamber for the time being. I do not want them to get hurt if the Akkeidii try anything.

"Legerohn may be able to tell us about the movements of the Erebim or what has been done to the Sunfall Sea, perhaps even about the verrandulum. *I want to let him suffer and understand that he cannot escape without my command. He may be more amenable to answering us after being imprisoned for a time."*

"He is a desecration. His life is not measured like yours."

"Is his life like the Azari's?"

"The former Prince of the Moresi's body will fail before the des-ecrater's does."

"We will not have to wait that long."

"His brother will seek him out." Sarokin sounded ominous.

————◆————

*"*THE QUEEN'S RIDERS HAVE *reached the Last Stronghold. Lokah Kriel has gone to meet them on the Plateau...*

"The other riders have left Carina alone with the Kriel while they tend to the great horses."

"What are they saying?"

"He apologizes for Aenguz's death, for failing to protect him. He recounts the death chamber ceremony to her. She runs to the sea wall. Lokah Kriel is following her. She climbs up onto the outer wall and

looks out over the sea. Lokah Kriel is giving her the Message Bearer's scabbard."

"What do they say?"

"Only the Sunfall Sea sees their words."

"What now?"

"She weeps."

"Leave them be." Thelen's heart ached for her grief.

55

RETRIBUTION

If there had been any eyes on the Prince of the Moresi, it would have looked like he hadn't moved. He sat on the angular bench at the back of the hexagonal cavity. He seemed to be engaged in meditation, a dark practice that seemed to have him communing with the black stone.

The intermittent trickle of water from the seam in the ceiling ran down a crease in the wall to a hole in the floor. It was a solitary and lonesome sound. The distant crash of the waves was lessened by the small, tapered window. The opening in the cell was wide, but it tapered to a small square not big enough for a head to poke through.

An angled square of light moved up the door. The sun was dropping into the Sunfall Sea. Legerohn did not raise his head to look at it. His head did not move, did not count the moments until nightfall. The days moved by, but the Prince was unmoved, as if time had grown meaningless to him, as if his course was set apart from those in the world around him. Only the half-eaten loaf of barrio bread gave any indication that he had moved at all.

He just waited. There was no pining or lamenting. He did not scream or call out. He simply waited in a resigned stillness.

The light turned to cold orange, and soon the darkness engulfed the space. If there had been eyes on him, they might have shuddered at the cold, bleak space. They might have held empathy for the prison the Prince of the Moresi found himself in.

Slight footfalls brushed the stone in the corridor. The basalt walls echoed even the slightest sounds.

Legerohn did not raise a curious ear. He did not look for a face in the narrow gap that was the only other opening to the cell.

More shuffles passed by. It made no difference to him. The night took hold.

Soft footfalls came to the gap. Legerohn did not raise his head.

The lock stone slid out. The heavy door turned open on its hidden fulcrum.

"Brother, I am here. You hid yourself well. Had I known earlier, we could have begun our final desecration of the Last Stronghold sooner."

"Where is the Azari Stroud?" the Prince asked. His head was still bowed.

"I stole down the stairs from the infirmary, and he was distracted from his post," the voice said.

"Ophiactii and Arkarua together," the Prince hissed.

"Yes, Arkarua. The cursed Akkeidii tried to keep me away, but I was able to steal away. Come, let us shame Tycho with our destruction of the Last Stronghold. And then we can ravage and burn Inverlieth."

Legerohn raised his head slowly. His eyes met the face of the familiar voice.

Chimere.

Ophiactii Chimere stared down at the Prince.

The Prince stared at the thing that had been Chimere.

Ophiactii Chimere's complexion changed. "You are not Arkarua." A gnarled sneer twisted across his face. "What is this?"

"Your end," Legerohn breathed.

Ophiactii Chimere checked the door, as if to confirm that it wasn't closing in on him.

"Yours, I think. Who can save you?" Chimere kicked out his left foot, and his boot flicked off of his foot. It snatched back in the air, held by a single thread. His foot was no longer human. Yellow scales wrapped the heel and much of the foot. The four smaller toes were withered and black, maggots writhing in between in the ashen places. The proximal toe was oversized and gruesome. At the tip of the toe was a short, sharp curved talon. Hair and dried blood were caked around it. It looked sharp enough to rip out a throat and silence any victim. He brought up his knee impossibly high and readied the foot to strike at Legerohn.

The Prince leaned back slightly but did not flinch or balk.

The Ruinwaster smiled with horrible glee.

Then the Ruinwaster torqued and writhed like a jolt had shot through him. He held in place, except for the unholy leg. It kicked out wildly at the Prince.

Legerohn leaned back out of range and watched as the daggered blade came through the Ruinwaster's chest. Blood covered it, but some of it wiped off on Chimere's shirt, and Legerohn could see the gleam of *montmorillionite* in the dark. The faint starlight found thin exposed patches of the silver metal.

A hand gripped Ophiactii's throat. The hand glinted. A heavy forearm pressed down on his shoulder like a vise. The Ruinwaster was pinned. A face came up beside him like the living face of night.

Aenguz Sidor.

"I am your doom, Ruinwaster. Your recompense for Saissha and Illia."

Ophiactii whipped and twisted violently, but Aenguz held him firm as stone between his metal arm and his *montmorillionite* weapon. "Return to your bleak gaol. We are done with you here. Earthmight is done with you. The earth is done with you. Return to your forever downward, your forever hell."

Arms and legs flailed wildly. "Don't send me back! Nooo!"

Aenguz squeezed his throat. "You cannot overcome the sacred metal. Your time on the earth has been too long. Be gone."

In a last effort, Ophiactii became more like Chimere again. He rasped through Aenguz's grasp, "Tahnka, please help me..."

Legerohn clenched his teeth. He took in the sharp dagger that poked out of Chimere's chest. "You are not Chimere. Be gone with you."

Aenguz crushed Ophiactii's throat, and his head dropped. With that, the fell spirit was drawn out of the moment and pulled into a tight maelstrom. A sudden but violent vortex wrapped in on itself. Chimere's body fell limp, and the livid shadow was gone.

Aenguz released Chimere's corpse and let the body fall. He left the weapon in his chest for good measure. The Dagba Stone was safely on the hook at the head of his weapon.

Legerohn stood and looked down on Chimere's body. "Poor Chimere." His grief dilated around the young Moresi. "How did you know it was him?"

"I did not know. I knew that whoever it was would be drawn to you if they thought you were a brother-twin Ruinwaster."

Legerohn's head swayed as he seemed to comb through all of his memories of Chimere. "He was not quite the same ever since the City of the Sho-tah. But I thought that it was due to his injury and all that he had endured."

Aenguz shared Legerohn's remorse for the young Moresi. "Ophiactii must have gotten into him during the summoning."

Aenguz drew out his weapon with care for the memory of Chimere. He let his sorrow free in the cell.

Legerohn stepped around the body and patted Aenguz on his chest. Aenguz gave a slight wince.

"Are you well?" he asked.

"Next time, let's use thicker wood." Aenguz knocked lightly on his own chest.

"Next time?"

Aenguz smiled with a quiet laugh.

"You have many surprises, my friend. Do you have any surprises to get us out of here?" Legerohn asked.

56

ESCAPE

Aenguz pushed the stone door closed and set the lock stone in place. He went to Braydehn's cell, pulled out the lock stone, and opened the door. A wave of relief flowed out of the cell. "What happened? What was that noise? I knew you would not leave me, but so many days had gone by."

"We will talk later," Aenguz whispered.

Braydehn went back into his cell and tied up the loaves of barrio bread in a blanket. He threw it over his shoulder and joined them in the hall.

Braydehn and Legerohn turned up the corridor.

"Wait, not that way." Aenguz closed Braydehn's cell door and set the block in place. "Follow me."

They looked confused, but they followed Aenguz farther into the corridor around the long, curved cell block.

The darkness of basalt was broken by the light of night. A door was opened to the outside, and a silhouette stood framed inside.

Lokah's familiar shape came into focus. He propped open the hidden door. A stone grate in the channel at the floor was propped up.

He waved the three men through. Then he let the door close behind them, and the stone grate fell back down into place.

Legerohn smiled in the night. Braydehn's eyes were wide and bright as stars.

"Stonemages," Aenguz said.

"Stonemages," Lokah echoed.

"The Stonemages would never make a gaol that they themselves could be imprisoned in," Aenguz said to Legerohn and Braydehn knowingly.

They stood in a rough-hewn channel carved into the rock that was open to the sky. Stars bespeckled the veil of night. They were still in shadow, but far more light than what they had left behind.

Lokah led the way and walked quickly down the walled ledge. It blocked the view from the sea, and the foundation of Earthmight blocked the view from the Spire above. The pathway was littered with detritus and sea grass.

It wound downward to the north side of the keep until it came to a cave-like opening. Violent surf drowned out their steps. Salt brine filled the air.

Lokah drew his weapon out and called white *montmorillionite* light to his weapon with words of lore.

They made their way down some steps until they came to a long, hollow chamber. One side was open. A half wall marked the bottom. Two figures were there.

Mandavu clutched his mace and relaxed when he saw Lokah. He maintained a low light from his mace. Beside him was a figure in a beige tunic. A black capelet was pulled backward over his head. It looked like the head was turned around completely on the body.

"Prince Legerohn," Mandavu said with a slight laugh. "Braydehn, good, you did not forget the bread."

"I did not forget, Lord."

Legerohn shook his head in disbelief. He walked to the hooded figure. "Stroud?"

"Lord Prince," the muffled voice replied.

Legerohn looked at Aenguz for an answer.

"He is a part of the embassy. We are all going back."

"What about Lord Chimere?" Braydehn asked.

"Chimere was the Ruinwaster Ophiactii," Legerohn answered glumly.

"Chimere?!" Mandavu said. His own disbelief knurled his face. "He insisted on going back to the infirmary tonight."

"It was difficult not to tell him, but you told us to trust no one," Lokah said dutifully.

"Wait," Legerohn asked, "what if the Ruinwaster was not Chimere?"

"Then I assumed Thelen would imprison him to find out where we had gone. We would wait a day, and then we would steal in and free him the next night. But now we cannot wait. Now we must hurry," Aenguz said. He handed his weapon over to Lokah, and his Kriel loremaster slid it into his oversized Akkeidii-tooled scabbard.

Lokah led the remnants of the embassy to the other end of the chamber. Mandavu guided Stroud by the arm.

On the opposite end, there were disintegrated tarps on the floor. And there, beside them, was an old longboat. It looked like it was older than the fishermen's current boats, like it was built in another age.

Lokah waved Legerohn over with a grin. Legerohn's eyes filled with wonder when he gazed inside. There, unwrapped across the bench seats, were four Gildelmun oars and a Gildelmun rudder. The *montmorillionite* light called a dim yellow light from the golden wood.

Questions filled his eyes. "How? Where?"

"Akkeidii Stonemages and Moresi craftsmen were friends back then too," Lokah said gladly. "They were hidden in the bottom of the boat."

Aenguz gazed in wonder at the boat with the Prince, and then, after a brief moment, he said, "Let's go!"

Lokah sheathed his weapon in with Aenguz's. Mandavu sheathed his mace and passed his scabbard with Saissha's braided staff to Lokah. The Kriel loremaster undid Aenguz's Akkeidii sword from his waist and stowed all their weapons at the bottom of the boat. Braydehn handed him the blanket-wrapped barrio bread.

They grabbed the old longboat and dragged it out of the hidden chamber and down the ramp that led to a narrow cove. White waves battered the rocky walls around them. A plain jetty, weathered by time, blinked in and out with the waves. They fitted the oars into their sleeves, and Legerohn fitted the Gildelmun rudder into the rear. Mandavu was careful with Stroud. The hooded Azari was completely dependent on him.

Water sloshed at their legs at intervals and jostled the boat. One by one, they climbed into the boat. Mandavu guided Stroud into the rear. Aenguz waved Legerohn into the front. Then the three Akkeidii and the lone Stair Guard pushed the boat to the edge. Frigid water drenched their legs. A salty, gelid spray saturated the air. They watched the waves crash in and out.

"The next one," Aenguz called over the rush.

"Aye," they answered.

Then, with the next surge, they held the boat in place, and then all four hopped in, rocked it, and the boat swelled down into the water.

They tumbled about as the longboat leaned away from the jetty. They kept the oars tight against the boat as it bobbed and shifted. The rush pulled them in toward the sharp crevice and then it pulled back, bore them along, and vomited them out into the shadow of the rock cliffs and starlit Sunfall Sea.

The Akkeidii spun around onto their seats.

Mandavu put Stroud's hands onto the rudder. Legerohn motioned to the Makan how best to position them. Then Mandavu took the two oars at the back and faced the rear. He rolled his shoulders and felt the weight of the oars.

Legerohn moved to grab one of the second set of oars, but Aenguz stopped him. "You have to guide us."

Legerohn nodded. The hooded Azari could only be told how to steer. Lokah and Braydehn grabbed one oar, and Aenguz took the other.

"Which way are we going?"

"North. Head north and keep as close to the shore as possible."

Legerohn climbed into the prow and called back "left" and "right" to Stroud until he understood which way to turn the rudder to drive the boat.

With their line set, the Akkeidii and Braydehn put their backs hard into rowing away from Earthmight.

They were near to invisible in the shadow of night. Legerohn kept their course straight. They rowed as if they were fleeing the Black Earth.

None could see them. None were looking for them. If there had been eyes on the old longboat, the speed that they achieved would have lived in sailors' tales forever. For the embassy, their only thought was the fastest escape.

Mandavu heaved and pulled. His prodigious strength was on full display. Lokah and Braydehn heaved with Aenguz and tried to keep pace with his *montmorillionite* arm. The boat lurched with each stroke. The Gildelmun oars shimmered like old gold.

They rowed through the night and settled into a fearsome pace. Legerohn guided them facilely, calling to Stroud over the Akkeidii.

The coast passed by them, and the hard cliffs softened. A thin shoreline emerged that gave way to rounded hillsides. Long hoary grasses rustled in the night wind. Dead fish lined the shore and lapped in the surf. Brine and fetor filled the air.

They rowed until the sky glowed in the east.

The boat slowed. The Akkeidii were all but spent. Braydehn's shoulders moved, but his arms were limp. Aenguz had to draw back the power in his arm for fear of pulling them out to sea. He needed to match what his comrades were doing.

He looked over to the shoreline in the vague light. There was an inlet - the outflow of a salt marsh.

"Legerohn, I think that is it," Lokah called.

Legerohn called back to Stroud. The hooded Azari turned the rudder and guided the boat faithfully.

They met the effluence from the sea. They rowed into the marsh with barely enough strength to overcome the current. Long grasses closed in around them as the river narrowed.

The keel scraped at the bottom.

"To the right," Lokah said.

Legerohn called back again to Stroud.

The boat dug into sand and rock. The exhausted Akkeidii hopped into the water and hauled the boat to the shore. Braydehn and Legerohn climbed out and helped them.

Stroud sat in the back with the reversed capelet covering his face. He looked macabre in the empty boat, as if he were a boatman for the damned.

Mandavu led him out of the boat, and they gave it one final heave and collapsed onto the shore.

In the first light of dawn, Aenguz, Lokah, and Mandavu laughed through their exhaustion like old warriors at the unlikelihood of their escape.

OLD FRIENDS

Lokah slung his scabbard with both weapons and handed Mandavu his scabbard with Saissha's Counsel Lord staff. He passed the bread to Braydehn. Aenguz took the sword Lokah had made for him and cinched it around his waist.

They hauled the ancient boat far out of the water to some boulders and rocks under the cover of willow trees. The Gildelmun oars and rudder were tucked under the bench seats after the boat was flipped over. Legerohn secured them as if he were hiding a treasure. "I will return for these one day. I will see that they are displayed in Inverlieth. I will find a place of honor for them there."

Once he was satisfied that the boat and the sacred wood within were safe, he asked, "Where do we go now?"

Lokah took the lead and guided the company upriver.

Aenguz came up to Stroud and Mandavu. "Do they know that we are gone? Are they aware that you are gone?"

"No, no one knows. The hall between the death chambers is nearly black at night and very dark during the day. No death stewards have come to the death chamber. If any came, they might be surprised by my absence, but they would not question the ways of the Azari. None of my people have noticed my absence, yet."

They had made it this far, but there was still a long way to go to get to the Cleve. Aenguz didn't doubt that if the One King ordered it, he could have Azari there before they reached the final passage home.

"Where is the One King and the One Army?"

"They are south of Llangollen. Azari surround the column."

Not only was he drawing the One Army farther away from Earthmight, he was also drawing it farther away from Corundum and any help they might bring back, if they survived the men of the garrison and the mystery of the Cleve.

They walked along the shore, just at the water's edge, surrounded by brush and slumbering trees. The morning air was cold, but the gentle breeze from the Sunfall Sea kept the atmosphere mild. Their steady pace helped to ward off the chill. Every moment they moved unnoticed by the Azari gave them an advantage.

Aenguz walked with Lokah, and Brayden walked with the Prince. They would need horses, if they could find them.

Stroud placed a hand on Mandavu's shoulder and followed like a blind man. They knew the general direction of the Cleve, but it was still days away, and there was the matter of the Sentinel to account for. What would he do once he saw them? Could Stroud subdue him? Could he kill him? With their powers, they would be evenly matched. Or would the witnessing Azari even condone a fight among their own?

The land opened up before them to their right. Wide snow-capped mountains rose in the distance to the north. Striations of clouds obscured the east. The fast-rising sun cast shafts up into them and then rose above them, muting the morning light.

They crested a rise, and there, in the near distance, were two Free People, riders for the Queen, and a half a dozen great horses saddled.

"Metzly!" Braydehn called.

Aenguz's heart leapt.

The company moved into a jog. Elation opened his heart as he recognized Carina beside her.

Carina's face warped into shock. Aenguz slowed to a stop and dared not come any closer. She gazed on the impossibility of Aenguz and froze.

Metzly was shocked, but her familiar surliness was still stamped on her face. "Pah!" she said in surprise. "You were killed!"

Lokah caught up to Aenguz. "I did not have an opportunity to tell her you were alive, only that we would need her help here. I dared not, for fear of the Azari."

"Carina…" he pleaded. He strode toward her carefully.

Carina untied something at the back of her saddle. She let Aenguz's scabbard drop to the ground.

Aenguz picked up the empty scabbard and reached for her horse, a gray and smoke-colored mare.

"Thank you for coming," Lokah said to Carina and Metzly. His tone was laden with shame and apology.

"The line of horses is set. If we hurry, we can reach Tormont Vale by midnight," Metzly said.

Carina's horse sensed her shock and pulled away from Aenguz. She continued to stare as the unreality of Aenguz's presence worked in her mind.

The company mounted. Stroud was helped up. Then Metzly and Carina kicked their horses into a full gallop.

They rode hard and fast, as if they were being chased. They pushed the horses even harder than the night they had tracked the Erebim. Aenguz wanted to talk to Carina, but they were running too hard.

By midday, the horses were nearly spent. They had slowed to a run, then to a fast canter. In the distance, Aenguz could see horses grazing placidly on the open hill. They looked up curiously at the riders coming toward them.

The racing company dismounted from their horses, unsaddled them, and saddled the fresh horses. Metzly waddled like an old woman on her wounded hip.

Aenguz called Carina, but she kept away. She climbed deliberately onto her horse and moved away while the company saddled their horses.

Stroud spoke up. "The Azari are aware that I am gone."

"When? When did they notice?" Aenguz walked over to the hooded Azari.

"It has not been long. They are searching the keep. They fear Oblivion has taken me."

"Do they know we are gone?"

"They know Mandavu, Lokah, and Chimere are gone. They look for them too. They have not searched the cells yet."

They were running out of time. How long before the Azari thought to check the cells?

They all looked at one another as if they were about to be discovered right there. They jumped onto their horses and galloped into the east. The sun fell at their backs and drew shadows on the land before them. They followed the hilly ground on the edge of a tree line at the base of the mountains.

At dusk, they came to another set of horses. They dismounted and saddled the fresh ones. Their spent horses wheezed and frothed. Carina and Metzly thanked the horses deeply before departing again as night came.

After several hours, riding by moonlight, Carina and Metzly slowed the horses to a walk. The company was exhausted and battered by the furious flight.

Carina guided them to some outbuildings that were little more than sheds, half stone and half timber. In the moonlight, they could see the quarter wall that segmented an area in a wide arc, like the place in Lihkit Vale where the great horses had gathered. There were a dozen horses within the half circle. They looked up lazily at the riders.

Metzly guided the company to the sheds. Carina dismounted carefully and walked away from them all. "We only have a few hours for rest. We ride again at dawn on these horses."

Aenguz went to follow Carina, but Metzly stopped him. "Tormont Vale was her home. This is the first time she has seen it since the invaders came. Leave her alone."

He ached to console her, but he heeded Metzly.

The exhausted company unsaddled the horses and went to the sheds. Lokah and Mandavu called heat to their weapons, and only a small light emanated. Braydehn passed around the barrio bread. The Akkeidii repeated their own mundane ritual and shared bread with one another.

Aenguz turned for his weapon and reached for his empty scabbard. He glanced at Lokah's scabbard with his own weapon hidden inside. Then he held out his arm and spoke the words of lore; light and heat glowed from his liquid silver arm.

It lit the faces around him.

"By Grieg!" Mandavu uttered.

Lokah set his weapon down and studied Aenguz's arm in awe.

They settled into beds of straw with Legerohn and Braydehn between them. They fell asleep quickly. Carina and Metzly slept in the other shed.

Aenguz was the last to fall asleep. What must she be going through?

He marveled at his arm and at the thrum of *montmorillion* lore that coursed through him. It did not feel like the miracle that it was though, because without the power to help Carina, it was useless to him.

58 VANISHED

"*What?! They are gone? What do you mean?*" Thelen signaled for them to be quiet and rode out and away from his personal guard. *The column was moving faster, but still had not found its rhythm. Biniam galloped up and down the line to urge them on.*

Once they were at a safe distance from others, Thelen told Hannoch and Sarokin to continue.

"They are no longer in the keep," Hannoch said, as if that cleared up the confusion for the One King.

They were maddening sometimes. "They left for the Cleve already? The people have not come to a consensus."

"Their supplies are still in the stables. Their horses are still there. No Azari sees them."

"How can that be?!" They were infuriating. "Where is Stroud?!"

"Stroud is lost to oblivion."

"What does that mean?"

"He cannot see, and we cannot see through his eyes."

"Is he dead?"

"It is the living death. Sightless. Alone. All black. Forever."

"How can they be gone?! How can you not know? What about the watch?"

"With the Keystone gone, there was no longer a need to keep a watch. There are fewer of us in the keep."

"Search for them!"

"We are."

How could they sneak out? Why? Thelen's nimble mind quickly confirmed the only exits in Earthmight. But no Azari had seen them. It was like they had died. The thought flashed like lightning.

"Check the boats. See if any are missing. They could have escaped through the death chamber and taken a boat."

Sarokin and Hannoch were silent.

Sarokin asked, "Where would they go?"

"They would go south and come up behind the very rear of the column, behind the supply train. We would never look for them there. There they could intercept the Stair Guard and take them with them to the Spine. Maybe to Lihkit. The Cleve is too dangerous."

Another thought came to Thelen. "Do any of the surrounding Azari see the Stair Guard?"

"No," they replied in unison.

59

IF THE WORLD REMAINS

Their pace did not slow. The great horses did not know where the company was going or why. They seemed to be playing at some racing game, trying to outdo one another in speed and endurance as they bore the company nearer to the base of the mountain wall. As the mountains of the north receded into the distance behind them, the Spine of the World grew before them.

It was a wall of gray cliff. The sharp peaks dominated the sky and then fell back out of sight. They loomed there, bleak and unforgiving. There were no foothills leading into the wall of rock that made up the Spine. The land undulated gently with brown grasses and patches of snow.

The black slit cut a line from top to bottom. It marked the face of the wall like a sword cut. The absolute edge and end of the world was here. The sun dipped behind a distant bank of complicated strata of clouds hurrying the dusk.

Stroud called for the company to slow.

The haggard company dismounted. They seemed as tired as the

horses that bore them. The slit of the Cleve dominated the cliff face just to the south of them. It was as foreboding as a guillotine. Stroud told them about the search in the west on the lands and shores between Llangollen and Earthmight. Free People and soldiers from the One Army looked for the company and the Dagba Stone. The moment they reached the Sentinel, the depth of their mistake would become known.

Metzly waved off the company from their horses. They would see to them. Metzly and Carina wrestled with the strain they had put the horses under. They tried to comfort them and assure them that their work was done. The company ate barrio bread on their feet in between breaths. They tried to shore up their strength and dispel the thought that it might be their last meal.

Stroud waited while they caught their breath and finished their hasty meal.

They worried about the remaining men of the garrison. Metzly gave Braydehn her axe, and Carina gave Legerohn her bow.

"Aenguz, I will only wound them. I will not kill those men."

"We will all try to not kill them, but not at the expense of ourselves," Aenguz stated, and looked to Mandavu and Lokah to confirm that they understood.

Mandavu and Lokah said, "Yes, lord," and then talked about how they might use *montmorillionite* to subdue the Sentinel.

"I will go to the Sentinel," Stroud said. "I will face him." He would go first. The others would wait for his signal to approach. The Sentinel would not take his eyes off the Cleve, but once he was approached, who knew what he might do?

"While he does that, we will meet the men of the garrison," Aenguz said. There were not enough of them, and Carina and Metzly were not going to help. He wouldn't take their help even if they offered it. They had done enough.

As they hefted their weapons and hardened themselves to meet their last challenge, Aenguz took the opportunity to go to Carina. Metzly moved to block him, but his hard gaze was greater than her surliness. She waddled aside.

Carina saw him and turned to face him. Her hard veneer was thinned by exhaustion and light sleep. Her eyes were motes of shimmering gold and silver. Her freckled cheeks camouflaged her pale face.

"Carina, I-" Aenguz started.

"What happened to you? How did you come back to life?"

"I had to fool the Azari in order to get away, so that we could attempt the Cleve."

"You were never going to stay, were you? Was everything between us a lie?"

Aenguz swallowed. The light was fading. Time was growing short.

"I saw you by the bridge when we first came down from the Spine. I saw you that first morning in Lihkit moving among the great horses. The horse we shared before the war came to your covert. Our time in Earthmight. I have ever sought to be with you, and hold you, and look on you. For my part, I have loved you every moment since that first one."

The rest of the company was anxious and ready to face their final challenges.

"If I could bring the world to heel and halt the doom that confronts it, I would. If there was no other reason, if I had no other responsibility, I would do it for you and for you alone. If so much did not depend on my charge, I would make a life here with you." Aenguz took a tentative step closer. His throat was dry. "But I cannot stay."

"Why not live here? Why not have a life with me here?" Desperation strained the corners of her eyes. Her voice wavered.

Aenguz held a parallel life in his heart for her - one where he did live with her, and they could make love under the stars. But the demands on him were too massive to be ignored. And he was tainted by Morgrom's charge. "I would not be welcome in the coverts or the homes of the Free People."

"We could find a place in a small vale to live. We could have a life together."

"And you would give up riding for the Queen? Give up the great horses and being with the Free People?"

Her eyes welled, and tears drained onto her face as the realizations struck her.

He stepped closer to her and took her hand. He looked into her eyes so that she could hear him. "Carina, I had a lot of time to think in the cell, and I realized something. I have been exiled from every place I have been since I was marked by the Woe Sower. The Last Emissary has no home. If I had lost my weapon to Earthmight, I would have become Hearthless among my own people. I think I sought to hide from that truth by being with you. Being with you was more a feeling of home than I have known since I left the Mashu. And I am grateful for it. Grieg knows that I am grateful for you. But I do not know if I will ever set foot on the mountains of the Mashu again. I do not know if I will survive the Cleve, but I must try. If I do survive, I do not know where this dire mark, this fell charge, will take me. If I were to stay, I know in my heart that it would not leave me or us alone, even if we hid in the smallest vale in all of the Lower Lands.

"My life is not my own to give. Morgrom saw to that when he burned the message into me. Know this..." He brought up his left hand and took her arm gently. "If the sun continues to rise over the Spine and the seasons continue to turn, if the moon grows and fades and the course of creation is righted once and for all, you will know that I have succeeded. Whatever I endure will be as much for you as for the whole of the Earth. Even if you were the last person on the Earth, I would still endure all of it for you, so that you might remain and have your life."

Silent tears streamed down her face. "Without you."

He ached with the pain he had caused her and was still causing her. He studied every dot on her face, drinking in her hazel eyes, now blurry through his own tears. Strands of tight curls escaped, wilting from beneath her helmet.

"Without me." He wrapped his arms around her and hugged her hard. She could not resist him. She fell into him, but she was weak. All life was gone from her.

He whispered in close to her, "I love you, Carina of the Free People, horse lord and chosen rider of the Queen of the Free People. If the world remains, know that I love you. Whatever may befall us in this war, know that I love you."

He took in as much of her as his heart and body could absorb. He noticed a firmness at her belly. He let her go, and her hands came together and covered her stomach. Tears streamed down her face.

Silent understanding sprouted in him, and his heart dropped. The life he might have had with her would never be. He took his empty scabbard and tipped it. The *mithrite* chain poured into his hand. He thought of a tangible connection to share with her. "Here, take this."

"What is this?"

"This is *mithrite*. It is a bond and an oath."

He placed it in her hands.

"It is a symbol of faith between Moresi and Akkeidii. It is an unbreakable chain. It will be a bond between you and me."

She looked like she might let it fall, like she did with his scabbard. It looked paltry in her hand. Moonlight made it glint like dusty diamonds.

"If you will not take it for us, then take it for Sorolokova on behalf of the Akkeidii. For the Akkeidii and the Free People, it is an unbreakable link. For me, for you and me, it is an unbreakable chain."

Mandavu's voice cut through the spell that surrounded them. "We need to act while there is still light for the others."

Aenguz pulled away from her.

Metzly rocked to Carina and consoled her.

Aenguz turned toward the others; he did not know how. More was ripped out and away from him in that moment than he could process or comprehend. A hole deeper than the pit of Carrowen Celd opened up in him.

The remaining leaders of the embassy hurried over the last rise before the mound where the Sentinel stood.

60

SENTINEL

Aenguz took Stroud's arm from Mandavu and guided him up the mound.

"We are close," Stroud said in a muffled tone tinged with awe or fear.

"Stand back. Wait here," Aenguz told the others.

"Wait," Mandavu said.

"I will go myself. Be ready for my call."

"I will not let you out of my sight," his First said emphatically.

"I do not know what will happen between these two Azari. This was my last gambit to get us past the Sentinel and into the Spine. If anyone among us has more power than this..." He held up his silver hand. "...then they can meet the battling Azari." Then he softened for his First. "Listen, if this fails, if I fail, then it falls to you two to pass through the Cleve and reach the Mashu."

Mandavu squeezed his mace. He seemed to be confronting his own perceived inadequacy. For all the strength and all the power of his *montmorillionite,* he could not confront the powers and forces that

Aenguz was called to. He deferred to Aenguz's orders, and his resistance against arguing or insisting further took more strength than any he could have provided Aenguz.

Lokah unslung his scabbard and drew out Aenguz's weapon. Aenguz slung his empty scabbard over his shoulder and carried his Dagba Stone-weighted weapon in his right hand. "It is still *montmorillionite*. It is still sharp. And though your arm is new, there is lore in it. More lore perhaps than even in our weapons."

"I hope I will not need either."

"We will be here. Call if you need us."

"I will."

He guided Stroud ahead of him partway up the hill.

"Here," Stroud said. "Stay behind me. Watch your hand."

"I will."

Aenguz worked at the knot on the black capelet. Then he pulled the hood off and took some steps back.

Stroud inched his head down to orient himself. He wiped his face. He seemed to blink.

Aenguz sank down to the grass and crawled behind Stroud until he could see the figure of the Sentinel Azari framed by the wall of the Spine and the towering slit of the Cleve.

"Wait here," Stroud said.

Aenguz watched as Stroud crossed to the Sentinel.

The beige tunic was in tatters. The Sentinel looked like a derelict. His skin was weathered and sun-burnished, dark as bronze. His unruly hair looked forever windswept, as though it had faced wind and rain for eons. The brittle brown grasses covered his feet and ankles. It looked like his feet had rooted deep into the earth. Stroud looked tall against the statue-like watcher.

"I see myself. Azari, who comes? I have taken the oath; my service is sacrosanct. I need no relief." The Sentinel's voice sounded like ice grinding on boulders.

"I come to release you. Your service is at an end."

"No one can end my faithful vigil for our people."

Aenguz inched closer, flexed his metal arm, and gripped his weapon tight, ready to spring. He wasn't sure how he might help Stroud, but he was ready to do anything to get the embassy past the Sentinel.

Stroud walked beside the diminutive Sentinel and mirrored his stance. They stared at the black line in the body of the Spine.

Aenguz could only guess what thoughts and realizations were flowing through all of the Azari at that moment. Would they pit these two against each other?

"Stroud." The Sentinel's voice scraped. "You were lost to Oblivion. Share your words with the Azari."

"I will share them with you first. I was not lost to Oblivion. I allowed myself to be obscured."

The Sentinel let out a slight gasp. "How did you come so soon from Earthmight?"

"I am not alone. I am beholden to Mono Lord Lana and the embassy from Corundum."

"You are the One for the Azari. You are our leader."

"I am. And I have taken on more purpose. I have chosen to serve the world and the cause of the Last Emissary."

"We are the Eyes of the World. We see what must be seen."

"Yes. That is right. And it is time now for us to see what lies within the Cleve."

Stroud and the Sentinel were silent.

Aenguz wondered what Thelen might be thinking, knowing that Stroud was at the Cleve.

Then Stroud pivoted in front of the Sentinel and looked him squarely in the eyes. "I, Stroud, One of the Azari, release you from your charge. Your service has been impeccable, your faith steadfast since our great loss. Now the time has come to reveal what bars the Cleve. Now we will know what is within the object of your vigil."

Stroud held out his hands and helped the Sentinel out of the earth that had surrounded his feet.

The Sentinel turned his head slightly but returned to the cleft. He looked down at the buildings of the garrison, then back at the slit. Up to the night sky, then back to the Cleve. He looked to Stroud and back again. An eon of muscle memory could not wholly free him.

Stroud exuded some form of empathy. He walked down the slope toward the Cleve with the Sentinel.

A panicked call came up from the garrison. Men poured out from a few of the many square stone shelters and scrambled toward the two Azari.

Aenguz signaled back to the others.

Mandavu and Lokah were there in an instant. Legerohn and Braydehn were right behind them. They walked to the top of the mound where the Sentinel had stood.

"What happened?" Mandavu asked, confused by the absence of a fight.

"Stroud ended the Sentinel's service."

The two Azari marched down the hill away from them toward the Cleve. A crude stone wall barred the bottom. At the near edge was a heavy wooden door bound with iron fittings.

The soldiers grew louder as they noticed the five dark figures standing. They started jogging to the Sentinel and Stroud. When they saw the five men, the bulk raced toward them.

Legerohn quaked. "Aenguz."

"Now," he said to Mandavu and Lokah.

His First and his loremaster raised their weapons high into the air, spoke the words of lore, and called white light to their weapons. Aenguz stood between them. Legerohn and Braydehn shielded their eyes.

The men of the garrison stalled and looked at one another for an answer. The men pursuing the two Azari stopped and turned. Then their courage returned, and they continued their pursuit. The others raced up the mound.

There was a rumble behind the soldiers. Weaving through the stone shelters were the Stair Guard, their scarlet cloaks like dark torch flames in the night. Nedenthal was at the fore. He galloped to the heels of the charging men of the garrison.

Braydehn hollered in joy.

Lokah and Mandavu readied themselves. White light still blazed from their weapons.

Nedenthal called on the men of the garrison to hold as they climbed the hill.

The Stair Guard ringed them, swords drawn. Braydehn ran out to stand within their circle.

"We do not wish to harm you!" Aenguz shouted in a commanding voice loud enough for all to hear. "Stand down, men of the garrison. Your fight is not with us. We all battle the Divider, the Woe Sower that seeks to pit us all against one another. Stand down!"

The men lowered their swords.

Aenguz walked forward through the circle and greeted their leader. Mandavu and Lokah followed suit. Legerohn lowered his bow and squared his shoulders. He met them like a true Prince of the Moresi.

Nedenthal and the other Stair Guard dismounted. Braydehn ran around and clapped his friends on the back.

The Stair Guard mixed with the men of the garrison and the leaders of the embassy. They left their horses with the men of the garrison.

The remnants of the embassy from Corundum walked after Stroud and the Sentinel to the entrance of the Cleve.

61

ONE SIGHT

They entered the dark confines of the Cleve. Stroud and the Sentinel led the way. Mandavu and Lokah brought a bright light to their weapons as they walked at the Azaris' backs. Aenguz drew his weapon. He was unsure what power might come from it, but he was careful not to let his metallic hand touch it. Legerohn stood behind him. The Prince was dour and firm. He laid an arrow across Carina's bow and scanned the dark. They waited beyond the threshold as the Stair Guard filed in.

When the last of the Stair Guard entered, the door behind them closed. The garrison soldiers sealed them in. They could climb back over the wall easily if they needed to; the wall was intended to only slow a rush from an invading force. But as the heavy, rickety door closed, there was a sense that they were being abandoned or forsaken. They were no longer a part of the Lower Lands.

The old, cobbled road was covered with dust and bramble. It told the company that no foot of man or animal had disturbed the ancient highway. The sheer rift was wide, and it reached up into the night sky like the walls of a temple dedicated to the god of night.

The Sentinel and Stroud led on, peering into the shadowy darkness. Ambient light from the stars cast a pale sheen on the obdurate schist. The Stair Guard drew their swords, and Braydehn wielded Metzly's axe. Their nerves bristled in the dark.

Nothing had crossed through the Cleve since the Last Battle - nothing since the Azari women and children were led to supposed safety by an emissary and lost forever. No travelers. No passersby. Stubborn, angry weeds grew here and there through seams and cracks in the road. The air was dusty, suitable for the rock alone. The symmetry between the striations on both rock walls echoed and mirrored the change between the Upper and Lower Lands. Close, but separate. The same, but far. Their footfalls echoed off the walls, and the sound seemed foreign in a place bereft of purpose.

Adrenaline bore them on into the Cleve, but the musty air and still atmosphere sapped their temerity. The road led up a gradual incline, and it had the effect of weighing them down, as if some nascent power resisted them.

They marched well into the night, taut as a bowstring. A half-moon blinked in the sky overhead as the undulation in the contour of the cliff top weaved in the night. Shadows and pale silver light shimmered like gossamer on a languid wind as if ephemeral veils dangled from the height.

The light from Lokah and Mandavu's weapons cut through the shadows and the mere veils. They strode behind Stroud and the Sentinel.

Aenguz lamented the absent power in his weapon. He could fight with it if he needed to, and he did have the sword Lokah had made for him. They would be useful against a conventional force. But he hoped he wouldn't need the power of the Dagba Stone. If he unleashed it again, as he had in the Spine, it might kill everyone around him. The thought gave him more dread than what might lie ahead on the abandoned road.

Late into the night, the road opened up, and the sheer walls peeled back.

"Wait here," Stroud said.

"Stay alert," Aenguz ordered.

Stroud and the Sentinel walked to the opening. Aenguz, Mandavu, Lokah, and Legerohn were poised and ready twenty paces behind them.

"I am glad we have the Azari with us," Mandavu breathed.

"Let your light go," Aenguz commanded.

They whispered words of lore, and their *montmorillionite* light withdrew back into their weapons.

Stroud and the Sentinel walked into the opening in step as if they walked in formation. They turned their heads apart and scanned the space.

"There are two *verrandulum* here," Stroud called back.

"Two *verrandulum*?" Aenguz uttered.

"The ground around them is undisturbed."

The Sentinel turned his head back, and then it dropped. He shifted, and his shoulders bobbed. His torso clenched as if he were heaving. His head turned wildly as if he were blind. Stroud scanned to his right, but there was no sense of panic. The two Azari were out of sync. Stroud stared ahead, and his shoulders sagged as if he were resigned.

"Stroud, what is it?" Aenguz called. He closed the distance to the Azari. Mandavu and Lokah were right behind him.

Stroud turned and looked back at Aenguz.

"What are you doing? They will see us!" Aenguz shouted.

"The One Sight is lost to us. We cannot see through the others. The Sentinel is disconnected. He has never been alone in this way." Stroud held the Sentinel's arms to try to calm him.

"I cannot see! I cannot see!" Panic was unwinding him.

Stroud called to Aenguz, "I have been alone for an age in Corundum. I learned to live without the eyes of our people."

Stroud spoke to the Sentinel with a compassion Aenguz had never heard from him.

"You will learn. You will survive. You can see me. You can see them."

"How do you-? The world is so small. I cannot breathe!" He began to hyperventilate.

Stroud grew stern. "You will live. I will show you how to live. I did not have the One Sight, and I survived. They do not have the One Sight, and they live."

"How?! How?! How?!" Panic made the Sentinel shrill.

"Look at me. See me. What you see is all there is to the world now."

Aenguz did not know how to comprehend the Sentinel's loss. He barely understood the Azari's power, and now that the Sentinel was more like him, more like everyone else, he seemed foreign.

"We will keep watch on the far side. Take your rest here. I will help the Sentinel see his duty. That will be enough."

The bereft Azari walked to the far end of the open space, stood together, and peered into the darkness ahead.

62

MEZEKIAH

"**S**et a ring," Aenguz ordered Mandavu, "and get some barrio bread to break."

Mandavu called up Nedenthal and the Stair Guard as Aenguz looked at the two *verrandulum* on either side of the space. Smooth alcoves were carved into the rock on either side like housings for a shrine. The cloud material they were fashioned from roiled smoothly within the thin legs and the scalloped roof. They seemed alive, but apart from the world.

The Stair Guard ringed around Aenguz, Mandavu, Lokah, and Legerohn. Nedenthal had them take a knee, eyes facing outward.

Mandavu brought Aenguz two loaves of barrio bread.

Aenguz perched his weapon carefully at his side. He tore a loaf in half, held either piece to his left and right in the Akkeidii tradition, and gave them to Lokah and Mandavu.

He broke the other loaf and handed half to Legerohn. The remaining leaders of the embassy walked around the circle and tore off a piece of the hearty bread, held it up to the left and right, and served all of the Stair Guard.

When they were done, they went back to the center of the cordon, faced one another, took a knee, and ate.

Aenguz perched his laden weapon against his thigh, along with Mandavu and Lokah, as they had been trained to have it ready. The half-moonlight and starlight made their *montmorillionite* gleam. His own weapon was not as clean as Lokah or Mandavu's, but silver still shone through the grime and smudges. Only the physical sharpness and whatever power immured or awakened the Dagba Stone remained in his metal. He hoped to at least get both safely to Inverlieth.

He watched the Prince of the Moresi bite into his barrio bread, and he saw the *montmorillionite* ring glint in the pale light - the ring that had saved them from the Sallow.

"Where did you come by that ring?" Aenguz asked in between bites. He had meant to ask, but he had been distracted by so many other things.

Legerohn turned the ring over to look at it. "This was given to the second Prince of the Moresi by your forefather. This was given to him by Grieg Sidor the Venturer."

"Holy Grieg," Lokah breathed.

"By the Sanctor," Mandavu said in awe.

"It is a long story. When we reach Inverlieth, I will tell you the whole tale." He took another bite with a smile on his face.

"Step Mark," one of the men said, facing the rear.

Nedenthal stood and walked over to him.

The soldier came to his feet. "I see something."

Aenguz stood, and the others rose with him. They walked to the rear of the circle.

Back in the darkness, something seemed to materialize in the shadows. Bridging the sheer walls just above their heads was what looked like two titanic tree trunks twisting around each other. They must have passed right under it, but Aenguz was sure nothing had been there before. Both ends gripped into the walls with root arms and tendrils pushing or pulling the walls together or apart. Flakes and flints of stone trickled down into piles on both sides of the road.

"Did we pass underneath that and not notice it?" Mandavu asked.

The trunks were moist, and they shimmered sickly nearer the top. A green-gray moss draped down in tatters. The mountain walls seemed to groan against the pulling or pushing strain.

Aenguz called back over his shoulder, "Stroud, do you see this?"

"What is that?" The soldier pointed.

From behind the trunk, something white and translucent moved. It was a ball at first, and then it unwound and lowered itself to the ground. It was thin and covered in delicate white fur. It moved slowly, like a sloth.

"Stair Guard! Form up!" Nedenthal barked.

The Stair Guard lined up shoulder to shoulder. Braydehn stood beside Nedenthal.

The translucent creature moved toward them slowly, deliberately. It had a small round head and short proboscis that appeared to sniff the air. Its eyes were black dots against its white fur. A nightmare-like phantom moving outside of the physical world.

"Keep an eye on the *verrandulum*," Aenguz called to Lokah and Mandavu, wary of the enigmatic portals. "Legerohn..." He considered for an instant. "Shoot it."

Legerohn raised Carina's bow and sent a shaft directly at the monster. The bolt flew right through it. He took another and shot it at the wrapped trunks. The arrow sailed into the dark.

"It is an image or a vision of some kind," he said eerily.

"Stroud, do you see this?" Aenguz called over his shoulder again.

The creature slunk to the edge of the open area. It reached down to the ground; its hands were tapered together in a kind of long claw. It grabbed at nothing, curled the claw, and pulled its hand back up to its proboscis. It nosed the air and grappled with it just above its curved fist. It seemed to draw at the air as if it were sucking the juice out of a fruit.

"What is this? What are we seeing?" Aenguz asked.

"I cannot say," Lokah offered.

"Stroud?" Aenguz looked back at the two Azari. There in the opening was the creature, white and opaque. It held the Sentinel in its hand. The probing nose was locked onto the Sentinel's face. The snout flexed and tensed as the Sentinel's body twitched.

Stroud stood staring into the darkness, gorgonized.

"Oh, my Grieg! Stroud!" Aenguz sprinted toward him.

Mandavu, Lokah, and Legerohn raced after him. A bolt flew over Aenguz's head, but the creature twisted and dodged it.

Ahead, in the distance, he saw a reflection like a black mirror. Stroud was frozen like a statue, staring into the eyes of his own reflection.

The thing dropped the drained and desiccated Sentinel and reached for the immobilized Azari. Stroud was taken up.

Aenguz jumped and grabbed onto his legs and was pulled up with him.

Mandavu threw his mace over his head at the creature's arm while uttering words of lore. The blow dashed its wrist. Stroud and Aenguz fell, tumbling to the ground in a heap.

Aenguz shouted, "Stroud! Wake up!"

Stroud blinked. His face was ashen, and words came out of him broken and stilted. "It... it... is the Ruinwaster Mezekiah, but it is in the form of a giant Whi-White Wy-Wyrak."

Behind them, screams and shouts erupted from the Stair Guard. Nedenthal and another Stair Guard were caught up by the reflection.

The soldiers swung through the vaporous white legs, but the arms were solid enough to assail the Stair Guard.

Lokah and Legerohn pulled Aenguz and Stroud clear while the Stair Guard scrambled to fight and free their men.

Mandavu ran to grab his mace. As he picked it up, Mezekiah caught him in its tapered claw, his mace pressed against his body. Lokah darted to him, but Mandavu was already in the air.

"Heat! Call heat to your weapon," he shouted above the din of the Stair Guard.

Mandavu groaned as the air was crushed from his lungs. He gritted out, "*Bring your heat from Earth's fiery forge, dispel all cold, winnowing form. Fire and flame in metal's heart.*" Then his lungs gave out, and the words stopped.

Mandavu's head lolled, and Mezekiah's snaking snout reached for him. Suddenly, his mace glowed yellow and orange. It scalded both Mezekiah and Akkeidii alike. Mandavu screamed from some reservoir of pain.

The creature dropped him, and Aenguz's First tumbled unconscious to the ground. The hot metal had burned through his clothes and scorched his flesh along the length of his body.

Legerohn let arrows fly in both directions, but the creature snatched the bow out of his hands and broke it. Mezekiah seemed to be able to be solid and ephemeral according to its need and its reflection.

Lokah ran to Mandavu and stood over him, daring Mezekiah to take the fallen Makan.

The Stair Guard rallied around the mirror image of the creature. Three Stair Guard had been caught, drained, and dropped. Nedenthal, too, was dead. The remaining Stair Guard swung at the air and were blown aside when the opposite claw became firm.

"Fall back!" Aenguz shouted. "Fall back!"

They fell back to the small area at the center.

Lokah used his blade and words of lore to carry Mandavu back to them. Aenguz drew his sword and handed it to Legerohn. Calamity and confusion filled the shrinking space.

Mezekiah moved in close, its reflection mirroring its steps. The company was caught.

It pulled back with its left arm, and the reflection behind it did the same. It was readying to take out the company with one final swipe.

Aenguz called out, "Get down!"

Everyone dropped to the ground.

As the claws snapped in from both sides, Aenguz grabbed one with his *montmorillionite*-coated arm, and he caught the other in the crook of his Dagba Stone-locked weapon.

Mezekiah squeezed Aenguz. The claws pressed in like pincers and lifted him up. Both blood-soaked snouts reached for him.

His arm was impossibly strong, but the tension threatened to tear his body apart. If he let his weapon touch his arm, he might kill all of them in an instant.

Mezekiah strained and flexed against the arm and the metal. Aenguz could not hold on. He gave in and bent like a reed.

The weapon grazed his hand. When they touched, an argent power erupted - the birth of lightning, but only for an instant.

The blast burned Mezekiah; the arms snapped over and under one another.

Aenguz flew and tumbled through the air, passed into the *verrandulum,* and vanished. His weapon was thrown out of his hand in the other direction, dropping into the other *verrandulum.*

The spell of the reflection shattered, and the translucent image of

Mezekiah vanished. The solid version of the world-bridging Ruinwaster was blackened. The charred White Wyrak scurried back under the tree and disappeared into some crack or hole.

Most of the company was dazed but alive.

Legerohn and Lokah blinked at one another.

Stroud was on his feet. He stared at the *verrandulum* where Aenguz had vanished. He looked at Legerohn, Mandavu, and Lokah as if to see if they were still intact. He seemed to weigh Aenguz's need against theirs. And then he closed the distance in a blink and leapt into the portal.

The blast had woken Mandavu. The scent of his burned flesh saturated the air.

He watched as Stroud blinked out of sight.

"Follow him!" he ordered Lokah.

"Where?"

"Just follow him!"

"What about the Dagba Stone?"

"It does not matter. Follow him. I will be right behind you."

Lokah gathered his courage and then ran into the *verrandulum* and disappeared.

"Help me up," Mandavu said to Legerohn. He grated against the pain, but his will to follow Aenguz was greater. "Get my scabbard."

Legerohn grabbed the scabbard with Saissha's staff lashed to it, and then he helped Mandavu up and positioned himself under his good arm. "You are sure you can do this?"

"I am not dying yet." Mandavu clutched his mace. The heat was all but gone from it.

As Legerohn and Mandavu shuffled toward the *verrandulum*, Mandavu called to the Stair Guard, "Come." But fear still held them. They could not move, and the shock of their dead friends stole their reason. Mandavu could see it. They would not follow. Nedenthal was gone, and Braydehn was pale as death.

Mandavu groaned with every step. The burn shot bolts of agony through him. "Go on to Inverlieth. You will find help there. Remember Mond? Ask for him. Tell him where we have gone. Tell him everything."

Braydehn managed a terrified nod.

"Let's go."

Mandavu and Legerohn limped to the *verrandulum* and fell out of existence.

HERE ENDS

THE EARTHMIGHT WAR

BOOK TWO

OF

THE ANNALS OF THE Last Emissary

THE STORY CONTINUES IN

BOOK THREE

OF

THE ANNALS OF THE Last Emissary

THE FINAL FORTITUDE

GLOSSARY

Aenguz: Warrior of the Sidor Clan. Son of Sairik, fallen Ruler of the Akkeidii. Also named the Last Emissary, Stone Finder, and Message Bearer.

Akkeidii: People of the Mashu.

Arkarua: A Ruinwaster. A possessor.

Azari: Remnant of the One Race. Bearers of the One Sight.

Baierl Clan: Clan of the Akkeidii from the line of Michael Baierl.

Bane of Corundum: Another name for the Well of Sorrows.

Black Earth, the: A hell.

Blasted Flats, the: A land eradicated by Tycho Ruinwaster.

Braydehn: A Stair Guard of the embassy.

Bremball: A Counsel Lord of Corundum.

Byrgir: Lord of the Baierl Clan.

Cairngorm, the: Southern point of the Lower Mashu. Burial ground for the Akkeidii Heroes of the Last Battle.

Carina: Rider of the Free People. Paramour of Aenguz.

Carrowen Celd: The Deepest Hole. Domain of Lord Morgrom.

Channi: Remille's wife.

Chimere: A Moresi.

Chosen Freeholder: Mystics charged with warding the treasures of the Earth.

Cleve, the: The former road between the Upper and Lower Lands.

cog: A primitive river boat.

Counsel Lords: Protectors of the Lands of the Earth.

corallel tent: Tent used by the Stair Guard, with a tall section and long section.

Corundum: Home of the Counsel Lords.

Creche of Life, the: Another name for the One Forest.

Crystal Citadel: Another name for Corundum.

Cuzzoul: A Stonemage master. Son of Curufin.

Dagba Stone, the: A powerful talisman used to channel the poiesis of creation. Lost in the Last Battle and found by Aenguz in the Well of Sorrows.

Dahlward: Lord of the Deerherds, father of Sairak, grandfather of Aenguz.

Dalmeida: Archer. Father of Illia.

Deerherd: A lore-wise Akkeidii adept in the ways of the Mashu and a tender of roe deer.

Divider, the: Counsel Lord name for Lord Morgrom.

Divine Oculum: A powerful ocular room in Corundum used to view the Lands of the Earth.

Dormund Treachery, the: A bitter betrayal during a Challenge. Reviled by the Akkeidii.

Draymondon: A great horse. Carina's first horse.

durann: Akkeidii Stonemage tool used to manipulate stone.

Earthmight: The last fortress built by the Remnant and unified peoples. Also called the One King's Keep.

Einki: Step Mark of the Stair Guard. Leader of the Stair Guard of the Embassy from Corundum.

Elin: Grain Steward. Mother of Illia.

Erebim: Servants of Lord Morgrom.

Finit Clan: Clan of the Akkeidii from the line of Estevobahn.

First Treacher, the: Moresi name for Lord Morgrom.

Flayer, the: Akkeidii name for Lord Morgrom.

Forhnthulen, the Stairs of: The long stair that leads to Corundum.

Galangall Wash: A bridge city built by the Hyrrokkin for Lord Morgrom.

Gambl Clan: Clan of the Akkeidii from the line of Lerxst.

Ganzir: A vast desert made by Tycho Ruinwaster.

Gildelmun: A rare potent long-lived tree of the Lands.

gingrass: An analeptic herb.

Glaize, the: A persistent mist that occluded Corundum and the Divine Oculum.

Gran Lake: Lake near Straathgard.

Great Southern Sea, the: The great sea to the south.

Grieg's Gate: A man-made headwater that bars entrance to the Upper Mashu.

Grieg Sidor: Hero forefather of the Akkeidii. Also called the Venturer.

Haag's Lake: Lake in the Lower Mashu.

Hallock: Champion of the Gambl Clan.

Hearthless: Shunned Akkeidii forbidden a home.

Heideren Vale: A vale on the shores of the Sunfall Sea.

Hertha: Dahlward-mate. Clan Mother of the Akkeidii and of the Sidor Clan.

Hernus Kriel: Hero of the Akkeidii. Best friend of Grieg Sidor.

hulk: A primitive river barge.

Hyrrokkin: Stone creatures thought lost in the Lands. Builders of the first structures.

Illia: Daughter of Elin and Dalmeida, a grain steward.

Inverlieth: Home of the Moresi.

Janelle: Chief Keep Steward of Earthmight.

Jorgen: Squire to Aenguz.

Kachota: Warrior of the Makan Clan. Son of Warrum. Brother of Mandavu.

Kaissene: Land of the Sallow.

Keystone of Creation: Another name for the Dagba Stone.

Kikey: Healer steward of Corundum.

Kriel Clan: Akkeidii Clan from the line of Hernus Kriel.

Lana: Mono Lord of Corundum.

Larau: Slocum's wife.

Last Battle, the: The old battle between Lord Morgrom and the Counsel Lords where Morgrom was thrown down and the Dagba Stone was lost.

Last Emissary, the: Honorific given to Aenguz by Lord Morgrom.

Last Stronghold, the: Another name for Earthmight.

Legerohn: The Prince of the Moresi.

Leono: A Straathgardian fisherman.

Lihkit Vale: Village in the Lower Land.

Llangollen: Seaside village in the Lower Land.

Lokah: Warrior and Champion of the Kriel Clan. Son of Ruel.

Lord Morgrom: Enemy of the Lands of the Earth.

Makan Clan: Clan of the Akkeidii from the line of Ryker.

Mandavu: Warrior and Champion of the Makan Clan. Son of Warrum. Older brother of Kachota.

Mashu, the: Mountain home of the Akkeidii.

Mashu, Lower: Lands south of Grieg's Gate.

Mashu, Upper: Lands north of Grieg's Gate.

Mere Gurudev: The Chosen Freeholder of the Ganzir.

Metzly: Rider of the Free People.

Mezekiah: A Ruinwaster.

Mia: Granddaughter of Mono Lord Venrahl.

Millin, the river: A river in the Mashu.

Mimirmere: Pool at Corundum beneath the Divine Oculum.

Mithrite: A rare metal fashioned by the Moresi akin to *montmorillionite*.

Mond: A Moresi. Warder of Legerohn.

Monguerra: Chief Grain Steward of Earthmight.

Montmorillion lore: Study and knowledge of the properties of *montmorillionite*.

Montmorillionite: Rare metal found only in the Mashu engendered with magical properties.

Moodley: A Deerherd of the Kriel Clan.

Moresi: People of Inverlieth.

morillion: A rare loam that possesses healing properties. Made of *montmorillionite*.

Nedenthal: Leader of the Stair Guard of the embassy.

Oasis of Ganzir: A secret place hidden within the Ganzir.

Oblivion: Azari name for Lord Morgrom.

Ochroch: A Hyrrokkin. Stonethrall.

Ondolfur: Warrior and Champion of the Finit Clan.

One Bridge, the: A remnant artifact of the One Race.

One Forest, the: The first great forest of the earth. Also known as the Creche of Life.

One King, the: Thelen, the Ruler of Earthmight.

One King's Keep, the: Another name for Earthmight.

One Race: The state of all the peoples of the Lands before the Division.

One Sight: Ability of the Azari to all share the same sight.

Ophiactii: A Ruinwaster. A possessor.

Oso, the: River between Gran Lake and the Wester.

Philamay: Thank you in Moresi tongue.

Pogacar: Step Mark of the Stair Guard.

purna: An immuring salve.

Ragbald: Warrior and Honor Guard of the Sidor Clan.

Rainbow's Creche: Another name for Mimirmere.

Reaver, the: Hyrrokkin name for Lord Morgrom.

Rehl: An Azari.

Remille: Champion of the Gambl Clan.

Remnant, the: Fractured races left after the dissolution of the One Race.

Ridder: Son of Ragbald. Champion of the Sidor Clan.

Roberge: Son of Lakaadon. Champion of the Baierl Clan. Older brother of Strey.

roona: An herb that aids in wakefulness.

Roula: Rider of the Free People charged with delivering the embassy.

Ruinwasters: Five powerful servants of Lord Morgrom. Banished to the Black Earth.

Rursh Keleg: An ancient road that leads from the City of the Sho-tah to the Stairs of Forhnthulen.

Saiga: A white herbivorous antelope.

Sairik: Lord of the Sidor Clan, Ruler of the Akkeidii. Polemarch of the Akkeidii Warriors. Son of Dahlward, Lord of the Deerherds.

Saissha: Counsel Lord and leader of the Embassy from Corundum.

salaage: A Warrior's practice with a *montmorillionite* weapon.

Sallow: The denizens of Kaissene, loyal to Lord Morgrom.

Selene: Sidor maiden betrothed to Aenguz.

Selvin: A Deerherd of the Sidor Clan. Brother of Selene.

Shattered Lands, the: Ruinwaster-destroyed lands in the southwest.

Shivic: A Ruinwaster.

Sho-tah: A Remnant people annihilated by Tycho Ruinwaster.

Sho-tah, the City of the: City ruined by Tycho for disobeying Lord Morgrom.

Shudaak: Son of Stellan. Champion of the Finit Clan.

Sidor Clan: Clan of the Akkeidii from the line of Grieg Sidor.

Silvercryst: Common name for *montmorillionite*.

Slocum: Son of Shurn. Champion of the Kriel Clan.

Sorolokova: Queen of the Free People.

Spine of the Earth, the: The north-south mountain range that divides the Upper and Lower Lands of the Earth.

Stonemage: A lore wise Akkeidii who studies the properties of stone and building.

Stokke: A Moresi.

Straathgard: City and region of Men.

Strey: Son of Lakaadon. Champion of the Baierl Clan. Brother of Roberge.

Stroud: Azari of Corundum.

Sunfall Sea: The sea in the west.

surasanskeld: Old lore used to fuse *montmorillionite* with bone.

Sutton: Chief Keep Steward of Earthmight.

Tanna: Chief Animal Steward of Earthmight.

Tahnka: Honorific for Legerohn among the Moresi.

Tavinahl: Lord of the Kriel Clan.

Telakot: Azari assigned to the Queen of the Free People.

Tormont Vale: A village in the Lower Lands.

trullen: The diminished offspring of the Hyrrokkin.

Tsurah: Reptile race loyal to Lord Morgrom.

Tycho: A Ruinwaster.

Tycho's Dune: A slow-moving dune east of the Ganzir.

Uran: Stair Mark of the Stair Guard.

Urning: Powerful beings loyal to Lord Morgrom.

Venrahl: Mono Lord of Corundum.

Venturer, the: Honorific for Grieg Sidor.

verrandulum: Ephemeral gateways of the One Race.

Vopal: Squire to Ridder.

wadi: A valley or ravine, dry except during the rainy season.

wakeel: A trustee, an agent.

Warrior: An Akkeidii with knowledge of *montmorillionite* lore and the ways of battle.

Warrum: The Makan Clan Lord.

Water bridge: An ancient means for relocating water.

Water Gate: Another name for Grieg's Gate.

Well of Sorrows: Shaft where the Dagba Stone was lost.

Wester, the river: A river in the Lands.

White, the river: A river in the Mashu.

White Deeps, the: The cold north where glaciers grow.

White Earth, the: A heaven.

White Wyrak: A monster from Azari myth.

Woe Sower: Common name for Lord Morgrom used by the peoples of the Lands.

World Stair, the: A remnant artifact of the One Race.

"So, don your armor, grab your shield

For now, the fighting is close at hand

When we all must fight for our sanity

...and it's kill...

...or be killed"

— Surrealist

ACKNOWLEDGEMENTS

It truly takes a village to bring a book to life.

I am once again indebted to Steven Piskula. He had an unflinching capability to tell me what wasn't working in this story.

Thanks to Steven Pressfield for commiserating with me about the problems I had with the first act. He helped give me the fortitude to do the hard work of restructuring it.

A big thank you to Dana Pittman, my poignant and insightful editor, for keeping me on track with the core of the story. Her direct and experienced feedback punctuated key points along the way.

Thanks to Ramona Eihai, Megan Joseph, and Robin Fuller for the line editing, copy editing, and proofreading. I am grateful for their help in cleaning up the manuscript.

Copy editing is a thankless task, but I thank my wife Jennifer anyway, who exemplifies the meaning of going over the pages with a fine-toothed comb.

A hearty thanks goes out to my beta readers: Tracee Hicks, Paul Hicks, Brenda Gran, and Bill Gran.

Thanks again to Jeff Brown for an amazing cover. I don't know how you do it, but your work catches people's eyes every time.

Thanks to Christine at Open Book Design for once again typesetting a gorgeous book.

A nod to Stefan Grabiński for the story, The White Wyrak, a truly memorable and terrifying tale and monster.

Thank you to the village of readers who have embarked on this venture and to those whom I have met at my book signings. I appreciate you giving of your time to the journeys of The Last Emissary.

The venture continues…

AUTHOR BIO

J. Jason Hicks studied English Literature, Political Science, and World Religions, with a focus on classic literature, at the University of Wisconsin Oshkosh. The Earthmight War: The Annals of the Last Emissary Book Two is his second novel. He lives in Tucson, Arizona with his wife and his dog Maya.

www.jjasonhicks.com

linktr.ee/jjasonhicks

PLEASE TAKE A FEW moments to leave a review. Authors rely heavily on reviews to increase the chances that new readers will learn about books they may enjoy. Thank you!

Connect with Jason on Instagram, Facebook, and his website.

Join the venture to receive Fantasy Friday posts and exclusive access to details about upcoming books, in-person signings, and more.

You may access all of the above information and more via my Linktree and this QR code:

No generative artificial intelligence (AI) was used in the writing of this work or cover art. The author reserves the rights for this work and cover art, which cannot be reproduced and/or otherwise used in any manner. The author expressly prohibits any entity from using this publication for purposes of training AI technologies to generate text or artwork, including, without limitation, technologies that are capable of generating works in the same style or genre as this publication.

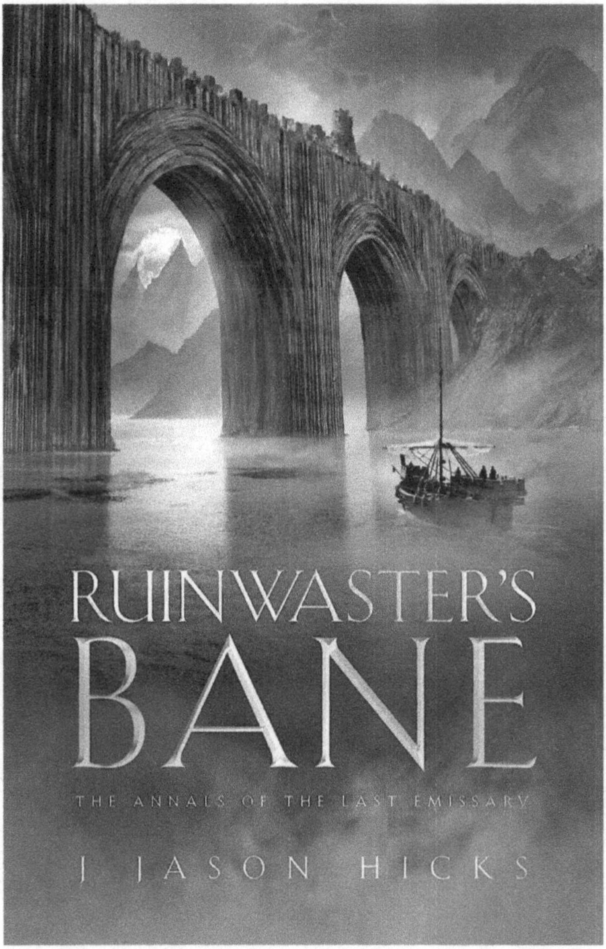